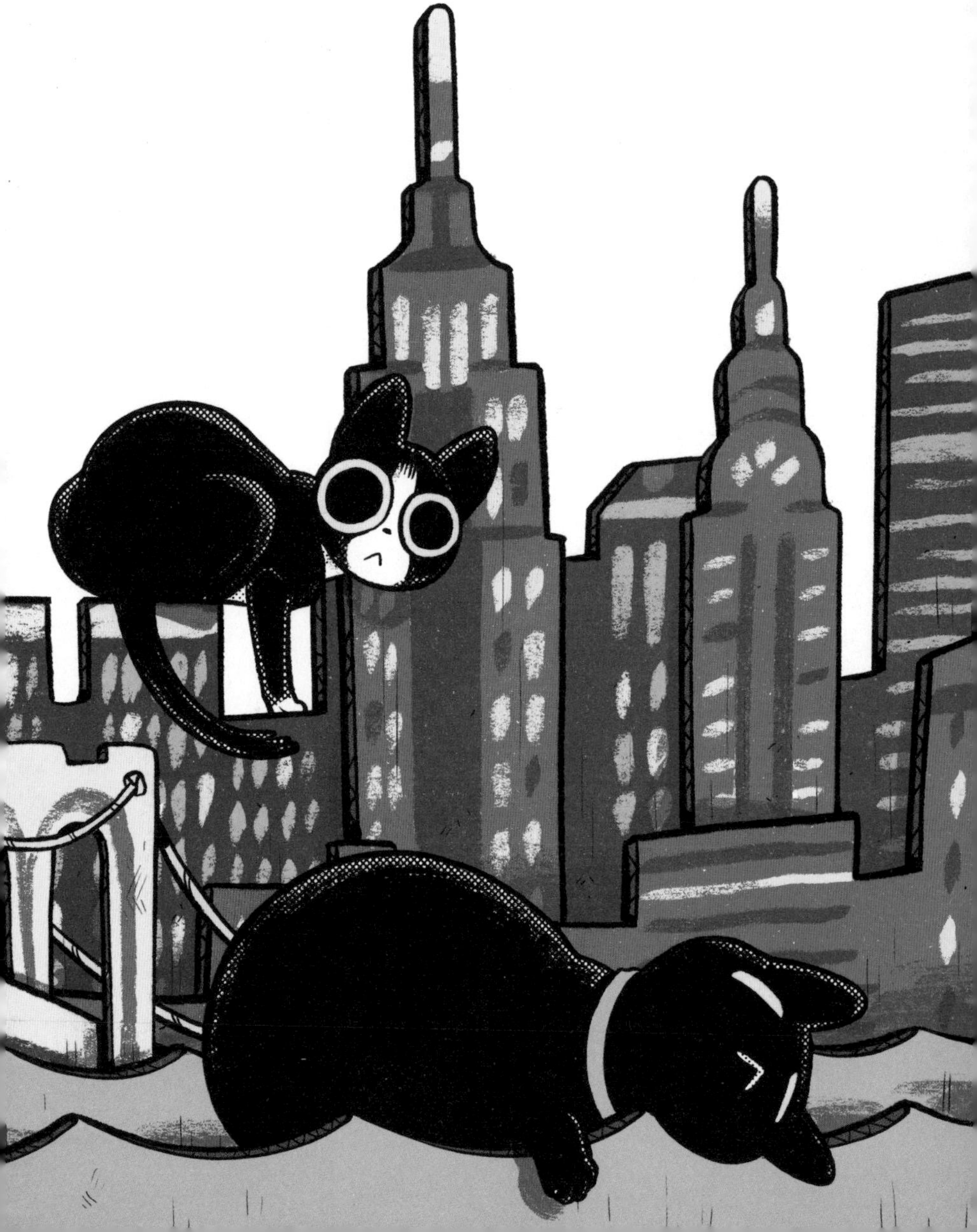

Edited by James Lucas Jones, Robin Herrera, and George Rohac
Book design by Yuko Ota, Ananth Hirsh, and Keith Wood

Published by Oni Press, Inc.

Joe Nozemack, publisher · James Lucas Jones, editor in chief
Andrew McIntire, v.p. of marketing & sales · David Dissanayake, sales manager
Rachel Reed, publicity coordinator · Troy Look, director of design & production
Hilary Thompson, graphic designer · Angie Dobson, digital prepress technician
Ari Yarwood, managing editor · Charlie Chu, senior editor
Robin Herrera, editor · Bess Pallares, editorial assistant
Brad Rooks, director of logistics · Jung Lee, logistics associate

1305 SE Martin Luther King, Jr. Blvd.
Suite A
Portland, OR 97214
U.S.A.

onipress.com
facebook.com/onipress
twitter.com/onipress
onipress.tumblr.com
instagram.com/onipress

johnnywander.com
@ananthhirsh
@aidosaur

First Edition: March 2017

Retail Edition ISBN: 978-1-62010-383-8 · eISBN: 978-1-62010-384-5

Artist Edition ISBN: 978-0-9980995-0-7 · Artist Limited Edition ISBN: 978-0-9980995-1-4

Our Cats Are More Famous Than Us: A Johnny Wander Collection, March 2017. Published by Oni Press, Inc. 1305 SE Martin Luther King Jr. Blvd., Suite A, Portland, OR 97214. Johnny Wander is ™ & © 2017 Ananth Hirsh & Yuko Ota. All rights reserved. Oni Press logo and icon ™ & © 2017 Oni Press, Inc. All rights reserved. Oni Press logo and icon artwork created by Keith A. Wood. The events, institutions, and characters presented in this book are fictional. Any resemblance to actual persons, living or dead, is purely coincidental. No portion of this publication may be reproduced, by any means, without the express written permission of the copyright holders.

Library of Congress Control Number: 2016952156

10 9 8 7 6 5 4 3 2 1

Printed in China.

FOR CONRAD & JOHN.

Thanks for the adventures,
on paper and off.

INTRODUCTION

I met Yuko and Ananth for the first time in 2009, shortly after they moved to Brooklyn to start a new chapter of their lives, both on the pages of *Johnny Wander* and off.

But I felt like I already knew them. It was as though we had already been friends for years. I could refer to the time George did that one thing, or Conrad said something witty, or John created a cantankerous riot (as John is wont to do). Even though I'd only read about these anecdotes in their comics, it felt like I had been there.

Writing autobio comics is tricky business. I've been putting my own life into the pages of my graphic novels for the better part of a decade, but I have the advantage of a 20-year retrospective lens, so I'm not constantly gleaning my present-day life for kernels of interest. Yuko and Ananth channel the everyday, the mundane, the highs and lows of navigating adulthood, and for this I admire them greatly.

Striking the right balance is key. It's not easy to let your readers into your daily life, essentially allowing them to read your diary, while also keeping things fresh, universal, and most importantly, funny. But they are funny people. They are warm and caring and smart as tacks. Yuko really does geek out full tilt about dragons, and then grabs her pencil to scribble them in her sketchbook. Ananth really does like sugar. And books. And the human condition.

The two of them really will take you in, feed you a big curry dinner, sit you down on their comfy couch for an hour or two of TV or video games, and write or draw with you. (While John does the dishes.) They will ride in the backseat of your car on the drive to TCAF, and listen to Phil Collins with you, and then write a comic about how you guys just wanted food, but could only find massage parlors. (And Horseland Emporiums. Yeah. What gives, Toronto suburbs?)

Johnny Wander is my favorite comic on the Internet. It's by two of my favorite people, both on the Internet and off. It's about roommates and work and life and dreams and reality. It's funny as heck. It's about two people wandering, together, through the labyrinth of early adulthood. The reader wanders with them, stopping along the way to pet cats in laundromats, duck into doorways to get out of the rain, and brew a quick cup of tea to enjoy with a friend. Yuko and Ananth are my friends, and after you read *Johnny Wander*, you'll feel like they're yours, too.

Raina Telgemeier, author of Smile
San Francisco, CA
May 2016

I.

I WISH to go a'wanderin',
A' wanderin' with you

What won'drous woods and wilderness
We'll go a'traipsing through

What kinds of creatures shall we see?
A wanderin', jus' you an me?
Birds and beasts from land and sea

While wanderin' with you.

sage advice

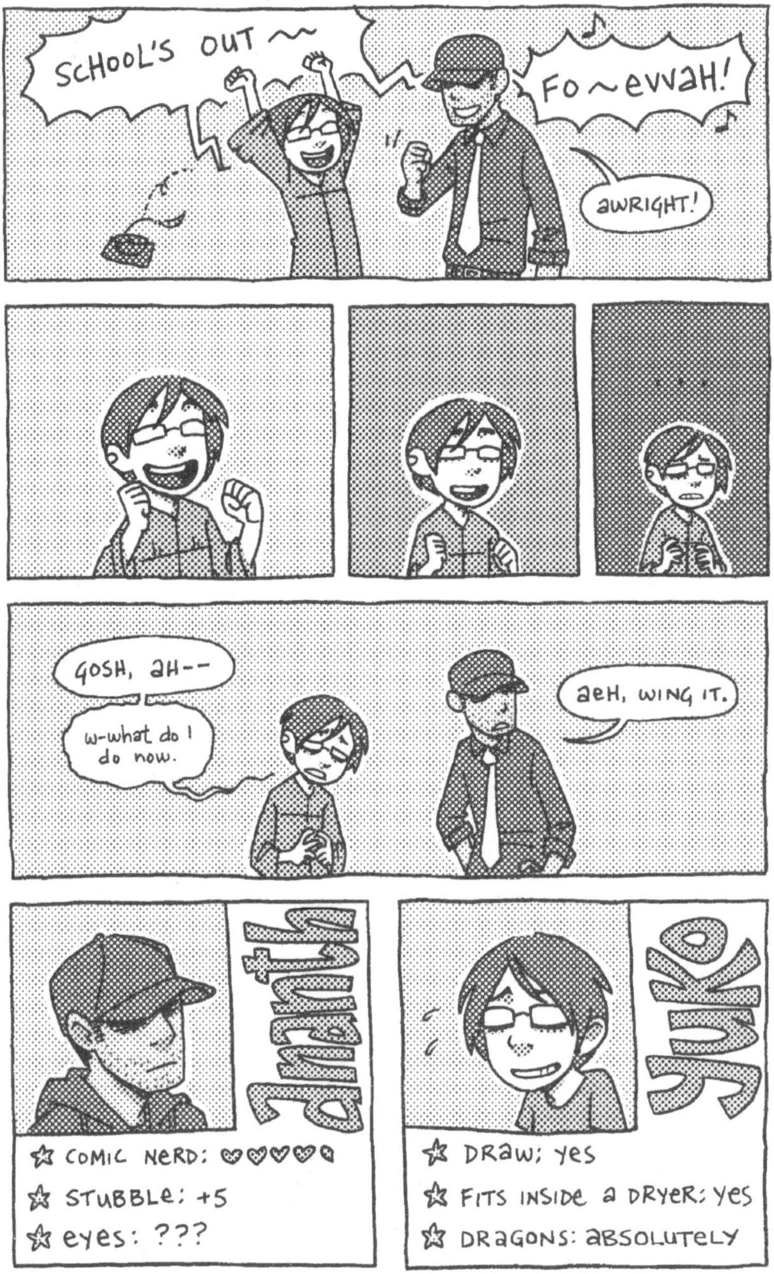
SCHOOL'S OUT ~~
FO ~ EVVAH!
AWRIGHT!
. . .
GOSH, AH--
w-what do I do now.
AEH, WING IT.
COMIC NERD:
STUBBLE: +5
EYES: ???
DRAW: YES
FITS INSIDE A DRYER: YES
DRAGONS: ABSOLUTELY

his parents must be so proud

a valid point

☆ HEIGHT: THE TALLEST
☆ MOOD: MILDLY ORNERY
☆ WE'RE NOT; PAYING TO
HEAT THE OUTSIDE what, were
you born in a barn or someth.

Puck Fair

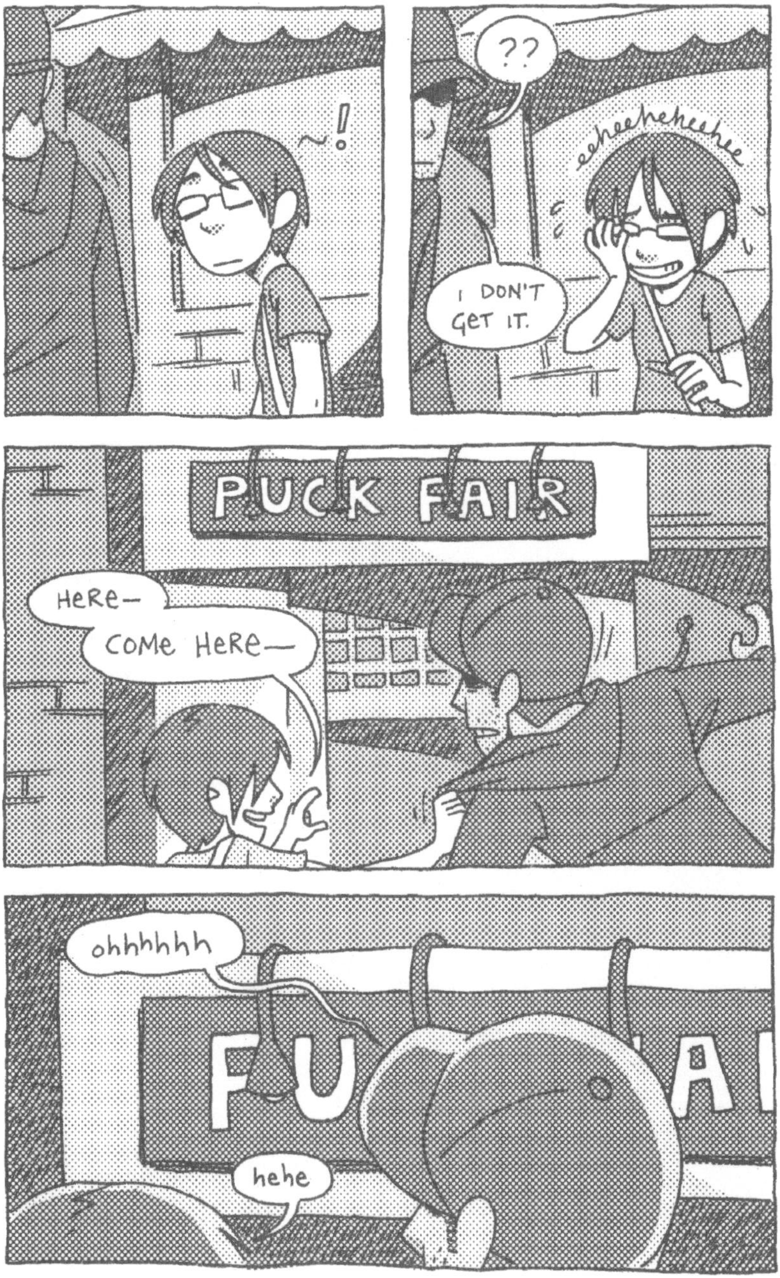
~!
??
eeheeheheeheehee
I DON'T GET IT.
PUCK FAIR
HeRe—
COMe HeRe—
ohhhhhh
FU
A
hehe

rest in pieces

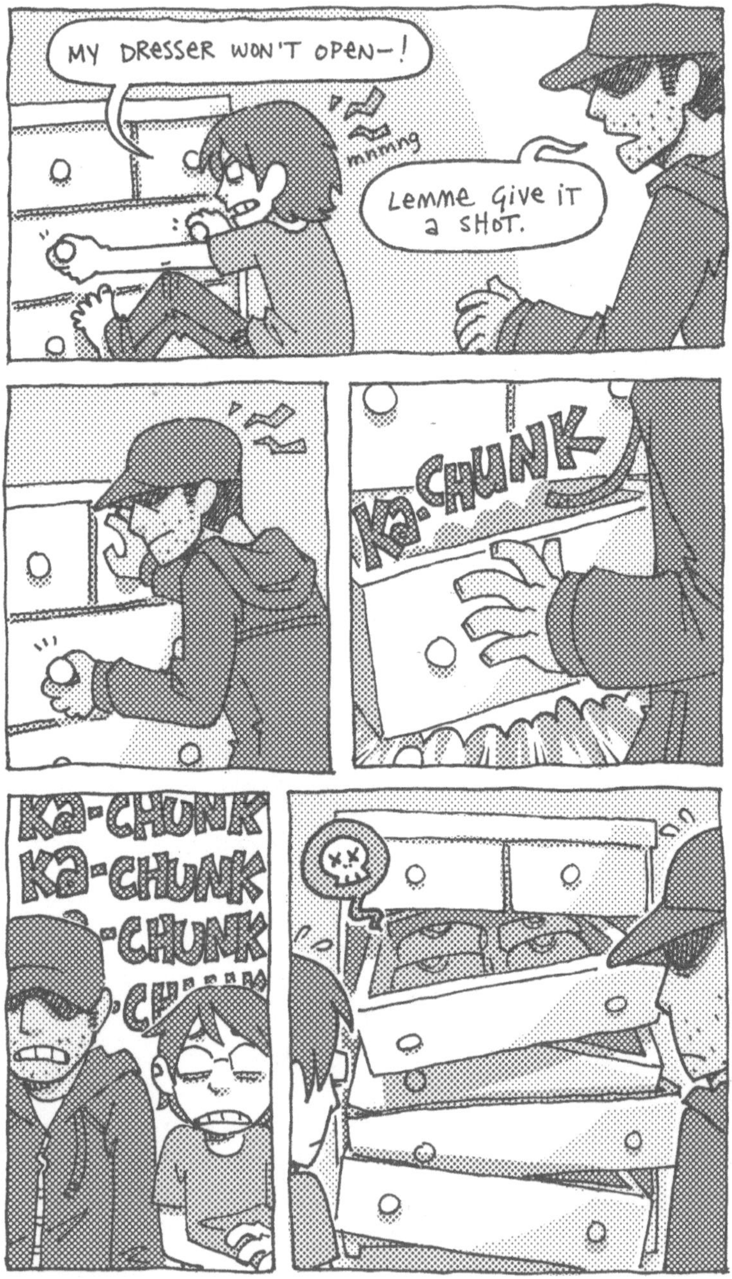
MY DRESSER WON'T OPEN–!
mnmng
Lemme give it a shot.
KA-CHUNK
KA-CHUNK
KA-CHUNK
-CHUNK

a face like sandpaper

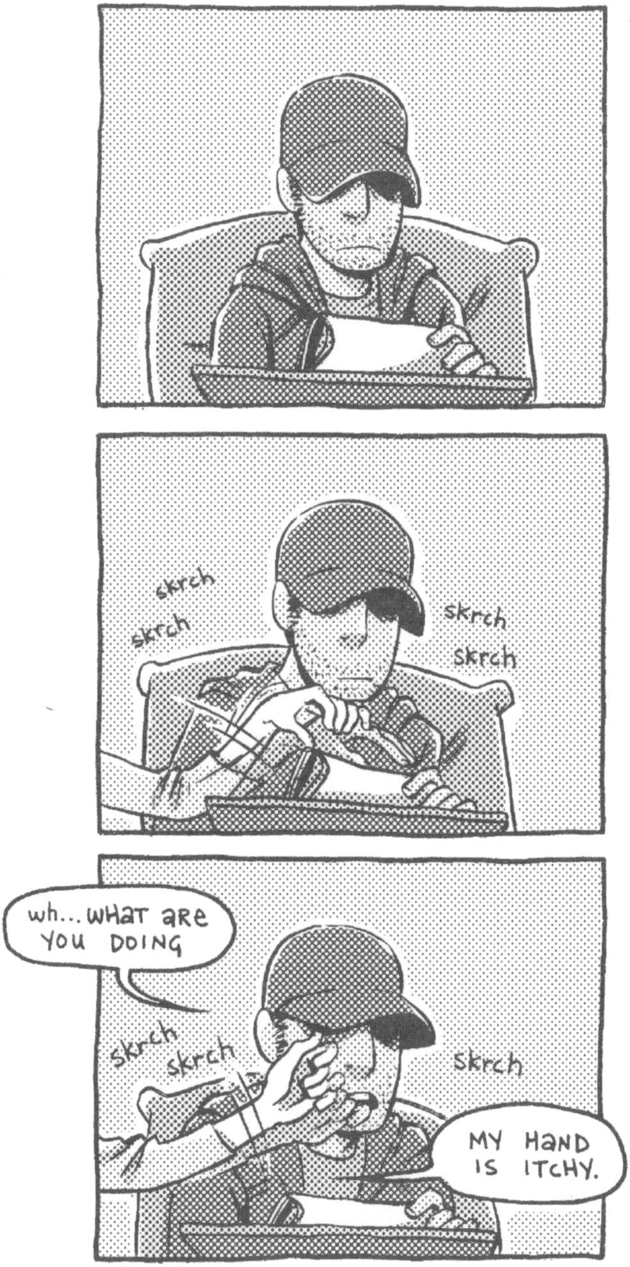
skrch
skrch
skrch
skrch
wh... WHAT ARE YOU DOING
skrch
skrch
skrch
MY HAND IS ITCHY.

boys are wimps

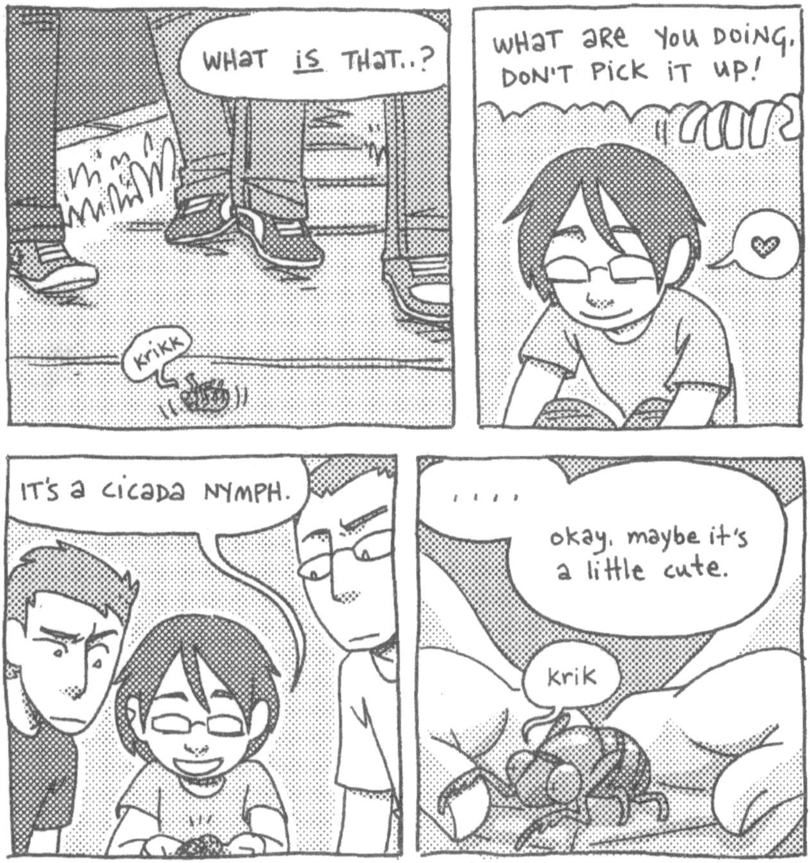
WHAT IS THAT..?
krikk
WHAT ARE YOU DOING. DON'T PICK IT UP!
IT'S A CICADA NYMPH.
....
okay. maybe it's a little cute.
krik

EPILOGUE:

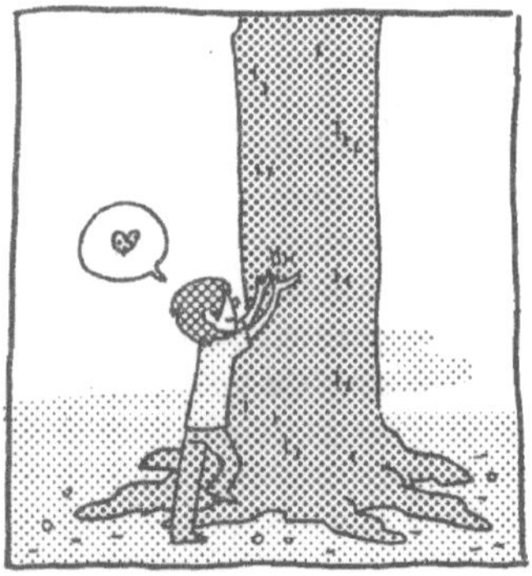

abandonment

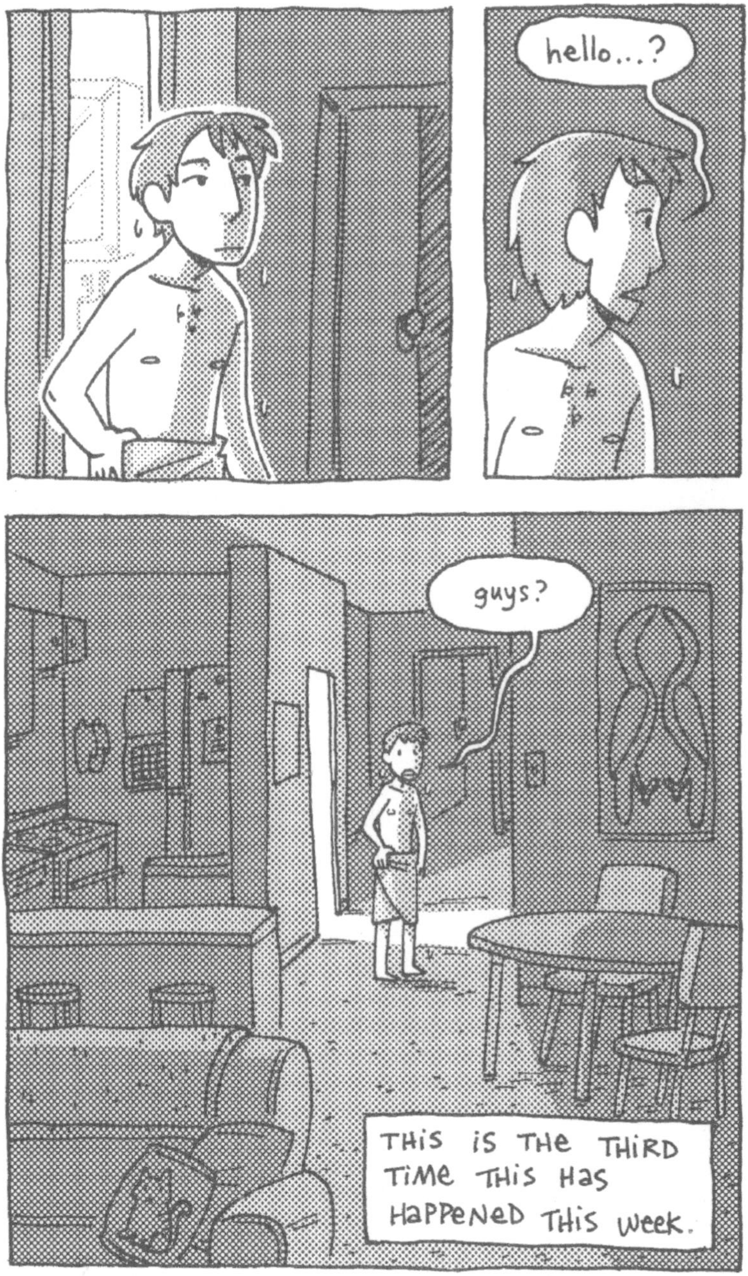

hello...?
guys?
THIS IS THE THIRD TIME THIS HAS HAPPENED THIS WEEK.

an open letter to all US registered voters

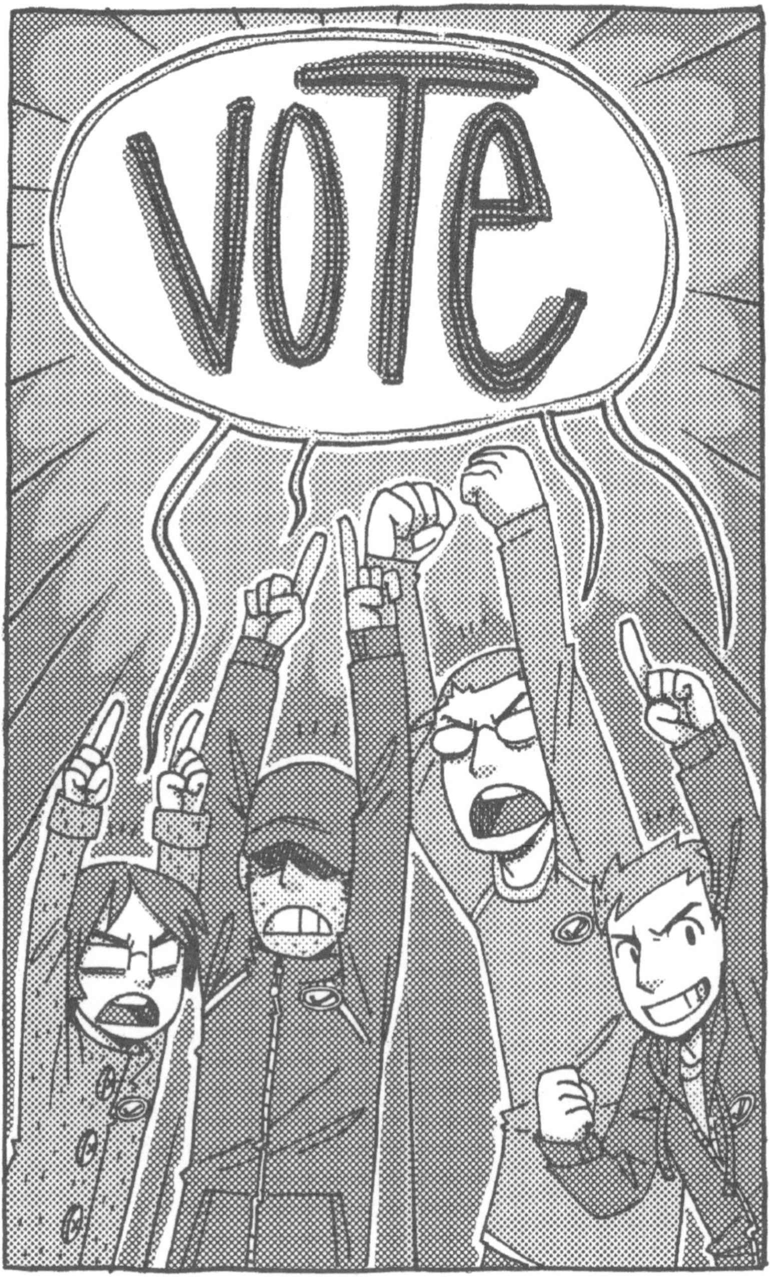
VOTE

spreading the wealth around

STEP 1: VOTE.

STEP 2: GET FREE FOOD.

STEP 3: REPEAT STEP 2.

exxxtreme furniture purchases

rest in pieces redux

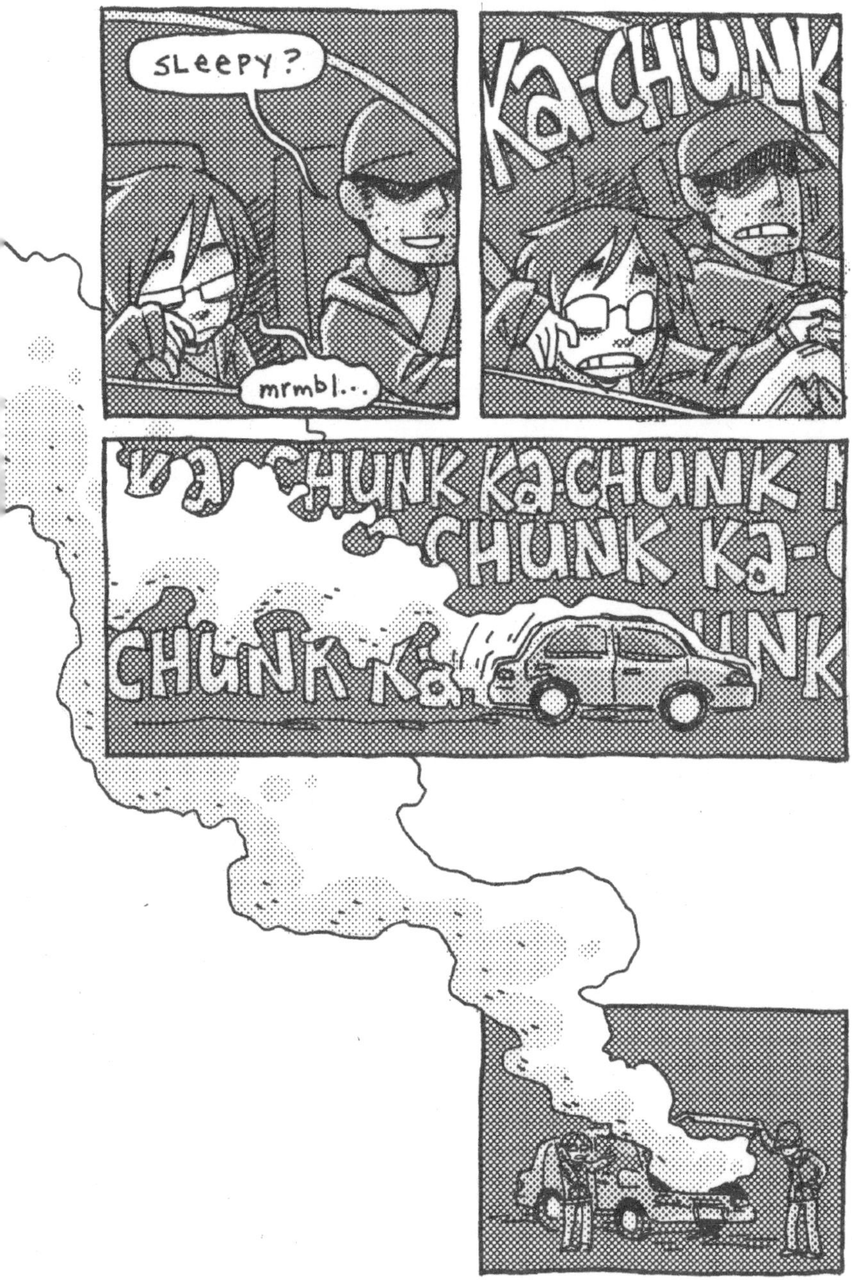
SLEEPY?
mrmbl...
KA-CHUNK
CHUNK KA-CHUNK
CHUNK KA-
CHUNK KA-
UNK

then i got curtains

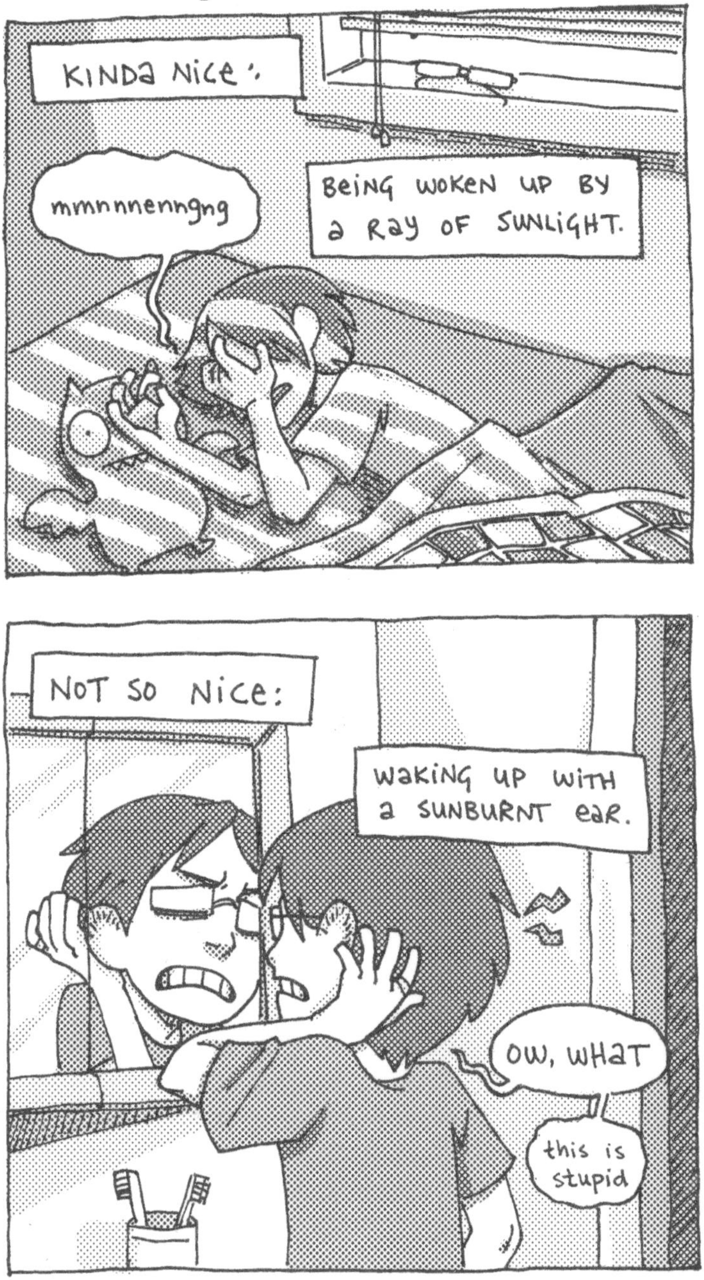
KINDA NICE:
mmnnnenngng
BEING WOKEN UP BY A RAY OF SUNLIGHT.
NOT SO NICE:
WAKING UP WITH A SUNBURNT EAR.
OW, WHAT
this is stupid

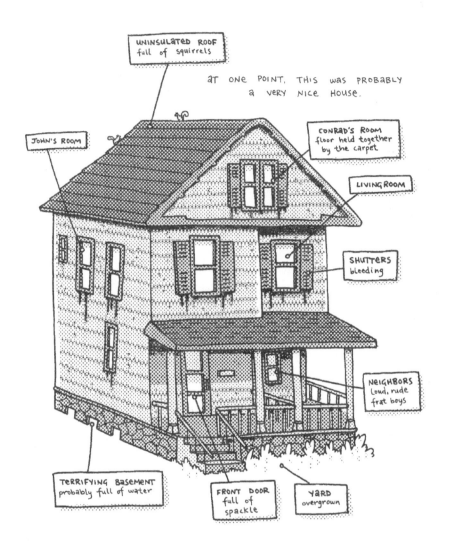

Before Maryland we lived in upstate New York, in a house the landlord repaired exclusively with spackle.

We named it SPACKLEHAUS.

in the walls

WELL, WE FINISHED MOVING IN.

SPACKLEHAUS MEMOIRS 1

HOW'S IT LOOK?

o-okay...

aw, WHAT'S UP?

THERE'S A HIDDEN ROOM—

I CAN SEE THE WINDOW FROM THE OUTSIDE, BUT THERE'S NO WAY TO GET TO IT....

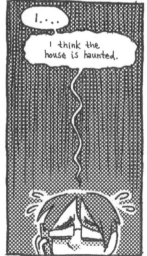

I....

I think the house is haunted.

WANT ME TO STAY ON THE PHONE WITH YOU?

NO...

skritter

skrch skritter

skrch

Yes.

ghosts might have been preferable

SPACKLEHAUS MEMOIRS 2

HEYY, MORNING!

SLEEP OKAY? ANY GHOSTS?

NOT REALLY.

also, shut up.

ANANTH.

wha?

THERE ARE SQUIRRELS.

IN THE WALLS

mygod.

the best sleepover ever

the first plague

we've found one cricket in our apartment—

every night for the past several weeks.

I have a running suspicion they're all the same cricket.

he only likes fake coffee

the most obvious course of action

theasaur

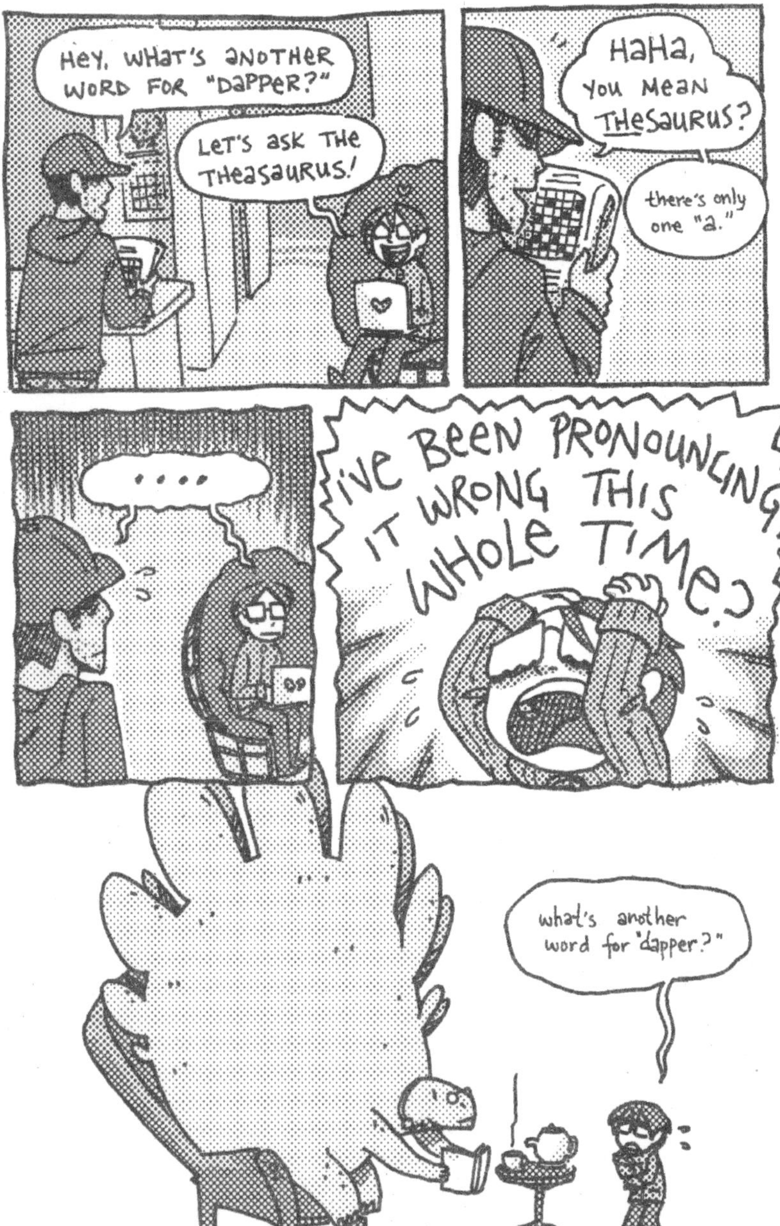

HEY, WHAT'S ANOTHER WORD FOR "DAPPER?"
LET'S ASK THE THEASAURUS!
HAHA, YOU MEAN THESAURUS?
there's only one "a."
....
I'VE BEEN PRONOUNCING IT WRONG THIS WHOLE TIME?
what's another word for "dapper?"

a netflix for books

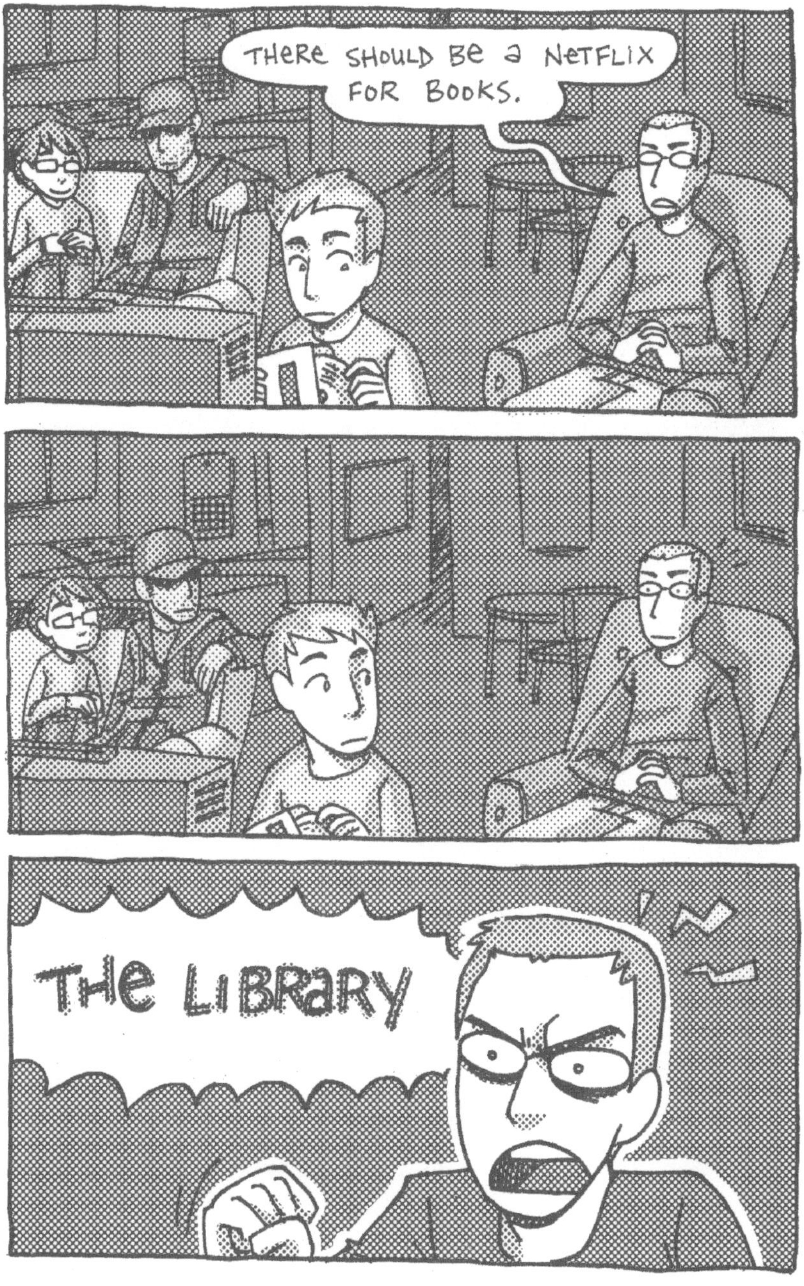
THERE SHOULD BE A NETFLIX FOR BOOKS.
THE LIBRARY

guilty until proven guilty

our neighbors think we are weird

STOP EATING RIBBONS

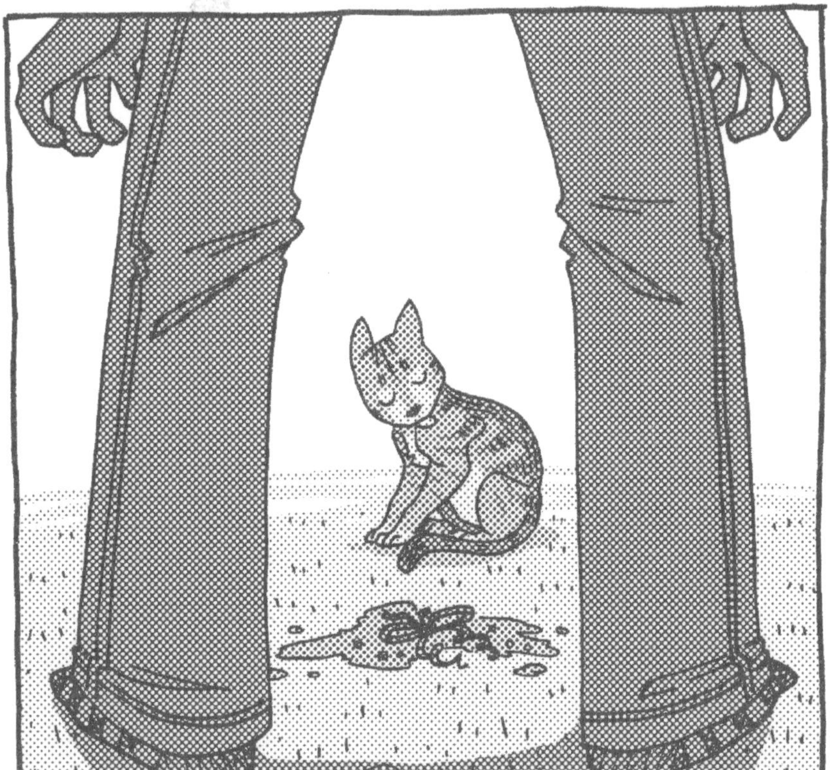

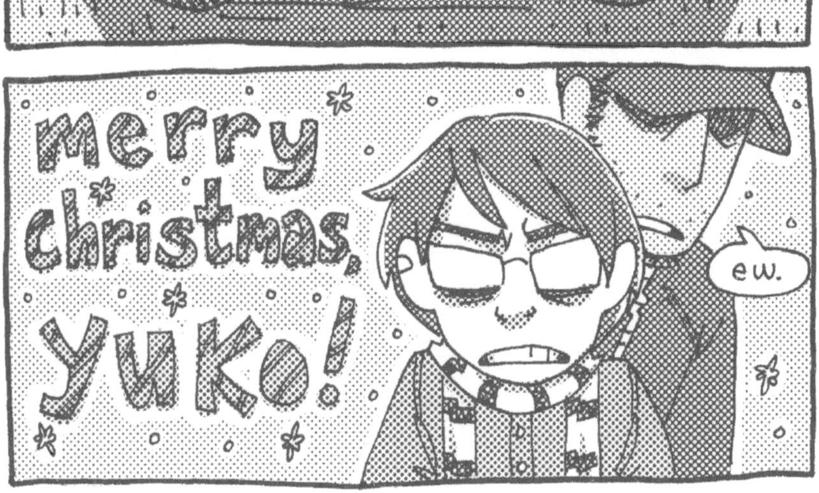
merry Christmas, Yuko!
ew.

read instructions before proceeding

あけましておめでとうございます。
happy new year

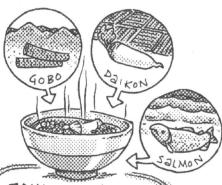

GOBO

DAIKON

SALMON

RENKON — pickled lotus root.

THE LOTUS FLOWER HAS TIES TO BUDDHA AND THEREFORE IS ASSOCIATED WITH GODLY BLESSINGS.

ZONI — mochi soup.

A TRADITIONAL SOUP MADE WITH RICE CAKE AND FOODS FROM THE THREE HARVESTED REGIONS OF JAPAN: MOUNTAINS, FIELDS, AND OCEAN. THIS IS MY FAMILY'S RECIPE.

INARIZUSHI — sushi rice in a sweet fried tofu shell.

ASSOCIATED WITH THE RICE GODDESS, INARI—IT IS SUPPOSED TO BE A FAVORED FOOD OF HER MESSENGER FOXES.

ZENZAI — sweet adzuki bean and mochi soup

EATING RED THINGS ON NEW YEARS IS SUPPOSED TO BRING GOOD FORTUNE. (A HANDFUL OF PEOPLE DIE EVERY NEW YEAR BY CHOKING ON MOCHI.)

not the first time this has happened

You Have To Make It Really Bad

happy birthday conrad

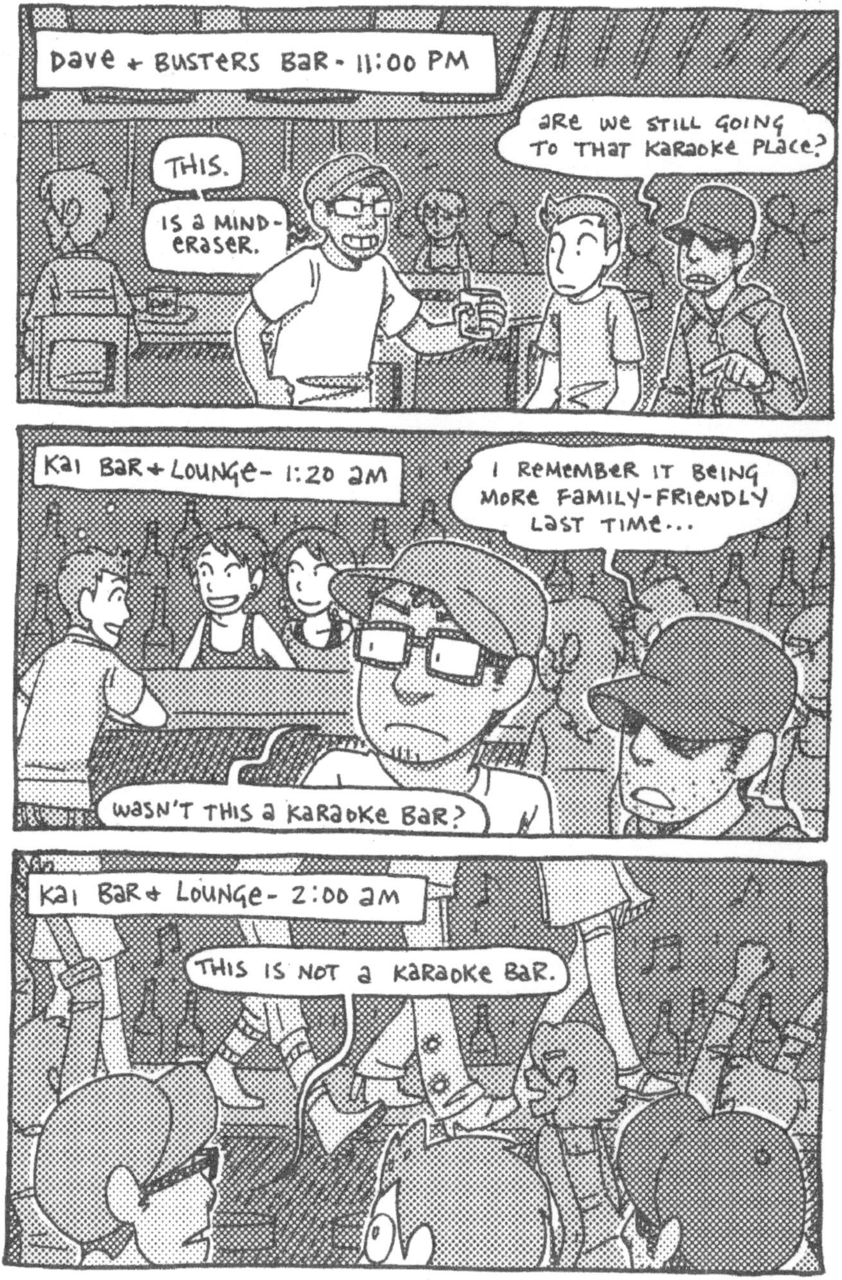
Dave + Busters Bar - 11:00 PM
THIS.
IS a MIND-ERASER.
ARE WE STILL GOING TO THAT KARAOKE PLACE?
Kai Bar + Lounge - 1:20 am
I REMEMBER IT BEING MORE FAMILY-FRIENDLY LAST TIME...
WASN'T THIS a KARAOKE BAR?
Kai Bar + Lounge - 2:00 am
THIS IS NOT a KARAOKE BAR.

various inadequacies

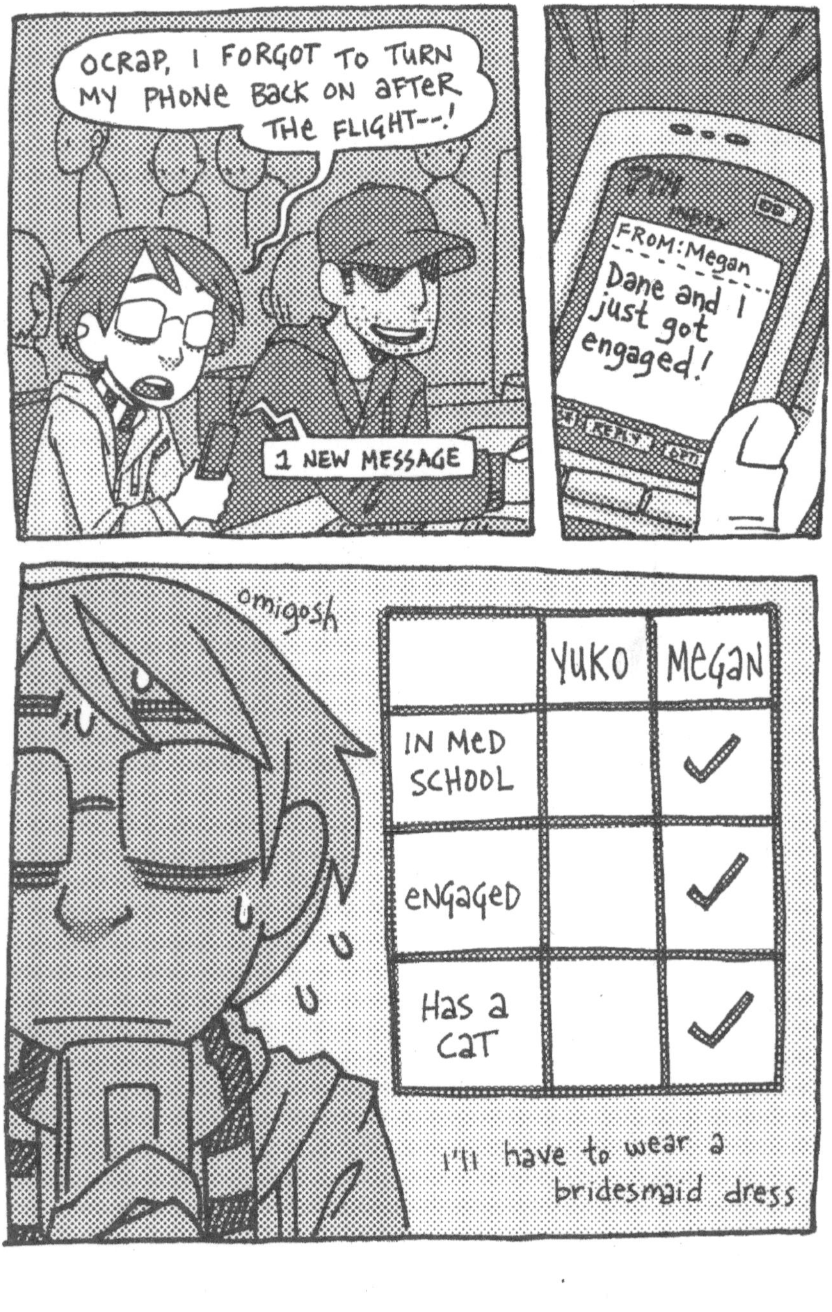
OCRAP, I FORGOT TO TURN MY PHONE BACK ON AFTER THE FLIGHT--!
1 NEW MESSAGE
FROM: Megan
Dane and I just got engaged!
REPLY
omigosh
YUKO
MEGAN
IN MED SCHOOL
ENGAGED
HAS A CAT
I'll have to wear a bridesmaid dress

fifth sense

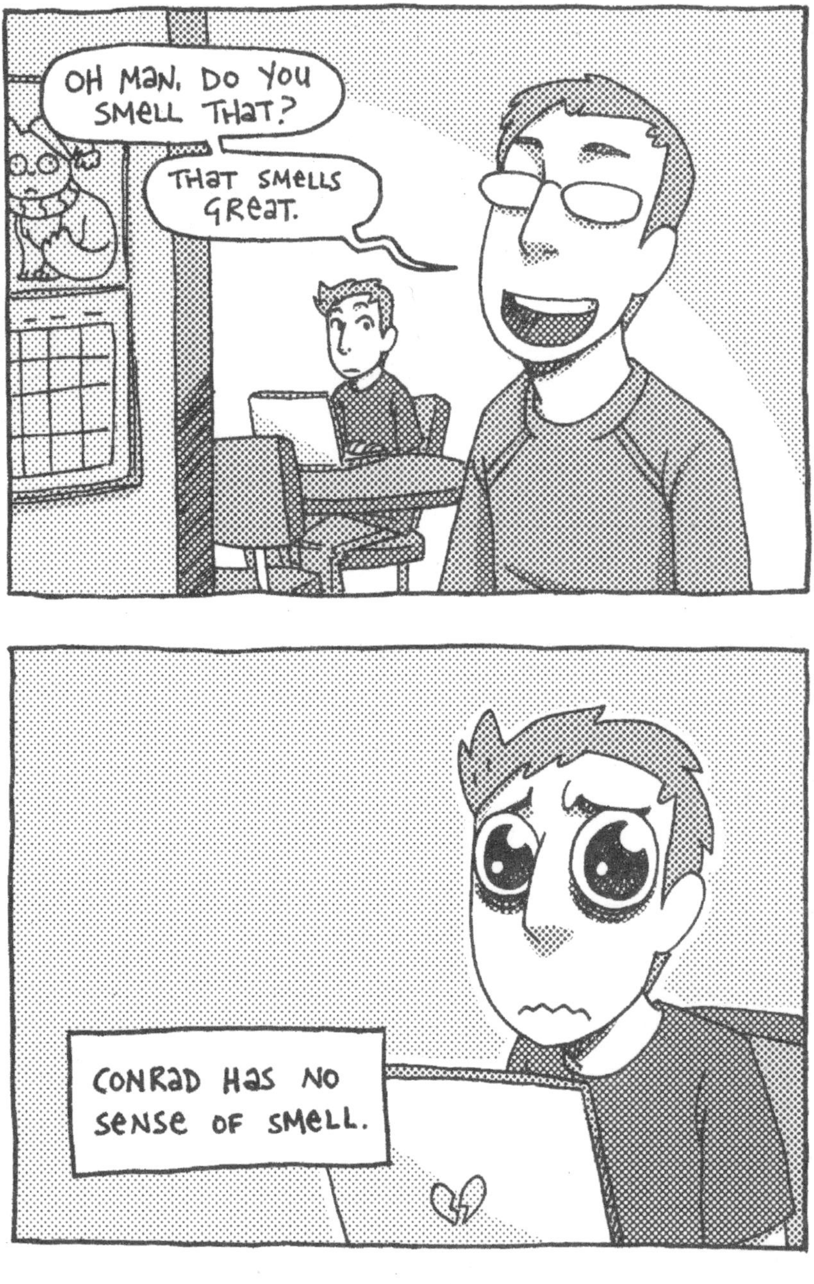
OH MAN, DO YOU SMELL THAT?
THAT SMELLS GREAT.
CONRAD HAS NO SENSE OF SMELL.

zoo LOLOLogy

buffaLOL

aLOLgator

goriLOL

fLOLmingo

eLOLphant

armadiLOL

saLOLmander

axoLOLtl!

coeLOLcanth!

ROFLope

hehe

without cable we cannot
be sure anyway

three dollar comfort

on the origin of knife fights

incorrect bread anatomy

initial y

deedledoodleee
HI DAD— I'M DRIVING.
HOW FAR HAVE YOU DRIVEN
er, MY ODOMETER SAYS 90 MILES OR SO.
SO YOU'VE DRIVEN FOR ONLY ONE HOUR?
....
stop assuming everyone drives just like you.

pink and purple poinsettia socks

cake wreck

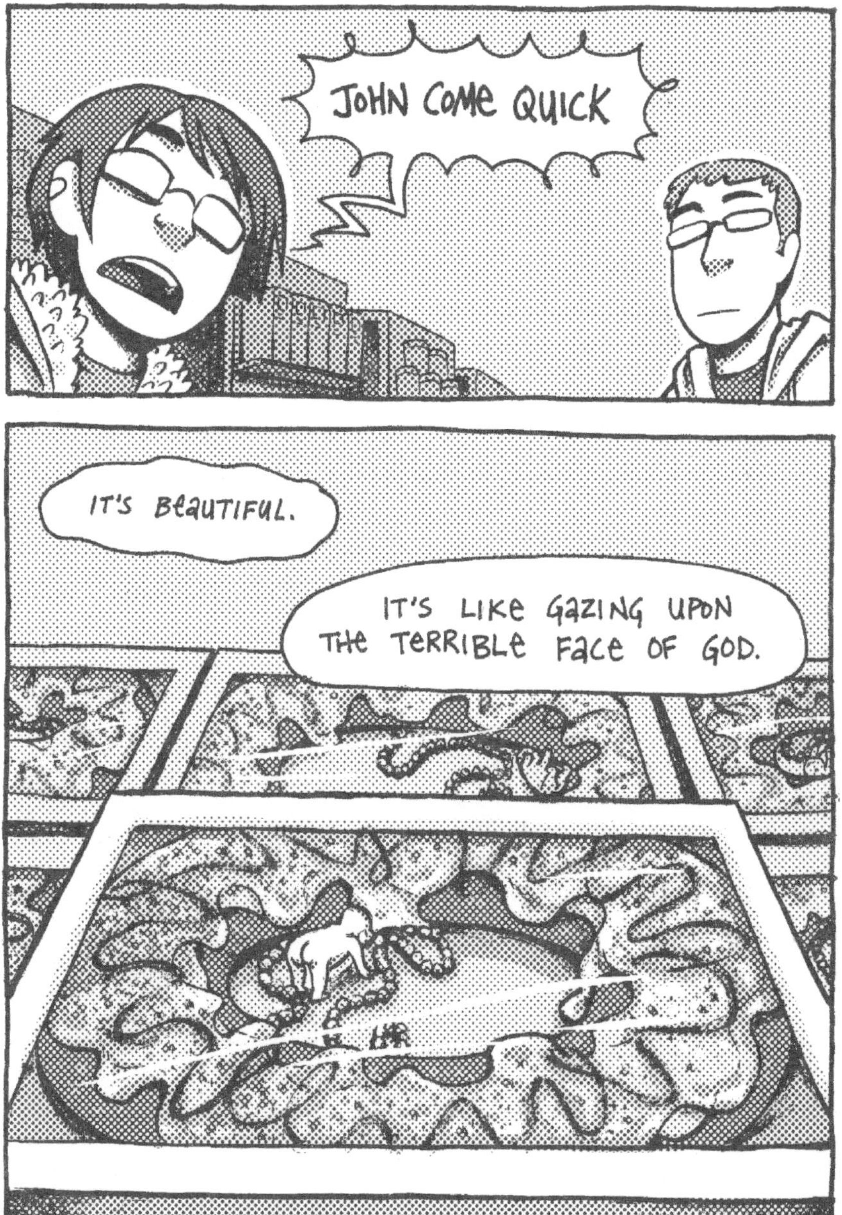
JOHN COME QUICK
IT'S BEAUTIFUL.
IT'S LIKE GAZING UPON THE TERRIBLE FACE OF GOD.

haircut tax

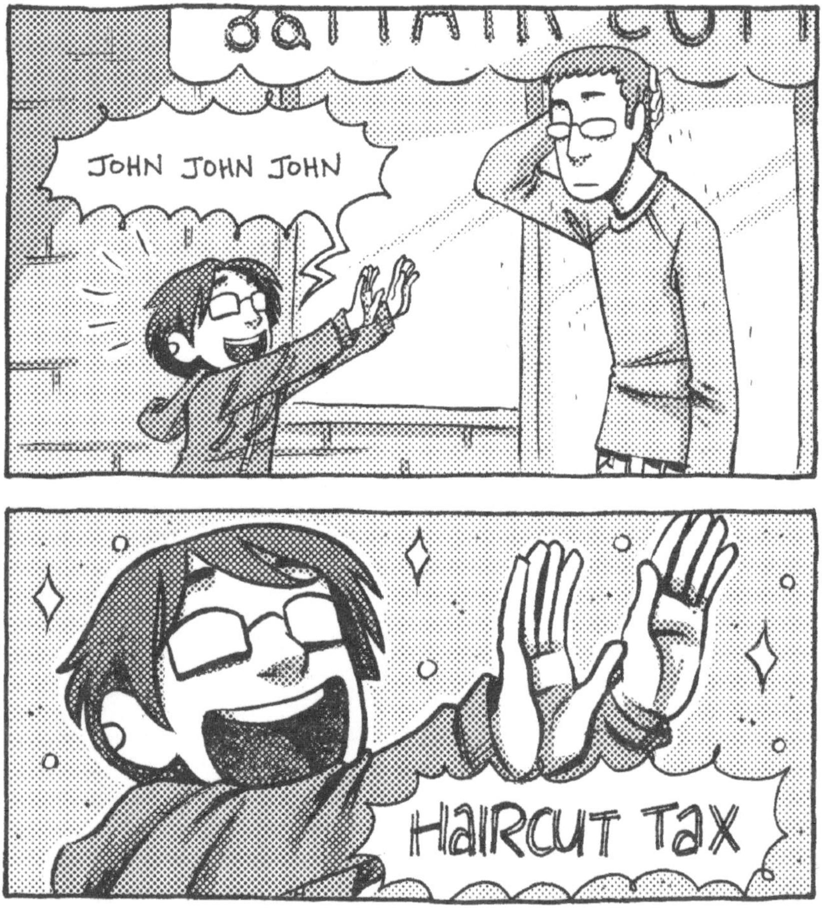
JOHN JOHN JOHN
HAIRCUT TAX

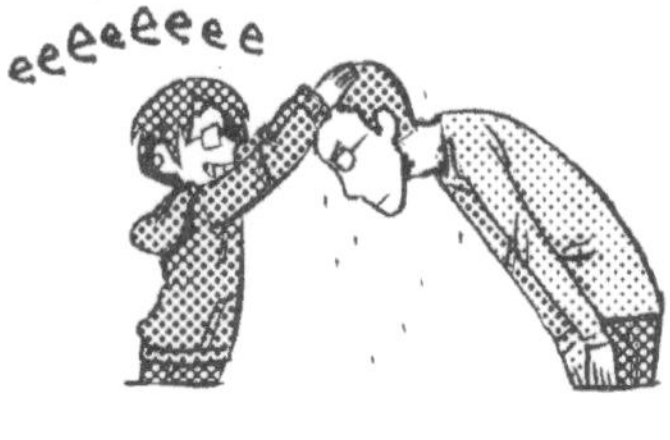
eeeeeeee

he named the houseplants

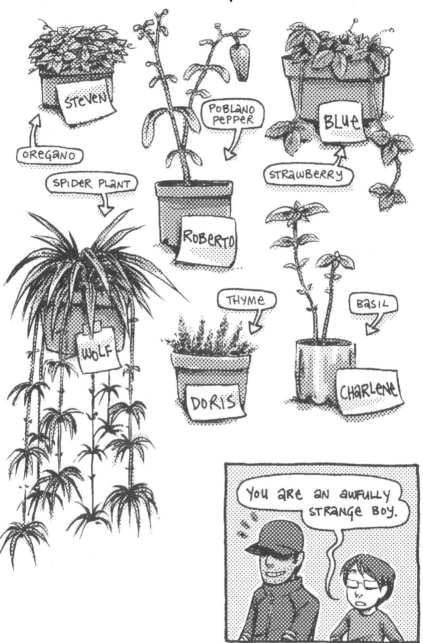

latitude change

MARCH 2008: ROCHESTER, NY

MARCH 2009: WASHINGTON DC

inscrutable language joke

where Yuko has to explain the joke:

鋤 焼き = SUKIYAKI, BEEF HOT POT.
PLOW COOK

大 好き = DAISUKI, TO LOVE
BIG LIKE

her computer died

HEY, WHAT'S THE PLAN FOR THIS WEEKEND?

WELL, I WANTED TO GET SOME WRITING IN— AND YOU HAVE TO WORK ON YOUR PAGES

WANTED TO SEE JESS THIS WEEKEND

AND WE COULD CATCH A MOVIE

ALSO, WE GOTTA DO OUR TAXES ON SUNDAY.

KA-CHUNK

AND THEN WE DID NONE OF THOSE THINGS.

homemade mace

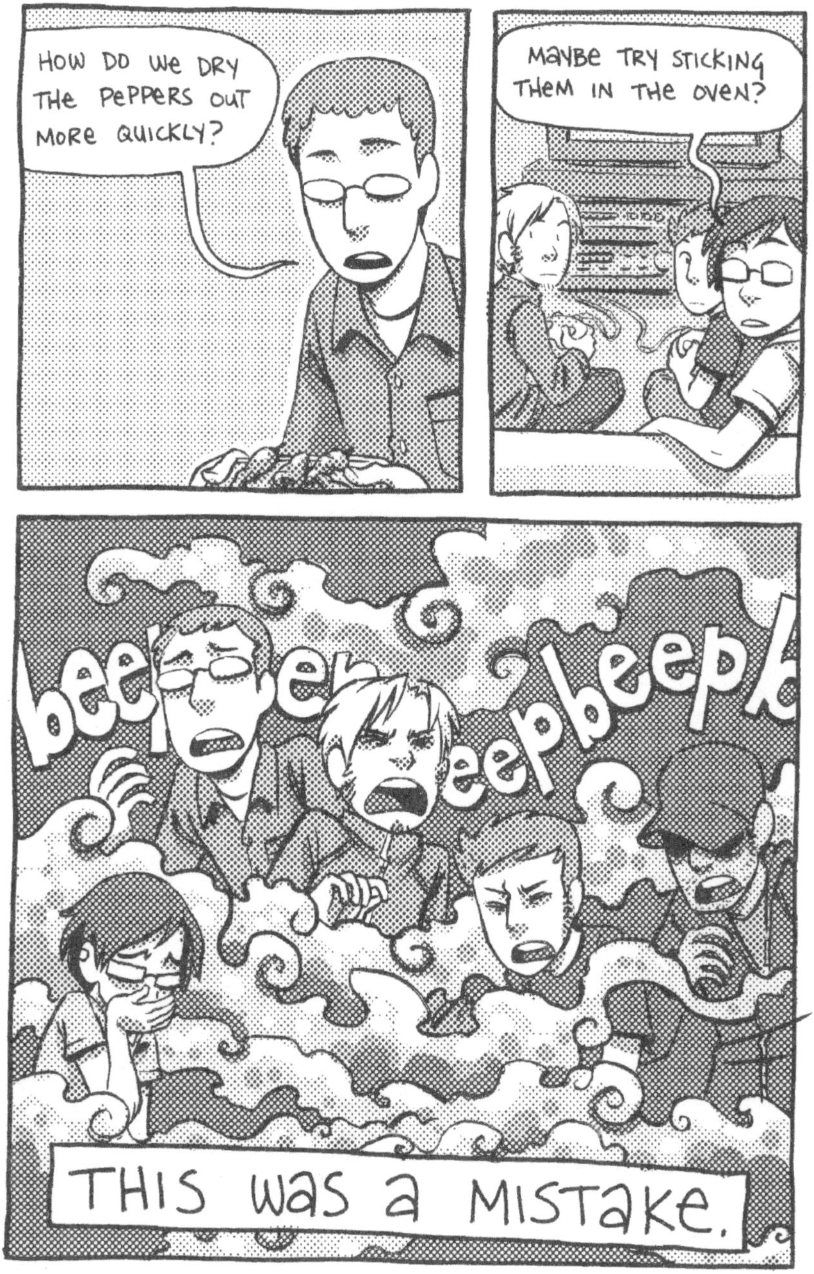

HOW DO WE DRY THE PEPPERS OUT MORE QUICKLY?
MAYBE TRY STICKING THEM IN THE OVEN?
beepbeepbeepbeep
THIS was a MISTAKE.

yuko's parents' cats again

things mika likes to do:

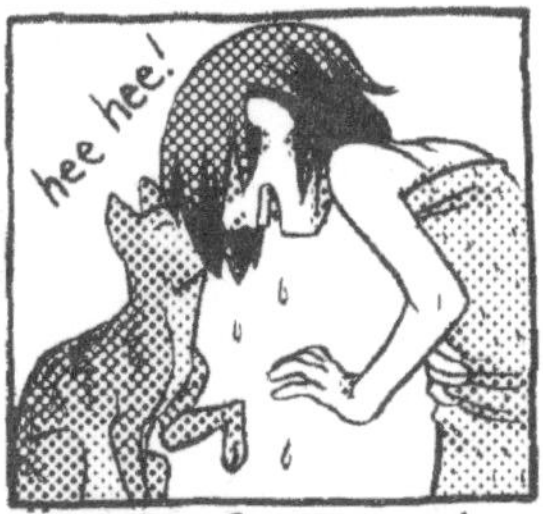
hee hee!

drink from wet hair

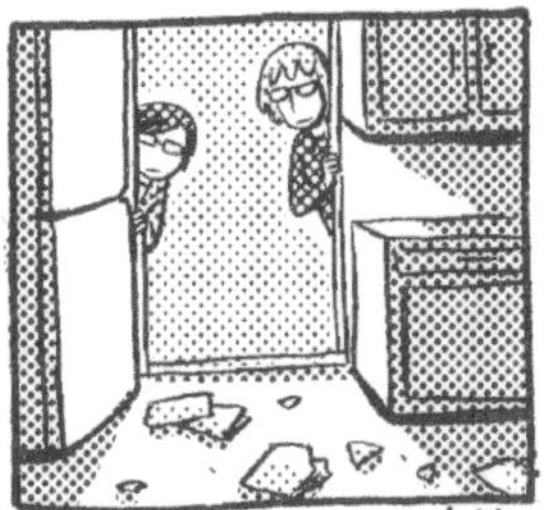

destroy things while no one is looking

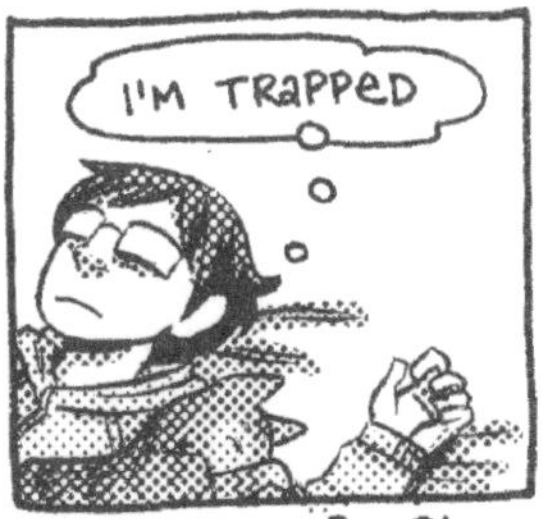
I'M TRAPPED

sleep on people, sometimes

things gonta likes to do:

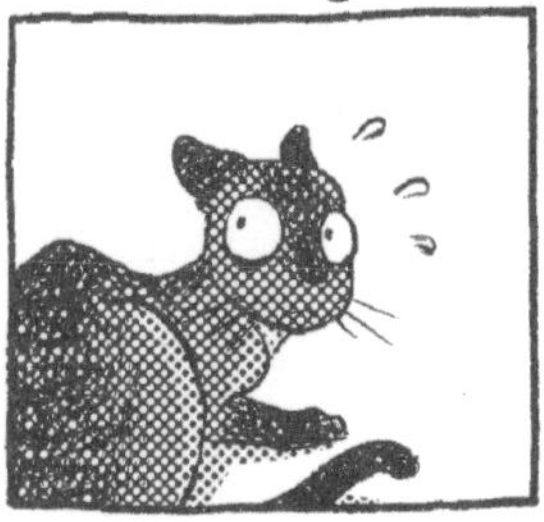

fret

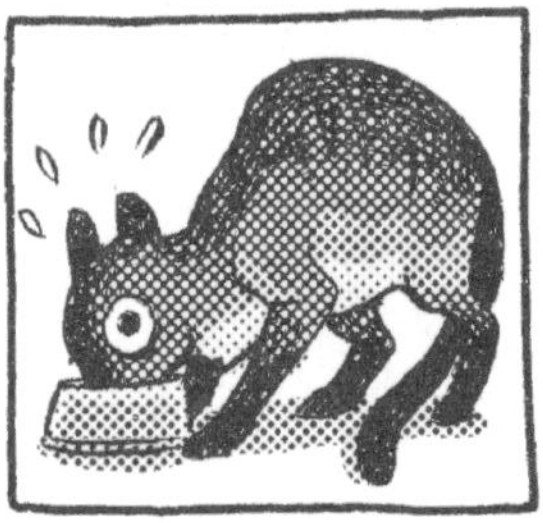

eat

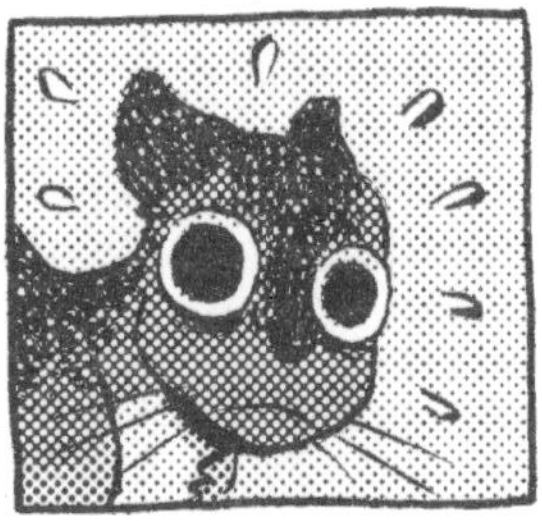

fret

things they both like to do:

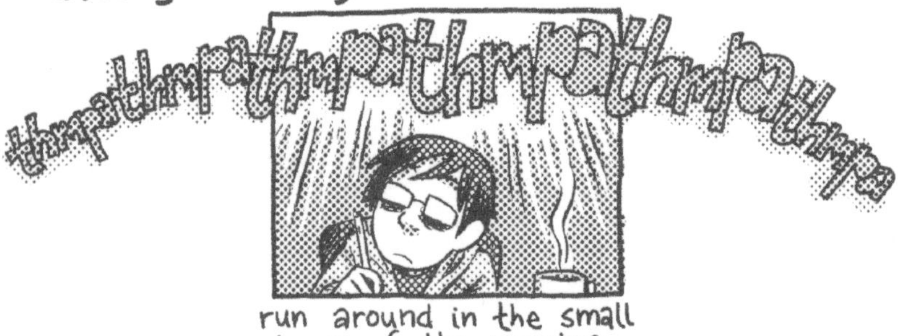

run around in the small hours of the morning

give or take ten years

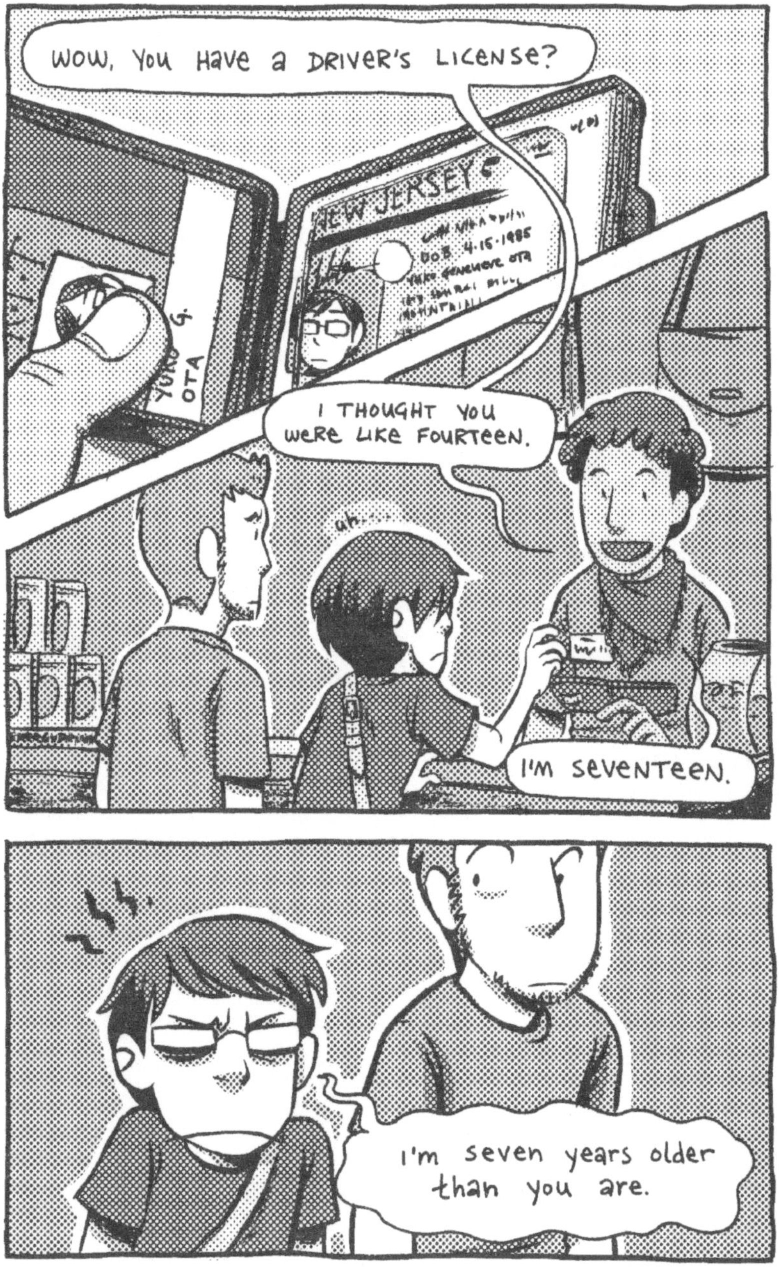
WOW, YOU HAVE A DRIVER'S LICENSE?
NEW JERSEY
YUKO G. OTA
I THOUGHT YOU WERE LIKE FOURTEEN.
I'M SEVENTEEN.
I'm seven years older than you are.

get ripped quick

ANANTH: 10 pullups

CONRAD: 7 pullups

JOHN: 7 pullups

YUKO: 3/4 pullup

ananth's tennessee plague

you were boat-adopted

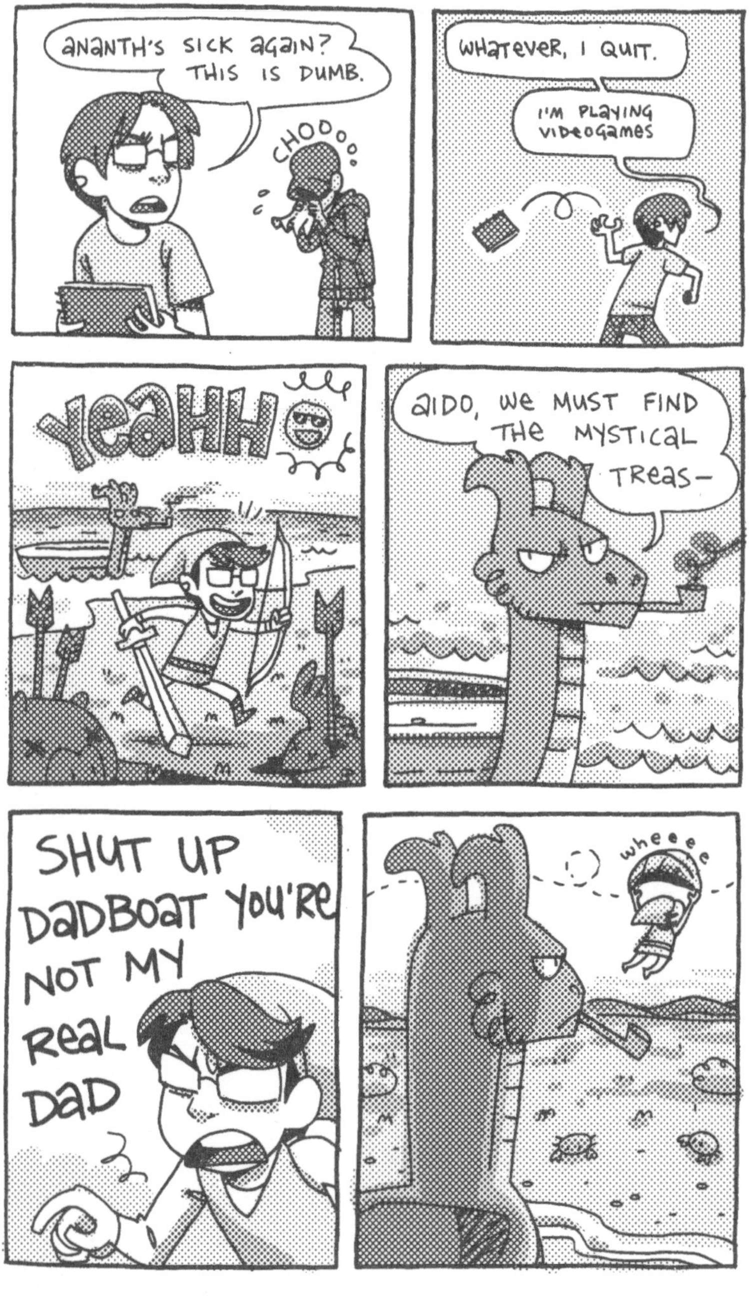
ANANTH'S SICK AGAIN? THIS IS DUMB.
CHOOooo
WHATEVER, I QUIT.
I'M PLAYING VIDEOGAMES
YEAHH
AIDO, WE MUST FIND THE MYSTICAL TREAS—
SHUT UP DADBOAT YOU'RE NOT MY REAL DAD
wheeee

aaaaaaaaaa

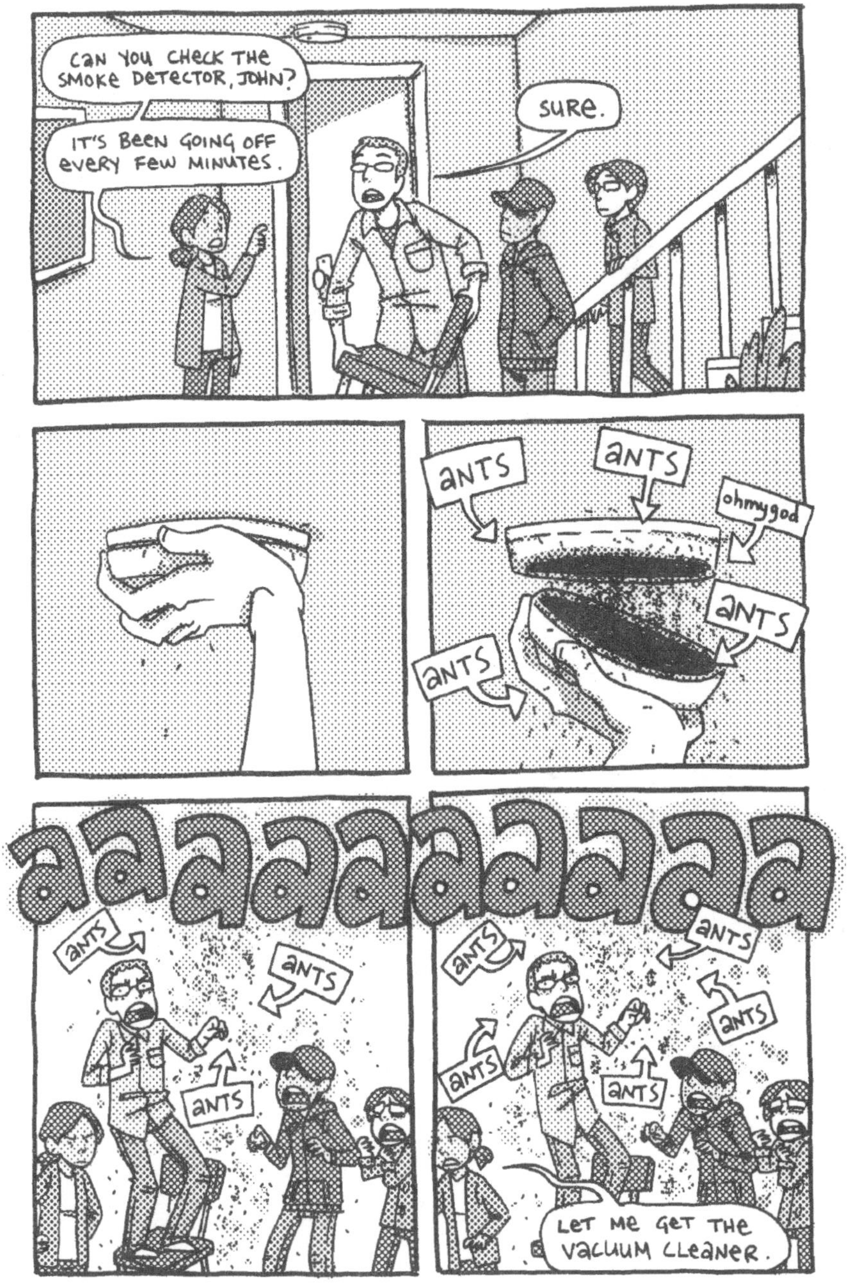
CAN YOU CHECK THE SMOKE DETECTOR, JOHN?
IT'S BEEN GOING OFF EVERY FEW MINUTES.
SURE.
ANTS
ANTS
ohmygod
ANTS
ANTS
aaaaaaaaaaaaaa
ANTS
ANTS
ANTS
ANTS
ANTS
ANTS
ANTS
ANTS
LET ME GET THE VACUUM CLEANER.

REM cooking

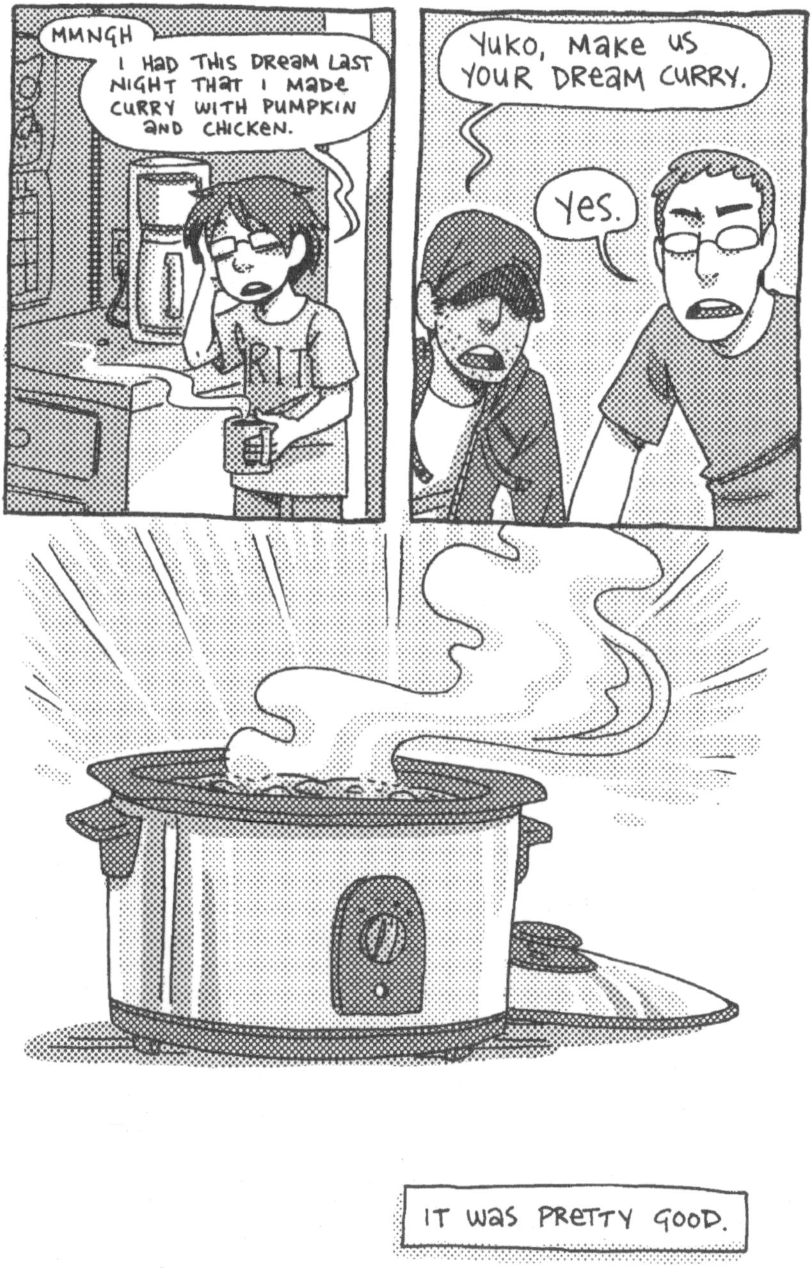
MMNGH
I HAD THIS DREAM LAST NIGHT THAT I MADE CURRY WITH PUMPKIN AND CHICKEN.
RIT
YUKO, MAKE US YOUR DREAM CURRY.
YES.
IT WAS PRETTY GOOD.

DREAM CURRY

This recipe makes enough curry for 6+ people, with leftovers. Quick to put together, no need to watch it, difficult to overcook... there aren't a lot of ways to mess this up.

Makes one giant 6 quart pot of curry!

INGREDIENTS
x2 Large chicken breasts, cubed (or more)
x1 15 oz can of pumpkin puree
x1 15 oz can of reduced sodium chicken broth
x1 8 oz box of S&B Golden Curry
x~4 carrots, peeled and cut into bite-sized pieces
x~3 big potatoes, peeled & cut into pieces
x1 Large onion, cut into large pieces
x~2 garlic cloves, diced
x~1 tbsp ginger (grated fresh or dried)
Cream or milk to taste

INSTRUCTIONS
1. Add all ingredients (except milk) to slow cooker.
2. Just barely cover all ingredients with water.
3. Cover and cook on high for 4-5 hours or low on 6-8 hours, stirring every few hours.
4. Add cream if desired.

Feel free to add or replace any vegetables. This will probably taste good with tomato, apple, sweet potato, peas, squash, eggplant, pepper, or whatever. There's no right way to make it.

If you want, you can eat the curry plain. Traditionally, you pour it over Japanese sticky rice, but you can also put the curry over regular white rice, ramen noodles, spaghetti, or whatever else you might want.

This is an ideal winter meal. It's stick-to-your-ribs warm and it'll keep in your freezer for-ev-er.

the thought that counts

john sets more things on fire

except for the cats and her mom

desperate times

SPACKLEHaUS memoirs 3

MaN, THaT'S a LOT OF GREaSE...

HE DID THIS FOR a YEaR.

harder better faster stronger

palpable discomfort

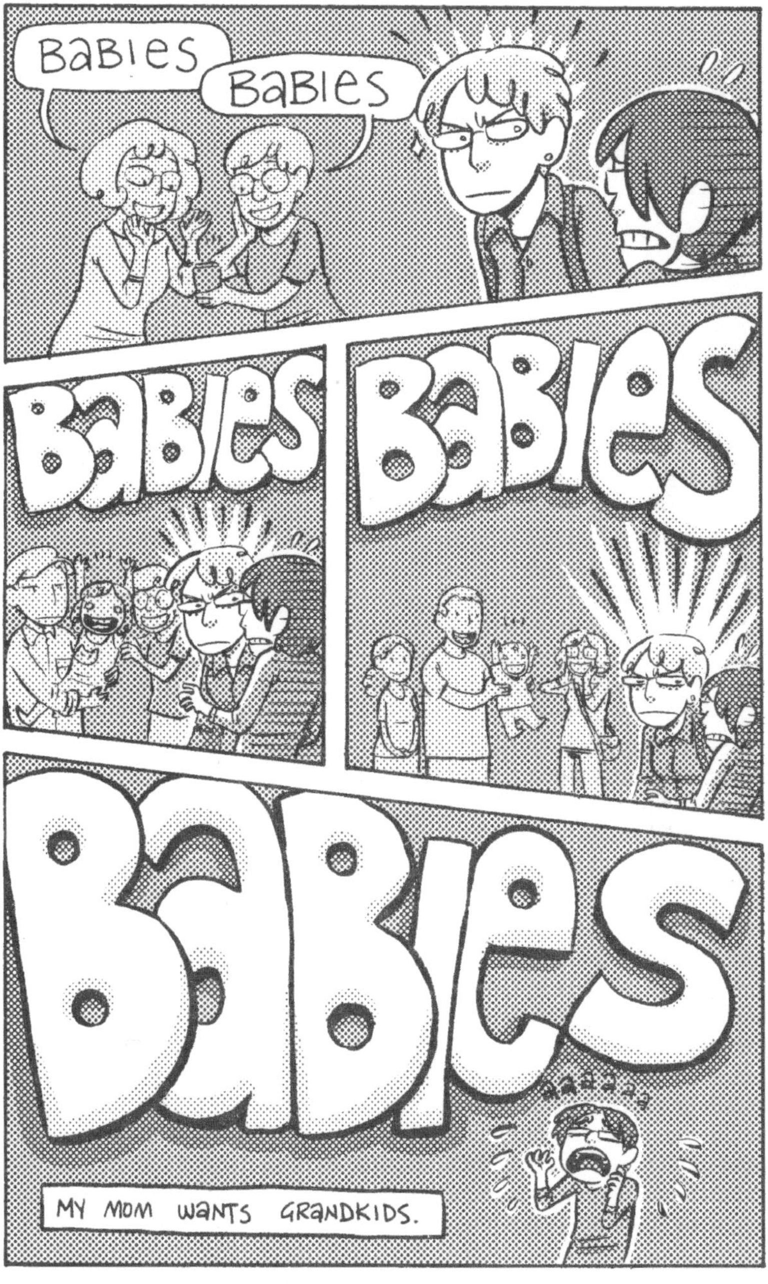
BABIES
BABIES
BABIES
BABIES
BABIES
MY MOM WANTS GRANDKIDS.

luckily they are all nerdy

on cats and burly ripped dudes

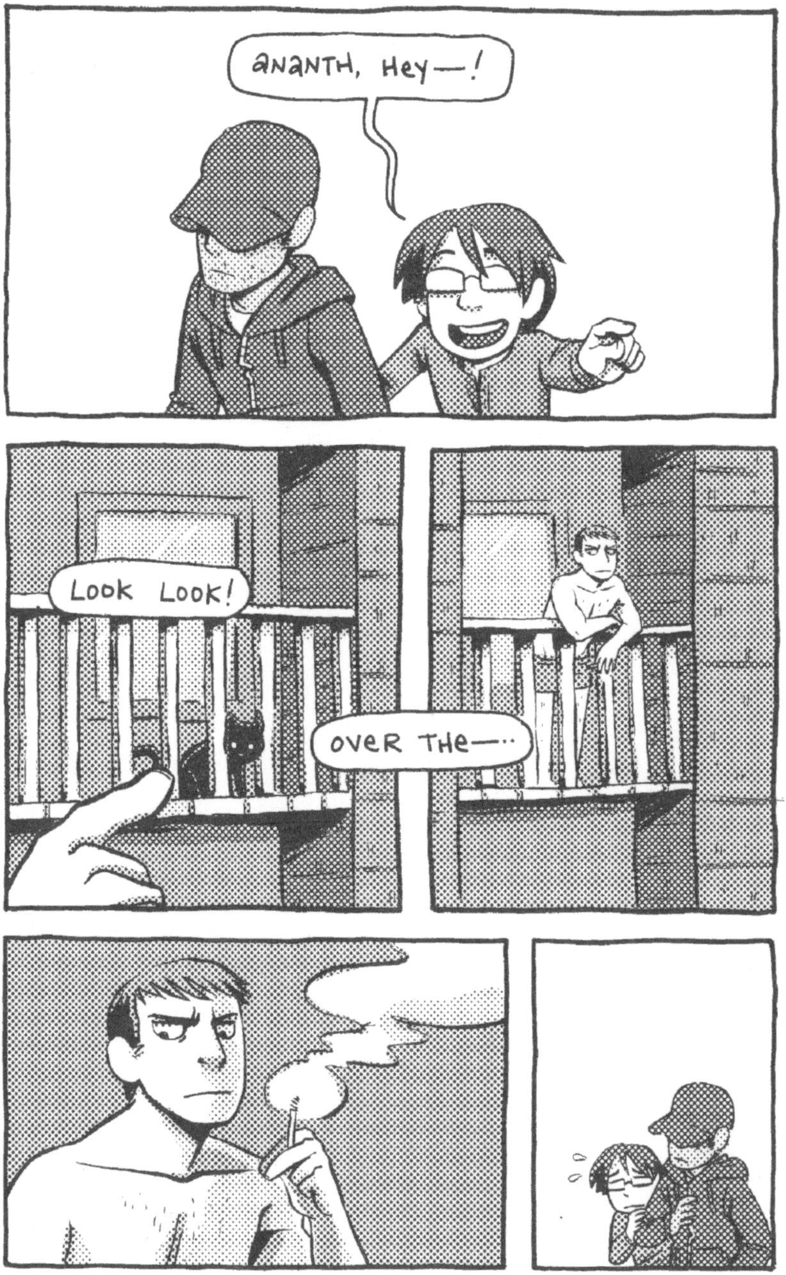
ANANTH, HEY—!
LOOK LOOK!
OVER THE—..

natural defense mechanisms

a lesson in appropriate attire

this keeps on happening.

she was pretty angry

STEEL NIBS AND I
ARE BREAKING UP.

she only likes real coffee

flights and flights of stairs

TRYING TO
TALK TO ME IN
JAPANESE IS LIKE
LISTENING TO ME SLOWLY
FALLING DOWN THE STAIRS.

then again, it's probably engrish

don't go back to rockville

foxes in the backyard

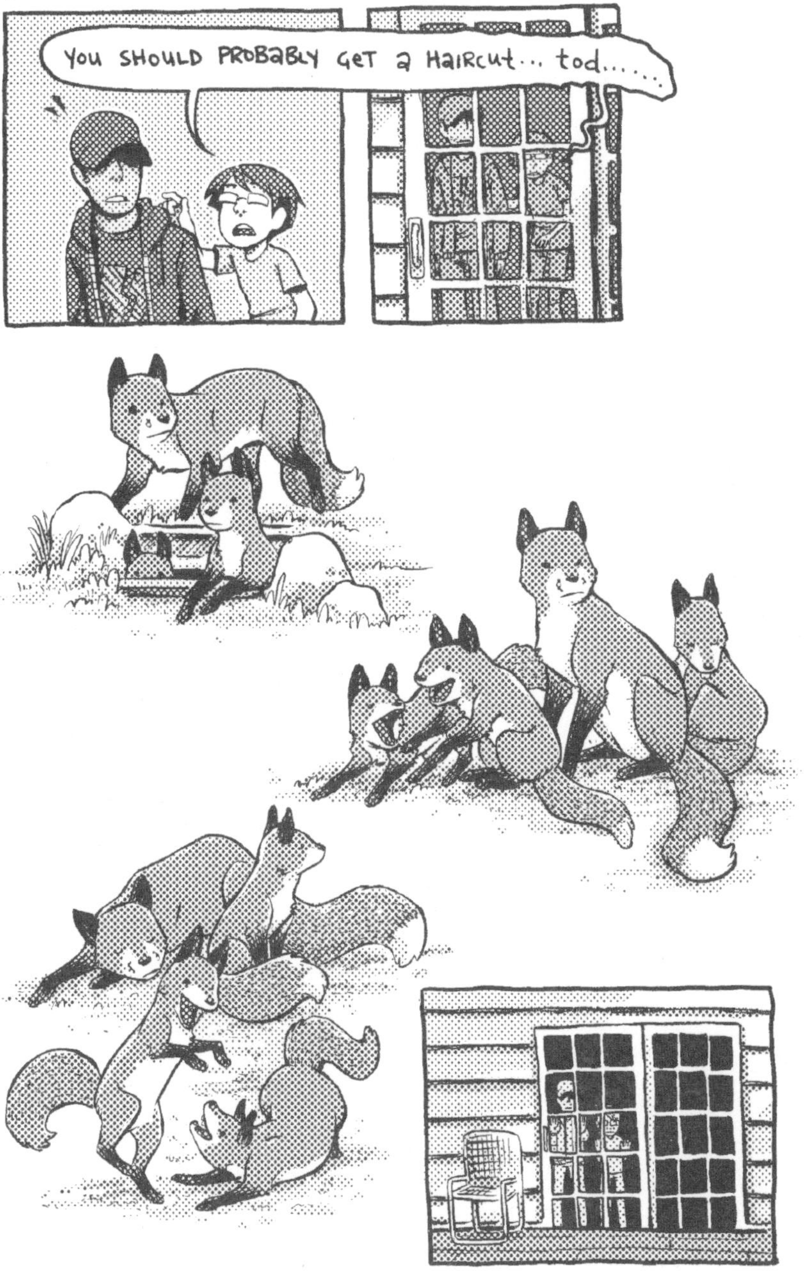
YOU SHOULD PROBABLY GET A HAIRCUT... TOD......

CUTE THINGS WE'VE SEEN ON THE SUBWAY LATELY

that can't be comfortable

at least we
can be assured
that Gonta will
never be eaten
by dinosaurs.

his pride, her passion

THERE WAS A WOMAN READING A ROMANCE NOVEL ON THE METRO.

SHE WAS AT ONE OF THE STEAMY PARTS.

why is it always my carpet

MORE THINGS MIKA & GONTA LIKE TO DO:

KLIKK

Crek crek crek crek

SPLUKK

aaaaaaaaa

VOMITING ON YUKO'S CARPET.

one bunny rabbit....

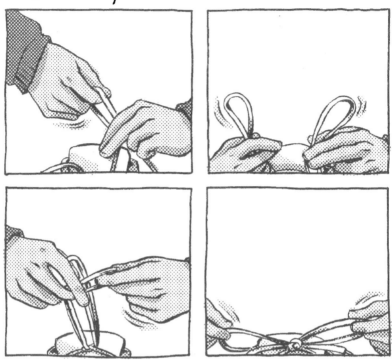

i still have to make bunny-ears to tie my shoes.

WHAT ARE YOU, SIX?

SH-SHUT UP

enjoy your four-hour flight

a weekend at connecticon

SOPHIE MET CHOCO.

YUKO LEARNED SOME THINGS.

AND THEN I JUST ADDED A BOX OF LEMON PUDDING TO THE BATTER.

YOU CAN DO THAT??

DAVE WON AT POKER

WHAT HE WON:

$11.26

one of his own business cards

sacks of potatoes

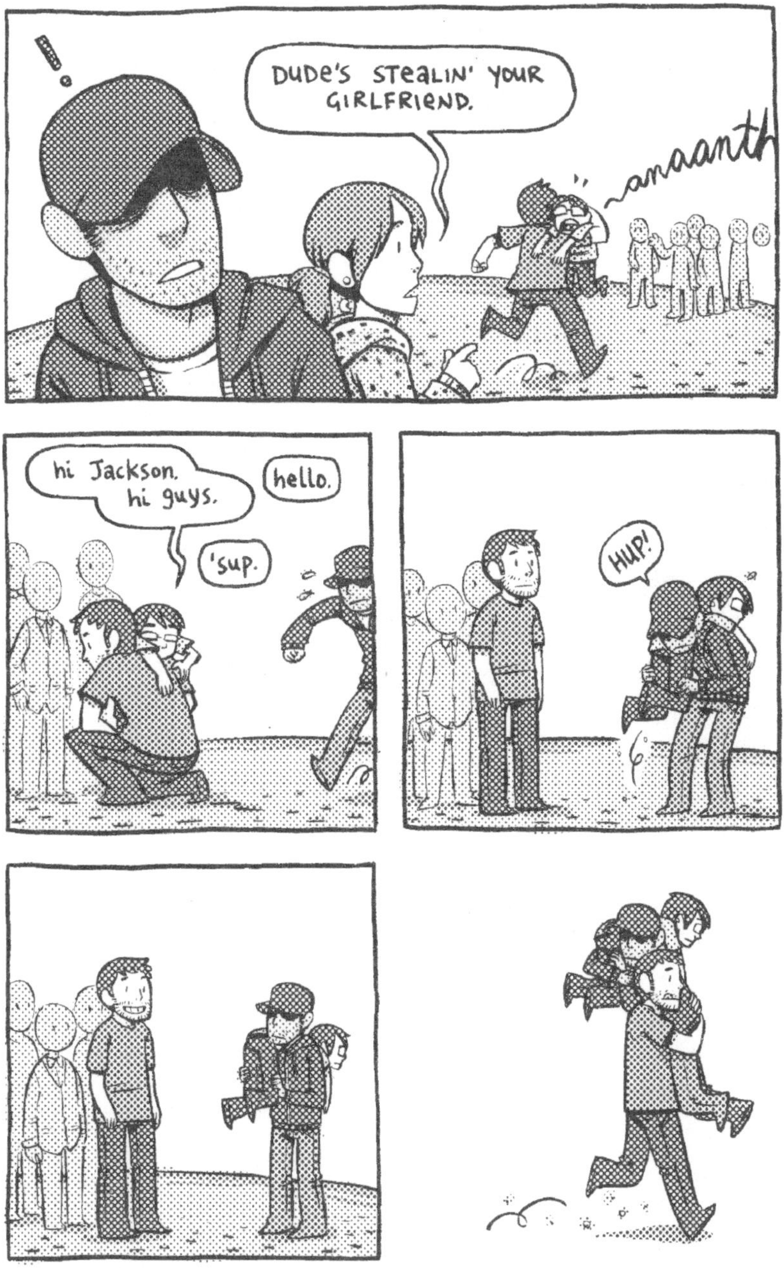
!
DUDE'S STEALIN' YOUR GIRLFRIEND.
~amaanth
hi Jackson. hi guys.
hello.
'sup.
HUP!

parental supervision required

so dumb

BOOKS
BOOKS
SEALED THE TAPE AND SCISSORS INSIDE.

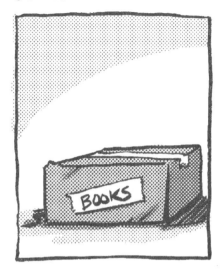

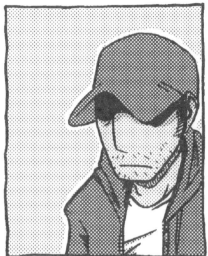

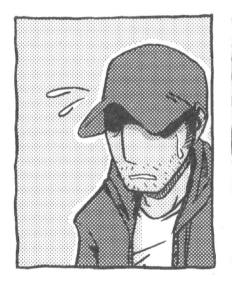

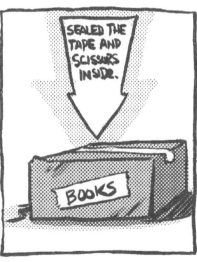

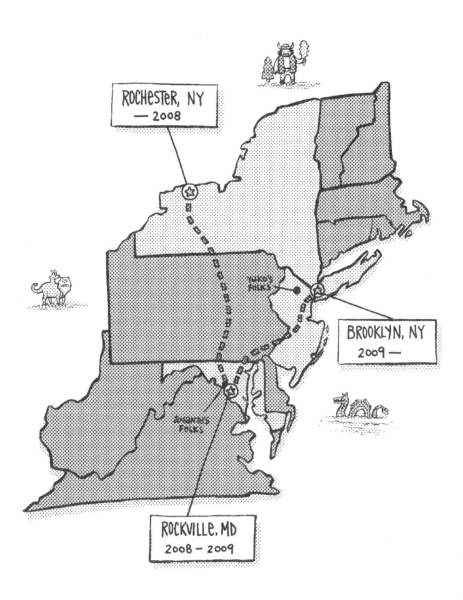

ROCHESTER, NY
— 2008

BROOKLYN, NY
2009 —

ROCKVILLE, MD
2008 — 2009

pardon our dust

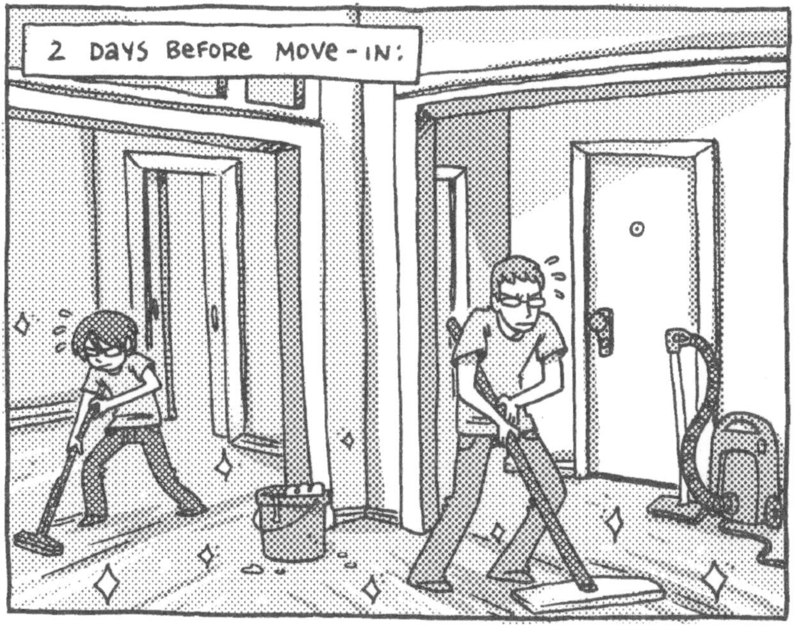
2 DAYS BEFORE MOVE-IN:

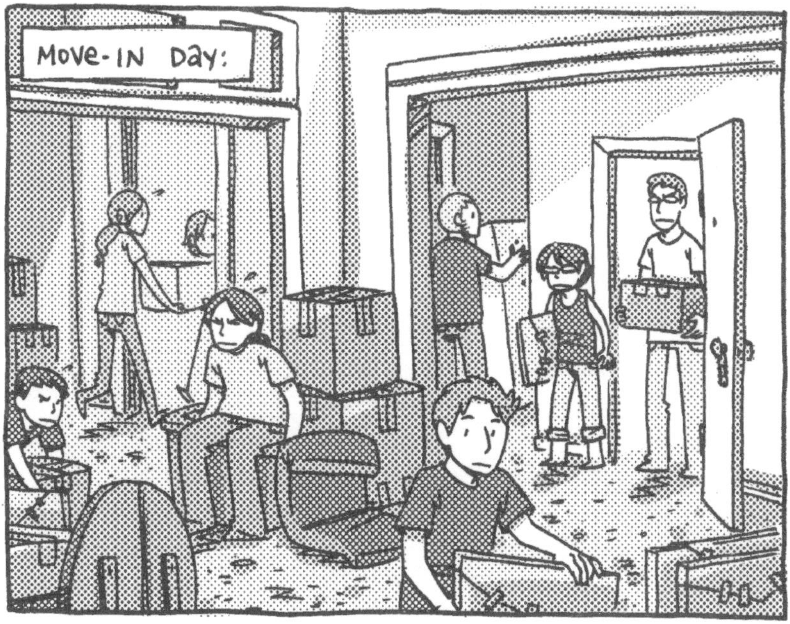
MOVE-IN DAY:

stairs forever

we now live on the top floor

of a five-story building

with no elevators.

it seemed like a good idea at the time.

the most terrible thing

at least it wasn't your head

I SWEAR, THIS IS GONNA HAPPEN ONE OF THESE DAYS.

well, maybe your head would've
been better

laundromat friends

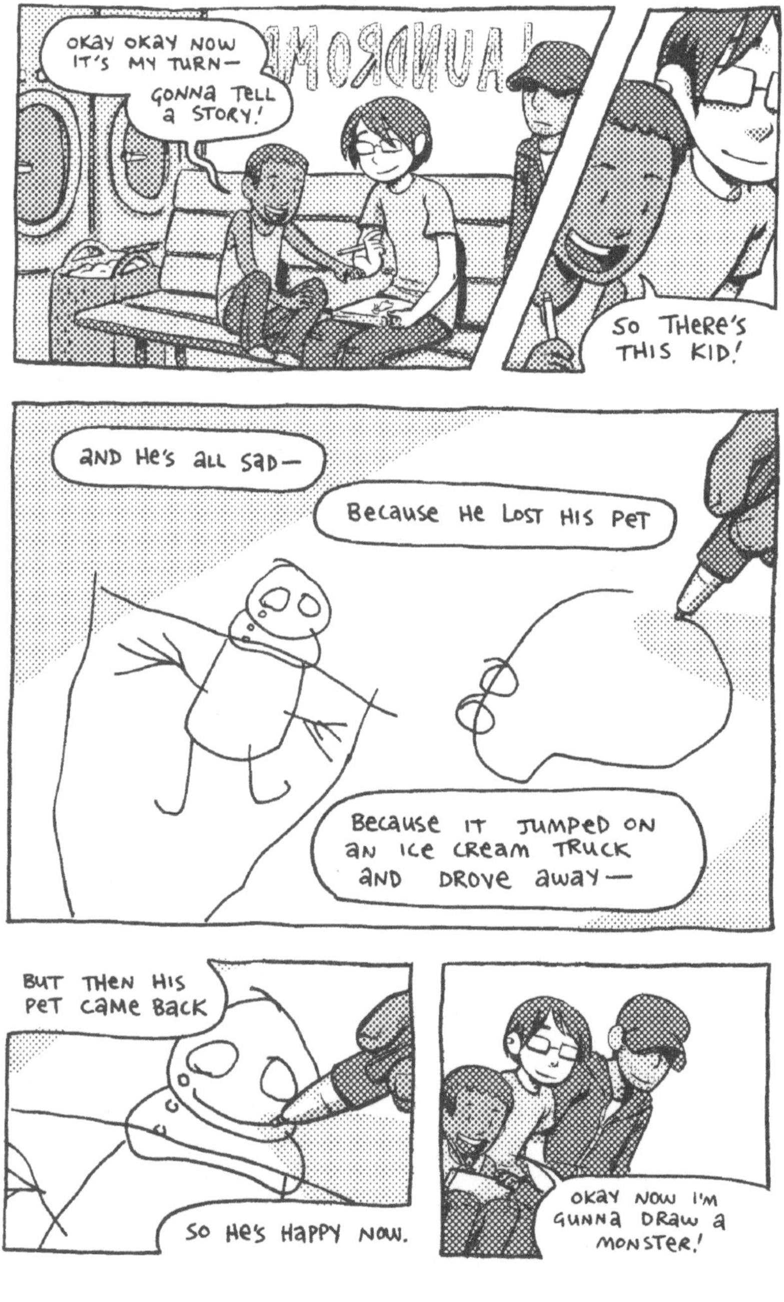
OKAY OKAY NOW IT'S MY TURN—
GONNA TELL A STORY!
SO THERE'S THIS KID!
AND HE'S ALL SAD—
BECAUSE HE LOST HIS PET
BECAUSE IT JUMPED ON AN ICE CREAM TRUCK AND DROVE AWAY—
BUT THEN HIS PET CAME BACK
SO HE'S HAPPY NOW.
OKAY NOW I'M GUNNA DRAW A MONSTER!

JORGE

AND THERE'S A TREE IN THE PARK AND A SQUIRREL AND A MOMMY BIRD BRINGING A WORM TO ITS BABIES AND THERE ARE EGGS IN THE NEST TOO AND THERE'S A SLIDE AND SOMEONE RIDING IT - NO IT'S TOO SHORT YEAH

WOW, I'M SUCH A GOOD ARTIST!

but how can I stay mad at you

how to ensure yuko never wears a skirt again

from planet panagarixa 7

BEFORE A WEDDING IN SOUTH CAROLINA

DID YOU GET THE RIGHT TUX?

Y-YEAH, BUT THEY SPELLED MY NAME FUNNY...

welcome to earth!

II.

WE'LL wander 'pon a pond'rous man,
His wide-brimmed hat held tall,

We'll sup amongst his heavy feet,
And find shade in his sprawl

Proposing to depart us three,
He'll decline dispassionately, or
Perhaps it will have been that he

Did not notice us at all.

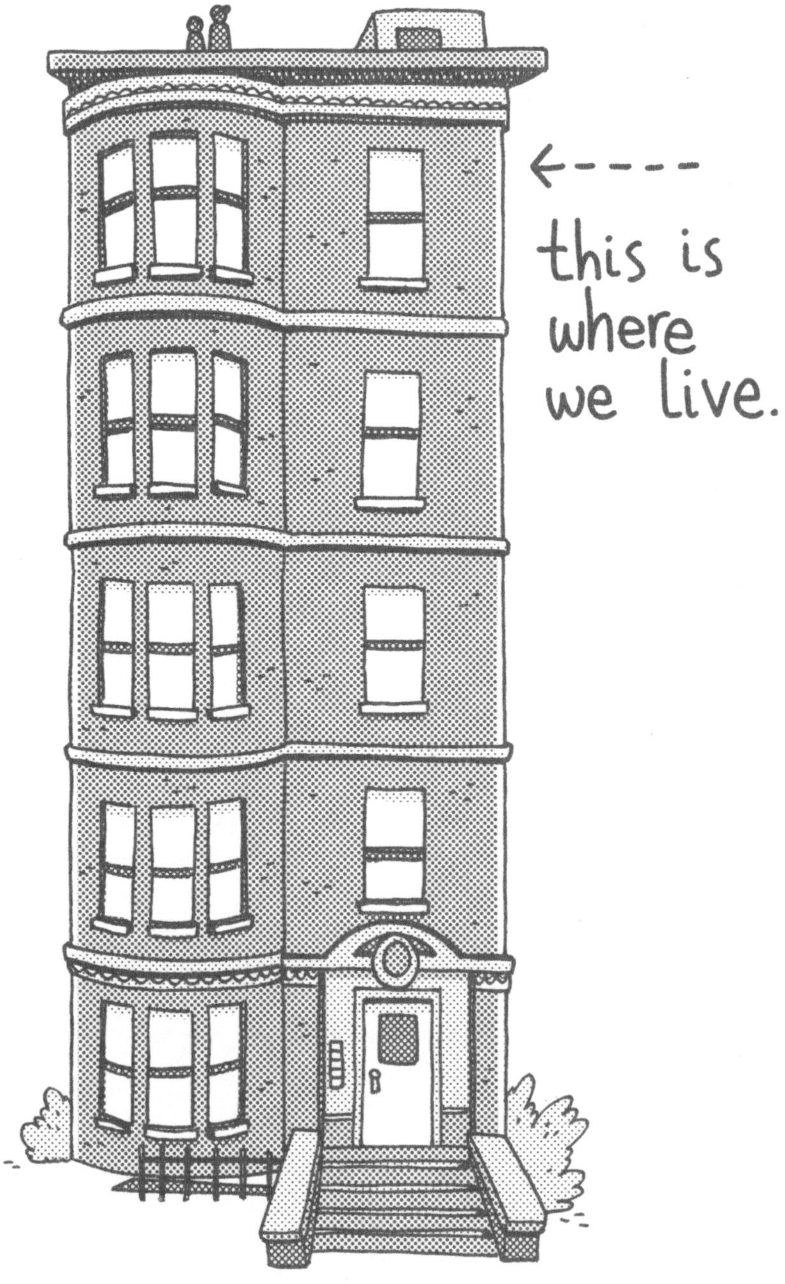
this is
where
we live.

escape to new york

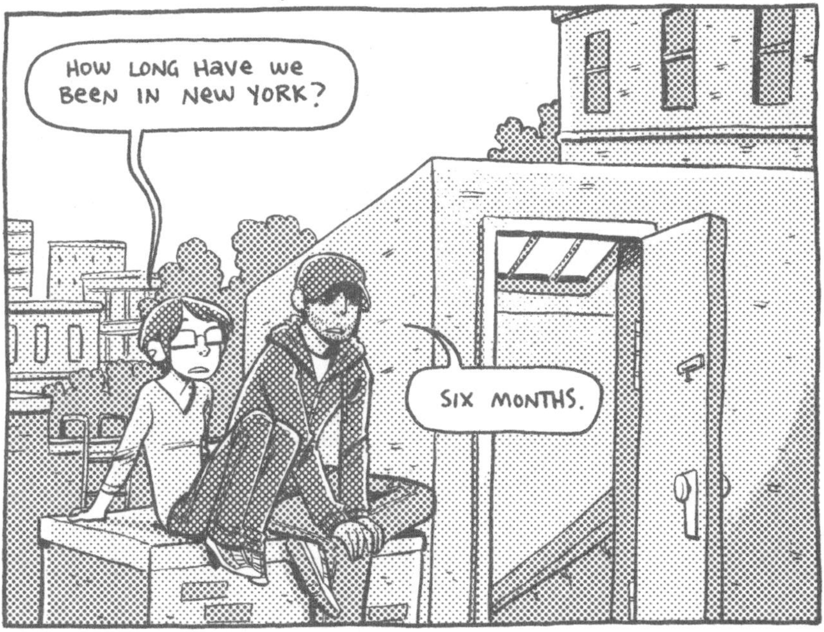
HOW LONG Have we Been IN New YORK?
SIX MONTHS.

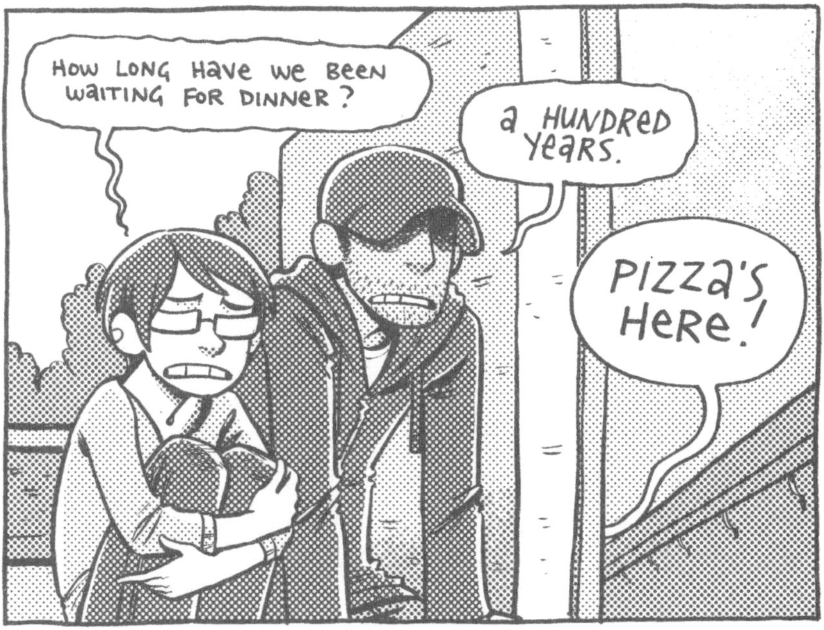
HOW LONG Have we Been waITING FOR DINNeR?
a HUNDReD YeaRS.
PIZZa'S HeRe!

don't burn the house down

but you don't live with us anymore

paleontoLOLgy

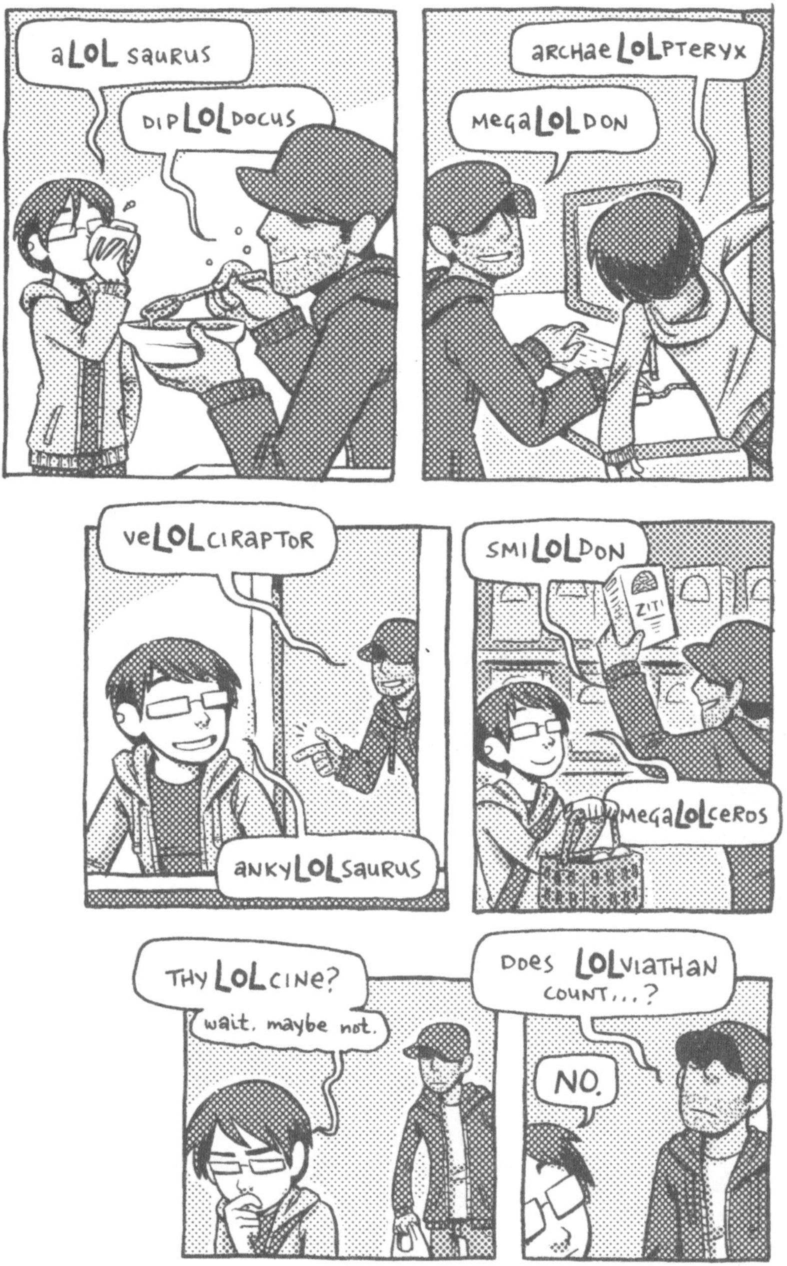
aLOL saurus
dipLOLdocus
archaeLOLpteryx
megaLOLdon
veLOLciraptor
ankyLOLsaurus
smiLOLdon
ZITI
megaLOLceros
thyLOLcine?
wait. maybe not.
Does LOLviathan count...?
NO.

hourly comics: october 6, 2009

1:20 AM

IT'S BEEN ANANTH'S BIRTHDAY FOR LIKE AN HOUR!

BUT ANANTH IS PLAYING LEFT 4 DEAD.

THERE'S LIKE 5 LBS OF M+M'S IN THIS THING

3:00 AM

COMIC IS DONE WANT TO DIE

9:30 AM

10:30 AM

man, my old inks are so inconsistent ...

PACKING PAGES FOR A COMICS EXHIBITION

11:00 am

DIRTY DISHES FROM
LAST NIGHT

CeReaL OUT OF a
COFFee CUP

11:30 am

GOD YOU KIDS
aRe SLOW.

aaa
SORRY!

GeORGe aRRIVeS!

12:45 PM

WAS THAT MARK WAHLBeRG?

PROBABLY.

We aRRIVe aT THe
VIaCOM BUILDING!

1:00 PM

dave   raina

♡ MeeT WITH Dave + RaiNa! ♡

I WISH YOU COULD'Ve
VISITeD WHeN IT WASN'T
SO... eMPTY....

THIS IS
awesome

OMIGOSH We'Re TOURING
NICKeLODeON MAGaZINe eee

NERDING ABOUT AVATAR

IT'S LIKE A SHRINE TO ████████████ AND ████████████████ HERE.

5:00 PM

full of free comics from Dave

GROCERY SHOPPING FOR CAKE INGREDIENTS

6:00 PM

what.

WHAT.

WOMAN FEEDING COMBOS TO HER DOG ON THE TRAIN D:

7:00 PM

WE SHOULD DO BIRTHDAY SUSHI SOON ♥ ♥

LET'S ALL DO BIRTHDAY SUSHI!

SO WE ALL DO BIRTHDAY SUSHI.

VVVVVBRRRRR.

BUT FIRST, WE HAVE TO DO DISHES. and vacuum.

8:00 PM

9:00 PM

YUKO & GEORGE MAKE A CAKE

I THINK THAT EGG WAS FERTILIZED.

DON'T TELL ANANTH.

oops.

10:00 PM

WORKING ON CONTRACT WORK WHILE CAKE COOLS.

11:00 PM

11:30 PM

FINISHING DEXTER SEASON 1

3:30 AM

Z*

*except for Conrad who pulled an all-nighter finishing work

दिवाली   DIWALI (in my family)

DIWALI CELEBRATES THE RETURN OF RAMA FROM EXILE, DURING WHICH HE DEFEATED THE DEMON KING RAVANA TO SAVE HIS WIFE SITA. HIS SUBJECTS LIT ROWS OF LAMPS (DIYAS) TO LIGHT HIS HOMECOMING. DIWALI MEANS "ROW OF LAMPS" IN SANSKRIT, AND IS CELEBRATED AS THE FESTIVAL OF LIGHTS.

A LAMP MADE FROM COTTON STRING WICKS AND GHEE (CLARIFIED BUTTER)

DIYA

PUJA (PRAYER) IS OFFERED TO LAKSHMI (THE GODDESS OF WEALTH), GANESH (THE GOD OF PROSPERITY AND LUCK), AND SARASVATI (THE GODDESS OF LEARNING).

PUJA

VARIOUS THINGS ARE OFFERED AS PART OF THE PUJA SUCH AS FRUIT, MITHAI (SWEETS), AND SILVER COINS WASHED IN A BOWL OF MILK. TILAK (A RED MARK) IS PUT ON THE FOREHEAD OF GODS AND THOSE PARTICIPATING WITH ROLI (VERMILLION).

YOU TOUCH THE FEET OF YOUR ELDERS AS A SIGN OF RESPECT — IN RETURN YOU RECEIVE BLESSINGS AND OCCASIONALLY GIFTS.

PRANAAM

these things happen sometimes

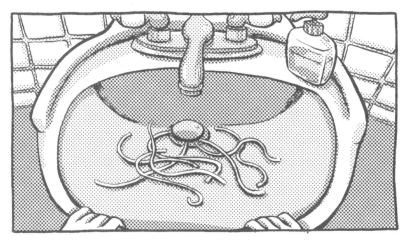

protomen @ trashbar

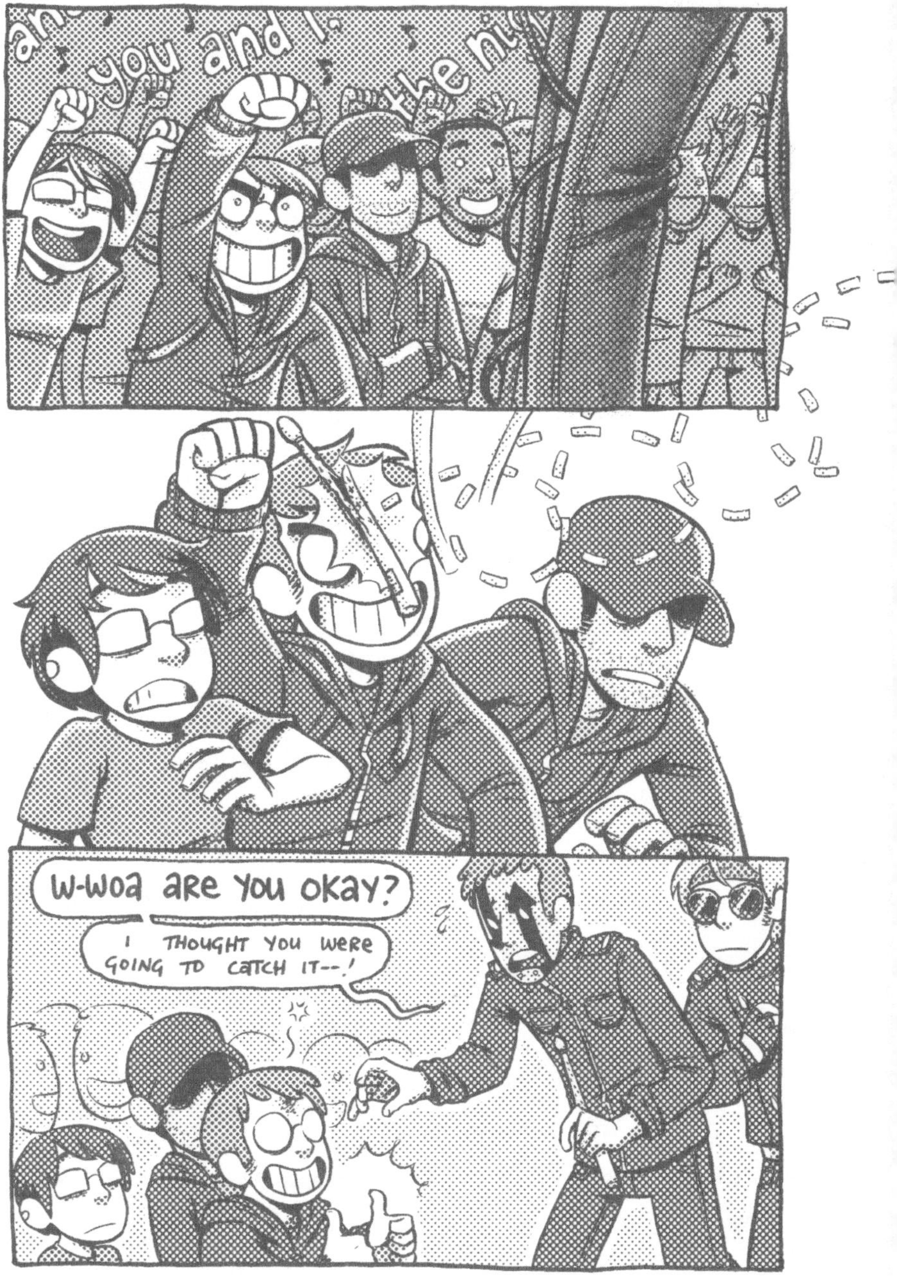
you and I
W-WOA ARE YOU OKAY?
I THOUGHT YOU WERE GOING TO CATCH IT--!

hand in the proverbial cookie jar

now he knows it's real

AND SO:

AND
LATER:

YUKO AND GEORGE GO TO GOODWILL

HEY HEY GUESS WHAT WE GOT

DID YOU GET ANOTHER STUPID MUG?

SH-SHUT UP HOW WOULD YOU KNOW

what they got:

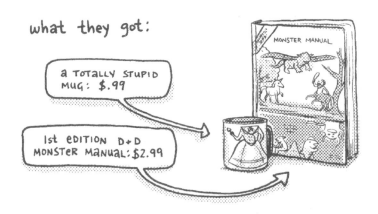

A TOTALLY STUPID MUG: $.99

1st EDITION D+D MONSTER MANUAL: $2.99

MONSTER MANUAL

CHRISTMAS MUG

BIRTHDAY MUG

PLASTIC INACCURATE
DINOSAUR MUG

BLACK CAT MUG

WILD STRAWBERRY MUG

SEDONA SUNSET MUG

WEIRD FRENCH
GOODWILL MUG

RABBITS IN
TREES MUG

GRUMPY DOLLAR-
STORE MUG

YUKO'S HIGH SCHOOL
GRADUATION MUG

GOODWILL GIRL MUG

GOODWILL "THIRTY
HURTS" MUG

full-contact comics

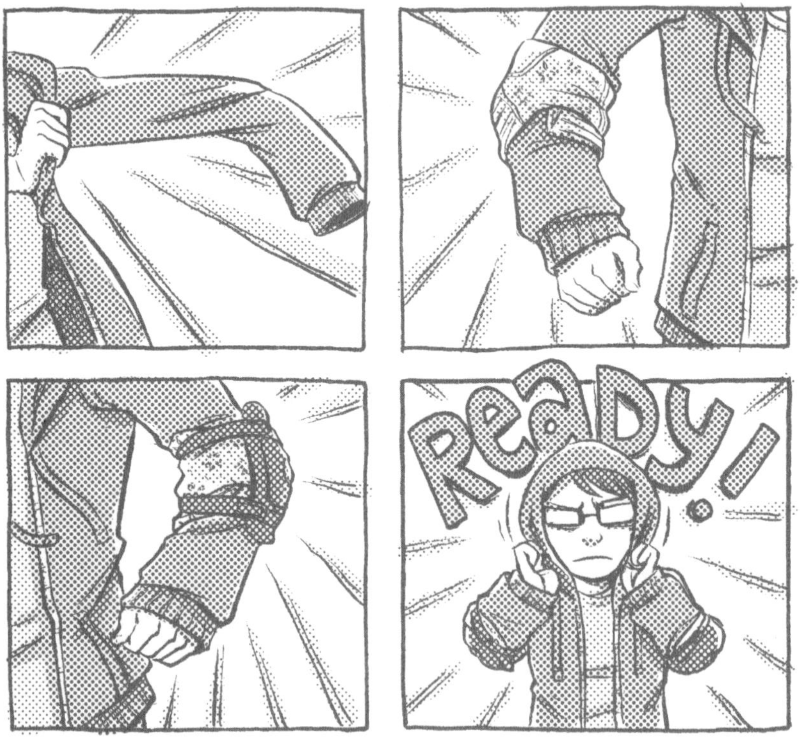
Ready!

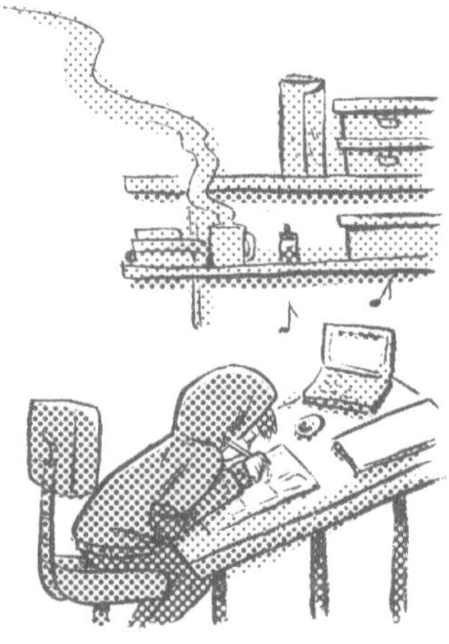

we're sorry john

OTHER THINGS JOHN TAKES SHOTS OF:

when did we even buy kiwis

speeed liiines

The ULTIMATE CLEMENTINE PEELING TECHNIQUE!

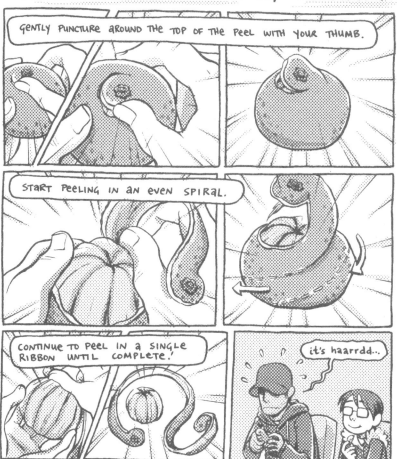

inept baby mouse

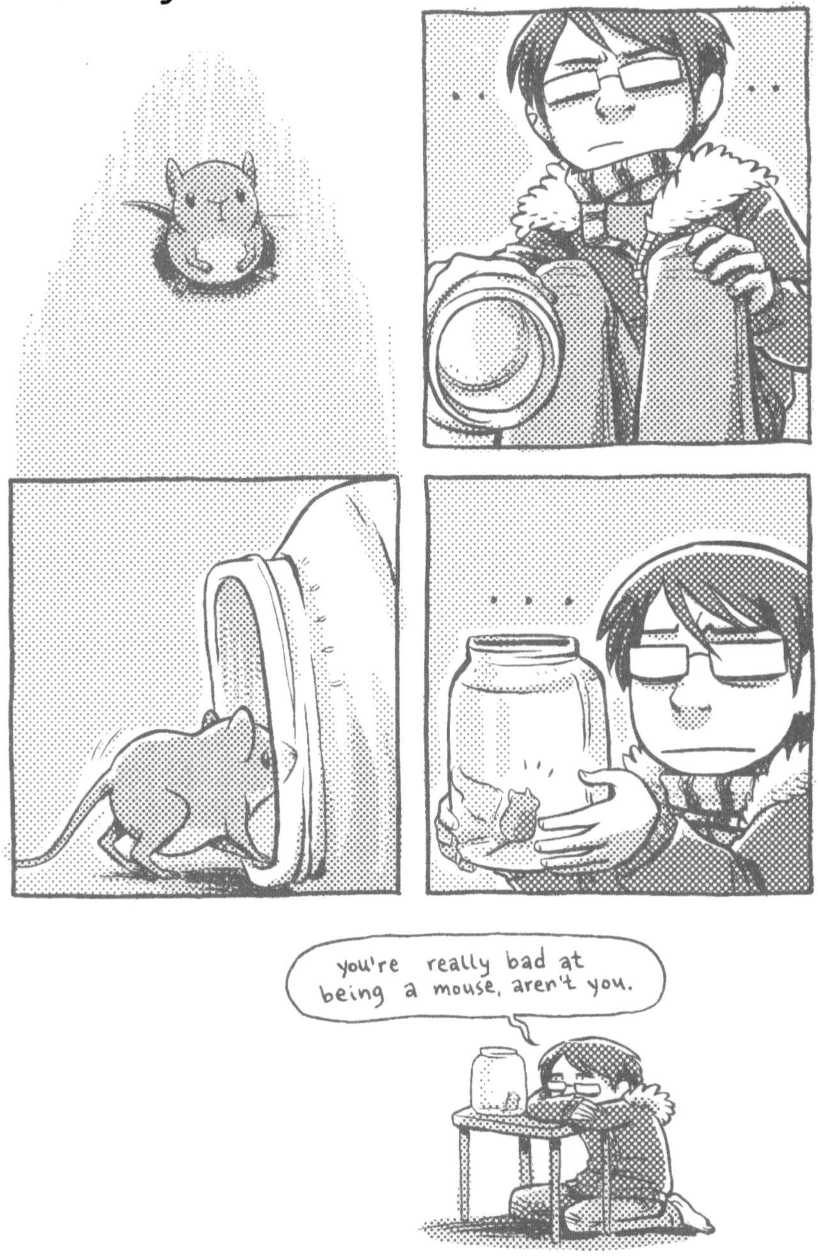
. . .
. . .
. . .
you're really bad at being a mouse, aren't you.

inept baby mouse II

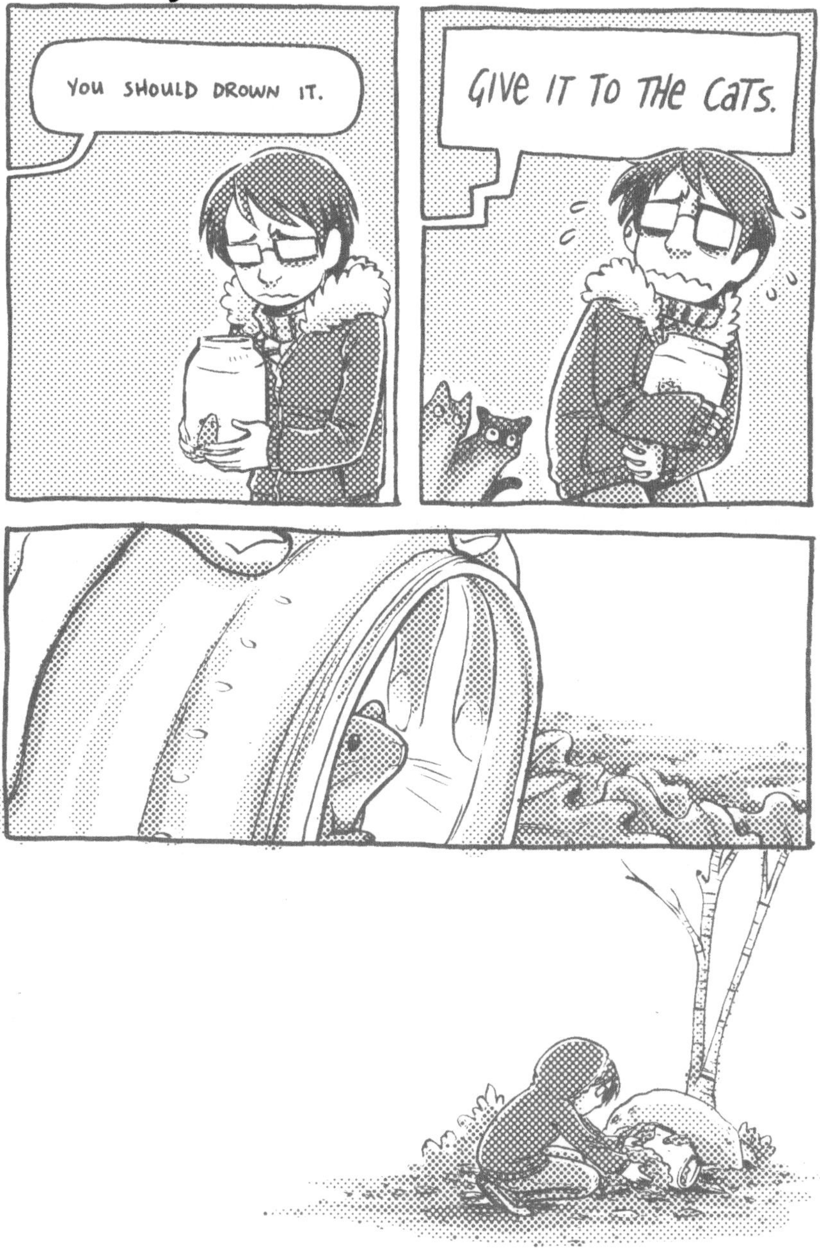
YOU SHOULD DROWN IT.
GIVE IT TO THE CATS.

on top of spaghetti all covered in cheese

FOR New
Years eve
we HaD a
BuNcH OF
FRieNDS
STay wiTH
uS...

BUT THE NEXT MORNING

VERY IMPORTANT QUESTIONS

WHAT'S THE DEAL WITH CONRAD'S HAIR?

WHAT WOULD HAPPEN IF GEORGE STOPPED SMILING?

127

MORE IMPORTANT QUESTIONS

WHAT IS BEHIND YUKO'S GLASSES?

WHAT DOES ANANTH'S FACE LOOK LIKE?

TERRIBLE CAT ODYSSEY

NOVEMBER— YUKO FOUND A RESCUE CAT THROUGH PETFINDER.COM.

DECEMBER— FINALLY GOT THE 10-PAGE APPLICATION.

TO MEET THE CAT.

HAD TO TRUDGE THROUGH THE SNOW TO GET A VET RECOMMENDATION.

JANUARY— FINALLY GOT APPROVED!

AFTER THREE MONTHS:

OOOWWW

the johnisms continue

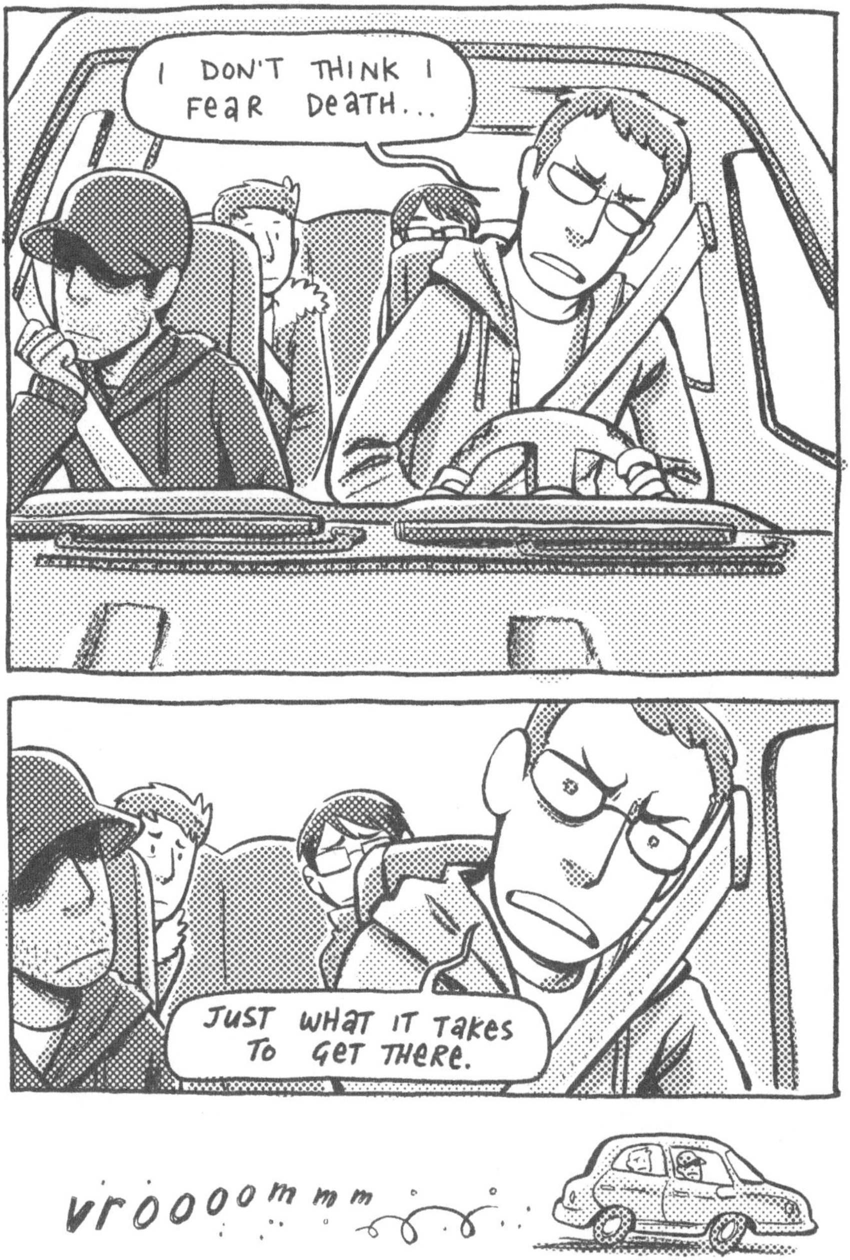
I DON'T THINK I FEAR DEATH...
JUST WHAT IT TAKES TO GET THERE.
vroooommmm

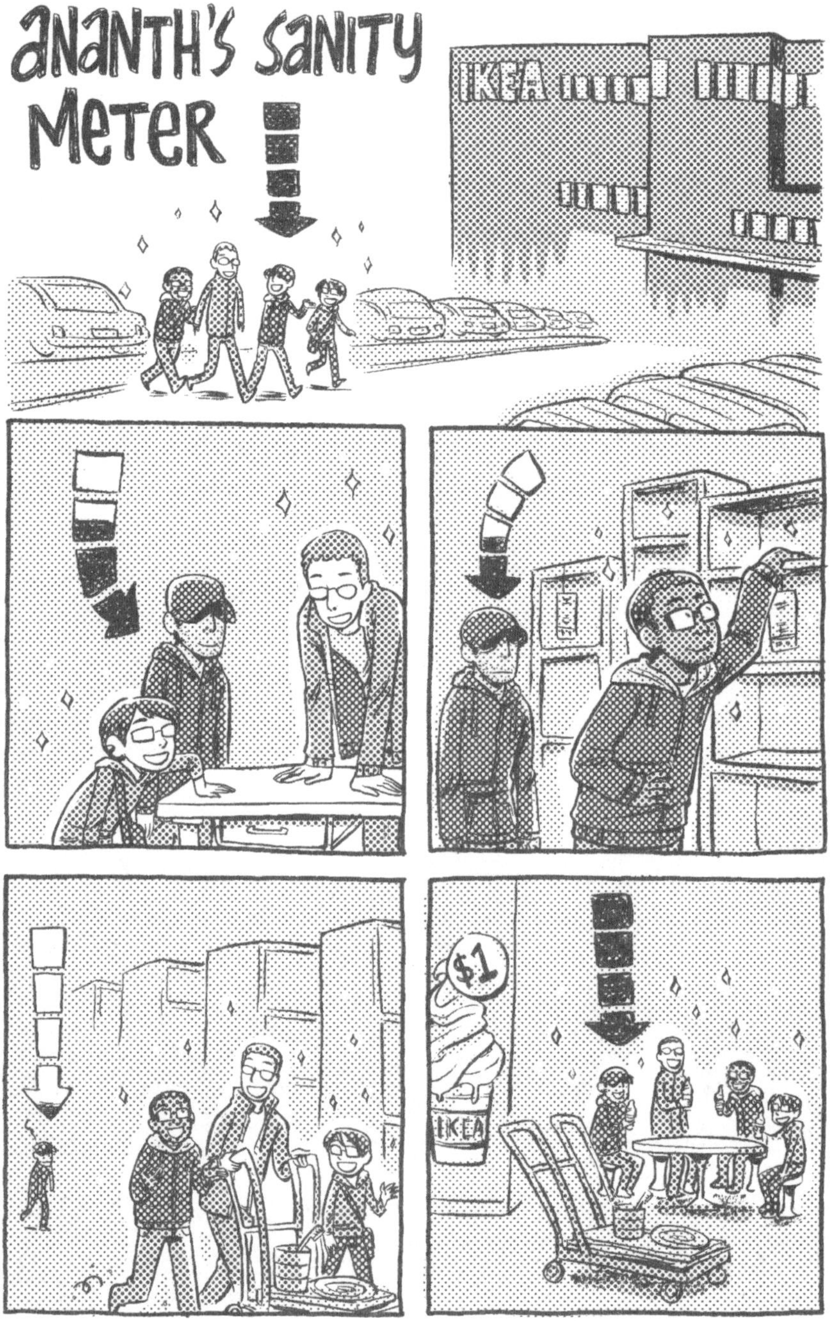
Ananth's Sanity Meter
IKEA
$1
IKEA

the triumphant return of wolf

ee, YOU BROUGHT THE SPIDER PLANT BACK! THANK YOU!

HERE, THESE FELL OFF.

AND NOW WE HAVE 15 SPIDER PLANTS.

HOW LAID BACK IS THIS CAT?

LET'S BOTHER IT

AND SEE HOW LONG IT TAKES FOR ME TO GET BITTEN.

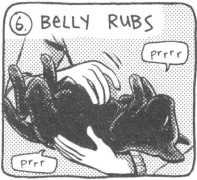

THIS OBVIOUSLY ISN'T A REAL CAT.

hourly comics: february 1, 2010

WENT TO BED WITH WET HAIR LAST NIGHT.

JOHN IS HERE!

TIME FOR BREADMACHINE!

OOPS, THE YEAST LATCH WAS PROPPED OPEN

EATIN' CEREAL, SHRINKIN' IMAGES FOR THE WEB.

ANANTH SET UP AN ONLINE SHIPPING ACCOUNT!

at the post office:

also my mom sent like 12 lbs of oranges.

The oranges are so acidic they hurt my teeth.

working on Megan's wedding invitation.

super calls me to let in the recently evicted tenants so they can check their mail.

MAKING TEA

DRINKING TEA, TALKING TO
ANANTH ABOUT SCRIPTS.

WRITING A LIVEJOURNAL
POST.

STILL WORKING ON THAT
THING FOR MEGAN.

AND THUMBNAILS.

AGH, I FORGOT — TODAY WAS ART GROUP.

DROWNING SORROWS IN CUTE CAT NAMES.

ANANTH LEAVES FOR HIS PARENTS' PLACE

BURNT THE TOAST (dinner)

WATCHING AWKWARD MACKIN' SCENES FROM MASS EFFECT 2

MAYBE I SHOULD START DRAWING MY HOURLIES.

138

WORKING ON JOHNNY WANDER COMIC INSTEAD

LISTENING TO ANGELS & DEMONS ON AUDIOBOOK.

INKING AND TALKING TO ANANTH ON AIM

THROAT IS FEELIN' SCRATCHY.

DRAWING HOURLIES.

THE MOON IS STUPENDOUSLY BRIGHT TONIGHT.

busy week.

well I guess conrad is home

YUKO'S TRAUMATIZING DENTAL MISADVENTURES

① BABY TOOTH PULLED BECAUSE IT WAS FUSING TO ADULT MOLAR. PERMANENT RETAINER AFTERWARDS.

② THE MUSCLE ATTACHING THE UPPER LIP TO THE GUMS REMOVED BECAUSE IT WAS PUSHING APART THE TOP INCISORS.

mowf

AGE 12: BRACES PUT IN FOR ABOUT A YEAR TO FIX THE GAP BETWEEN FRONT TEETH.

the insides of my cheeks are bleeding.

AFTERWARDS, A RETAINER.

AGE 15: AFTER GETTING FOUR CAVITIES IN THE SAME TOOTH, DENTIST DECIDES TO CROWN IT.

it's poorly formed, like there's a fold in the enamel.

it's gotta go.

BUT FIRST, ROOT CANAL

bwrrkrkgg

(GOT TO BRING THE NERVES HOME!)

142

age 19: WISDOM TEETH ARE IMPACTED AND NEED REMOVAL

But your tonsils are too inflamed, so we'll have to take those out first!

WHAT

TONSILS OUT. LAID UP FOR TWO MONTHS, LOST 12 LBS.

I can see every one of my ribs....

SURVIVED ON INSTANT MASHED POTATOES, ICED TEA, AND CODEINE.

THROAT HEALS, FINALLY ALLOWED TO GET WISDOM TEETH OUT!

Surprisingly painless!

age 22: PERSISTANT CHRONIC PAIN IN THE OLD CROWN

You can't possibly have pain in that tooth, there's no nerve! Unless there's an airbubble of bacteria inside causing an infection...

whuhf.

AND SO,

ROOT CANAL #2

BWRRKRKGG

SIGNIFICANTLY MORE PAINFUL THAN THE FIRST ONE!

ROOT CANAL HELPS NOTHING! EVENTUALLY YOU BECOME USED TO THESE THINGS.

it only really hurts when I brush my teeth.

the end
for now

SO THE DUDES IN THE NEIGHBORHOOD THINK ANANTH IS A JERK.

on self-incrimination

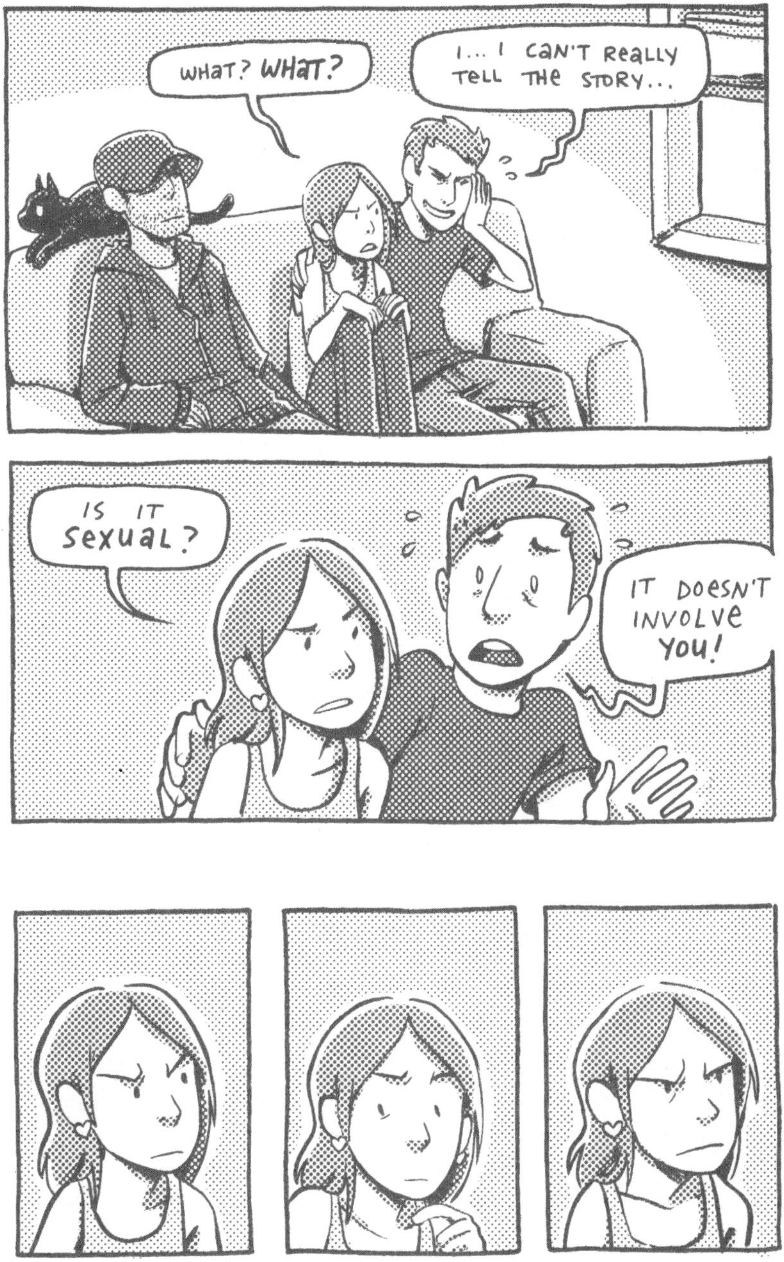
WHAT? WHAT?
I... I CAN'T REALLY TELL THE STORY...
IS IT SEXUAL?
IT DOESN'T INVOLVE YOU!

as foretold

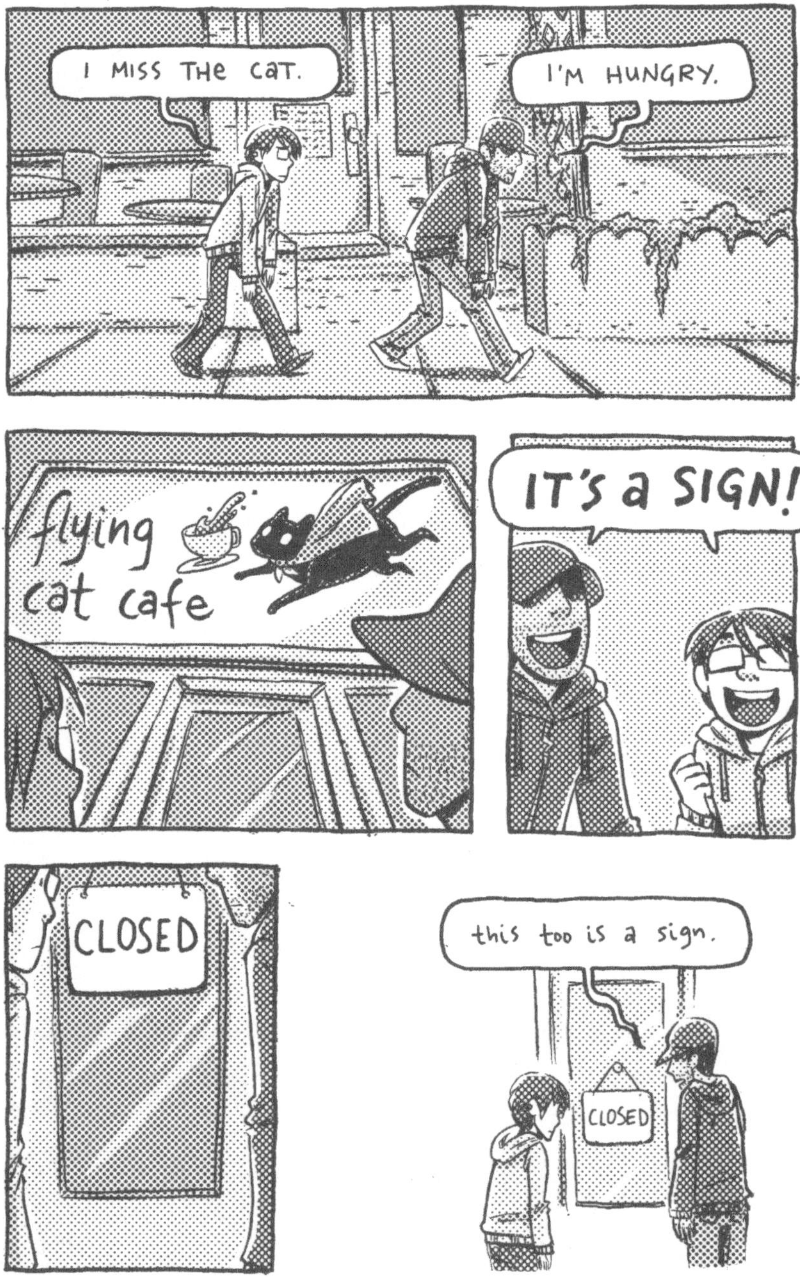
I MISS THE CAT.
I'M HUNGRY.
flying cat cafe
IT'S a SIGN!
CLOSED
this too is a sign.
CLOSED

ambulance cat

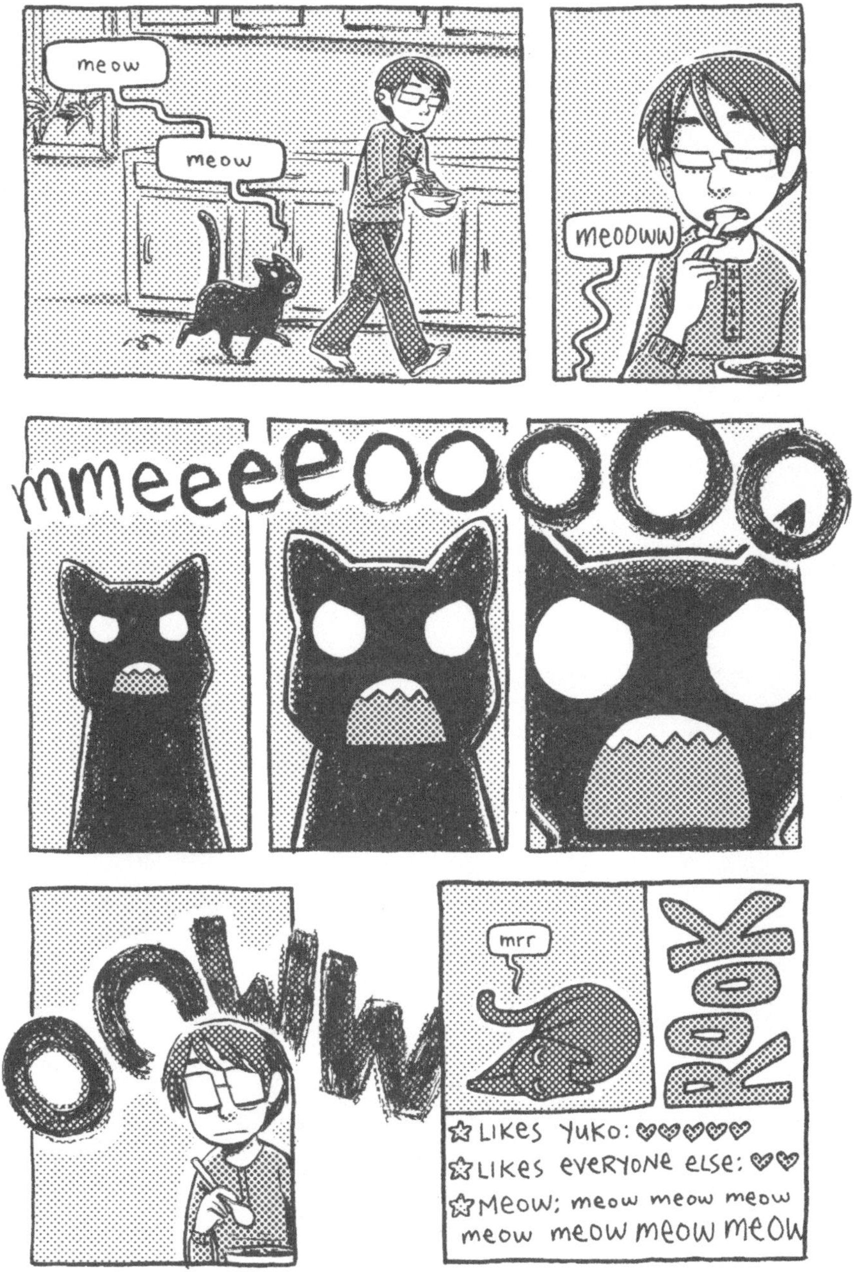
meow
meow
meooww
mmeeeeoooooo
ooww
mrr
ROOK
LIKES YUKO: ♡♡♡♡♡
LIKES EVERYONE ELSE: ♡♡
MEOW: meow meow meow meow meow meow meow

Ladies only

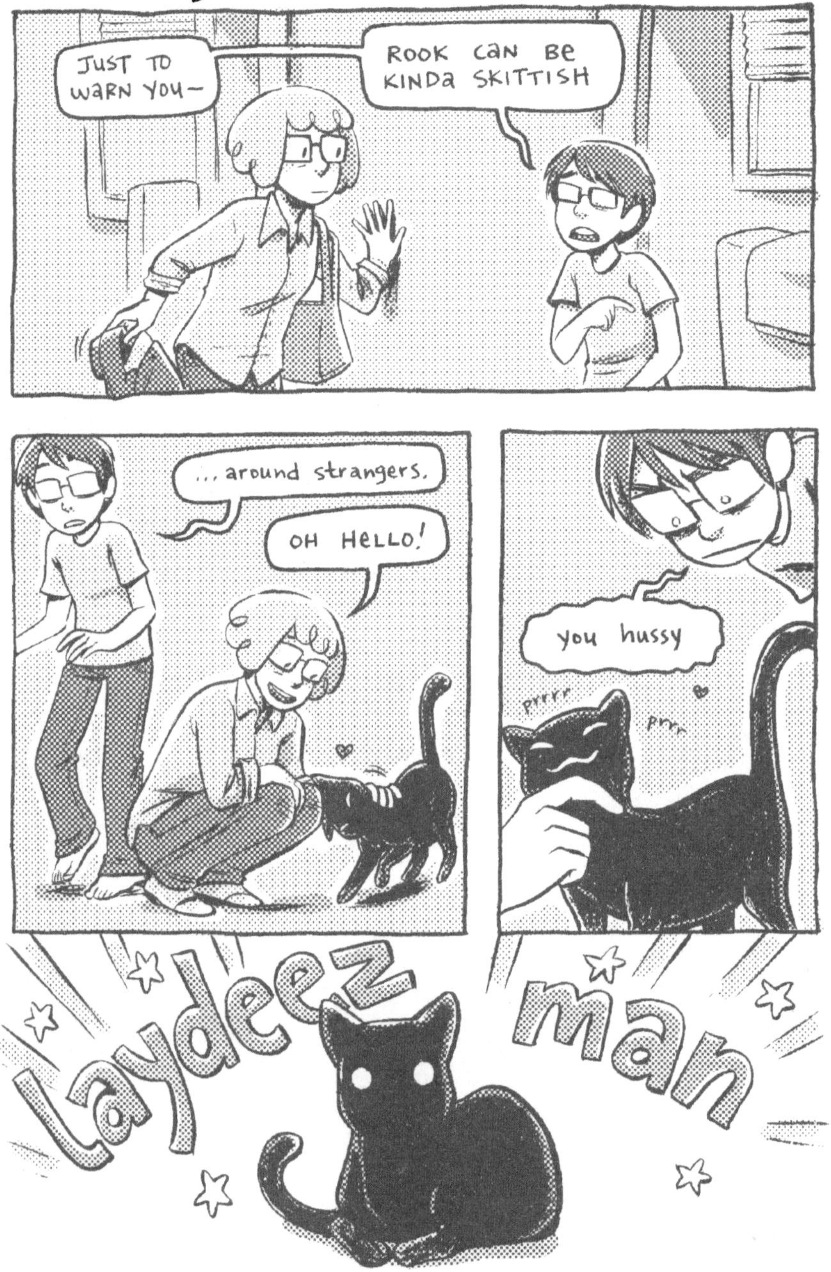
JUST TO WARN YOU—
ROOK CAN BE KINDA SKITTISH
...around strangers.
OH HELLO!
you hussy
prrrr
prrr
Laydeez man

like $200 of tinkertoys

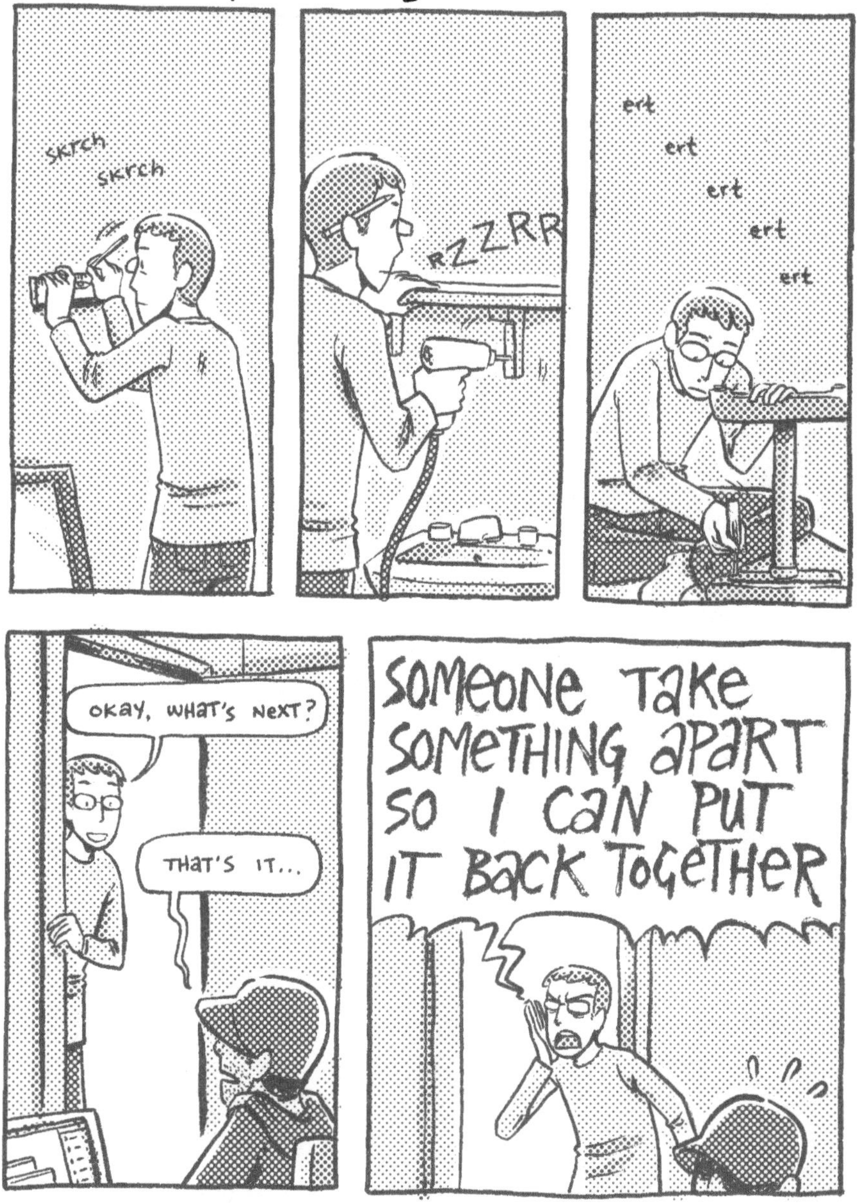
SKRCH
SKRCH
RZZRR
ert
ert
ert
ert
ert
OKAY, WHAT'S NEXT?
THAT'S IT...
SOMEONE TAKE SOMETHING APART SO I CAN PUT IT BACK TOGETHER

one man's trash

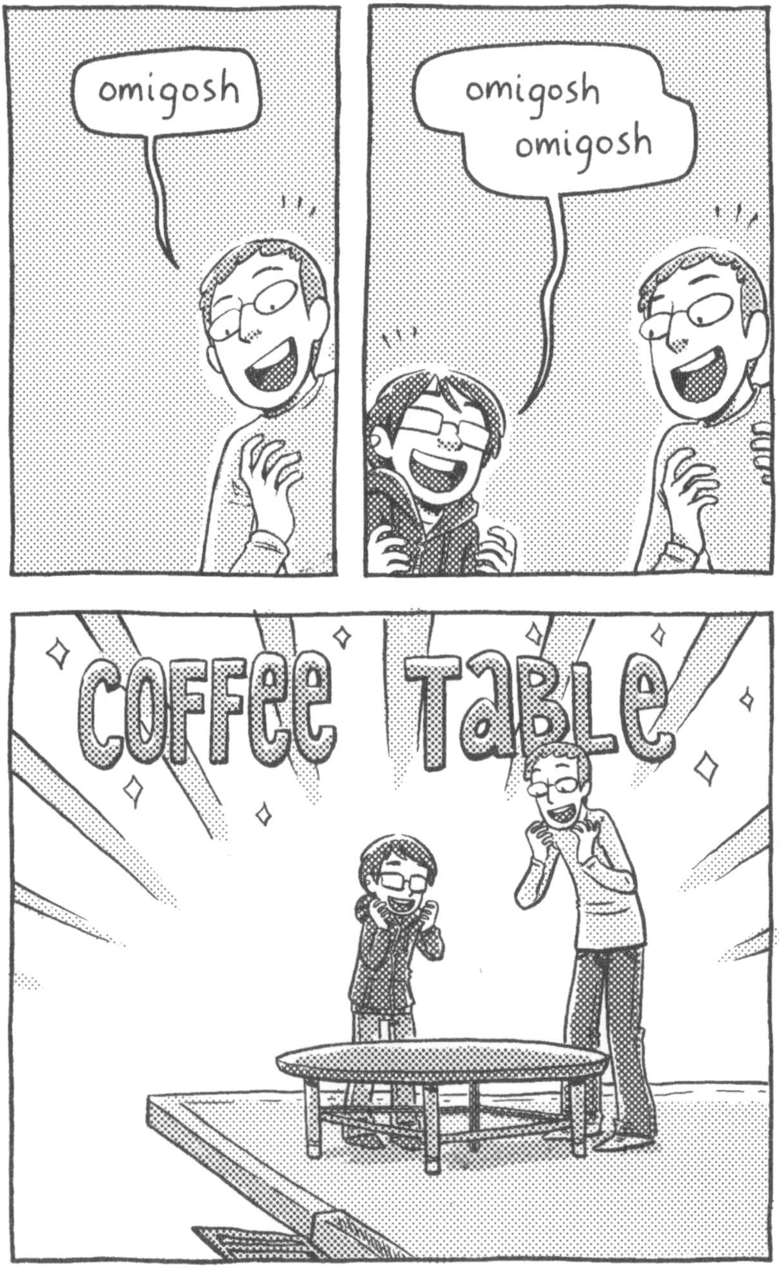
omigosh
omigosh
omigosh
COFFEE TABLE

SPACKLEHAUS MEMOIRS 4
the landlord

YOU MIND IF I SMOKE IN HERE?

um

OF COURSE NOT, IS MY PROPERTY!

CAN I TALK TO YOU ABOUT THE BASEMENT?

EHHHHH, STEP INTO MY OFFICE!

. . . .

uh, thanks for coming by....

EYYYY, YOU MIND IF I DRINK UPSTAIRS?

nothing some epoxy won't fix

because we sure weren't going to eat them

nothing personal

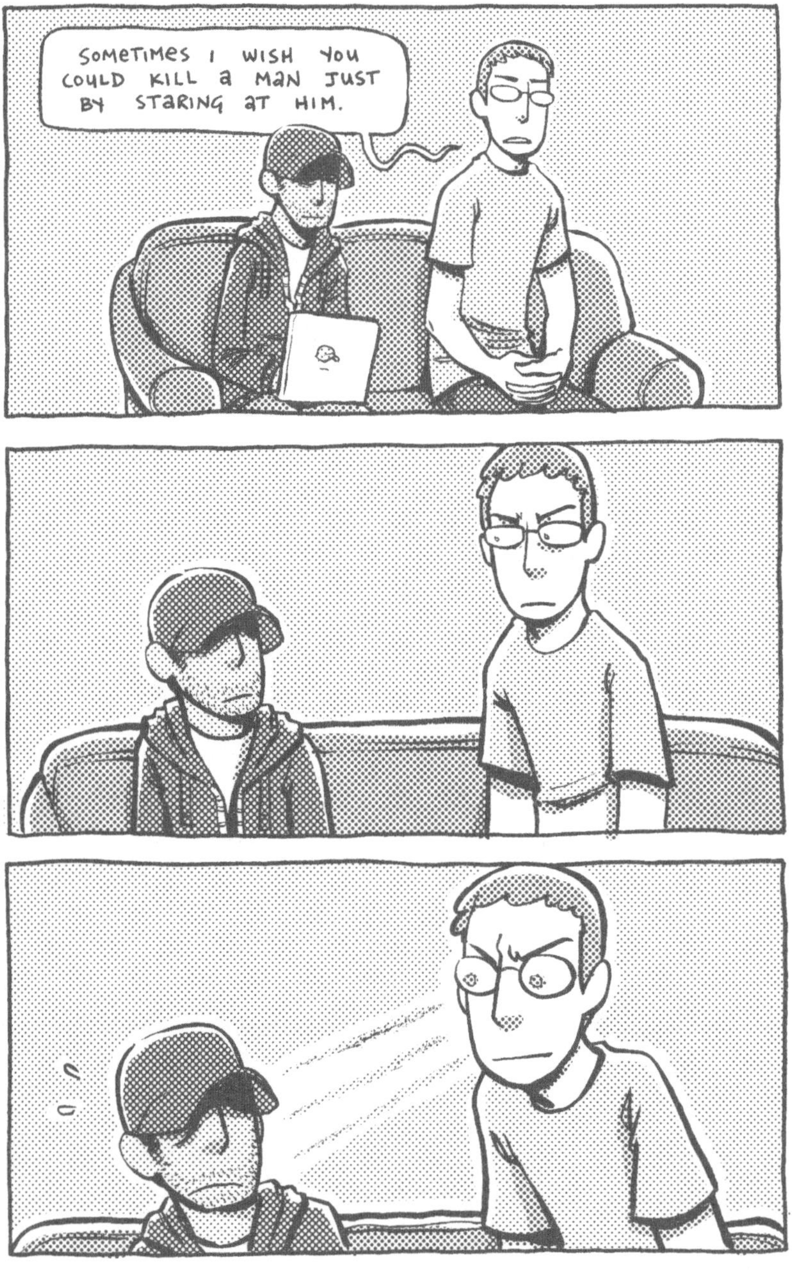
SOMETIMES I WISH YOU COULD KILL A MAN JUST BY STARING AT HIM.

THINGS ROOK WILL EAT
GIVEN HALF THE CHANCE

marinara sauce

ice cream

yogurt

flies

eggs

soup

soy sauce

miso paste

rice

ROOK! GET DOWN!

coffee grounds

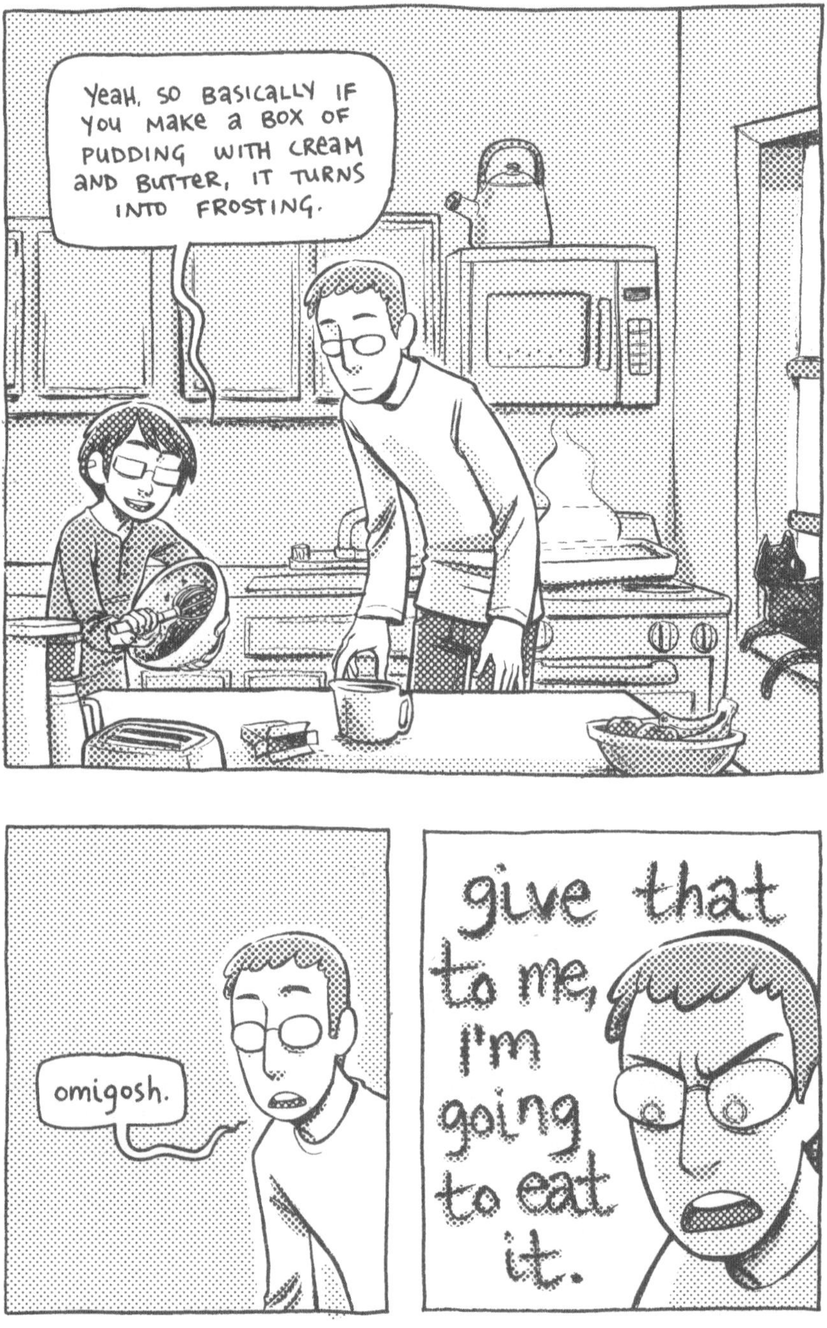
YEAH, SO BASICALLY IF YOU MAKE A BOX OF PUDDING WITH CREAM AND BUTTER, IT TURNS INTO FROSTING.
omigosh.
give that to me, I'm going to eat it.

SPACKLEHAUS MEMOIRS 5

HEY GUYS! THIS HOUSE CAME WITH AN INDOOR WATERFALL!
R... REALLY?
ALSO, THE BASEMENT IS FLOODED.

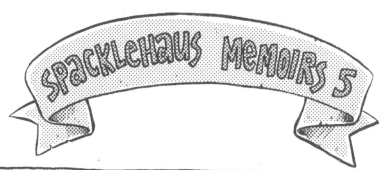

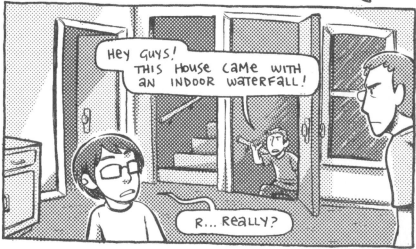

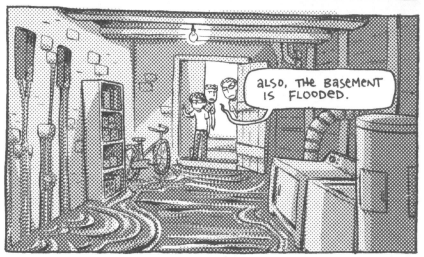

he's still the best super we've ever had

I CAN'T TELL
IF THE SUPER IS
MAKING FUN OF ME

FAIRLY UNEVENTFUL 14-HOUR TRAIN RIDE FROM TORONTO TO NEW YORK

8:00 AM— TAKING THE TRAIN FROM TORONTO BACK TO NYC!

BYE, TK!!

9:00 AM: . . . .

10:00 AM: . . . .

11:00 AM— OH GOSH WE'RE CROSSING THE BORDER

the reason for your visit?

wuh?

12:00 PM— BORDER GUARD IS STILL INTERROGATING PEOPLE.

please come with me, ma'am

1:00 PM— MOVING again! WE VISIT THE CAFÉ CAR.

this coffee is awful.

2:00 PM— TAKING DOWN SOME FUTURE STORY IDEAS.

3:00 PM— THE GUY ACROSS FROM US WON'T STOP SINGING...

ohh my daaarling...

4:00 PM— I KEEP ON FALLING ASLEEP WITH MY GLASSES ON AND MESSING UP THE FRAMES.

5:00 PM— THE TEENY JANITOR CARTOON IN THE BATHROOM KINDA LOOKS LIKE A DEVIL.

Be consider
the next p
and clean

6:00 PM— THUMBNAaaaIIIILLSS

skrch
skrch

7:00 PM— THE WOMAN BEHIND US IS SO LOUD THAT WE HAVE TO CHANGE SEATS.

and you know, I was on the train com
on February 25th when the snow wa
and Obama, he's been spending money l
my husband, you know what he says a
but you know what the Bible says abo
and the Hudson river lits just up a
I grew up i a city so there's not
you know w time got into the
it was afte 3am, weather wass

8:00 PM — TEENY LIGHTHOUSE ON THE HUDSON RIVER.

9:00 PM — WE'RE GETTING ANTSY.

aaa we've been here for over twelve hours aaaa

fidget
fidget
fidget

10:20 PM — WE'VE ARRIVED AT PENN STATION.!!

yes

I'm hungry.

visiting the mountsberg raptor centre

THIS IS TEDDY, ONE OF OUR BARRED OWLS.

SHE WAS HIT BY a CaR...

...WHICH RESULTED IN a BLIND EYE AND BRAIN DAMAGE...

...AND LEFT HER UNUSUALLY DOCILE.

she fell asleep.

eee ee

z

also special thanks to:

PAWGWA

TAKENYA

ECHO

OTUS

BEAN

HUTTON

and the Mountsberg Raptor Centre!

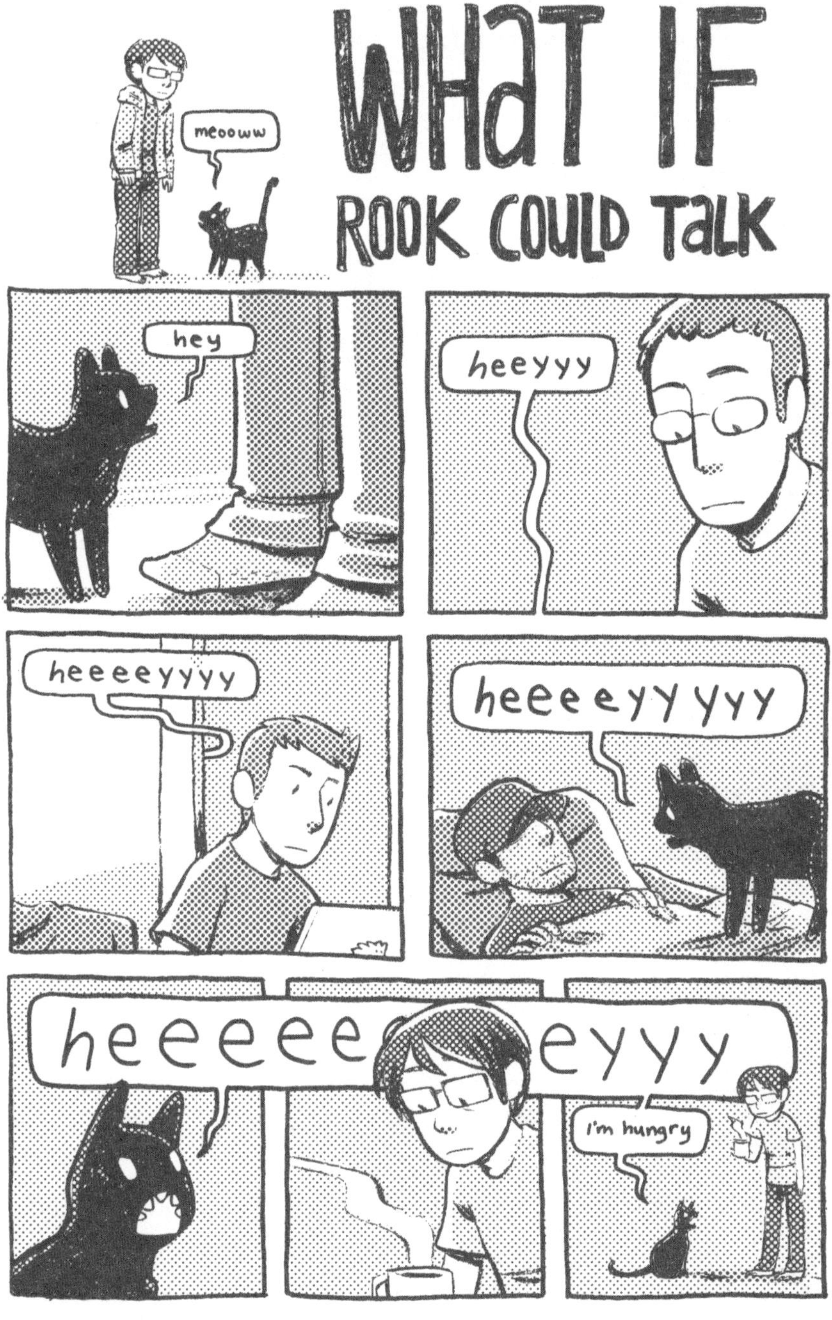
WHAT IF
ROOK COULD TALK
meooww
hey
heeyyy
heeeeyyyy
heeeeyyyyyy
heeeeeeyyy
i'm hungry

an alternate interpretation

rest in pieces revolutions

woes of a fifth-floor tenant

THE BEST PART OF MOVING A COUCH

IS SITTING ON IT AFTERWARDS.

but we were out of lighter fluid

the most delicious of the cingulatas

how bout them noodles

BUT WE KEEP WATCHING
FORENSICS SHOWS
OVER DINNER anyway

the sheddingest cat

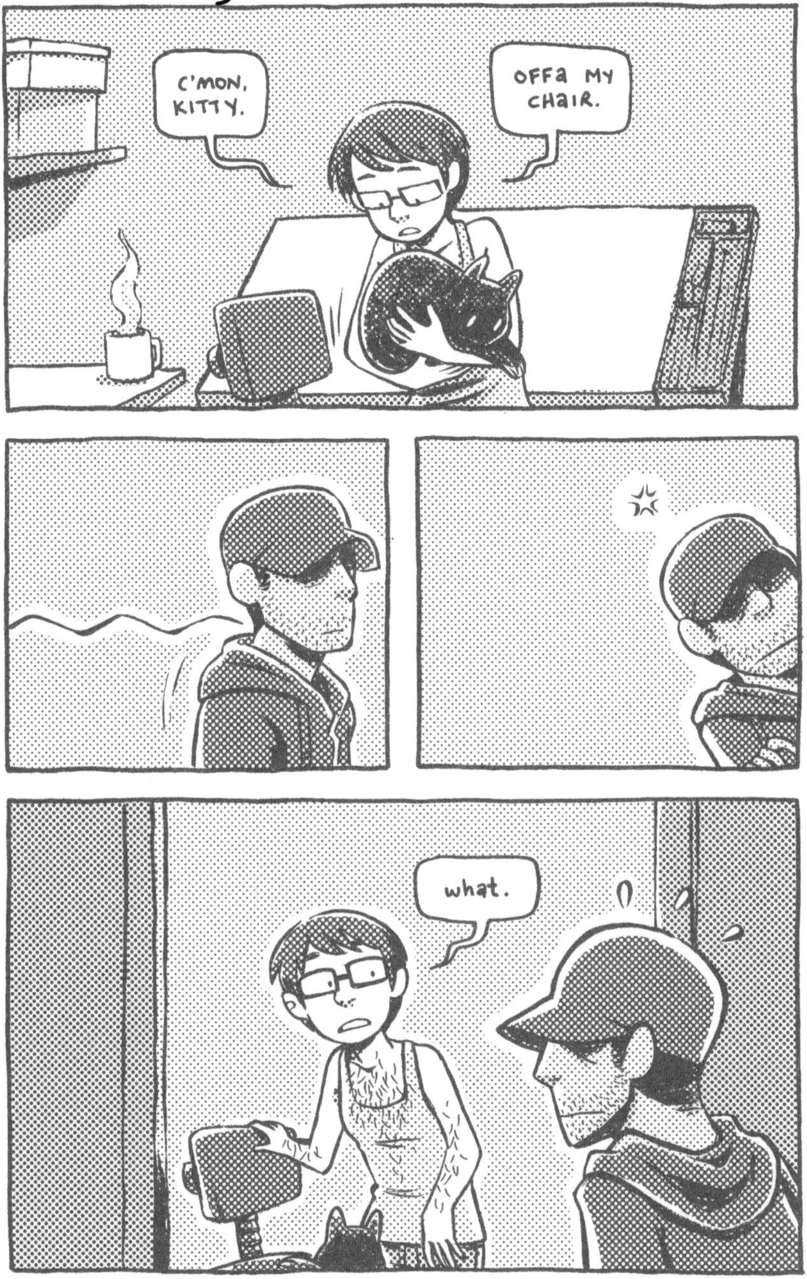
C'MON, KITTY.
OFFa MY CHAIR.
what.

bad: having a stye on the inside of your eyelid

worse: holding a hot compress to your face in sweltering heat

the great escape

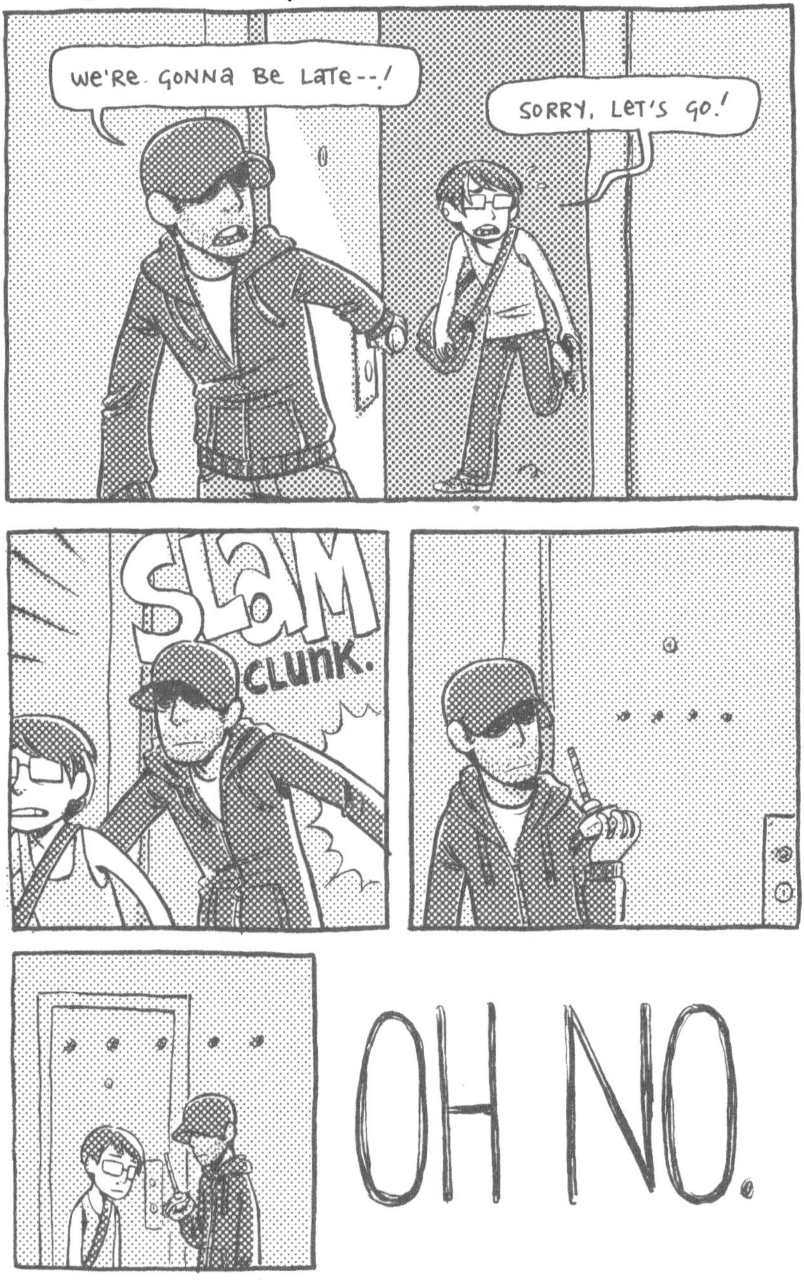

WE'RE GONNA BE LATE--!
SORRY, LET'S GO!
SLAM
CLUNK.
OH NO.

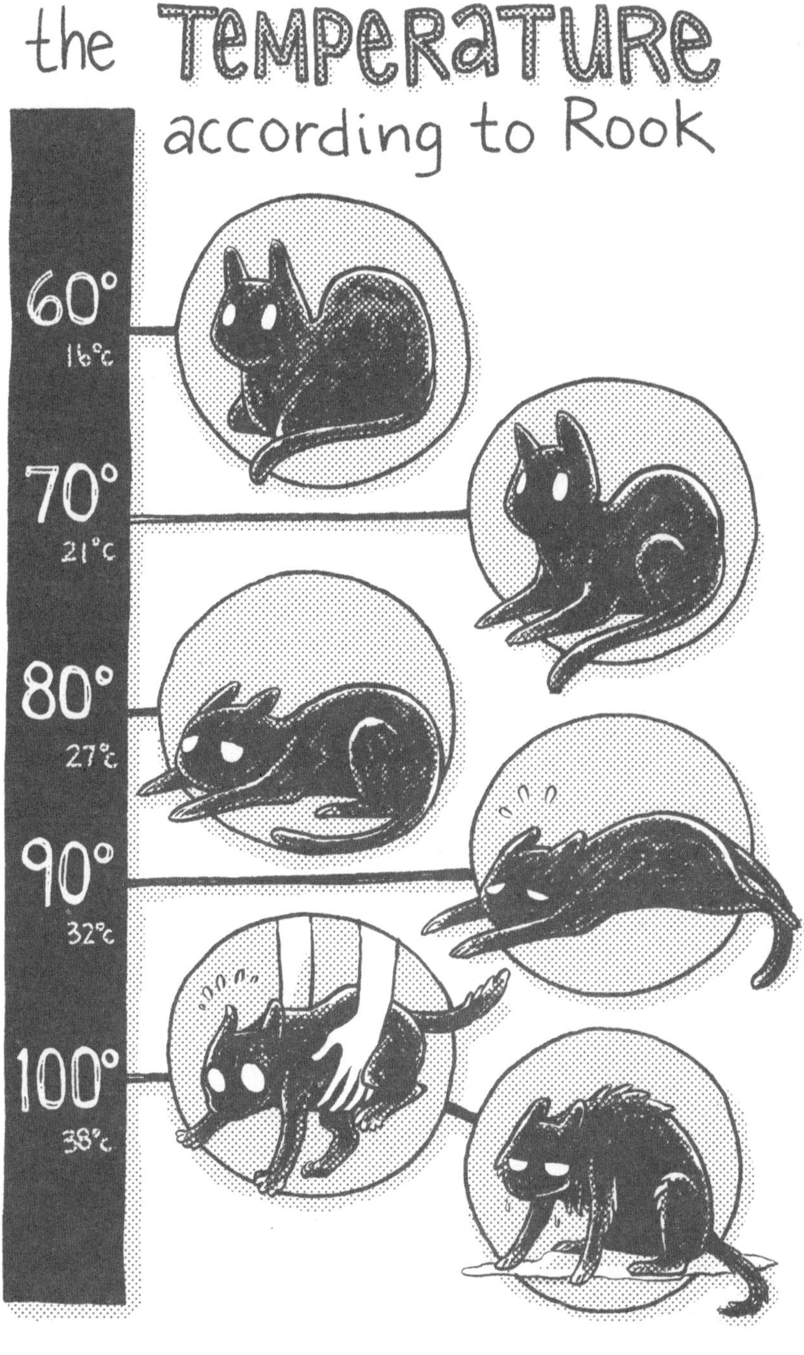
the TEMPERATURE according to Rook
60° 16°c
70° 21°c
80° 27°c
90° 32°c
100° 38°c

when it rains

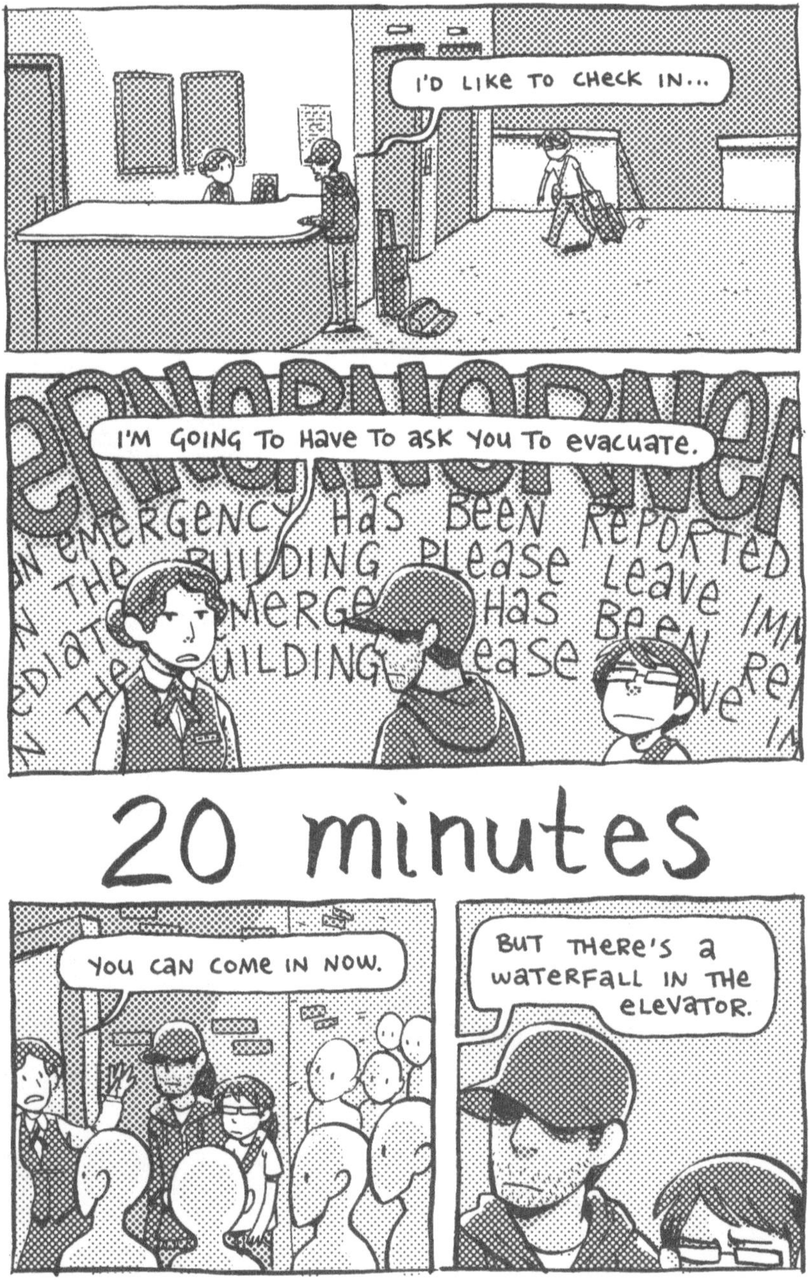

I'D LIKE TO CHECK IN...
I'M GOING TO HAVE TO ASK YOU TO EVACUATE.
EMERGENCY HAS BEEN REPORTED
THE BUILDING PLEASE LEAVE
20 minutes
YOU CAN COME IN NOW.
BUT THERE'S A WATERFALL IN THE ELEVATOR.

driver's tan

Driver's tan,
Driver's tan,
From my shoulder to my hand

Drove around,
Windows down,
Now my left arm is all brown.

the integral first step

the same terrible wavelength

but bookshelves are heavy

battlecat

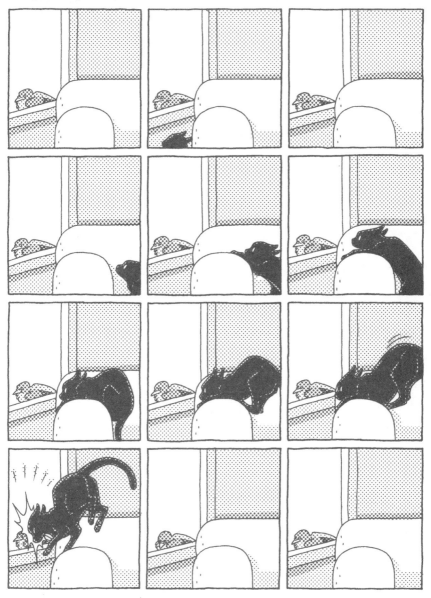

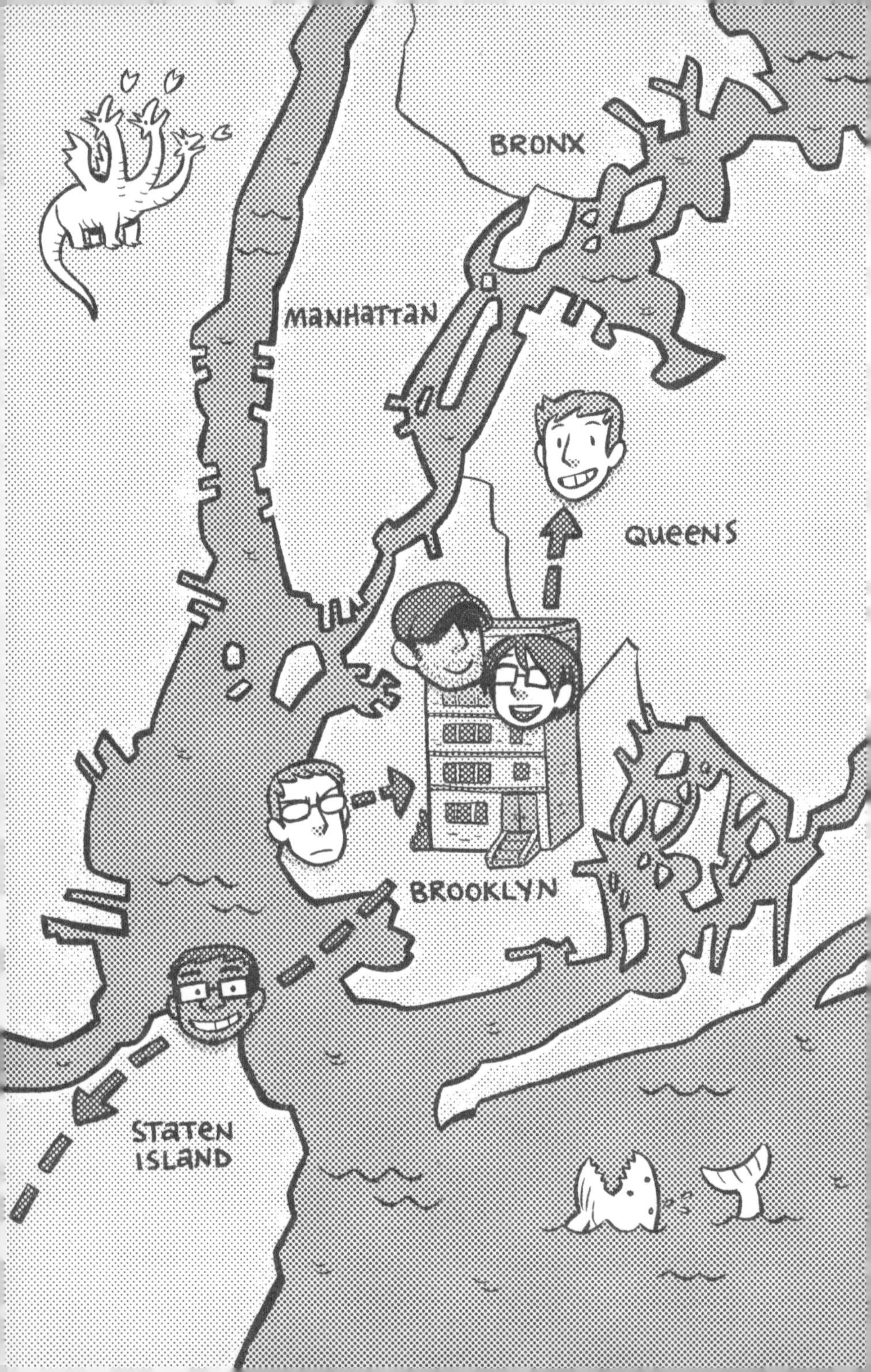
BRONX
MANHATTAN
QUEENS
BROOKLYN
STATEN ISLAND

but I don't have a mortgage

wookie of honor

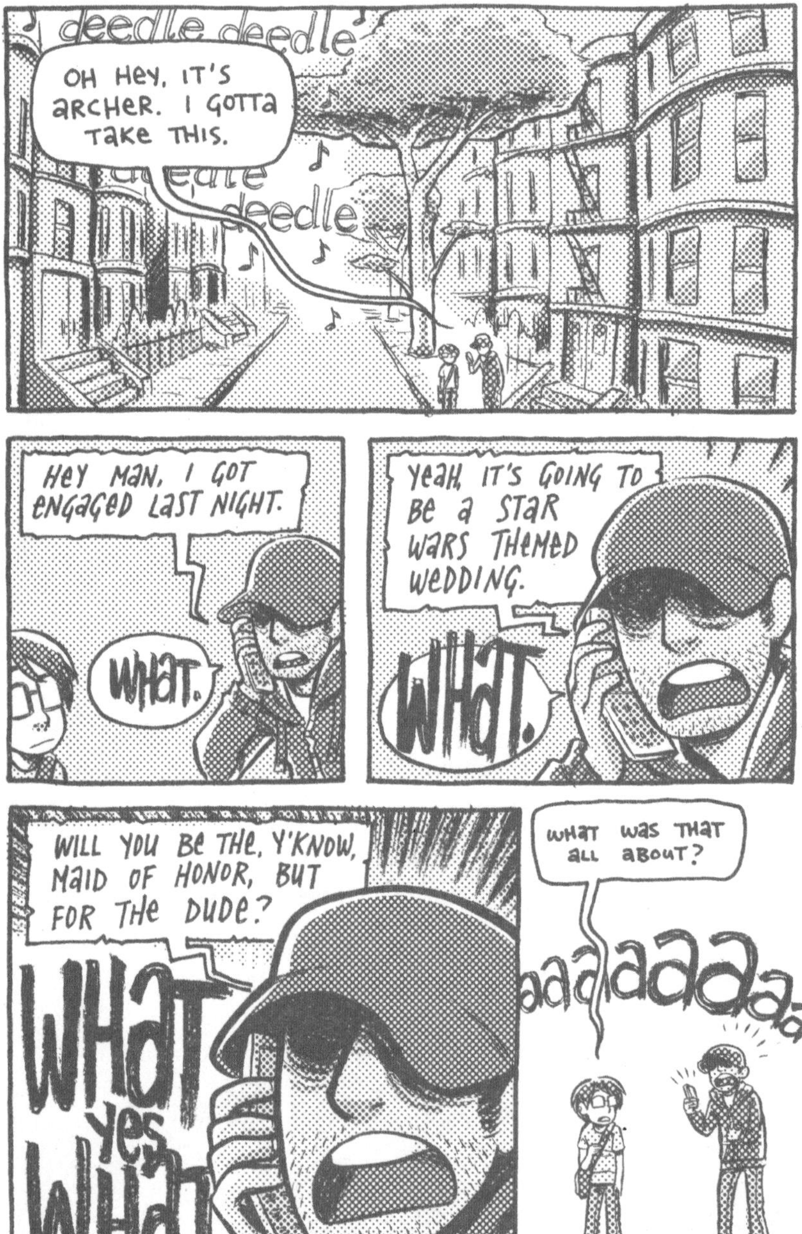
deedle deedle
OH HEY, IT'S ARCHER. I GOTTA TAKE THIS.
deedle
deedle
HEY MAN, I GOT ENGAGED LAST NIGHT.
WHAT.
YEAH, IT'S GOING TO BE A STAR WARS THEMED WEDDING.
WHAT.
WILL YOU BE THE, Y'KNOW, MAID OF HONOR, BUT FOR THE DUDE?
WHAT
YES
WHAT
WHAT WAS THAT ALL ABOUT?
aaaaaaaaa

ananth showers with his hat

AND SO: SHOWERS

AND THEN: THE SUBWAY

i don't trust it

THOSE PLUMS LOOK GOOD...

ONEYCRISP APPLES
GALA APPLES
FUJI APPLES
FRUIT PUN PLUMS

MANGOES
CANTALO
RRIES
BLUEBER

WHAT'S ... THAT...?

FLAVOR GRENADE
2.9D/LB

NO.

IT'S TOO DANGEROUS

motivational speaker

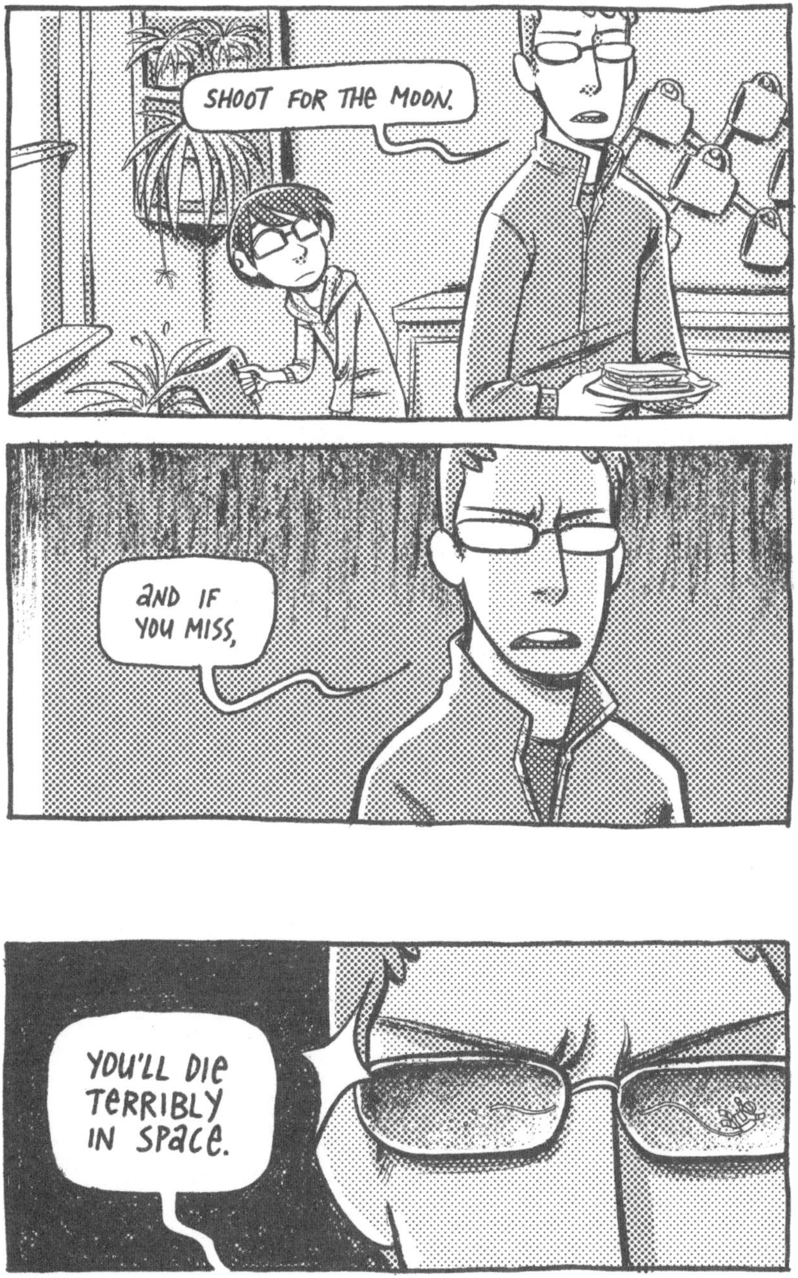
SHOOT FOR THE MOON.
AND IF YOU MISS,
YOU'LL DIE TERRIBLY IN SPACE.

good thing: y/n

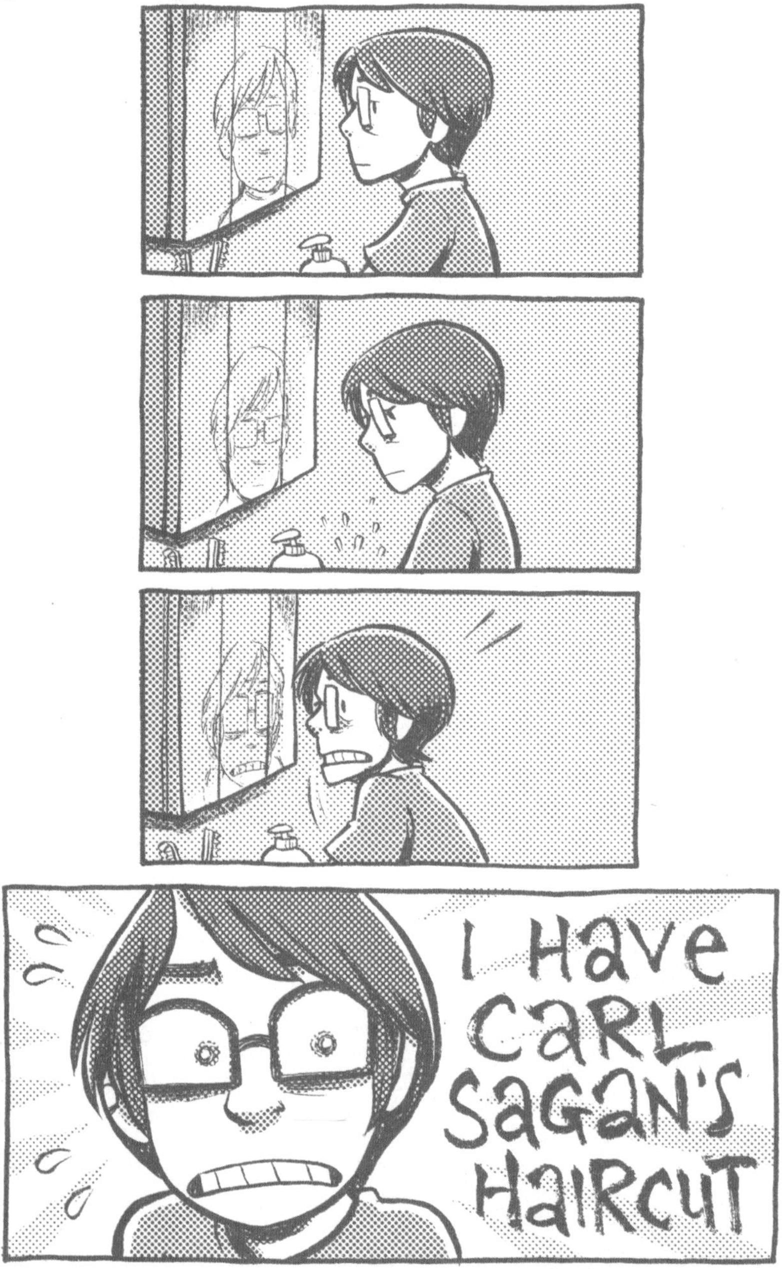
I HAVE CARL SAGAN'S HAIRCUT

yeeahh
well at least you don't have his eyebrows.

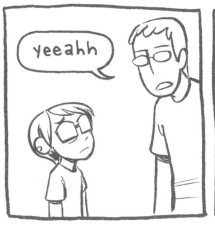

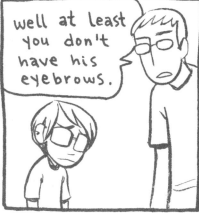

the tomatoes are dead, long live the tomatoes

BUT SOON:

R.I.P. 2010-2010

CAT -versus- DOOR

CAN THEY OPEN IT?

MIKA

yuko's
mom's cat

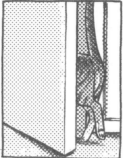

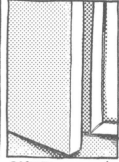

RESULT: yes!

ROOK

mow

MOWW

MYOOWW

. . .

RESULT: eventually!

GONTA

yuko's
dad's cat

clik

RESULT:

. . . .

189

oh no don't do that

eegk, subway fingers!

and this is how you get sick.

fwoooo

thank you, pterodactyl crazy band

LET'S HELP KC
eaT NOODLES!

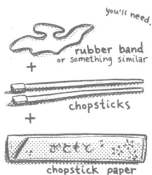

you'll need:

rubber band
or something similar

+

chopsticks

+

chopstick paper

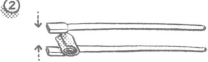

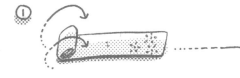

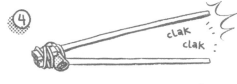

OKAY, NOW YOU'RE SET!

sweetie pie the sweet potato

and so,

welp

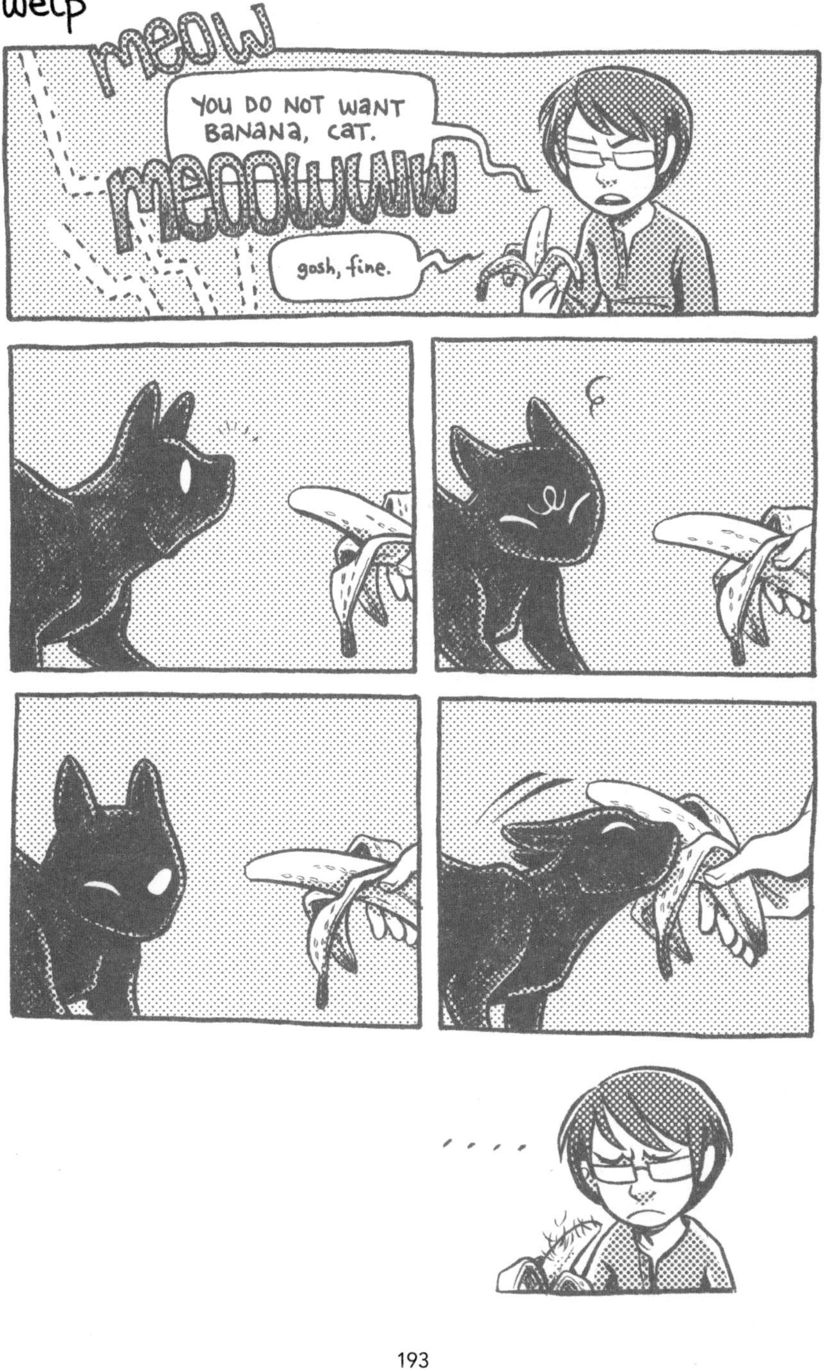
meow
YOU DO NOT WANT BANANA, CAT.
MEOOWWWW
gosh, fine.
. . . .

george has a posse

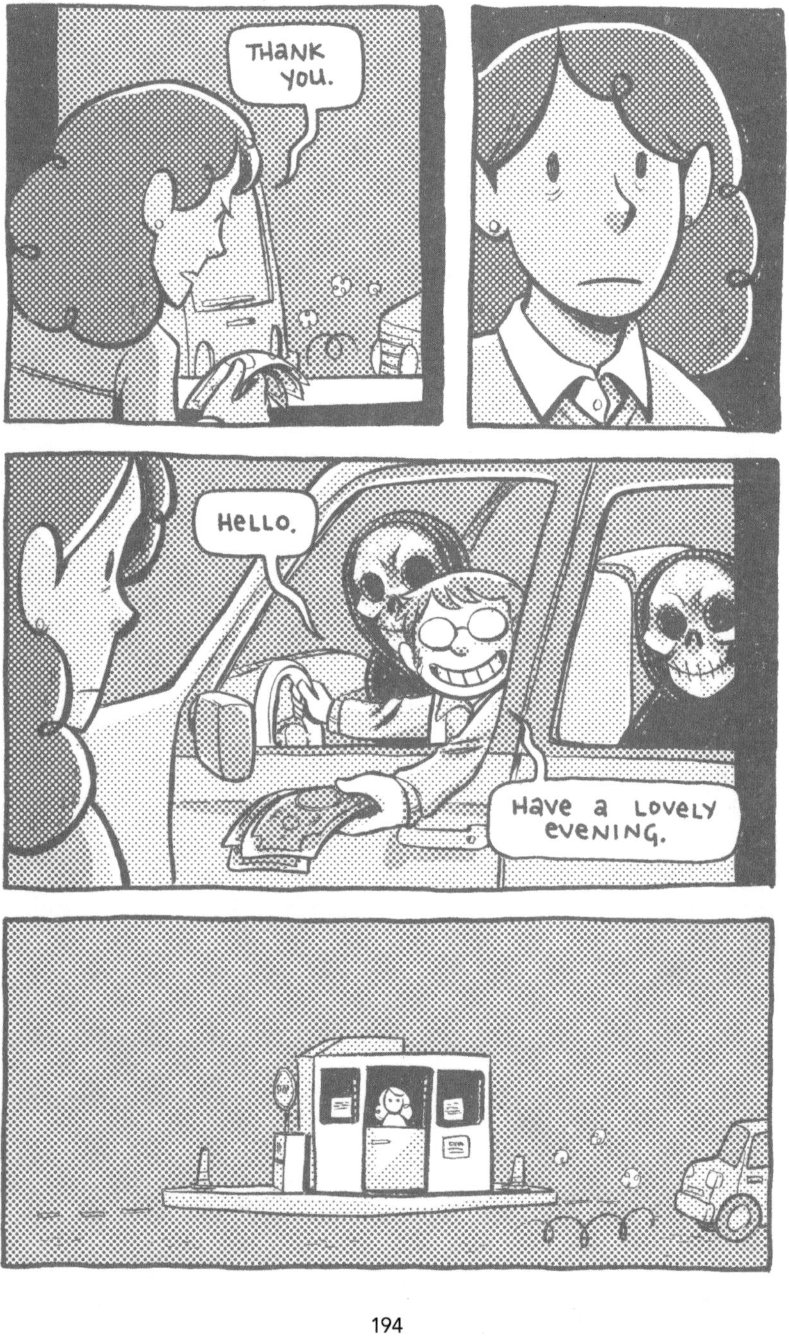
THANK YOU.
HELLO.
HAVE A LOVELY EVENING.

highlander in port authority

HOW YUKO GOT INTO SCIENCE AND STUFF

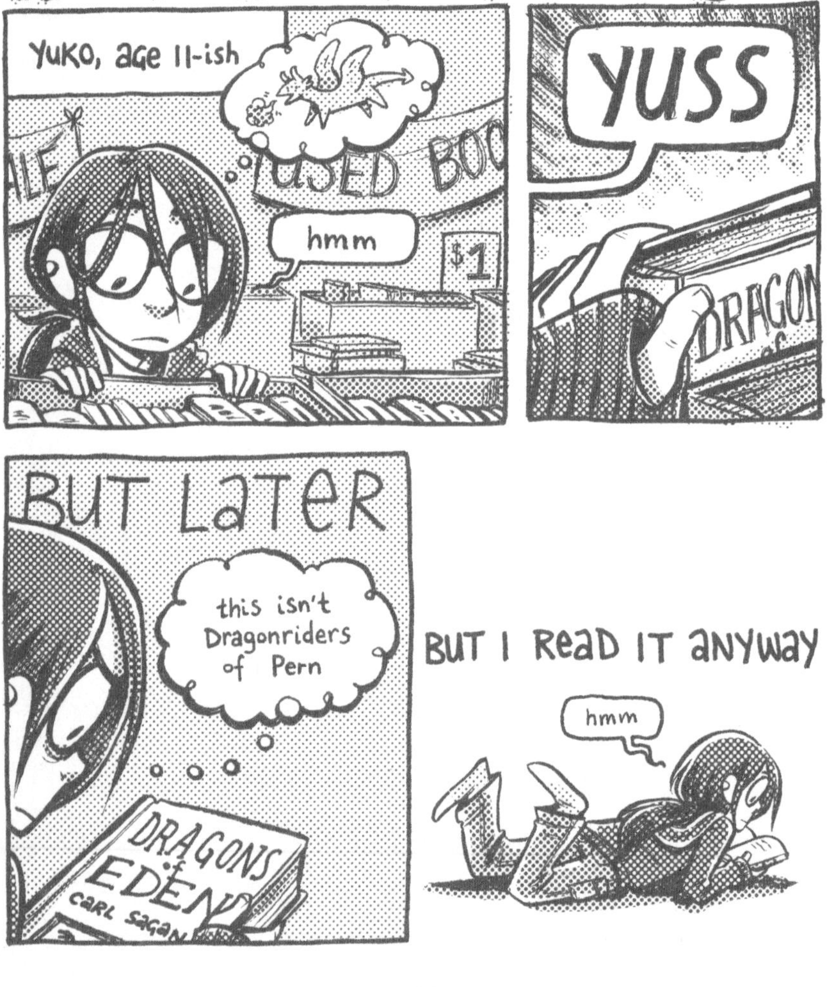
YUKO, age 11-ish
USED BOO
hmm
$1
YUSS
DRAGON
BUT LATER
this isn't Dragonriders of Pern
DRAGONS of EDEN
CARL SAGAN
BUT I READ IT ANYWAY
hmm

your jeers only make him stronger

drawing the drawing hand that is drawing you

cat-meras

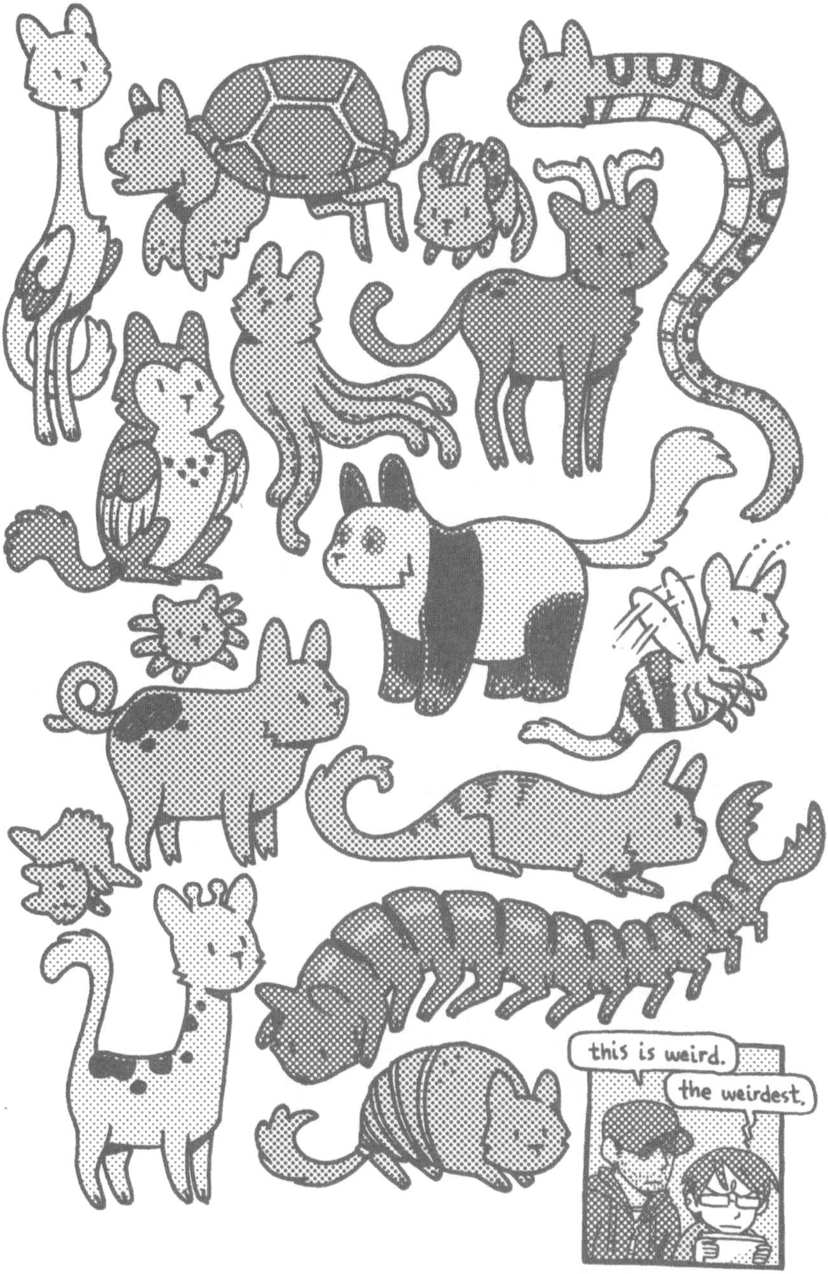
this is weird.
the weirdest.

right, guys?

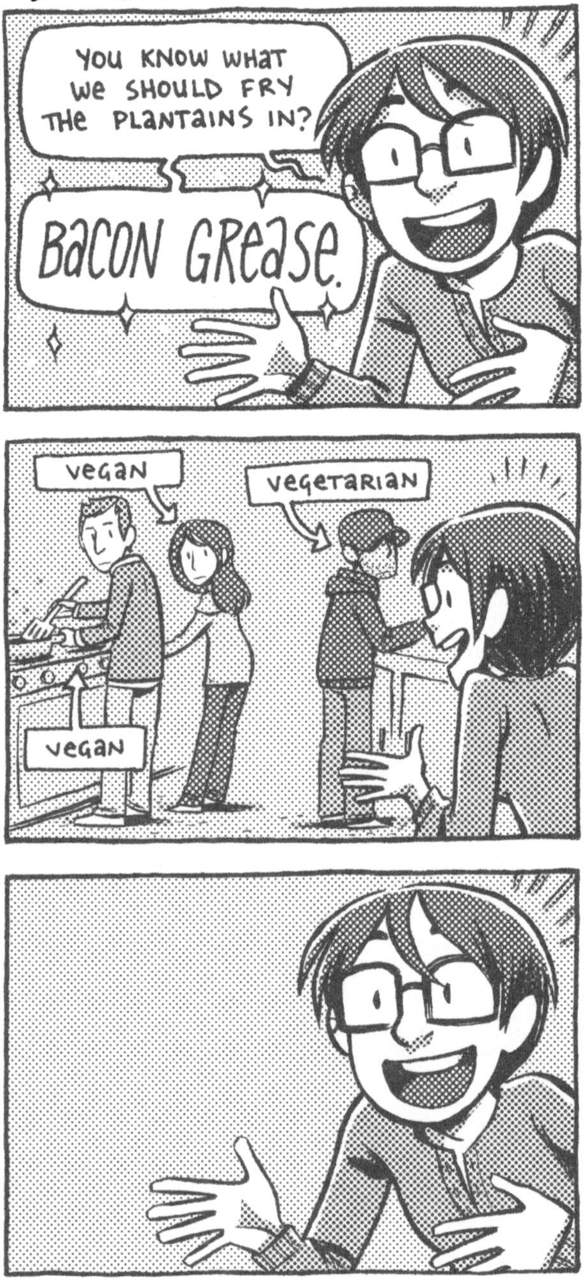
YOU KNOW WHAT WE SHOULD FRY THE PLANTAINS IN?
BACON GREASE.
VEGAN
VEGETARIAN
VEGAN

bridesmaid dresses is hard

all quiet on the western bus

beer-scented car freshener

nutella: the sriracha of sweet foods

THERE IS NO WAY THIS CAN GO WRONG

WELL OKAY MAYBE NOT

oh eww.

BECAUSE THE OIL IN THE NUTELLA SEPARATES.

THERE IS NO HEAT IN THE APARTMENT

also the internet is down.

what I am wearing inside the apartment RIGHT NOW:

I hate everything.

wool hat

scarf

hand warmers

camisole

thermal shirt

another shirt

stupidly thick socks

thermal hoodie

leggings

jeans

and underwear I guess.

terrible terrible food science

but in all seriousness

how did we get two dozen eggs anyway

but I'm your only... oh.

WHERE IS MY DAUGHTER
ah, I'm... ...
NOT YOU
THERE SHE IS

DRIVING ON THE BACK ROADS

 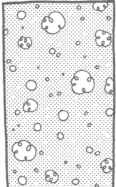 

BAKING EXPERIMENTS

made sweet potato-Banana bread for my parents.

meh..

GOT a New HaT FOR CHRISTMAS

CHRISTMAS GIFT BIAS

YUKO GOT:

hat

paper cutter

ANANTH GOT:

books

pajama pants

ROOK GOT:

GIANT CAT HOUSE

GIANT BIRD FEEDER

MILLET

DON'T SPILL THE MULLET!

A MULLET IS A HAIRCUT.

BIRD FEED

REALLY? I'VE NEVER HEARD OF IT.

HERE.

BIRD FEED

oh.

...mullet

EXCITING NEW YEAR CELEBRATION

11:00
WATCH GIRLY ANIME

♪ kissu kissu fall in rabbu ♪

12:00
WATCH THE BALL DROP, DRINK PRE-MADE MARGARITAS

10   9   8   7

bleh

12:05

z   z   z   z

look that gift horse right in the mouth

speaking from experience

meanwhile, in queens

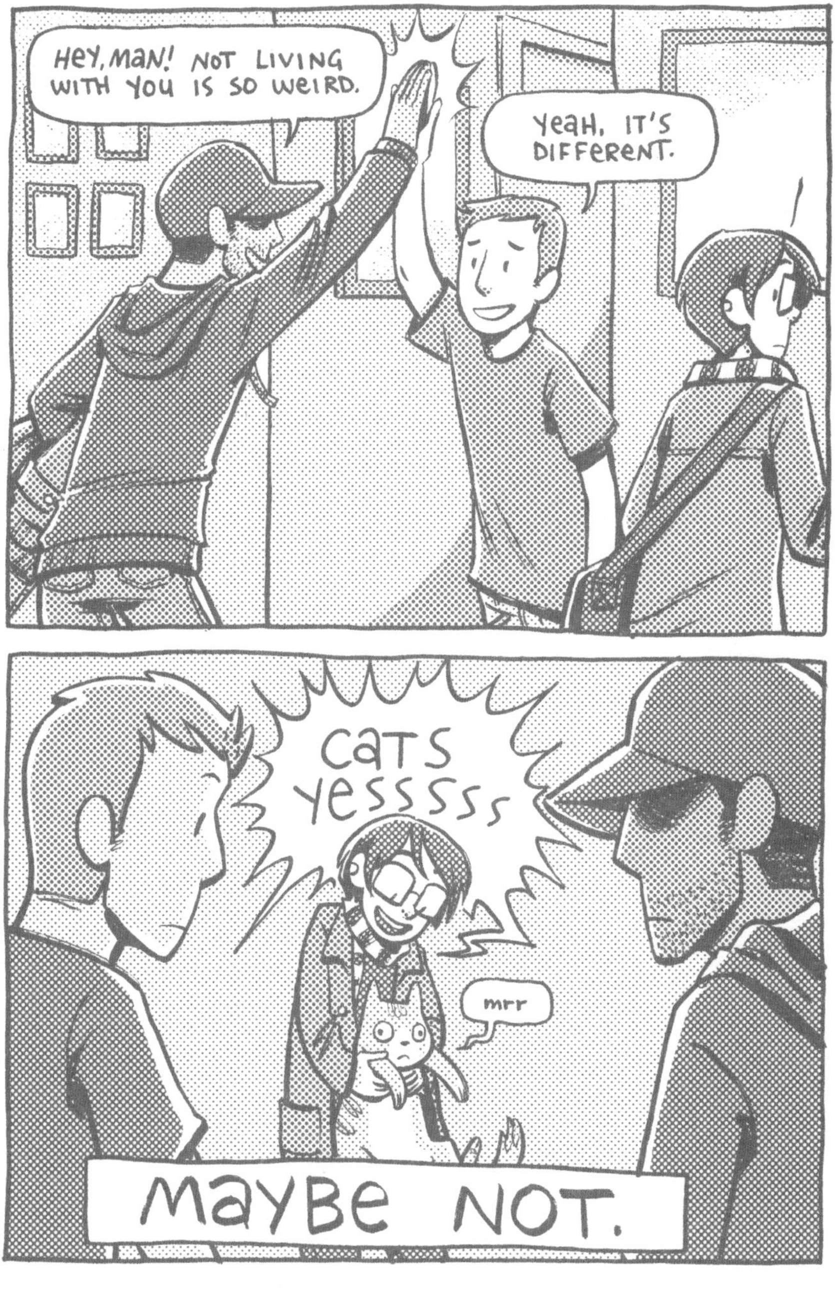
HEY, MAN! NOT LIVING WITH YOU IS SO WEIRD.
YEAH, IT'S DIFFERENT.
CATS YESSSSS
mrr
MAYBE NOT.

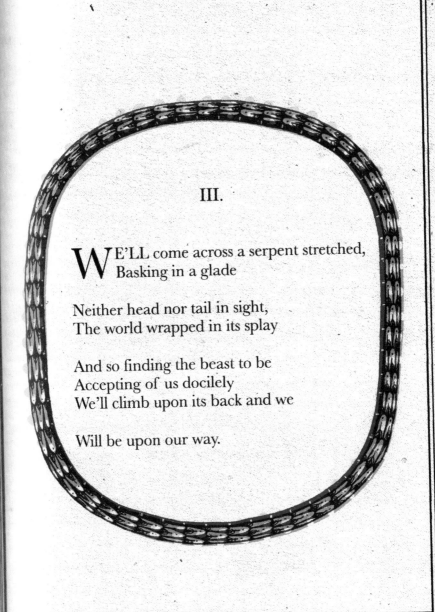

III.

WE'LL come across a serpent stretched,
Basking in a glade

Neither head nor tail in sight,
The world wrapped in its splay

And so finding the beast to be
Accepting of us docilely
We'll climb upon its back and we

Will be upon our way.

prelude to a ballad

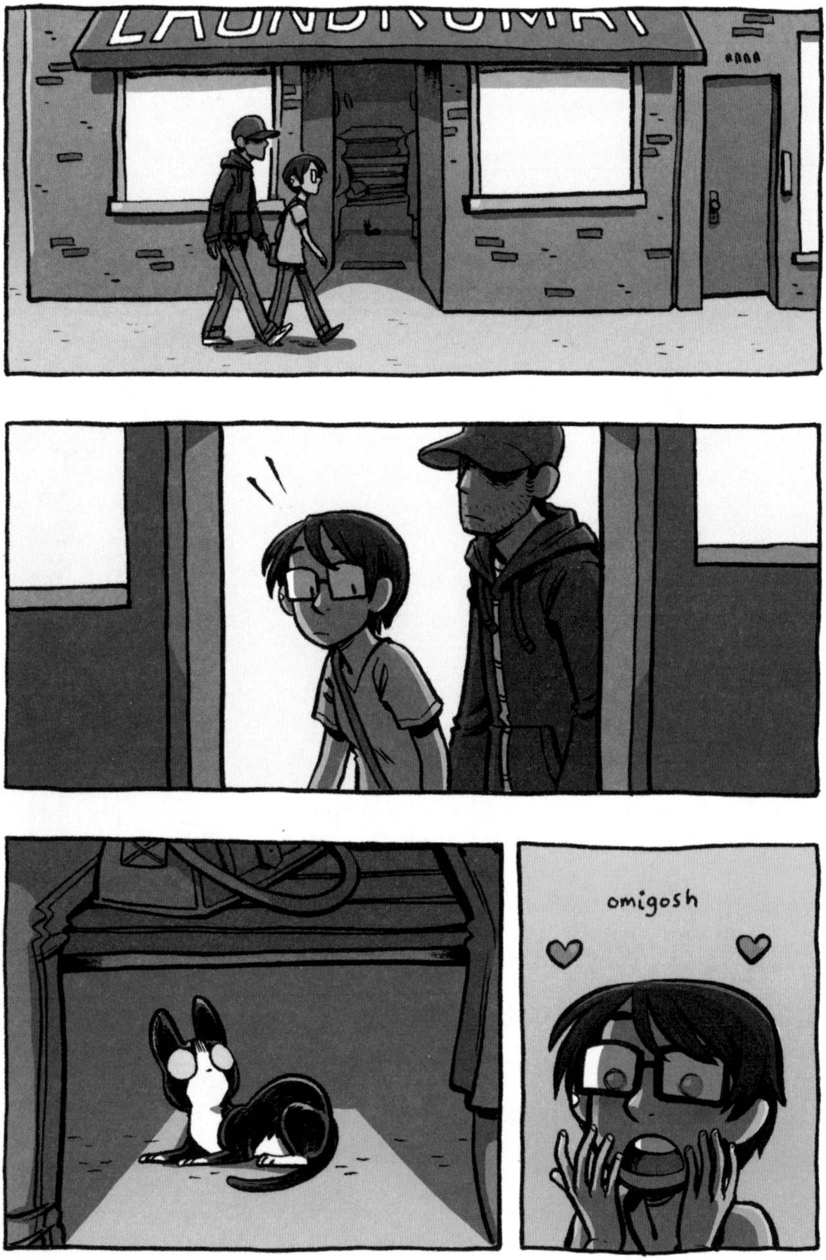
omigosh

monochrome

WINTER

SUMMER

AND SOON
ENOUGH

CMY cat

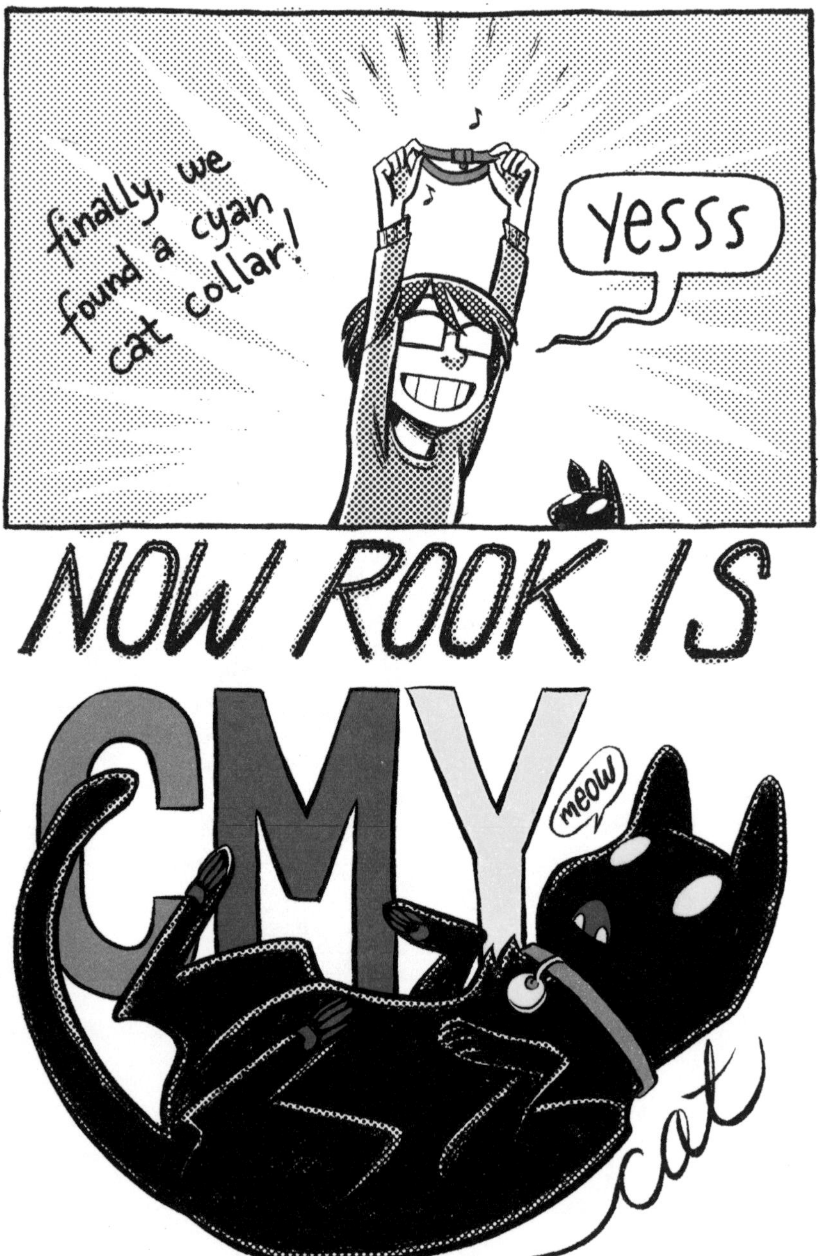
finally, we found a cyan cat collar!
YESSS
NOW ROOK IS
CMY
meow
cat

hand-face coordination

oh the horror

now we have to buy a new pork loin.

the ballad of laundry cat

a secret for the ages

IS THIS REAL? CHEESEQUAKE IS A REAL PLACE?

CHEESEQUAKE
SERVICE AREA 2 MILES

KEEP RIGHT

MAYBE IT'S SHORT FOR SOMETHING.

CHESAPEAKE QUAKERTON?

CHEESE AND QUAKERS.

LET'S NOT TELL ANYONE ABOUT THIS CONVERSATION.

mm

222

hourly comics: february 1st, 2011

10:00 am

WAIT, TODAY IS HOURLY COMICS DAY?

tak
tak

BUT I'M ALREADY DRAWING COMICS!

I'M DRAWING COMICS RIGHT NOW!

11:00 am

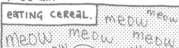

eating cereal.

meow meow meow meow meow meow meow meow meow meow meow meow meow meow meow

ROOK WANTS TO LICK THE BOTTOM OF THE BOWL.

12:00 PM

WAS GOING TO MAKE THE BED, BUT THE CAT IS ASLEEP ON IT.

z

he looks like laundry.

1:00 PM

MY THROAT'S BUGGING ME, SO ANANTH MADE ME TEA.

slrp

ONE OF THESE DAYS, I'M GOING TO ACCIDENTALLY DESTROY ALL OF MY COMICS.

like 20 pages of originals

2:00 PM

instant ramen ↓

leftover curry ↓

CURRY RAMEN SSPLURP

stop that

i'm trying to get work done

223

3:00 PM

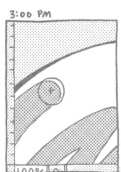

GAHH

meow meow meow meow meow meow meow meow meow meow

YOU DON'T EAT FOR TWO MORE HOURS

4:00 PM

I DON'T WANT TO GO GROCERY SHOPPINGGG

buhhh

BUT I PROMISED I'D MAKE A FUNFETTI CAKE FOR TOMORROW'S D+D GROUP.....

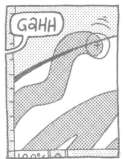

funfetti funfetti funfetti funfetti funfetti funfetti funfetti funfetti funfetti

5:00 PM

funfetti funfetti funfetti funfetti funfetti funfetti funfetti funfetti cake FUNFETTI

6:00 PM

DON'T LET HIM FOOL YOU, I FED HIM WHILE YOU WERE OUT.

meow meow meow meow meow meow meow meow meow meow meow meow meow meow meow

7:00 PM

DICKING AROUND ON THE INTERNET OR WHATEVER

La La La La

and then I went to bed.

HOURLY COMICS: FEBRUARY 1ST, 2011.

extended ballad of laundry cat

kitten quarantine

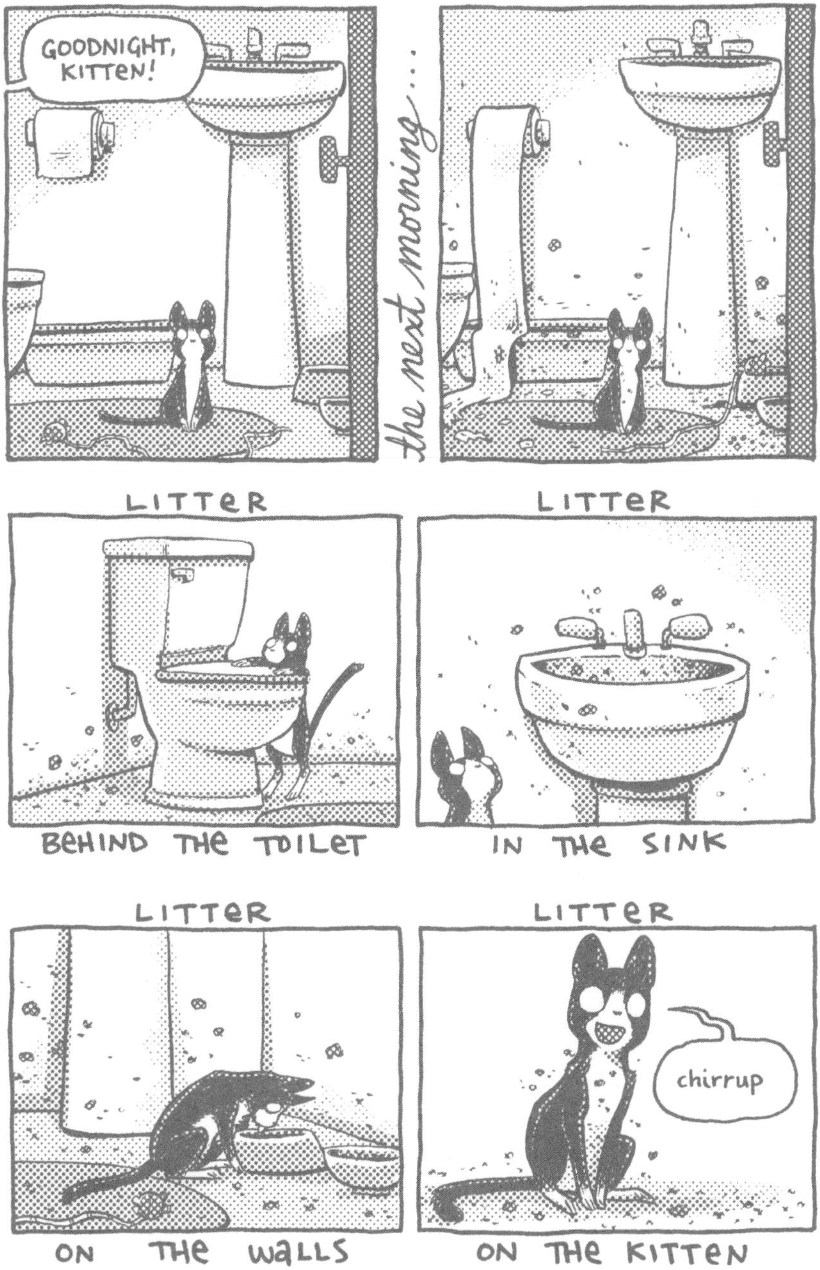
GOODNIGHT, KITTEN!
the next morning...
LITTER
BEHIND THE TOILET
LITTER
IN THE SINK
LITTER
ON THE WALLS
LITTER
chirrup
ON THE KITTEN

almost

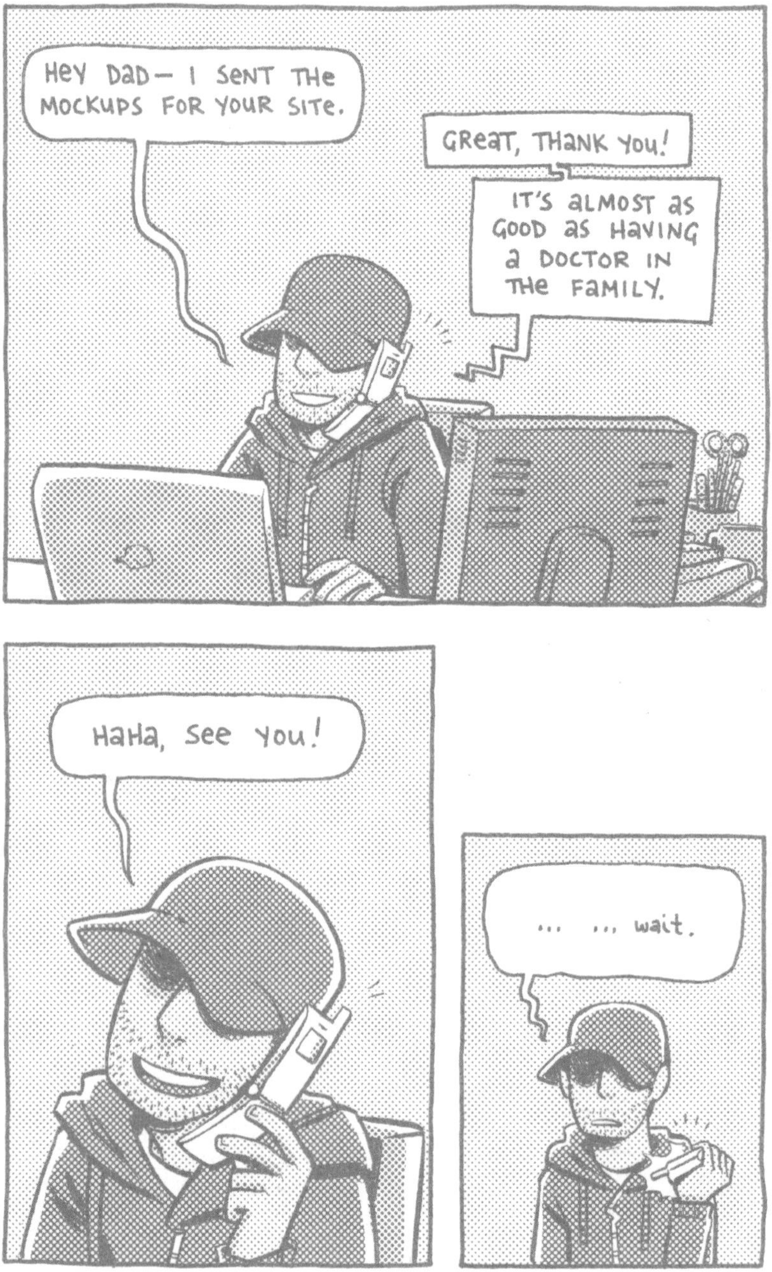
HEY DAD— I SENT THE MOCKUPS FOR YOUR SITE.
GREaT, THaNK YOU!
IT'S aLMOST aS GOOD aS HaVING a DOCTOR IN THE FaMILY.
HaHa, See You!
... ... wait.

combustifier

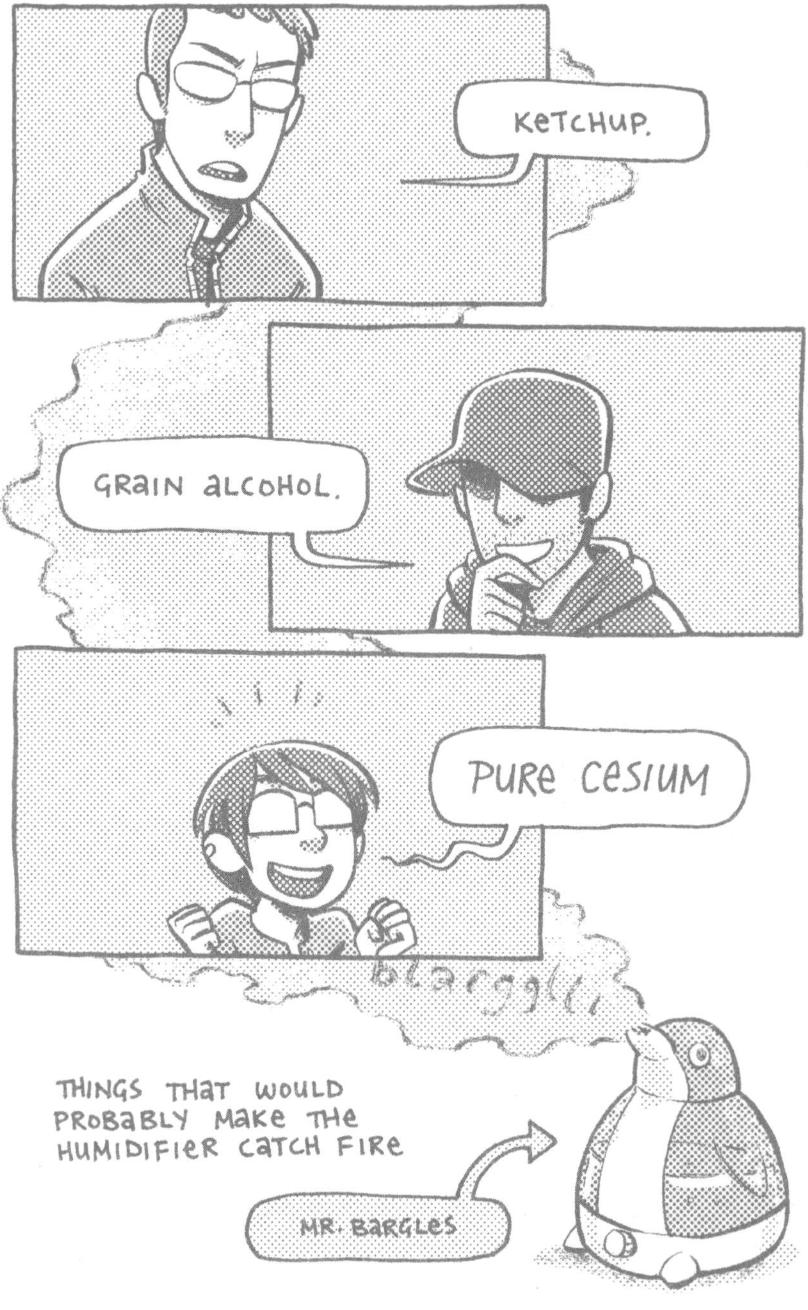
KETCHUP.
GRAIN ALCOHOL.
PURE CESIUM
THINGS THAT WOULD PROBABLY MAKE THE HUMIDIFIER CATCH FIRE
MR. BARGLES

should've taken the ferry

the surest path to friendship

1. approach

2. engage

3. ignore

4. rub on some stuff

5. engage again

6. ignore

tick tick tick tick

excuse me sir, we can keep your luggage behind the counter.

oh, sure.

anything in here, y'know, ticking or whatever?

just my clock collection.

what does it meeean

I HAD THE WEIRDEST DREAM LAST NIGHT.
mm.
BREAD & BUTTER
THE MUG
THE SPOON
THEY FIGHT CRIME

naming the kitten

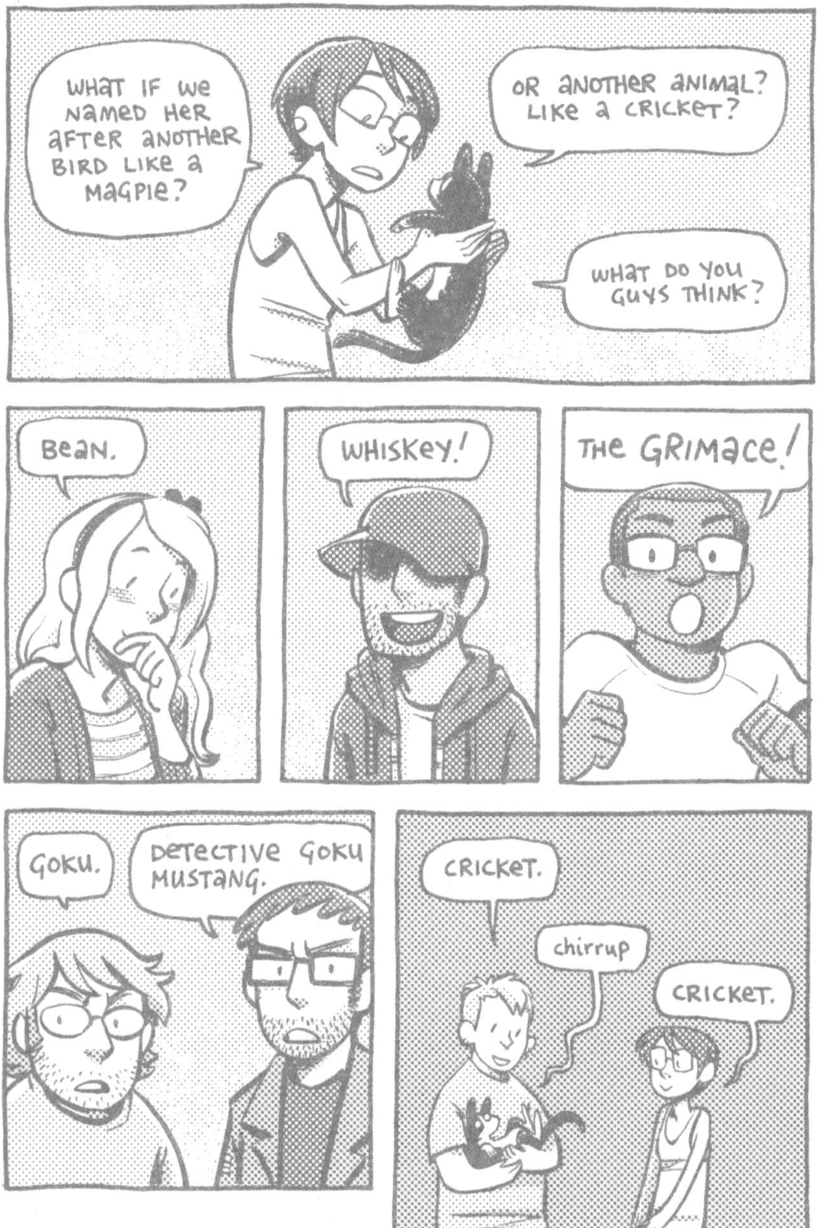
WHAT IF WE NAMED HER AFTER ANOTHER BIRD LIKE A MAGPIE?
OR ANOTHER ANIMAL? LIKE A CRICKET?
WHAT DO YOU GUYS THINK?
BEAN.
WHISKEY!
THE GRIMACE!
GOKU.
DETECTIVE GOKU MUSTANG.
CRICKET.
chirrup
CRICKET.

nearly burning down the apartment part fifty jillion

and so:

octopuses, not octopi

I HATE OCTOPUSES.
AN ANIMAL THAT GROSS HAS NO BUSINESS BEING THAT SMART.

HOW TO DRAW CRICKET

① draw a circle

② add two triangles

③ and two smaller circles

④ draw an upside-down heart

⑤ add a cat body

⑥ yay you're done!

☆ small:
☆ cute:
☆ smart:

urgent matters

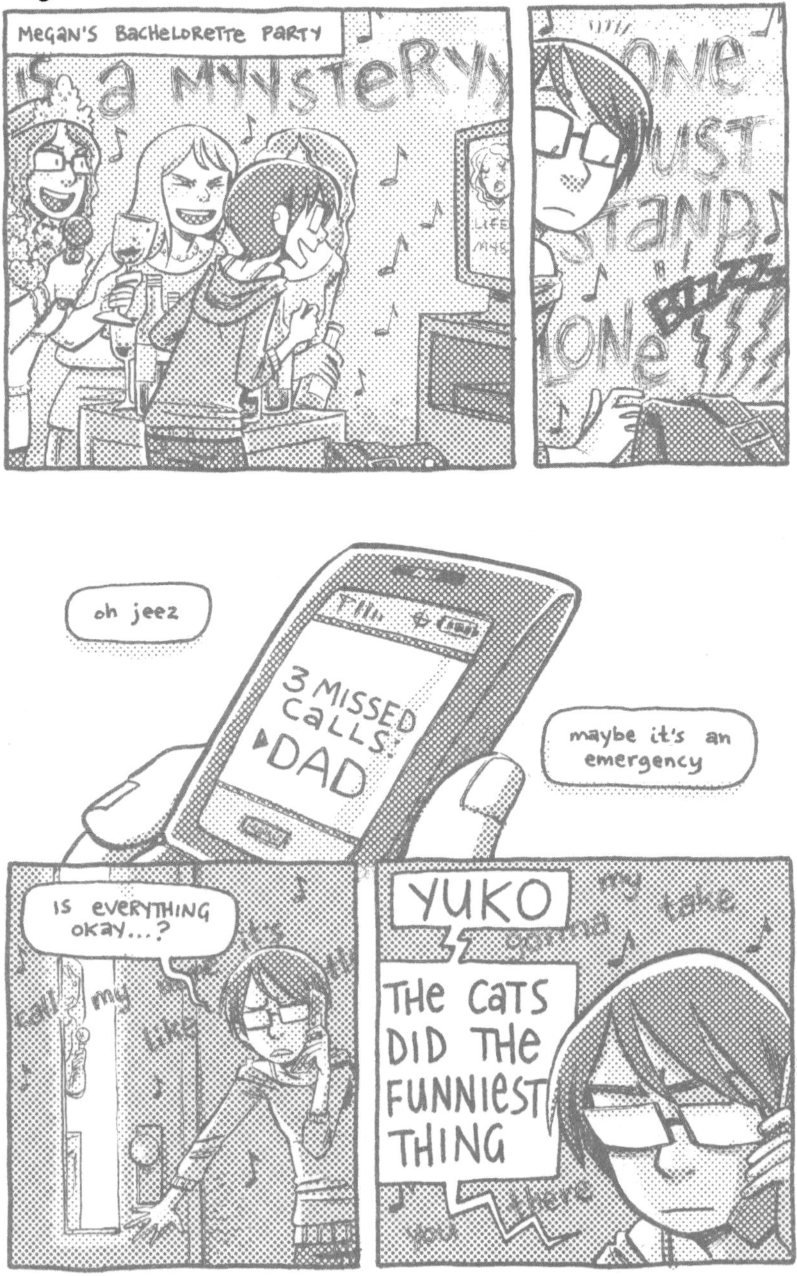
MEGAN'S BACHELORETTE PARTY
IS A MYYSTERYY
ONE MUST STAND ALONE
BZZZZ
oh jeez
3 MISSED CALLS: DAD
maybe it's an emergency
IS EVERYTHING OKAY...?
YUKO
THE CATS DID THE FUNNIEST THING

when rook met mika

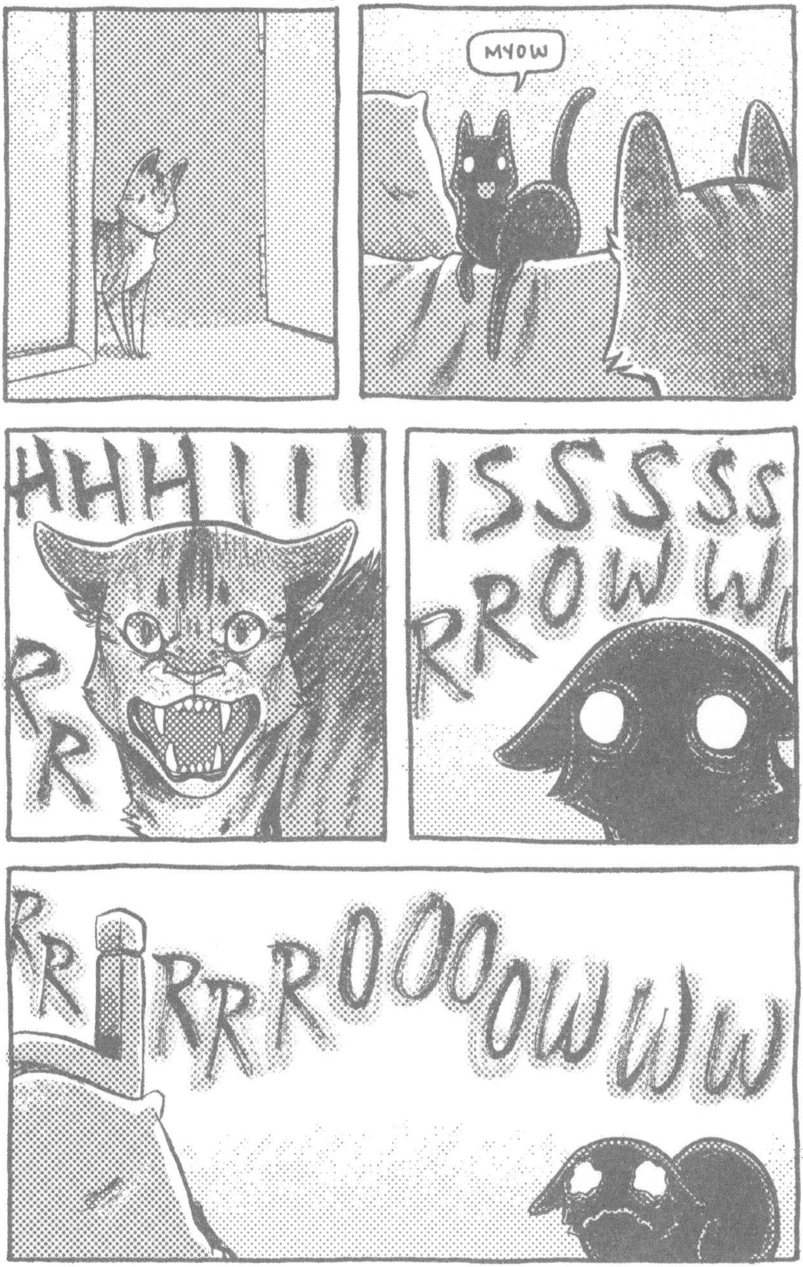
MYOW
HHH!!!
RR
ISSSSS
RROWW
RR
RRROOOOWWWW

when rook met gonta

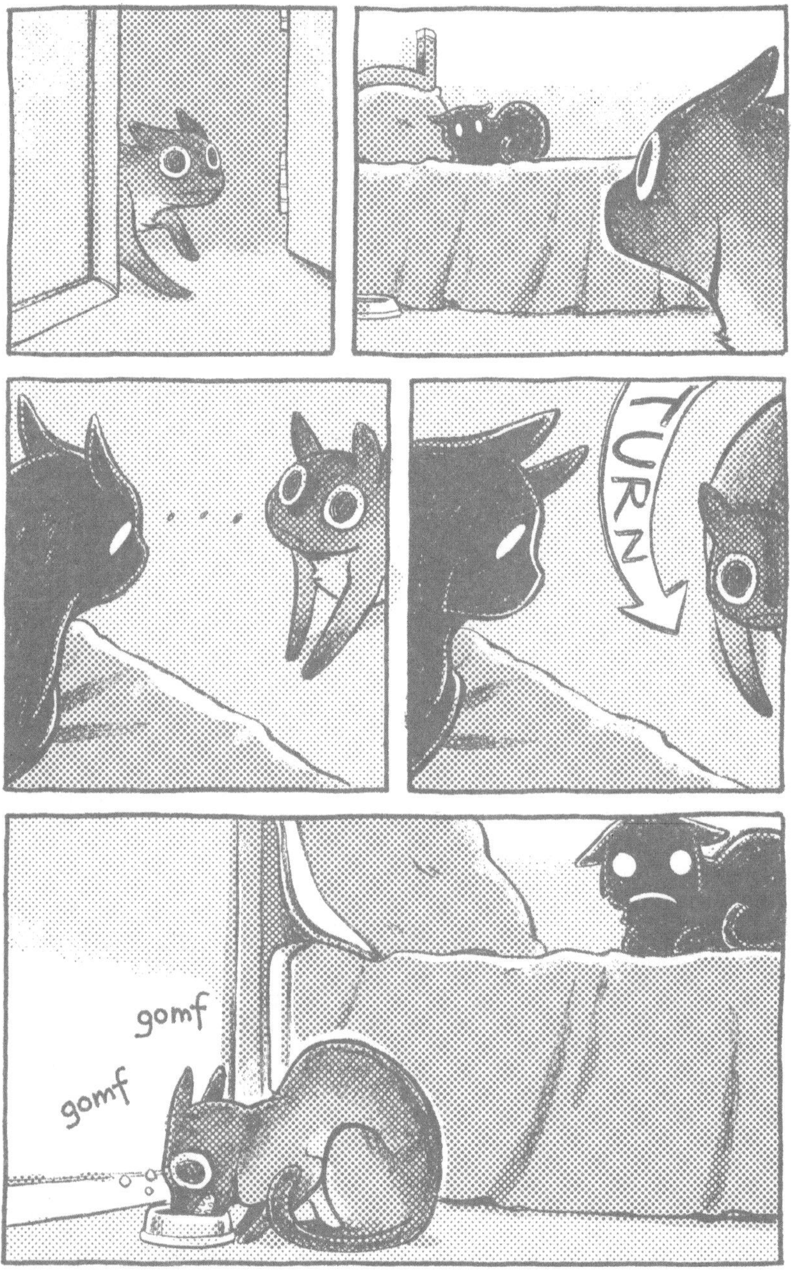
. . .
TURN
gomf
gomf

maid of honor

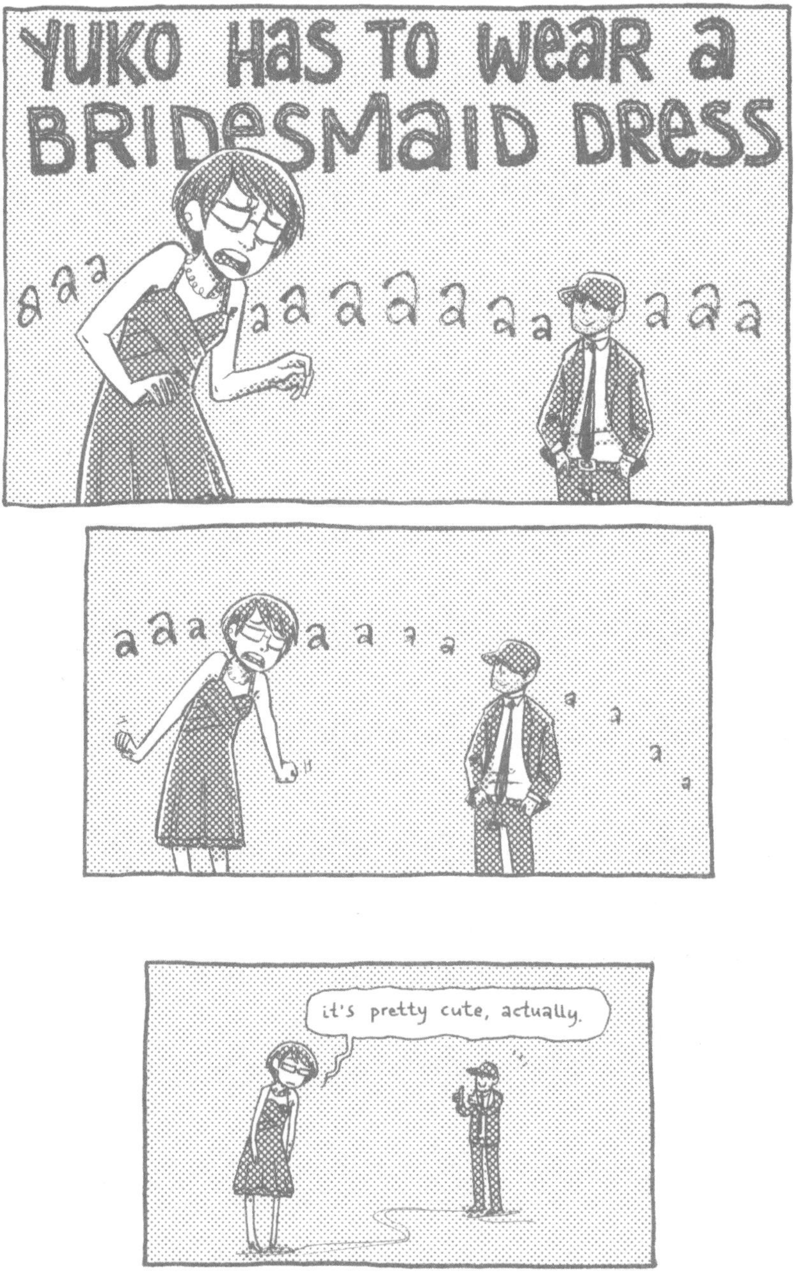
YUKO HAS TO WEAR A BRIDESMAID DRESS
aaaaaaaaaaaaaaaa
aaaaaaaaaaaa
it's pretty cute, actually.

don't get any ideas, mom

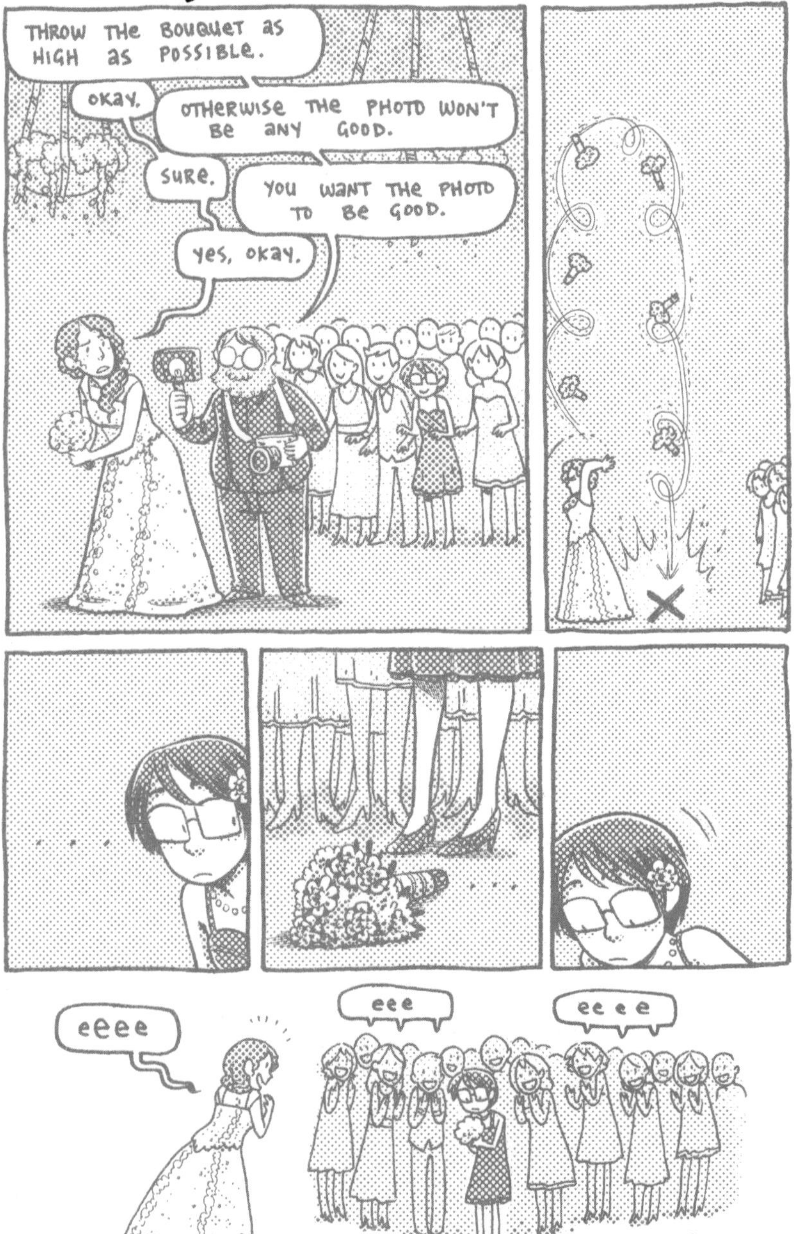
THROW THE BOUQUET AS HIGH AS POSSIBLE.
OKAY.
OTHERWISE THE PHOTO WON'T BE ANY GOOD.
SURE.
YOU WANT THE PHOTO TO BE GOOD.
YES, OKAY.
eeee
eee
ee e e
WELP.

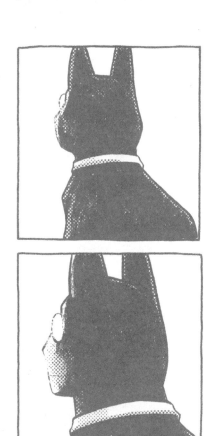

happy april fools!

carnivore-blocked

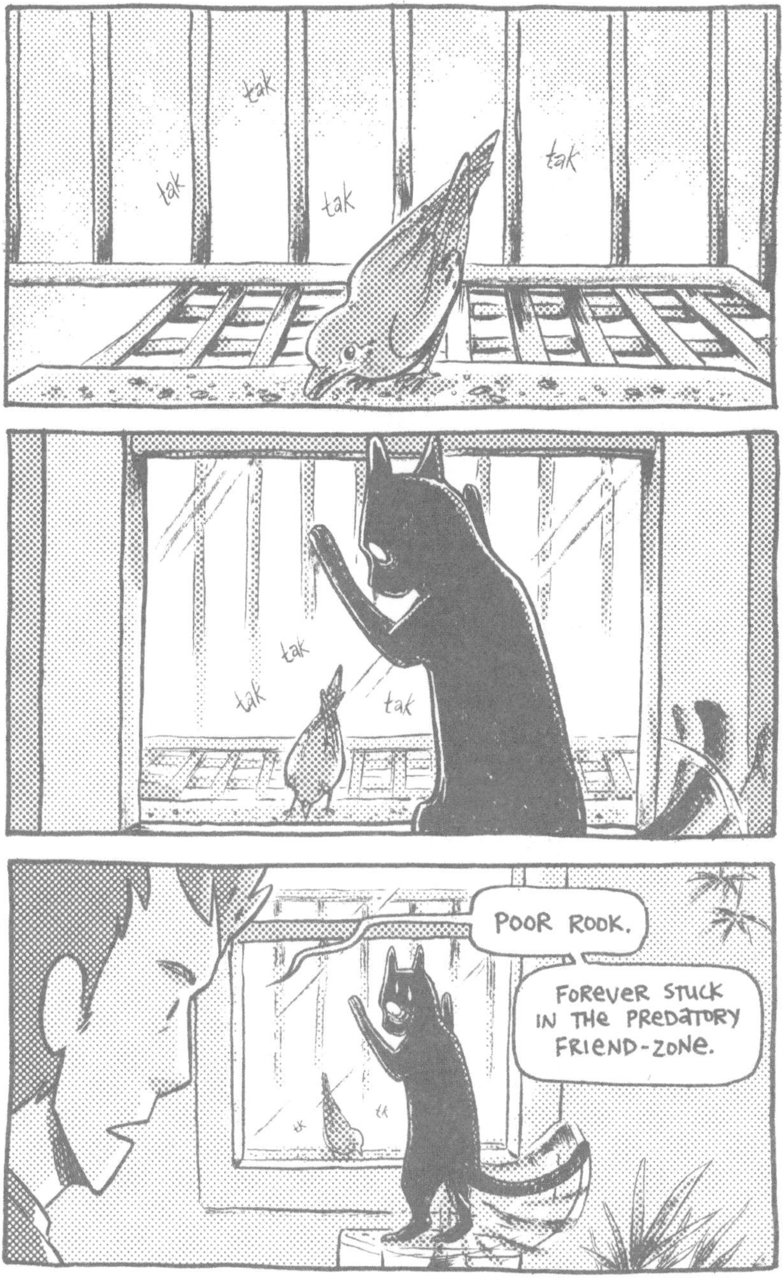
tak
tak
tak
tak
tak
tak
tak
POOR ROOK.
FOREVER STUCK IN THE PREDATORY FRIEND-ZONE.

the return of sweetie pie

5 DAYS LATER:

cake sagan

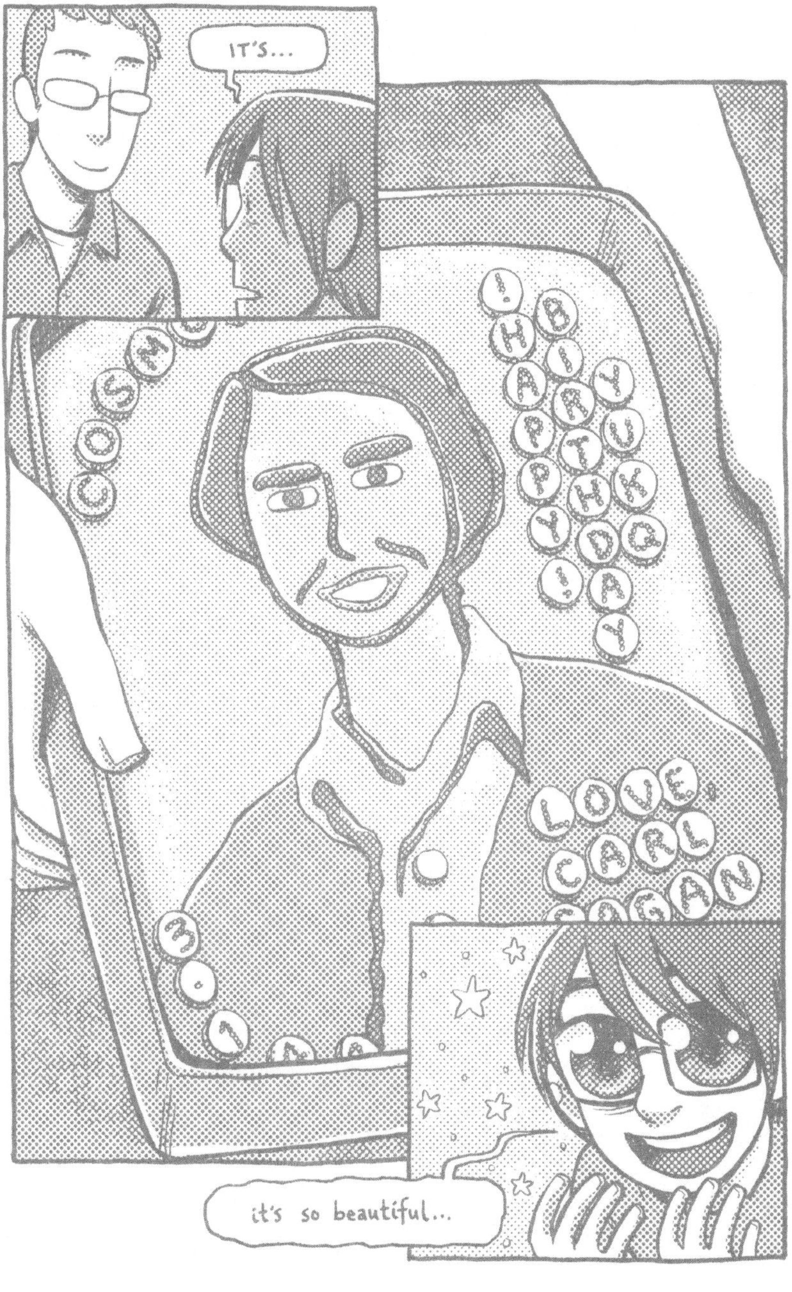

IT'S...
it's so beautiful...

bargle

BROUGHT TO YOU BY ASIAN ALCOHOL INTOLERANCE

thanks, nihilism dad

I HEARD YOU GOT SICK OVER THE WEEKEND
IT'S YOUR FAULT, DAD! IT'S BECAUSE OF YOUR DUMB GENES.
YOU SHOULD THANK ME. EVERYONE WILL DIE SOME DAY. SOME PEOPLE GET TO SOONER THAN OTHERS

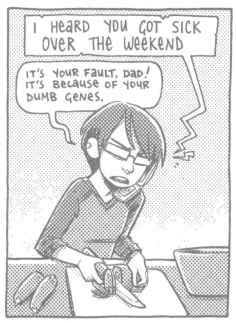

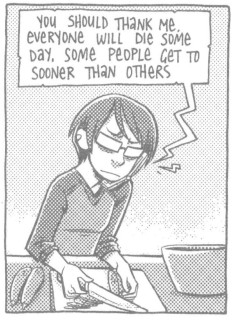

cat booger

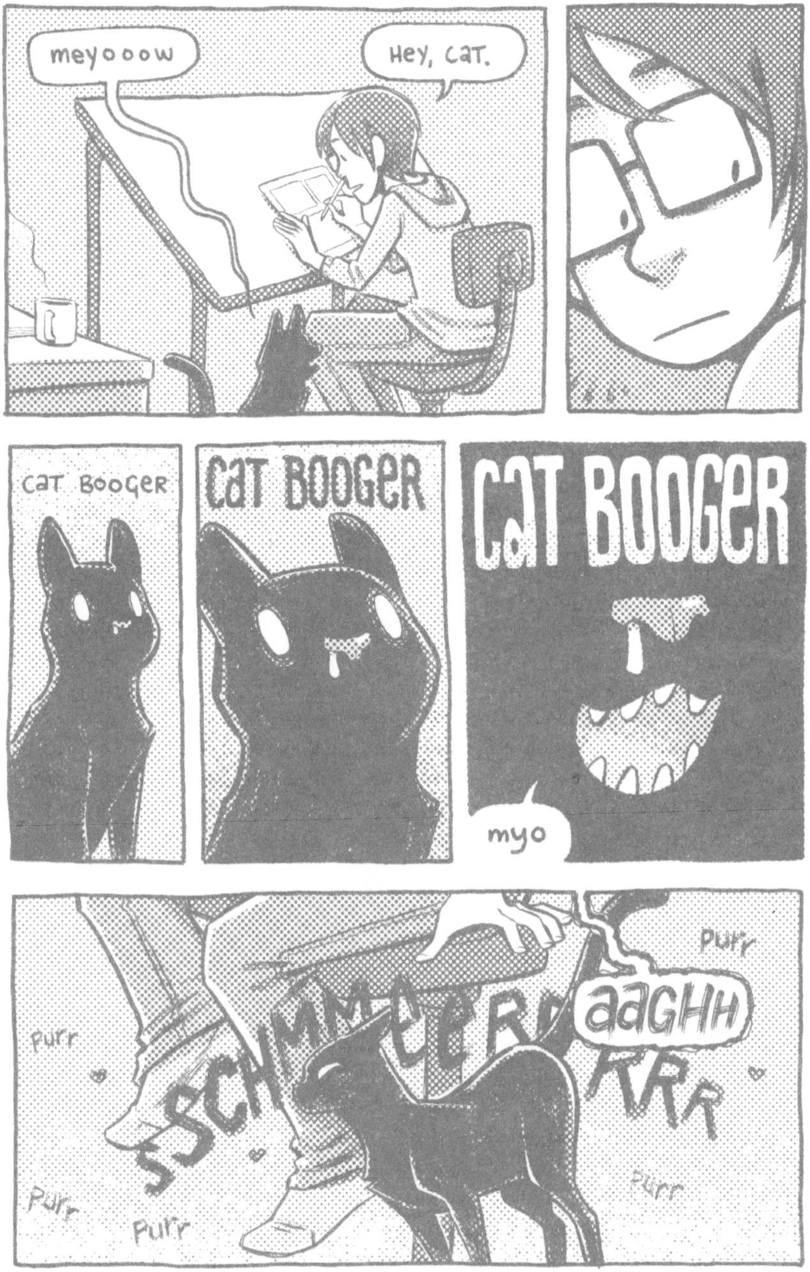
meyooow
Hey, cat.
cat booger
CAT BOOGER
CAT BOOGER
myo
purr
SSCHMMEERRRRRr
aaGHH
purr
purr
purr
purr

drinking problem

BA DUNPP
BLUHH
... there's a bridge there.
THANKS.

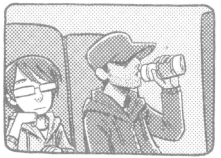

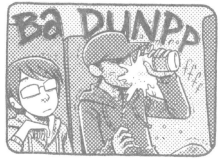

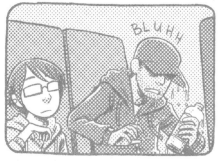

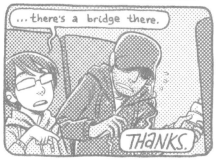

the call is coming from inside the houussee

gas station snacks for dinner

BUT NO FOOD.

where everybody knows your name

snickerdoggle

YOU GUYS SHOULD COME OUT HERE, THERE'S A TINY BROWN DOG WITH an UNDERBITE!

a SOMETHING-DOODLE.

ee!

a SNICKERDOODLE?

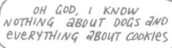

OH GOD, I KNOW NOTHING ABOUT DOGS AND EVERYTHING ABOUT COOKIES

saxocat

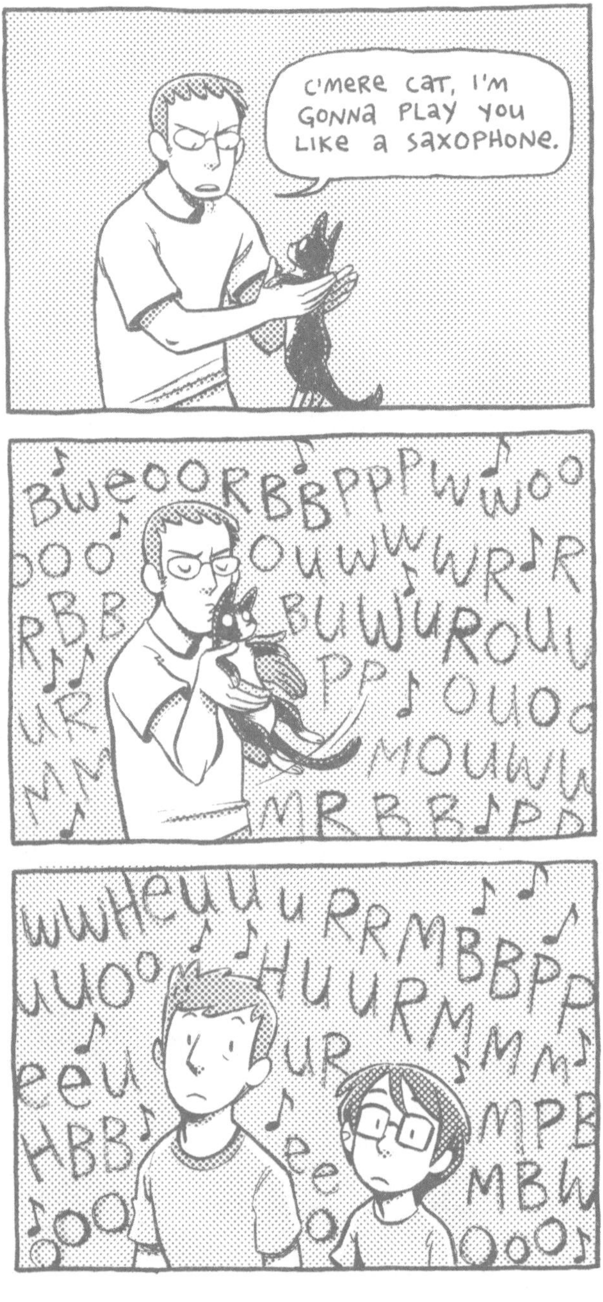
C'MERE CAT, I'M GONNA PLAY YOU LIKE A SAXOPHONE.
BWEOORBBPPPWWOO
OUWWWR
BUWUROU
PP OUO
MOUWU
MRBBPP
WWHEUUURRMBBPP
UUO HUURMM
UR
MPB
MBW
OOOO

puppy shower

YUKO, WILL YOU TEACH US HOW TO DRAW PUPPIES?

DRAWIN' PUPPIES

should have learned flag semaphore

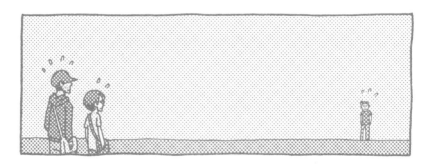

a few of my favorite things: TOUGH GUY EDITION

tough guy walking
sparkle dog

tough guy carrying
sparkle backpack

THAT WEIRD ECTO-COOLER SMOOTHIE THING THAT JOHN MAKES:

BLEND TOGETHER:

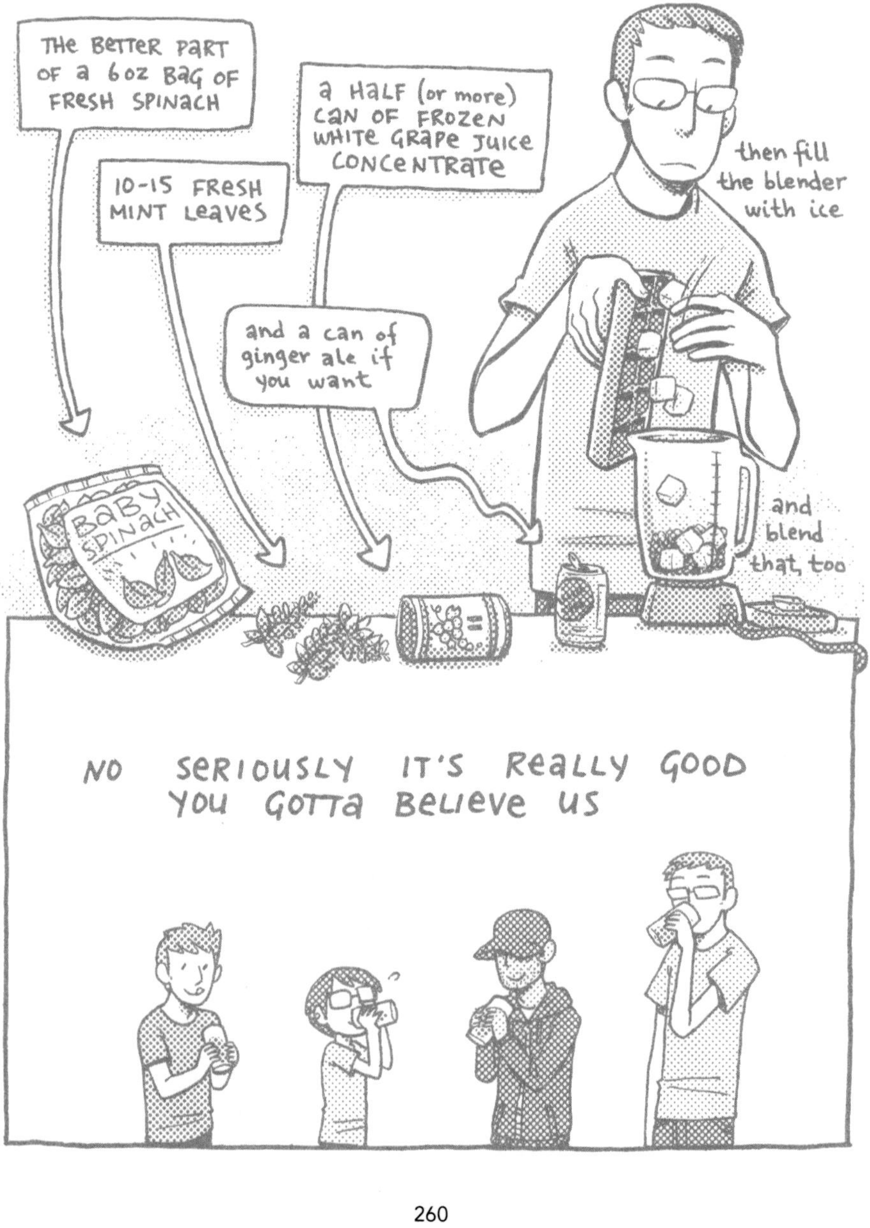
THE BETTER PART OF A 6 OZ BAG OF FRESH SPINACH
10-15 FRESH MINT LEAVES
A HALF (or more) CAN OF FROZEN WHITE GRAPE JUICE CONCENTRATE
and a can of ginger ale if you want
then fill the blender with ice
and blend that, too
BABY SPINACH
NO SERIOUSLY IT'S REALLY GOOD YOU GOTTA BELIEVE US

another day, another person mistaking yuko for a teenager

nope

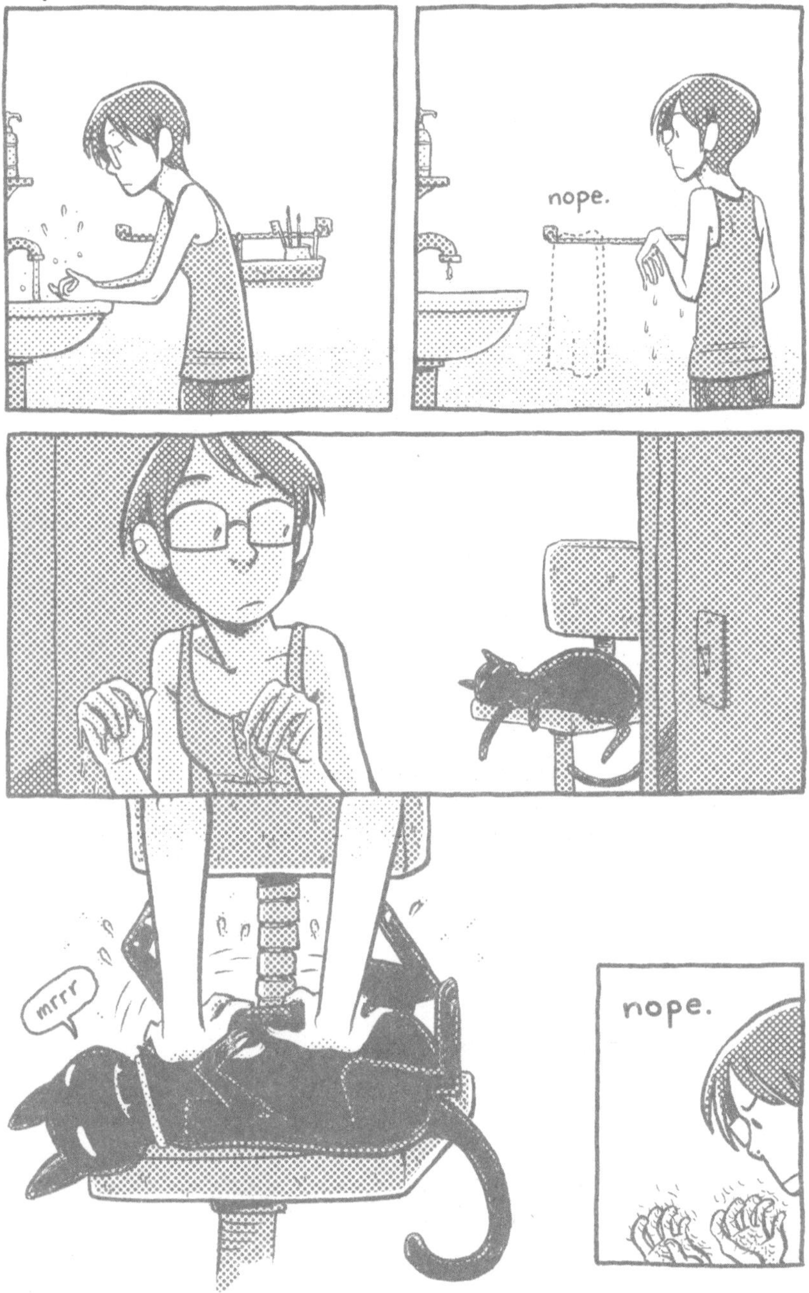
nope.
mrrr
nope.

good thing we just took up rock climbing

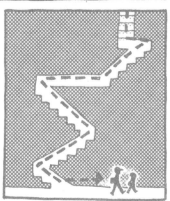

a few of my favorite things: SUBWAY MUSICIANS VERSION

FIVE-PIECE MARIACHI BAND IN FULL REGALIA

TIME-TRAVELING '80S RAPPER
(I didn't know they still made those shirts)

the time we drag-raced hulk hogan

cat ice tray

OH NO

THE CAT IS MELTING

meowwww

whew,
that was
a close
one.

AND SOON:

not the first, not the last

every o'clock shadow

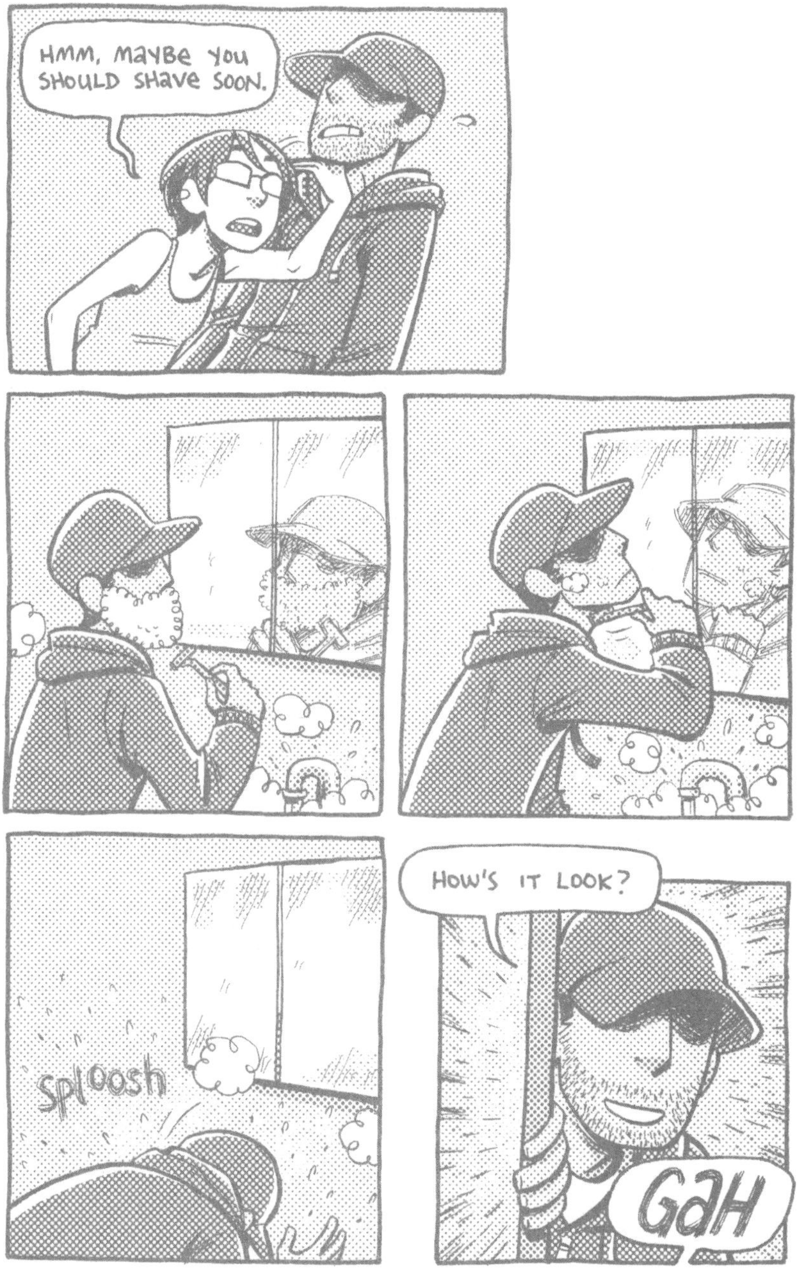
HMM, MAYBE YOU SHOULD SHAVE SOON.
SPLOOSH
HOW'S IT LOOK?
GAH

save yourself

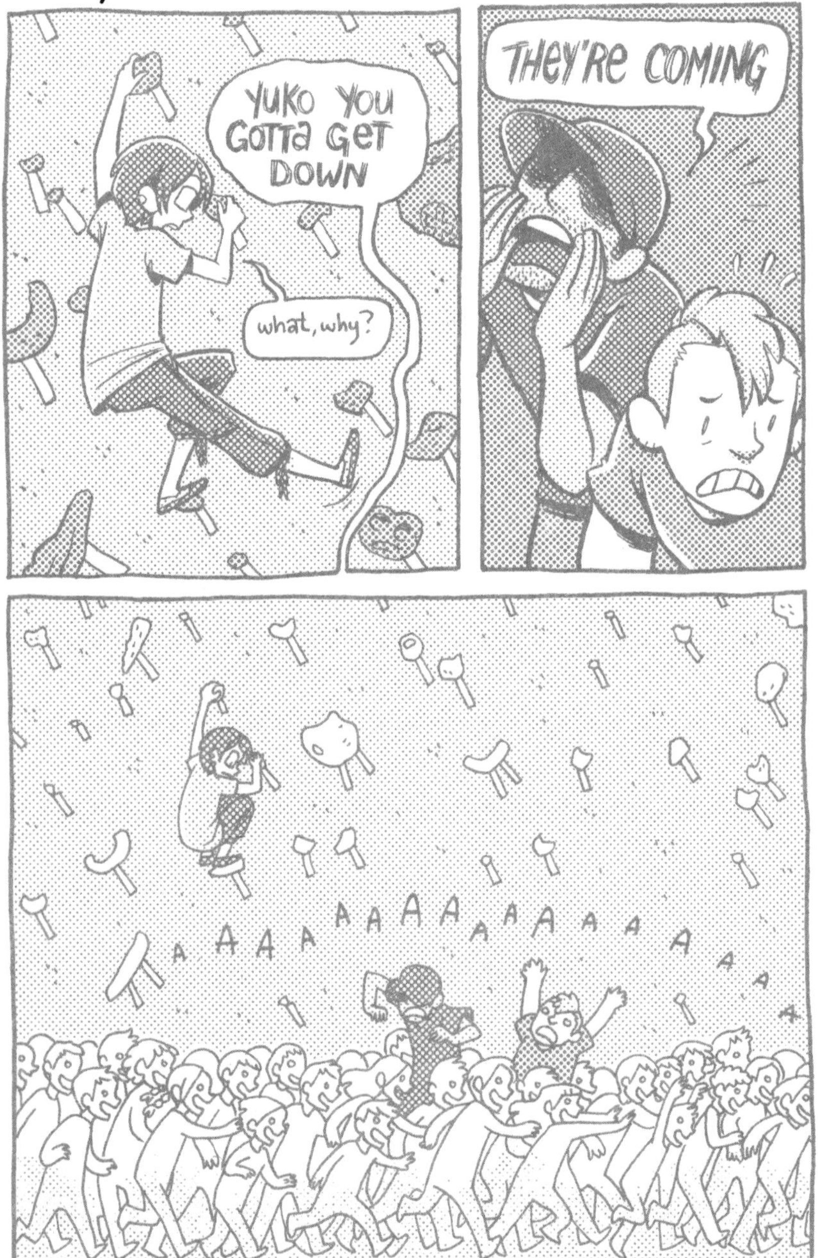
YUKO YOU GOTTA GET DOWN
what, why?
THEY'RE COMING
A A A A A A A A A A A A A A A A A A A A

stoppit, cat-dad

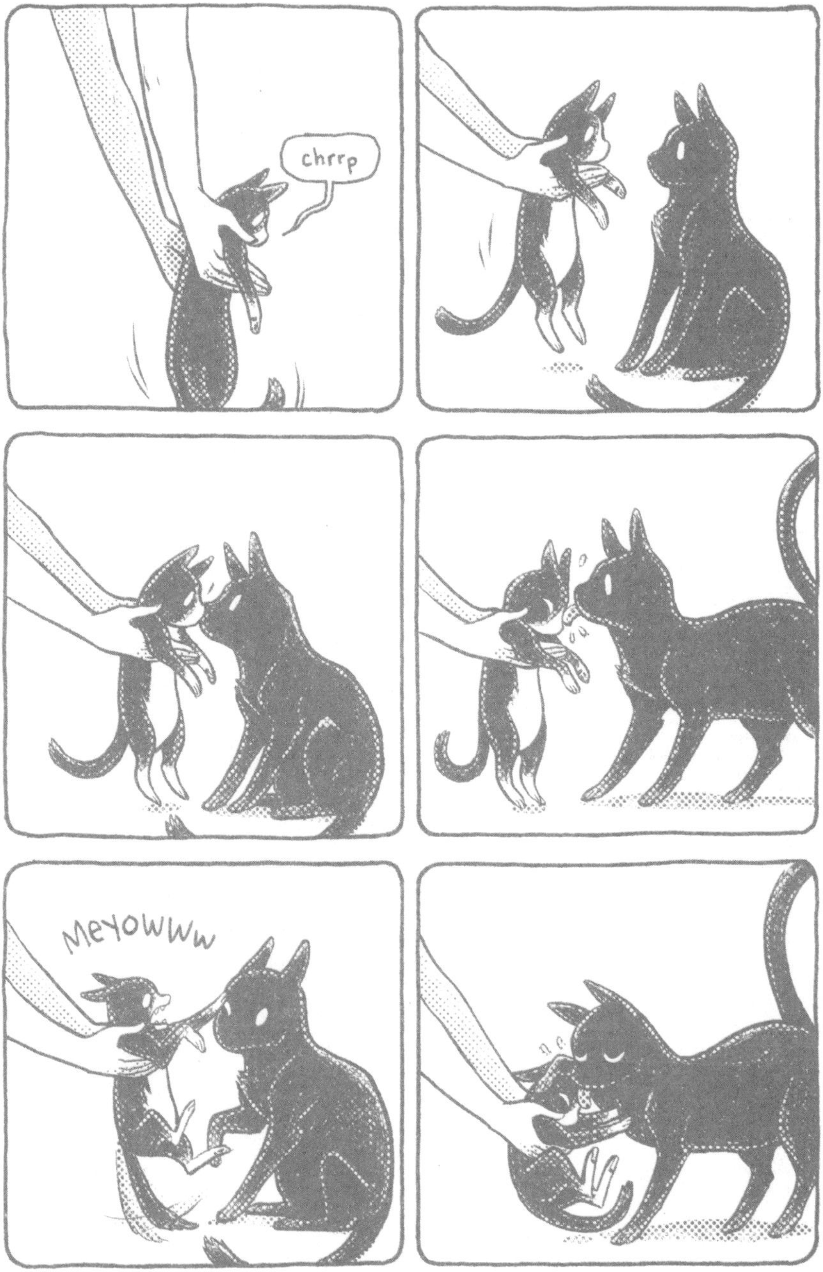
chrrp
MEYOWWW

taking it off

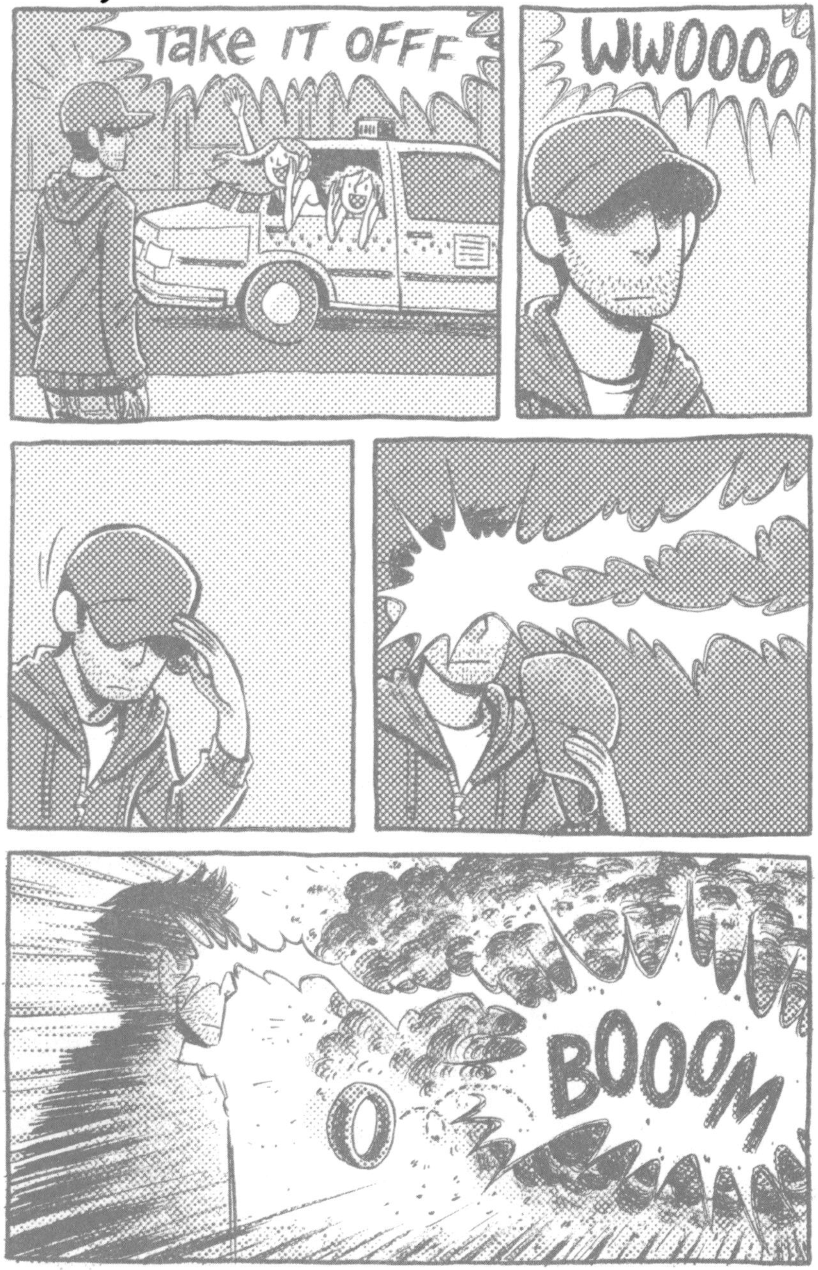
TAKE IT OFFF
WWOOOO
BOOOM

lock your doors

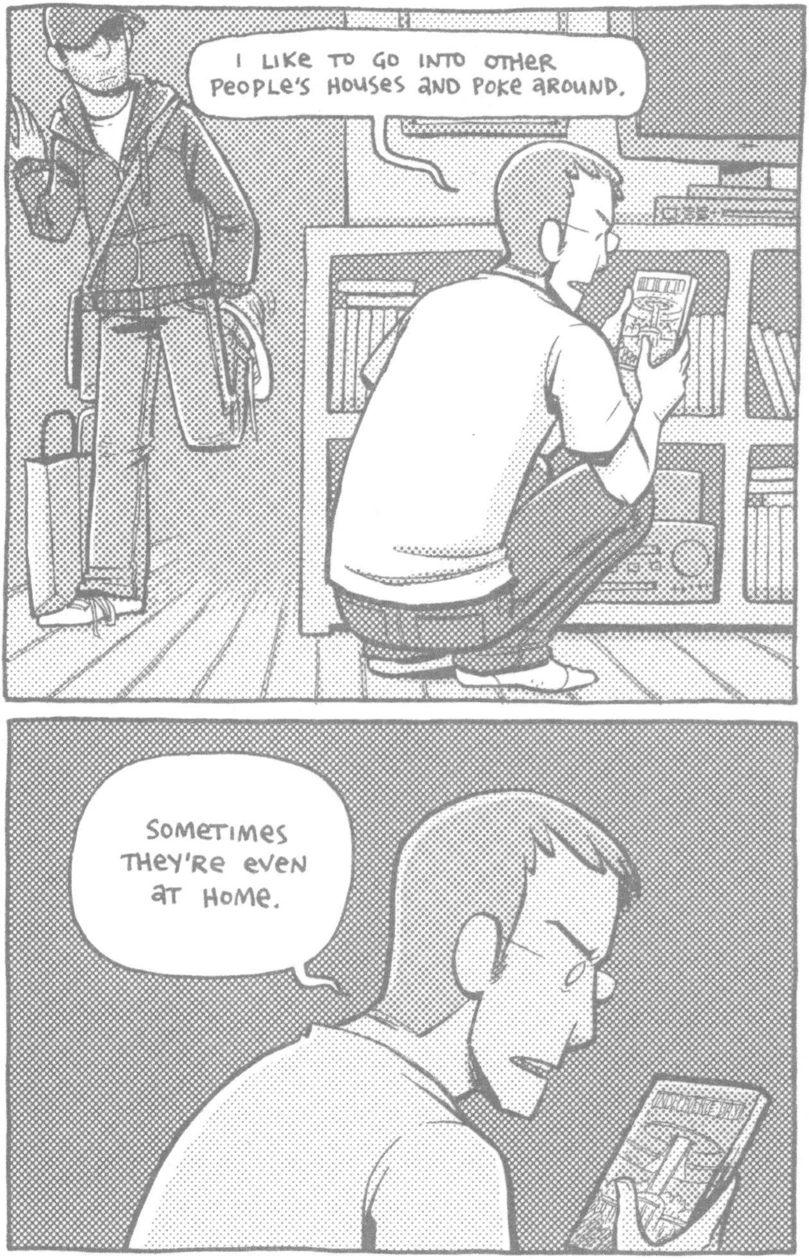
I LIKE TO GO INTO OTHER PEOPLE'S HOUSES AND POKE AROUND.
SOMETIMES THEY'RE EVEN AT HOME.

uncharted

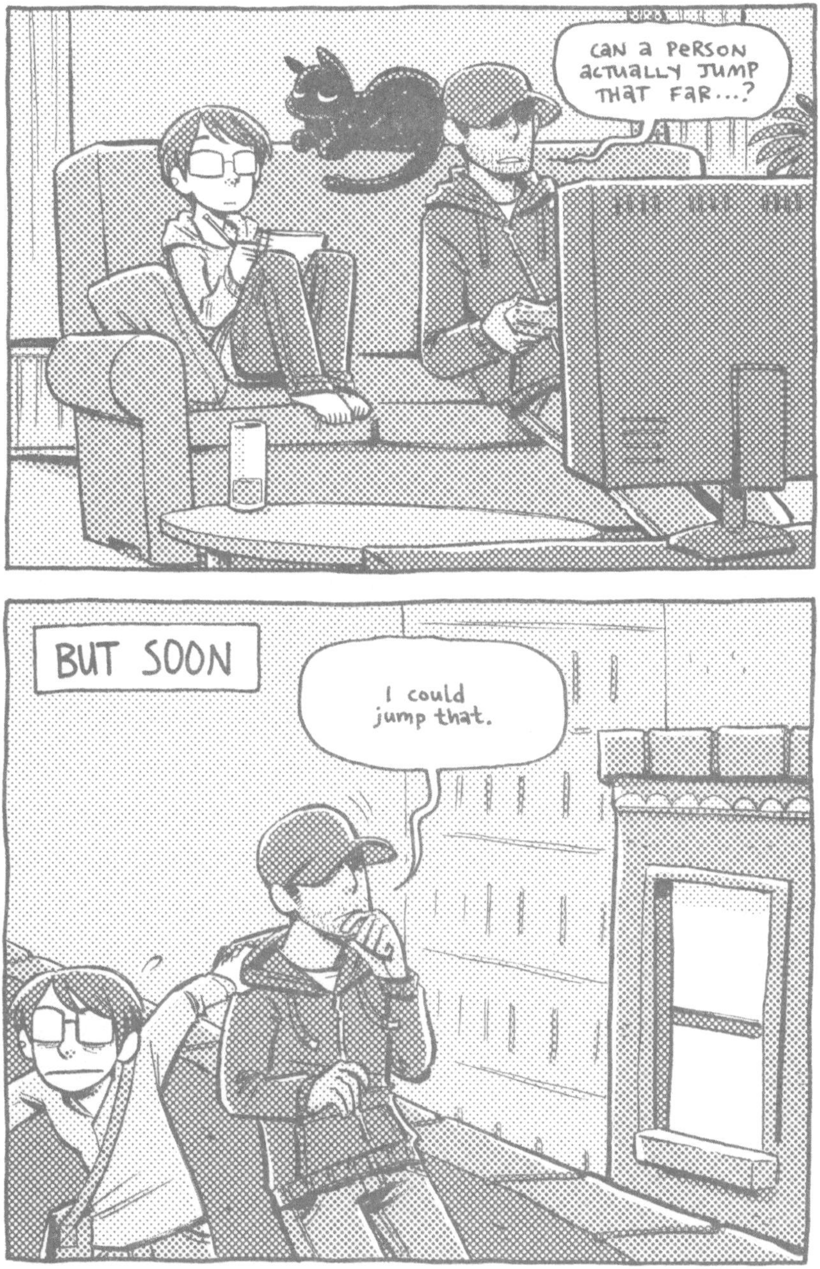
CAN A PERSON ACTUALLY JUMP THAT FAR...?
BUT SOON
I could jump that.

international man of mystery

MEANWHILE IN TAIPEI

magical buried treasure

chair sniper

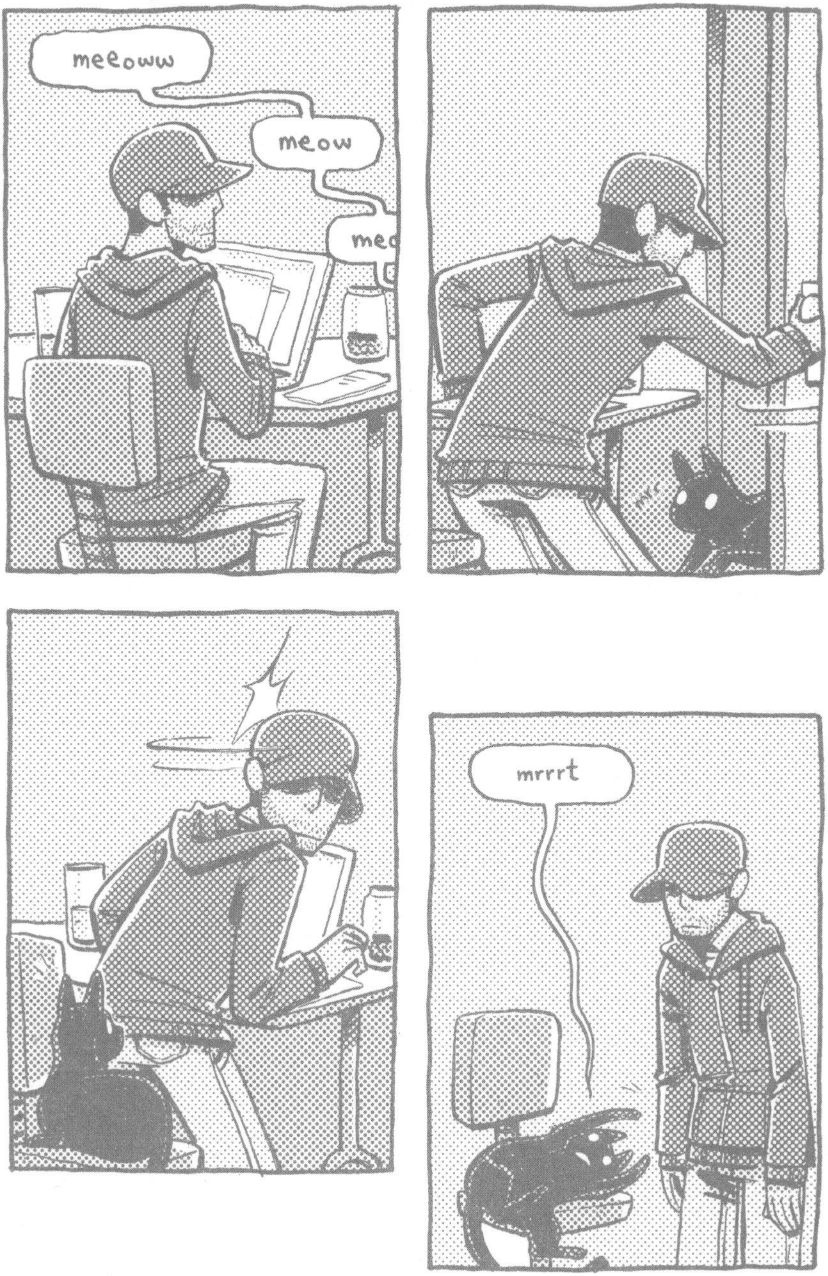

meeoww
meow
me
mrrrt

why did they put them all next to each other

peanut blarghr

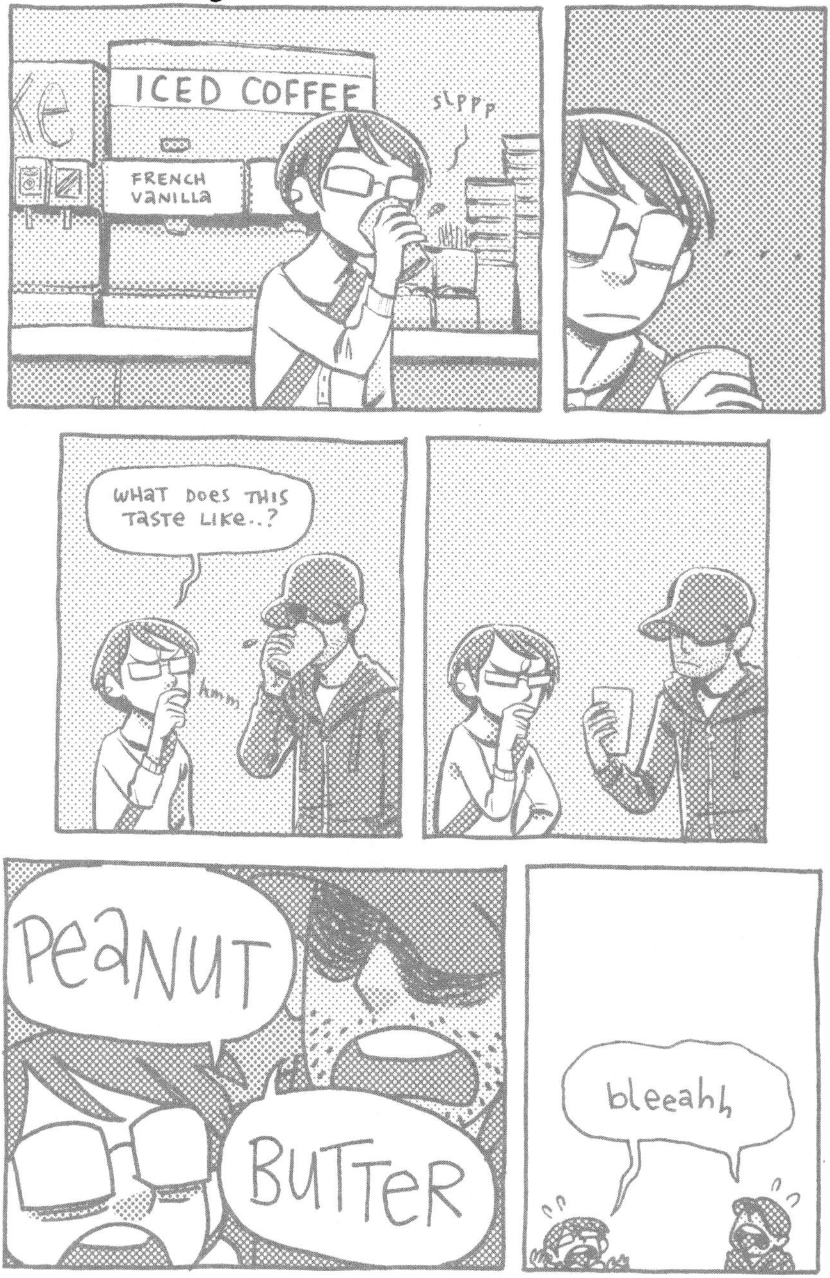
ICED COFFEE
FRENCH VANILLA
slppp
. . .
WHAT DOES THIS TASTE LIKE..?
hmm
PeaNUT
BUTTeR
bleeahh

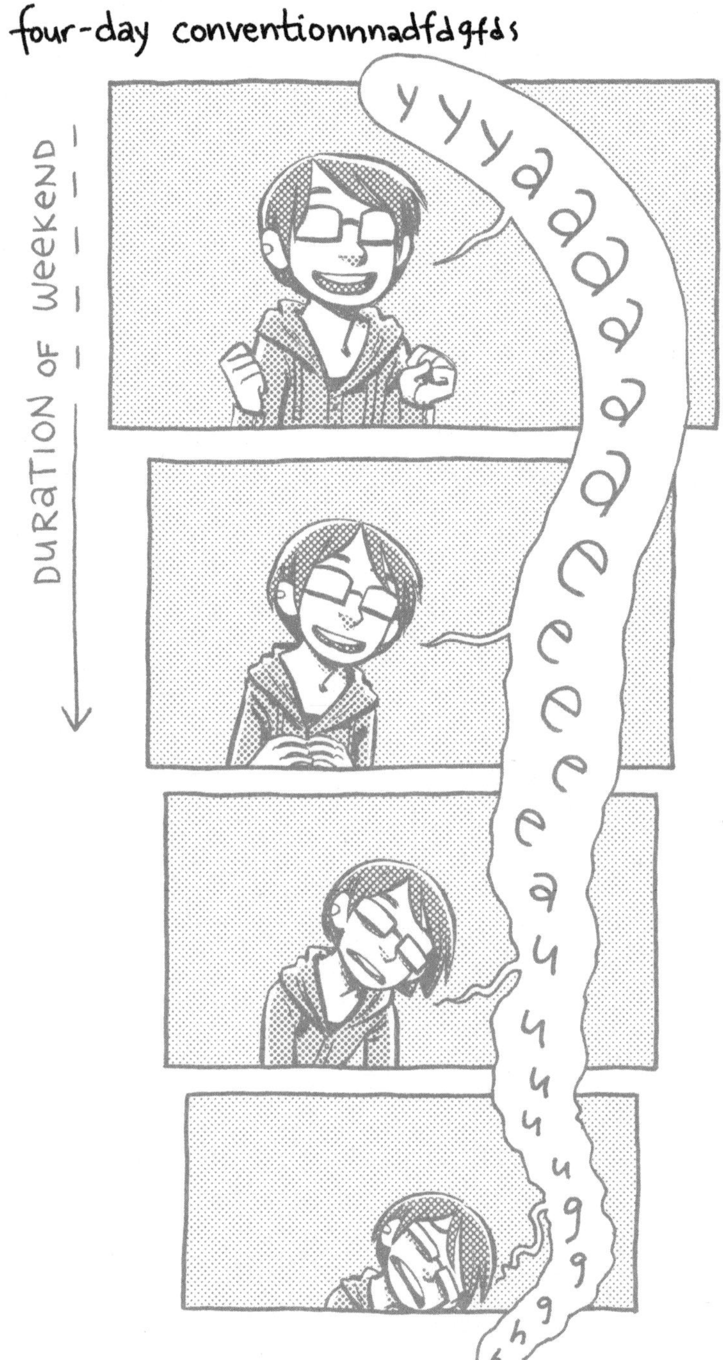
four-day conventionnnadfdgfds
DURATION OF WEEKEND
yyyaaaaaaeeeeeeauuuuugggg

peppermint bargles

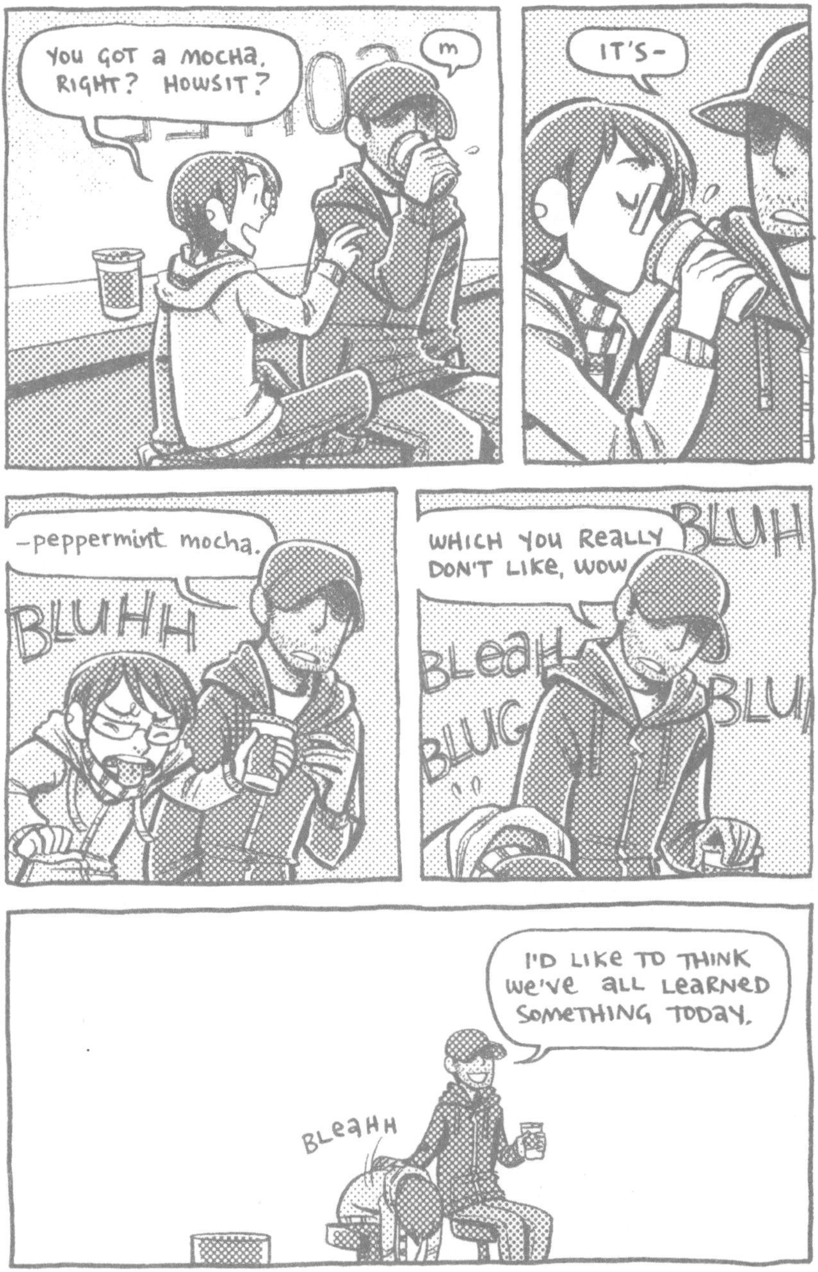

YOU GOT A MOCHA, RIGHT? HOWSIT?
m
IT'S-
-peppermint mocha.
BLUHH
WHICH YOU REALLY DON'T LIKE, WOW
BLUH
BLEAH
BLUG
I'D LIKE TO THINK WE'VE ALL LEARNED SOMETHING TODAY.
BLEAHH

all freight elevators are haunted

party cone

CRICKET GOT
SPAYED LAST
WEEK.

CLONK

CLONK

myert.

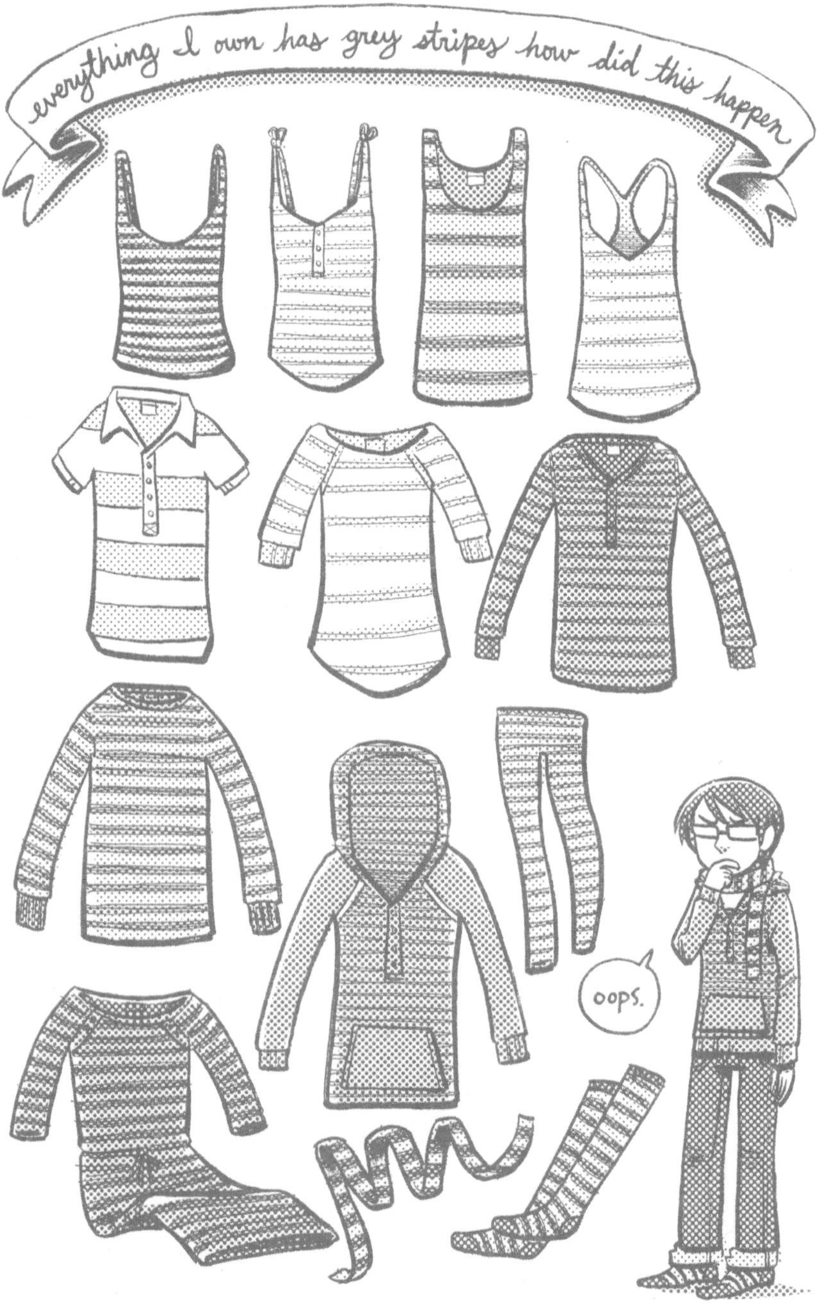
everything I own has grey stripes how did this happen
oops.

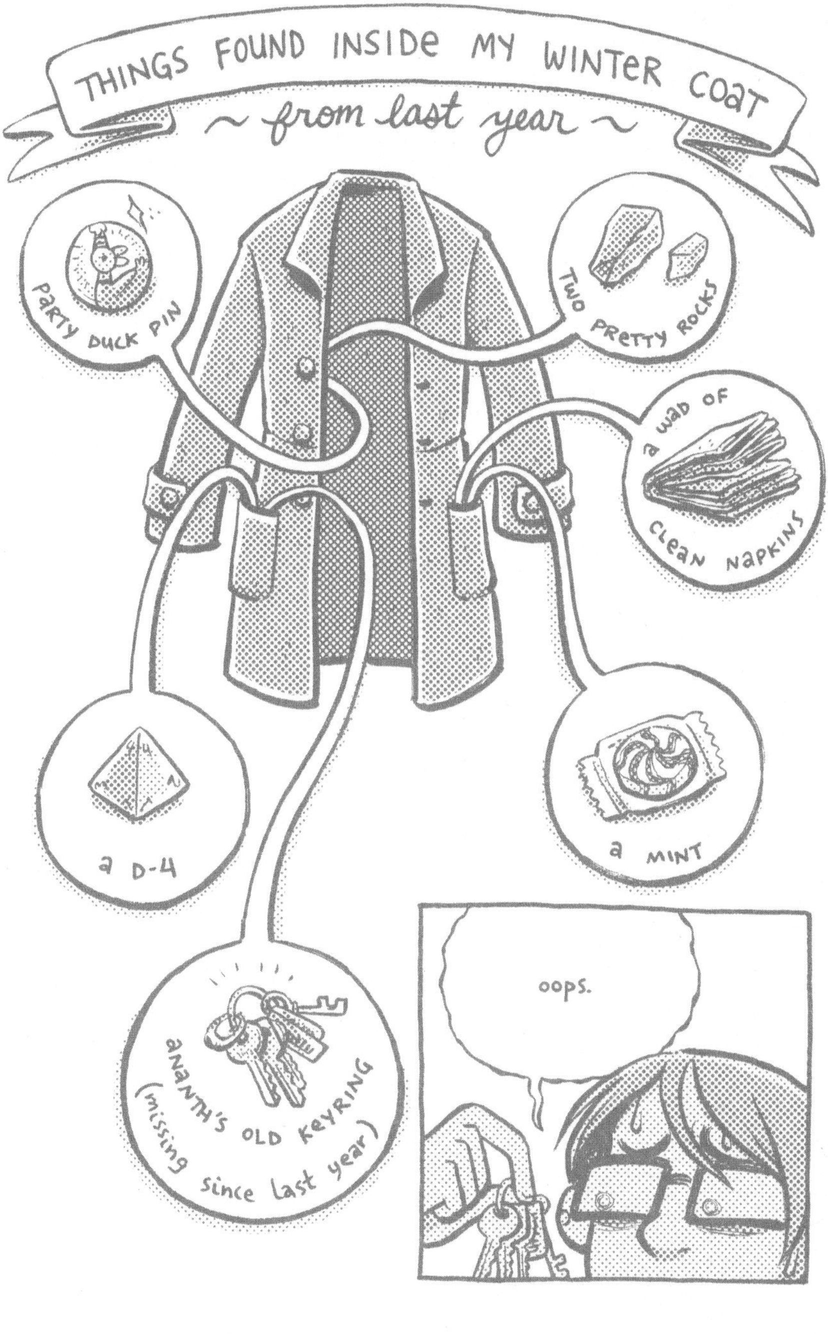
THINGS FOUND INSIDE MY WINTER COAT
~ from last year ~
PARTY DUCK PIN
TWO PRETTY ROCKS
A WAD OF CLEAN NAPKINS
A D-4
A MINT
ANANTH'S OLD KEYRING (missing since last year)
oops.

cat-rad

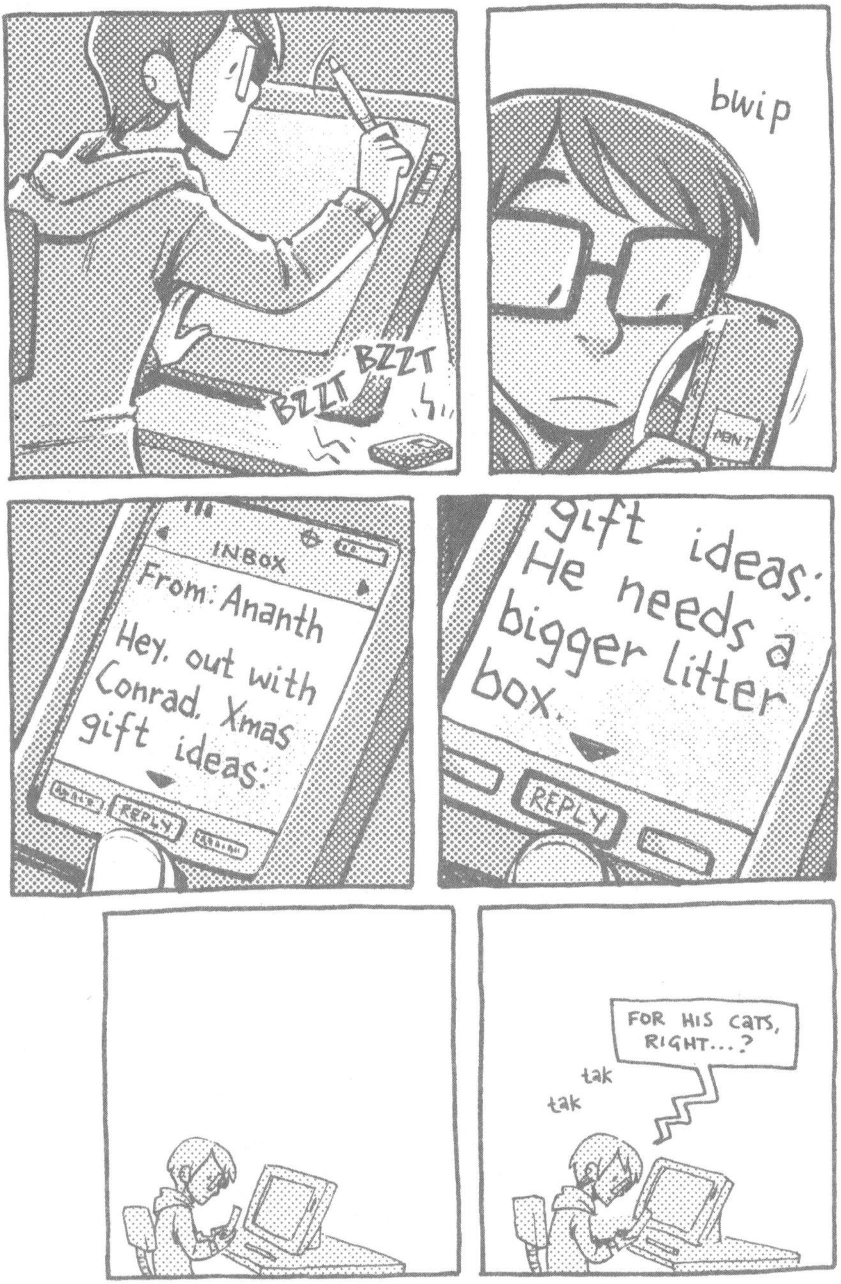
BZZT BZZT
bwip
INBOX
From: Ananth
Hey. out with Conrad. Xmas gift ideas:
REPLY
gift ideas:
He needs a bigger litter box.
REPLY
tak
tak
FOR HIS CATS, RIGHT...?

The Midas Touch
BUT WITH CAT HAIR

needs about ten packs of sugar

we are going to be best friends

it runs in the family

SORRY MOM, GIMMIE A SEC.
KSHHSSHH
KSHKKSSHH
OH, ARE YOU MAKING DINNER..?
GENERIC O'S
I, UH. I'M SORT OF.
I'M HAVING CEREAL.
HAHA, THAT SOUNDS GOOD.
GENERIC O'S
AAAAA I'M SO SORRY I'M SUCH A TERRIBLE ADULTAAA
OH NO, I WAS BEING SERIOUS.
I JUST HAD CEREAL FOR DINNER.

laundry rich

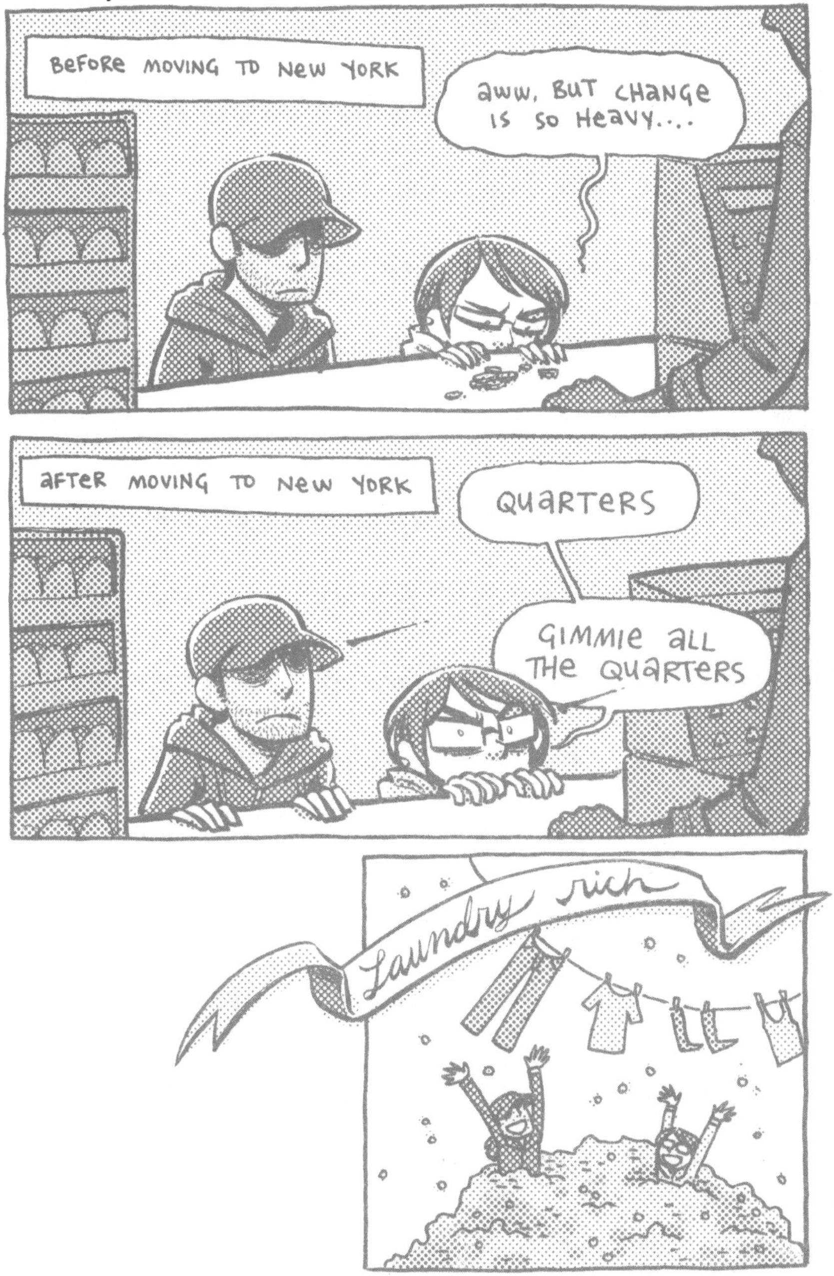
BEFORE MOVING TO NEW YORK
aww, BUT CHANGE IS SO HEAVY....
AFTER MOVING TO NEW YORK
QUARTERS
GIMMIE ALL THE QUARTERS
Laundry rich

teeny fractal buddy

IT...

IT LOOKS JUST LIKE A MANDELBROT SET...

I CAN'T WASH THAT OFF
...

AND THEN MY DESK WAS NEVER CLEAN AGAIN.

yes

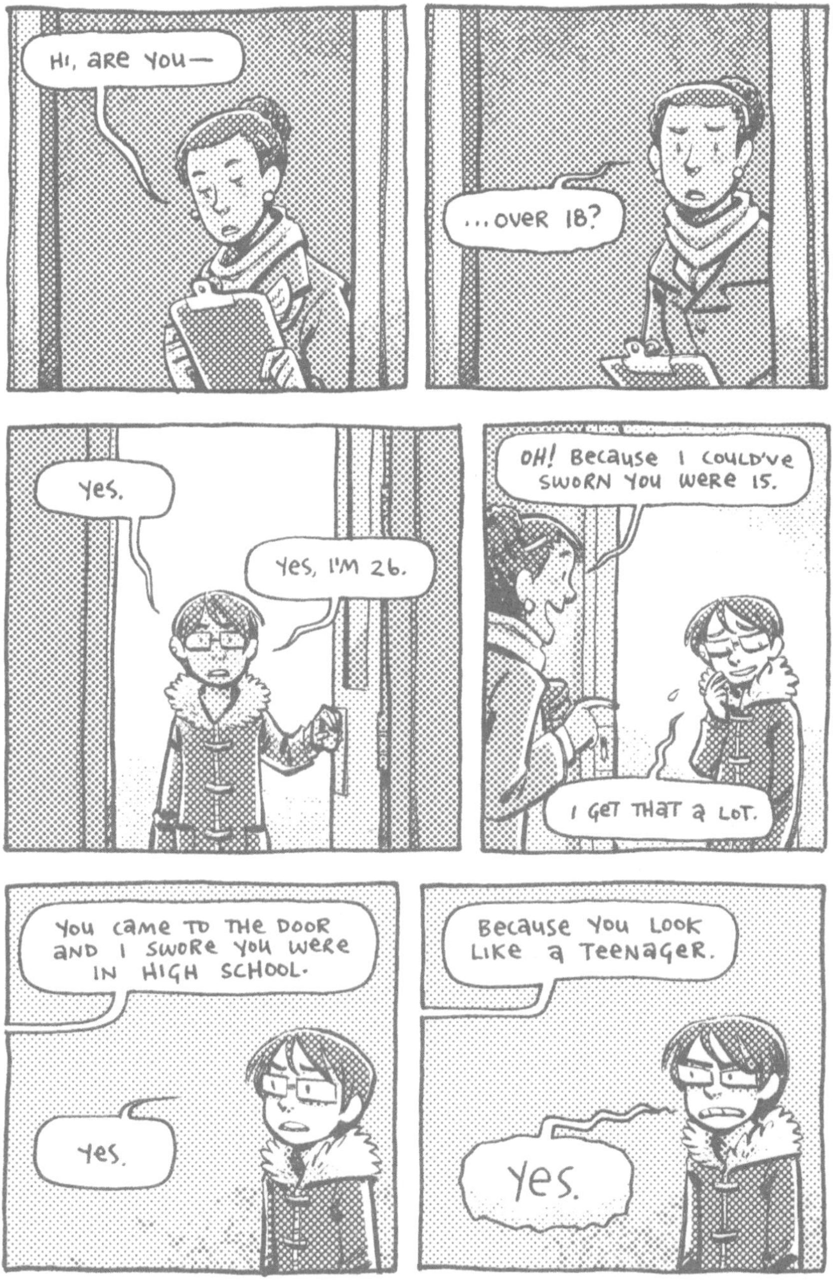
Hi, are you—
...over 18?
yes.
yes, I'm 26.
OH! Because I could've sworn you were 15.
I get that a lot.
You came to the door and I swore you were in high school.
yes.
Because you look like a teenager.
yes.

roadtrip soundtrack

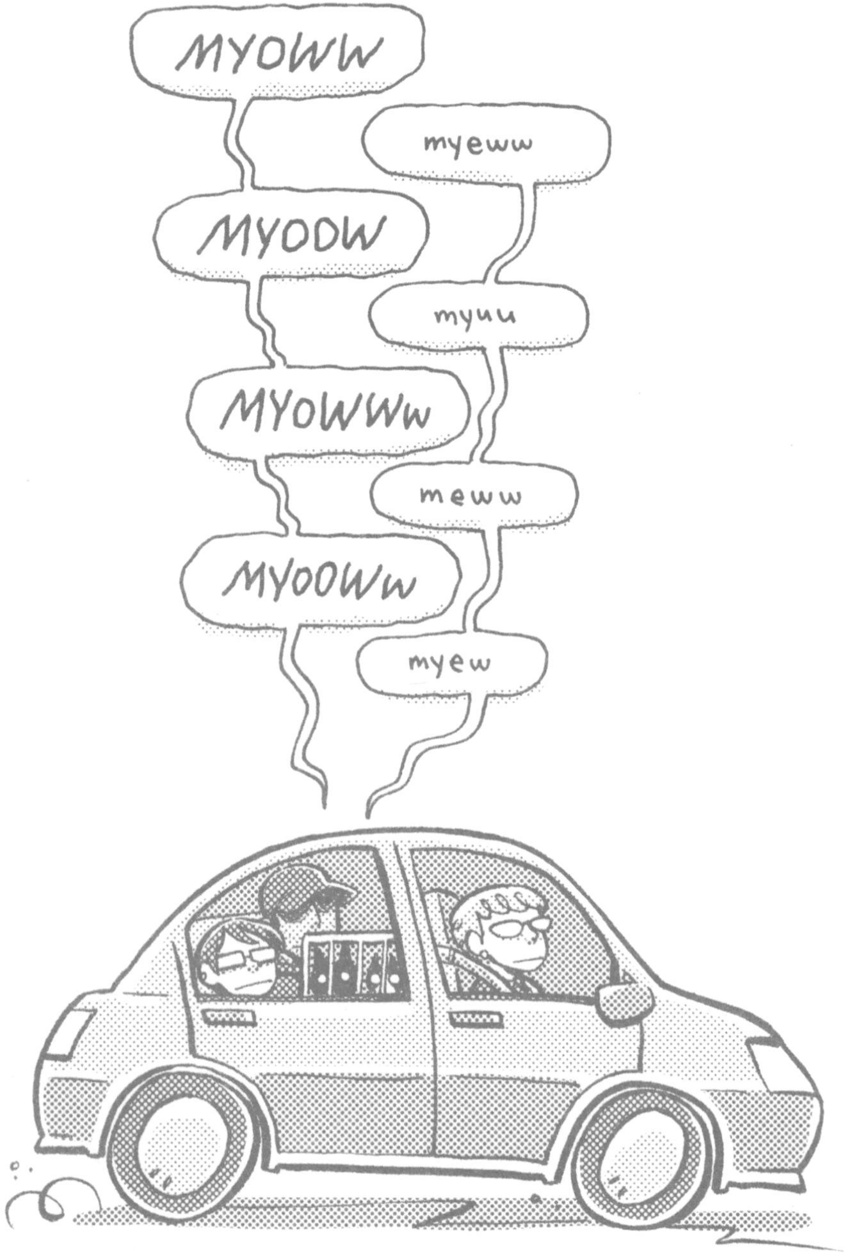
MYOWW
myeww
MYOOW
myuu
MYOWWW
meww
MYOOWW
myew

merry christmas, mom

hmm.

merry catsmas

LET'S MAKE A SANDWICH!

with yuko's dad

TAKE TWO SLICES OF LEFTOVER PIZZA

pepperoni

anchovy

COVER IN KIMCHI

KIMCHI

MICROWAVE

:30

r r r   r   r r r

enjoy!

kitten of a hundred names

how can you be unhappy while wearing a cupcake hat

cat burglar in the making

and so:

on hubris

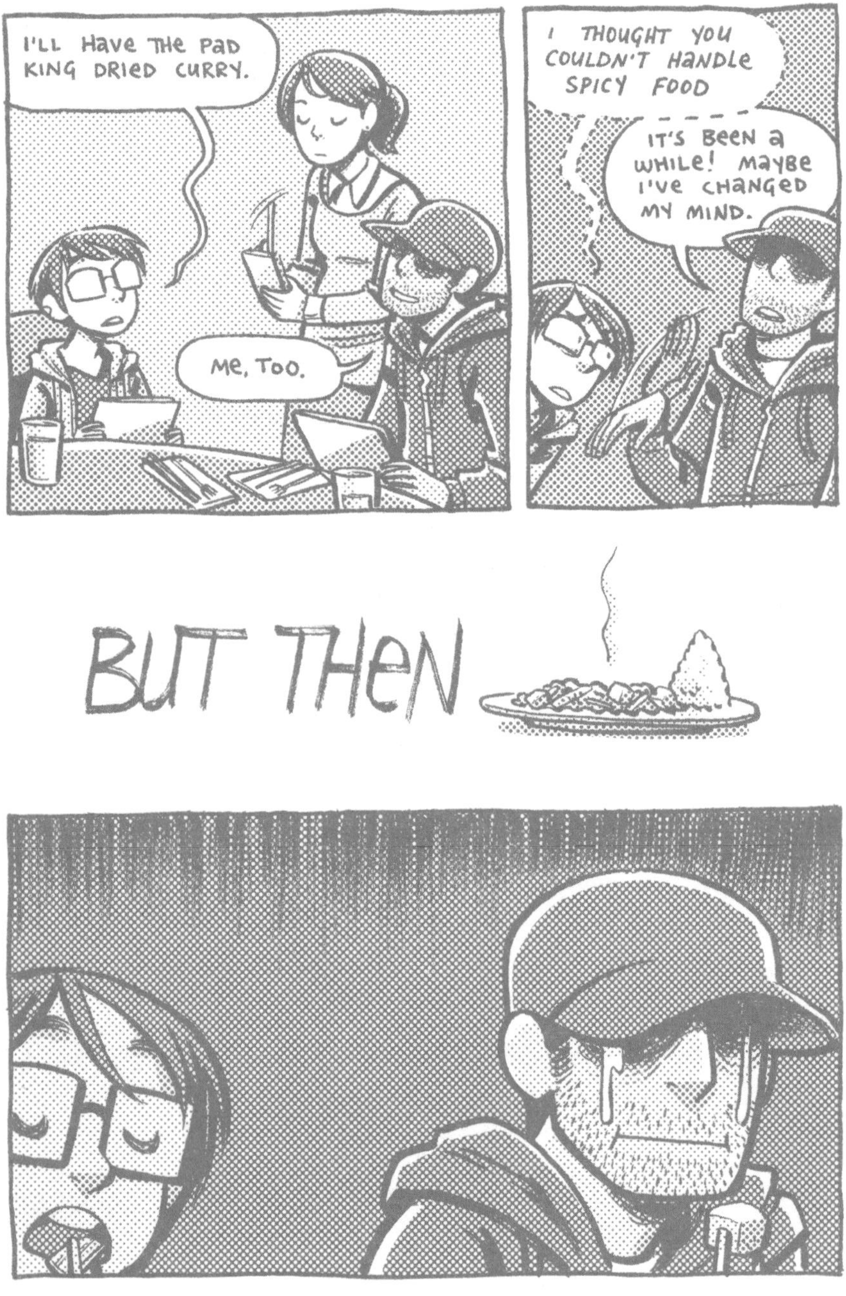
I'LL HAVE THE PAD KING DRIED CURRY.
ME, TOO.
I THOUGHT YOU COULDN'T HANDLE SPICY FOOD
IT'S BEEN A WHILE! MAYBE I'VE CHANGED MY MIND.
BUT THEN

tai chi-ing up the wall

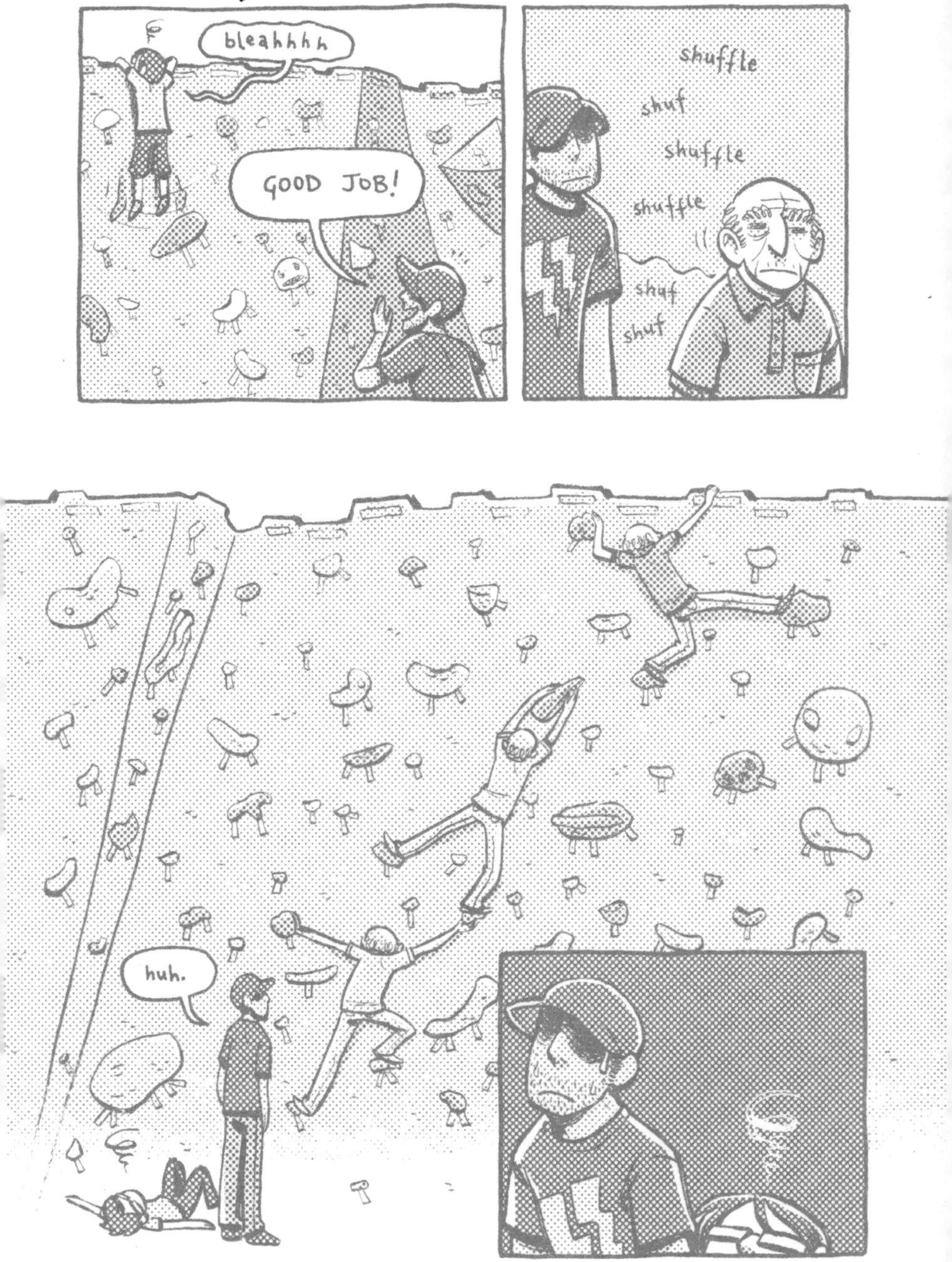
bleahhhh
GOOD JOB!
shuffle
shuf
shuffle
shuffle
shuf
shuf
huh.

water cat

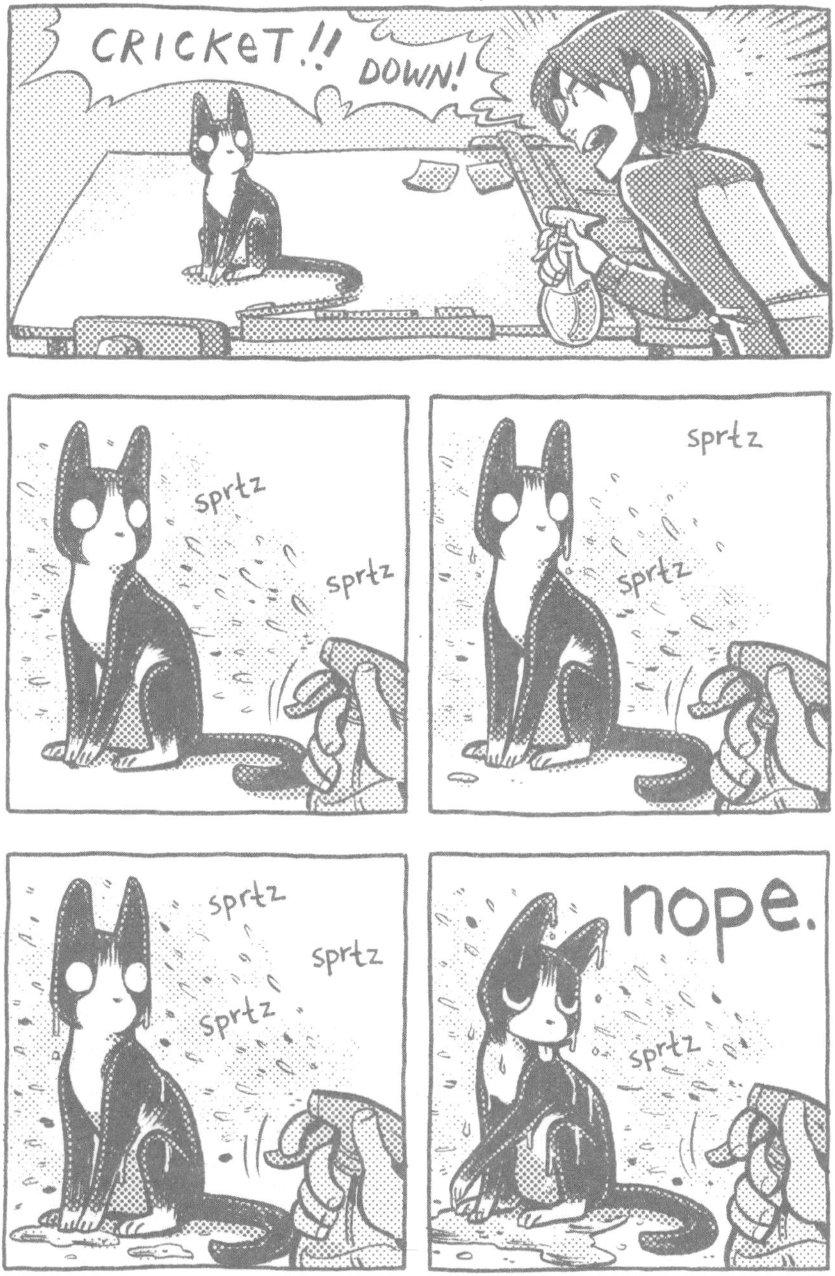
CRICKET!!
DOWN!
sprtz
sprtz
sprtz
sprtz
sprtz
sprtz
sprtz
nope.
sprtz

shirt cat

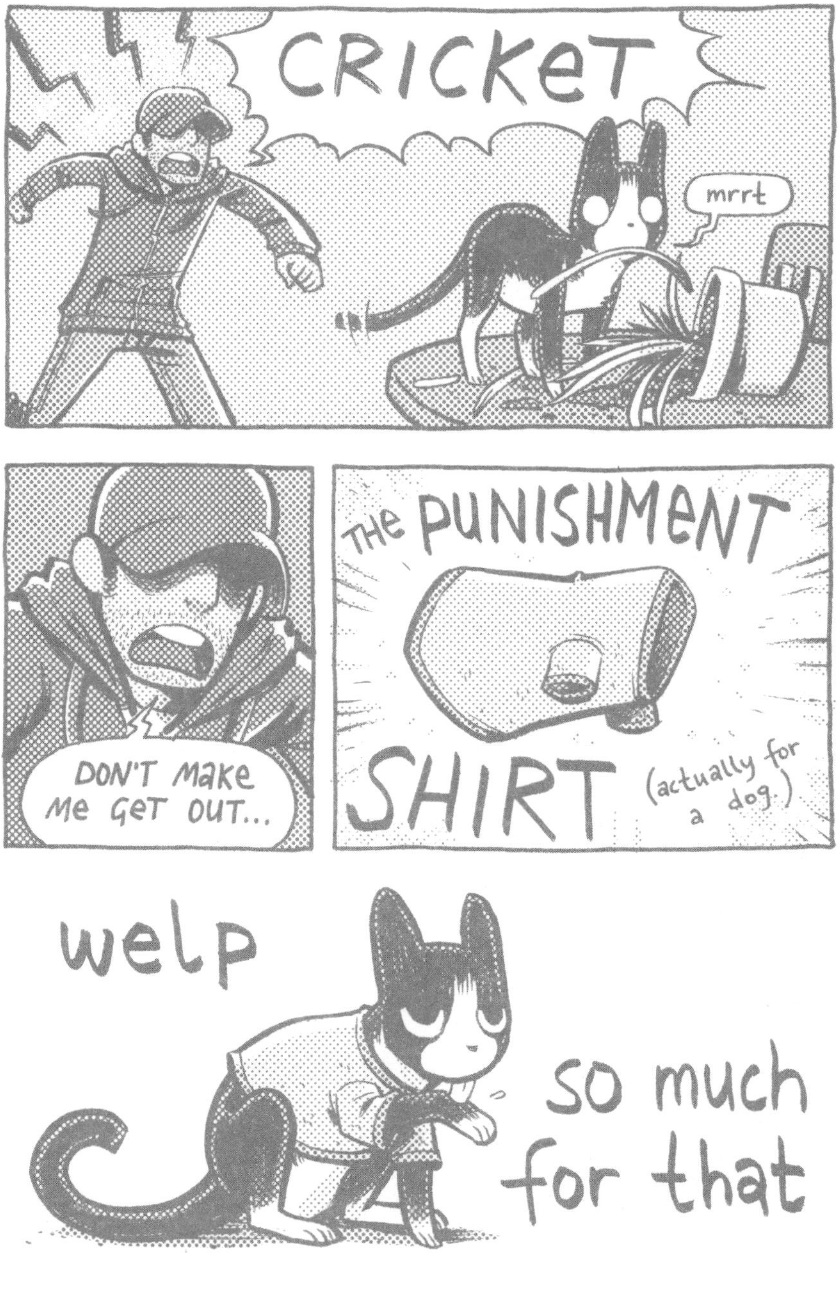
CRICKET
mrrt
DON'T MAKE ME GET OUT...
THE PUNISHMENT SHIRT
(actually for a dog.)
welp
so much for that

punishment shirt

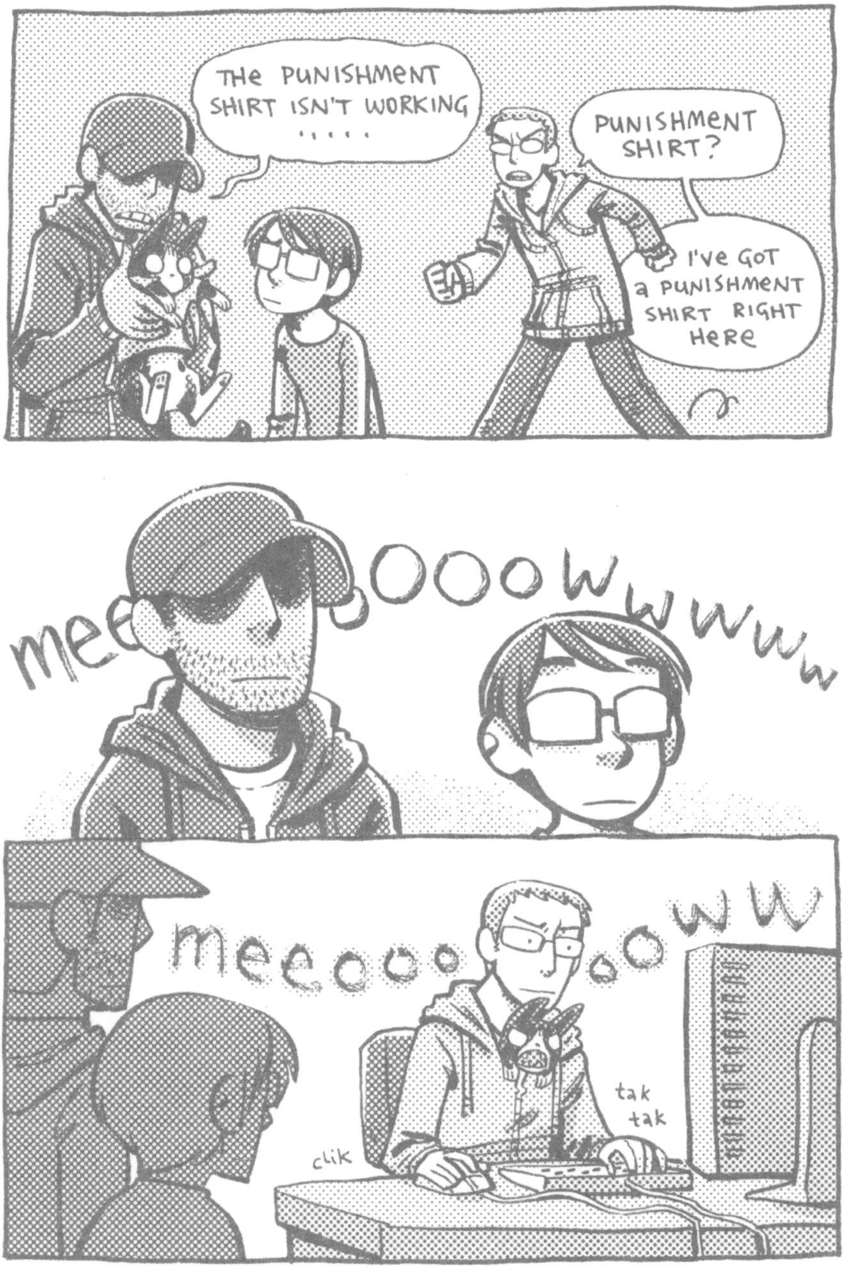
THE PUNISHMENT SHIRT ISN'T WORKING
. . . . .
PUNISHMENT SHIRT?
I'VE GOT A PUNISHMENT SHIRT RIGHT HERE
meeOOOOWWWWWW
meeooo...ooWW
tak tak
clik

c'mon I was checking my e-mail

taking compliments like a pro with yuko

bassinet chariot

hee hee hee hee hee hee

?

THERE'S SOMETHING WRONG WITH THAT BABY

307

schrödinger's book

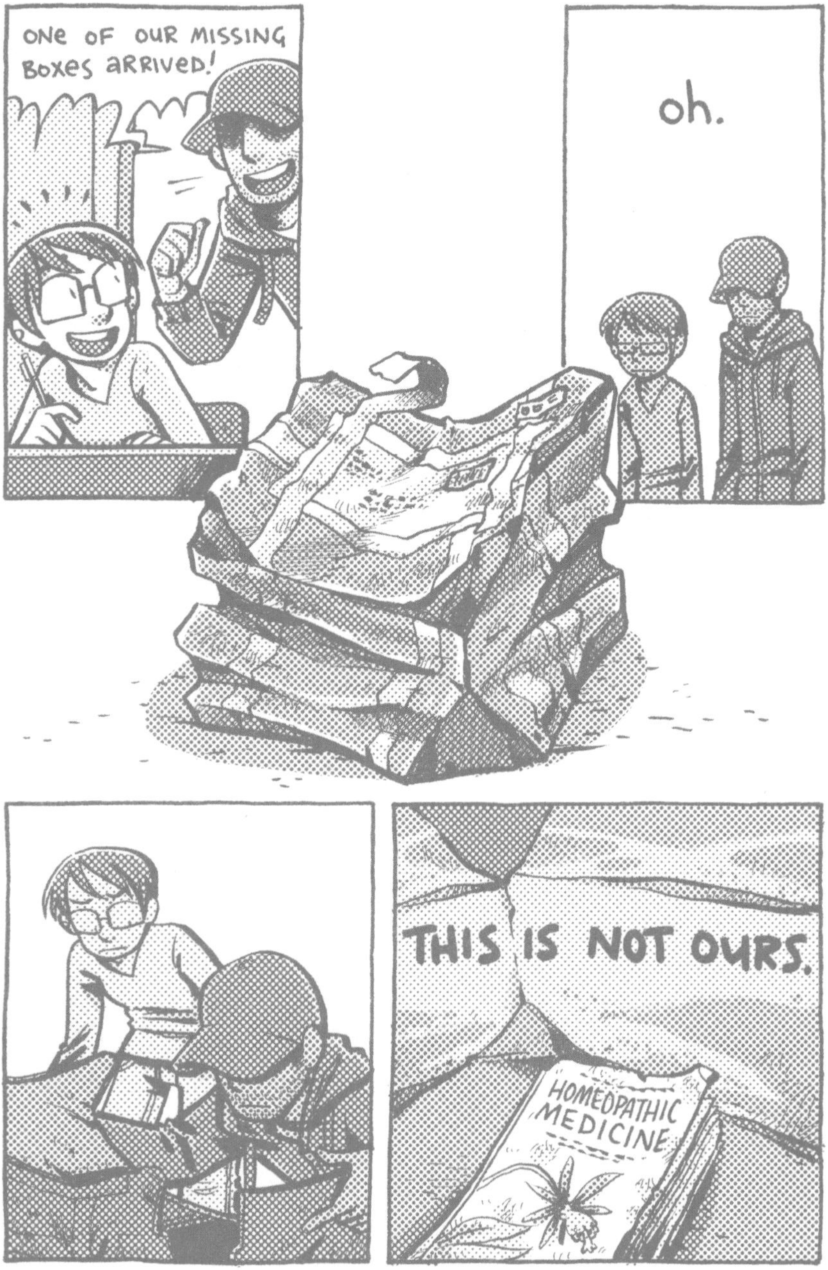
ONE OF OUR MISSING BOXES ARRIVED!
oh.
THIS IS NOT OURS.
HOMEOPATHIC MEDICINE

this is not my beautiful box

hunger games

OKAY, I THINK I'M DONE.

THESE ARE...

ALL COOKIES.

I'M SO HUNGRY

FRIENDS DON'T LET FRIENDS
SHOP HUNGRY

greasy pizza bro

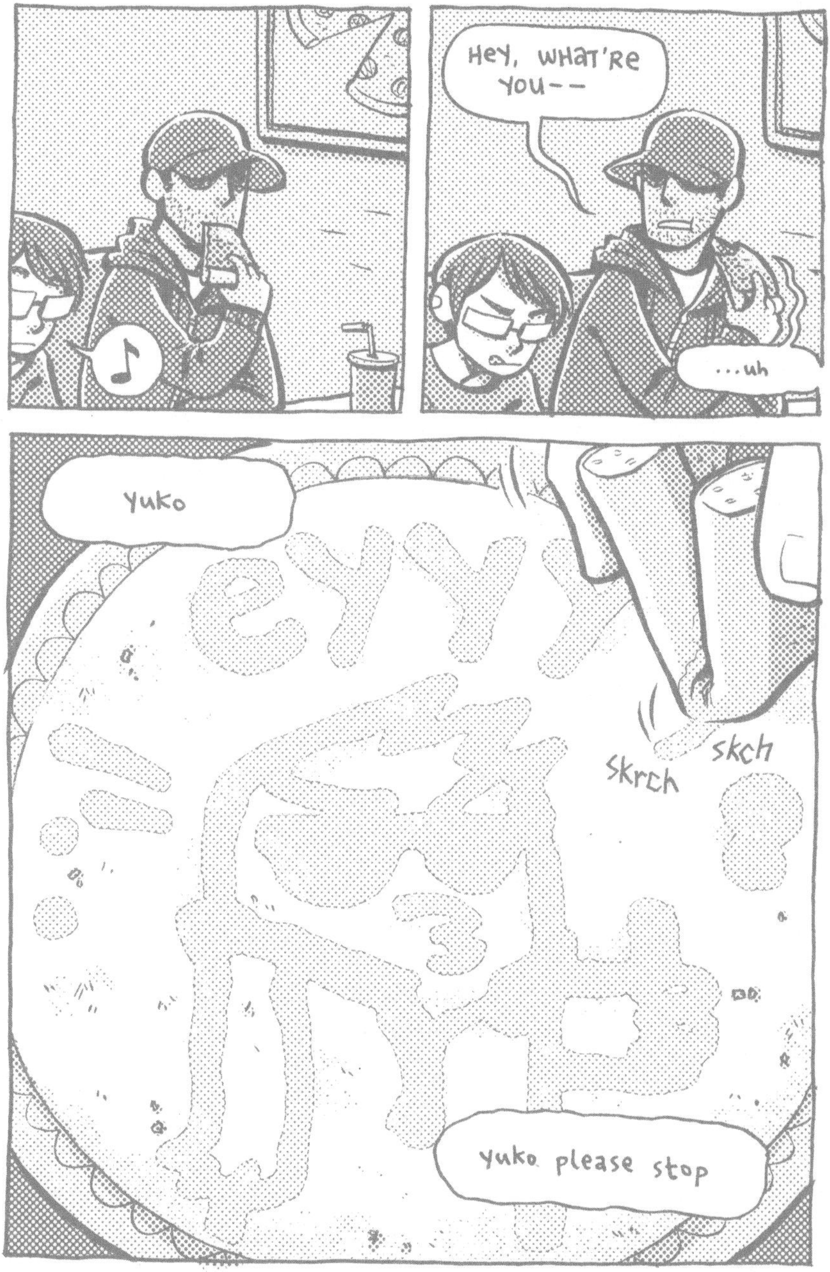
♪
Hey, WHAT'RE YOU--
...uh
yuko
skrch
skch
yuko please stop

serious art discussions

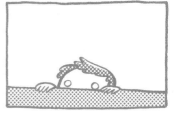

the urban climbing deer

I LIKE THE FLOWERS.

MARIGOLDS ARE SUPPOSED TO KEEP PESTS AWAY.

SO LIKE... DEER?

YES, LIKE DEER.

the most wonderful time of the year

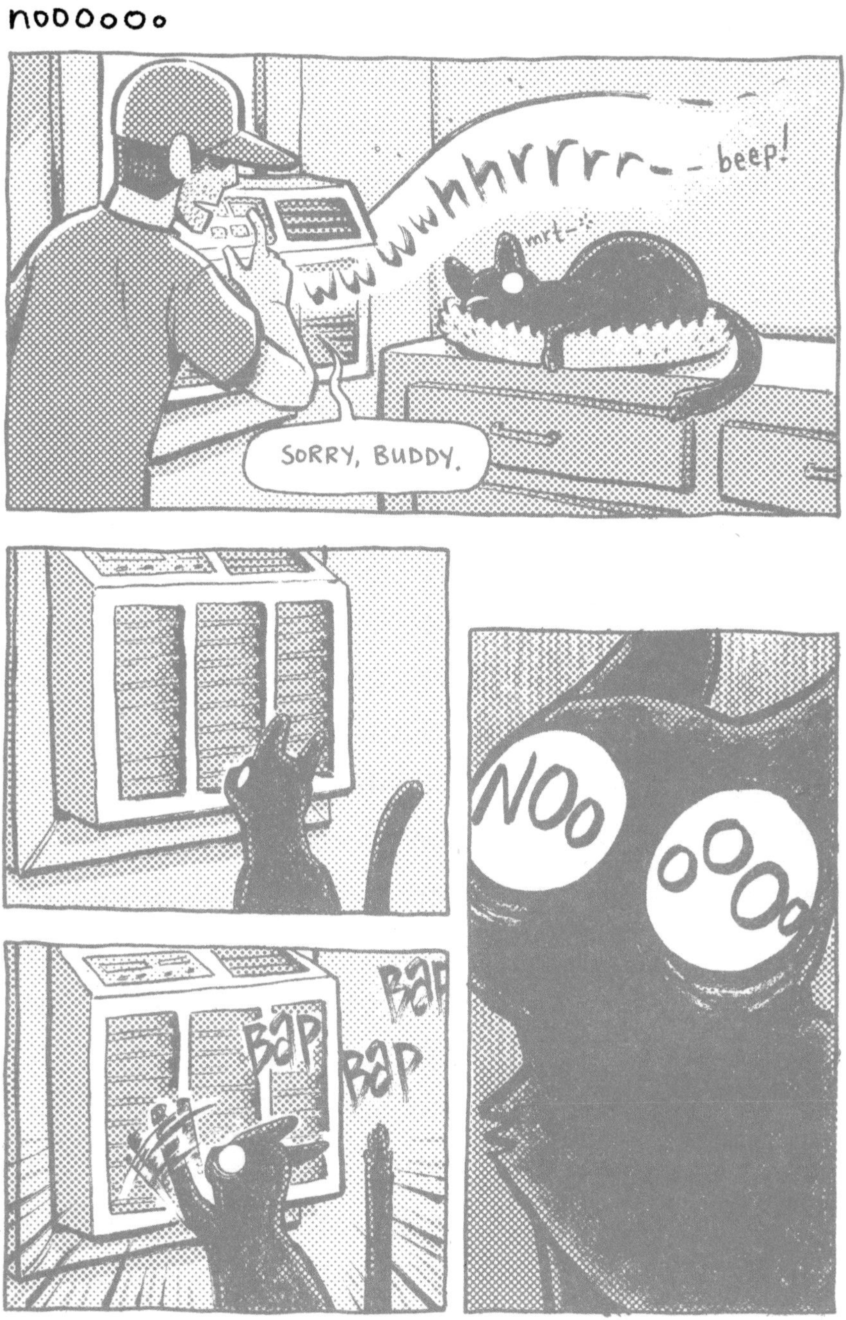
noooooo
wwwwhhrrrrr--beep!
mrt-
SORRY, BUDDY.
BAP
BAP
BAP
NOOoooo

a funny thing happened on the way to the movies

SQUEEZE THE DECK.

OKAY.

THAT'S NOT YOUR CARD, RIGHT?

NO.

LOOK IN YOUR WATCH.

OH, THE LINE'S MOVING.

IT WAS NICE TO MEET YOU!

YOU KNOW THAT WAS DAVID BLAINE, RIGHT?

WHAT

with love from cat

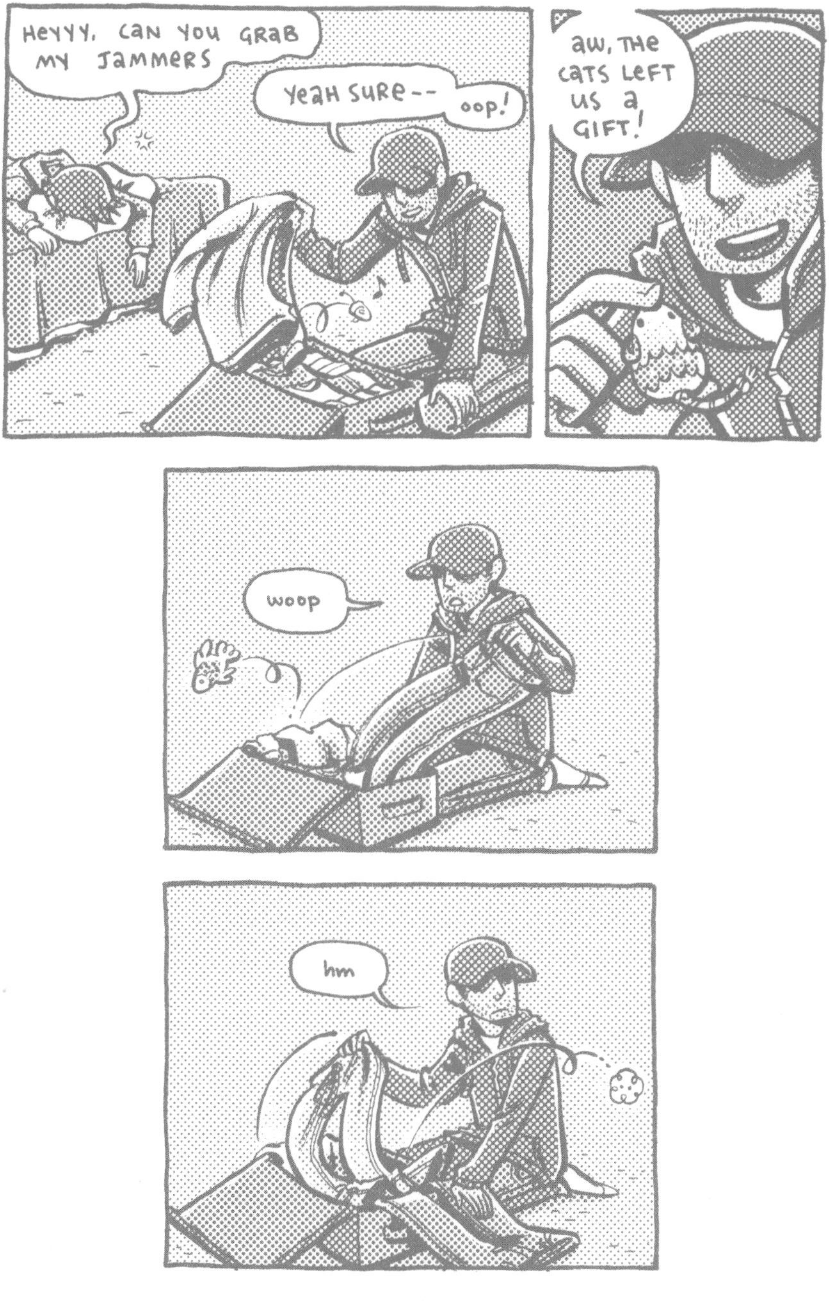
HEYYY. CAN YOU GRAB MY JAMMERS
YEAH SURE--
oop!
aw, THE CATS LEFT US a GIFT!
woop
hm

a dangerous addiction

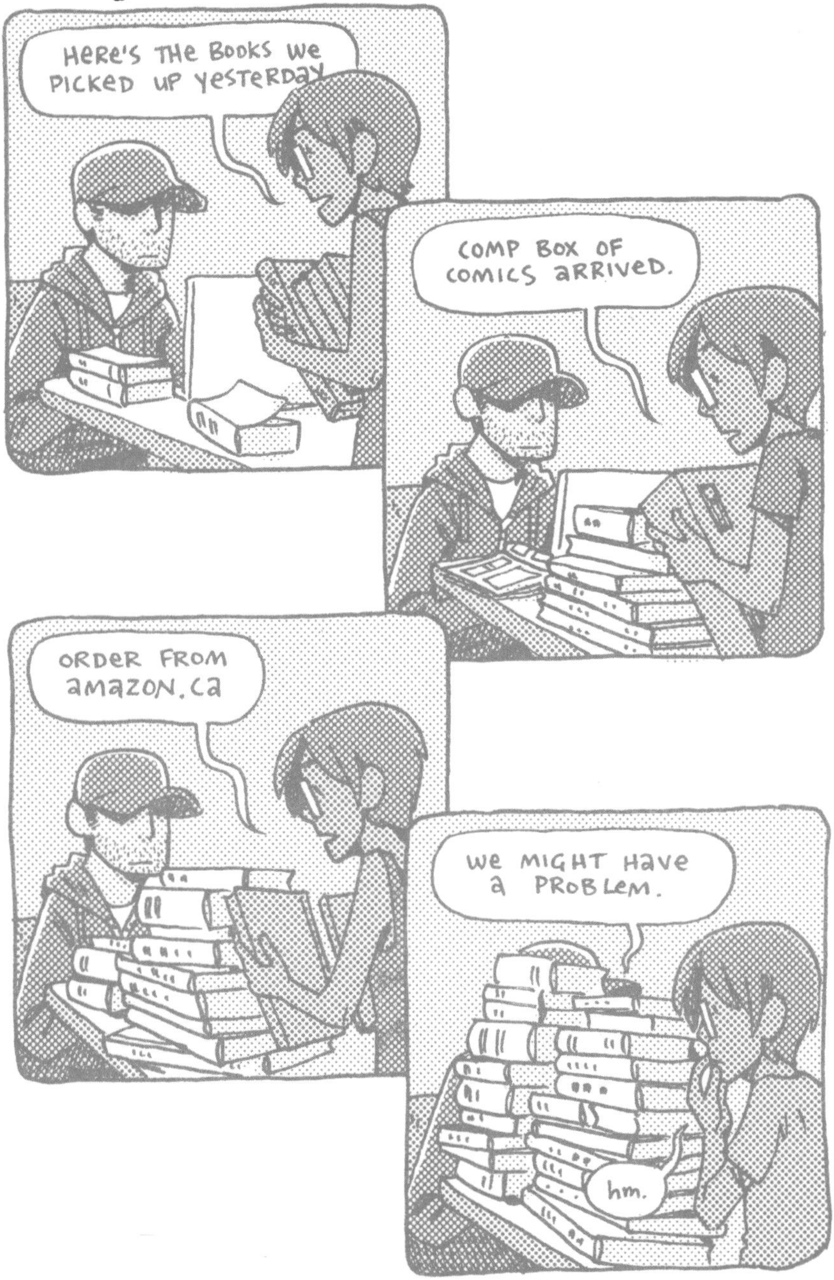
HERE'S THE BOOKS WE PICKED UP YESTERDAY
COMP BOX OF COMICS ARRIVED.
ORDER FROM amazON.ca
WE MIGHT HAVE a PROBLEM.
hm.

a pleasant drive

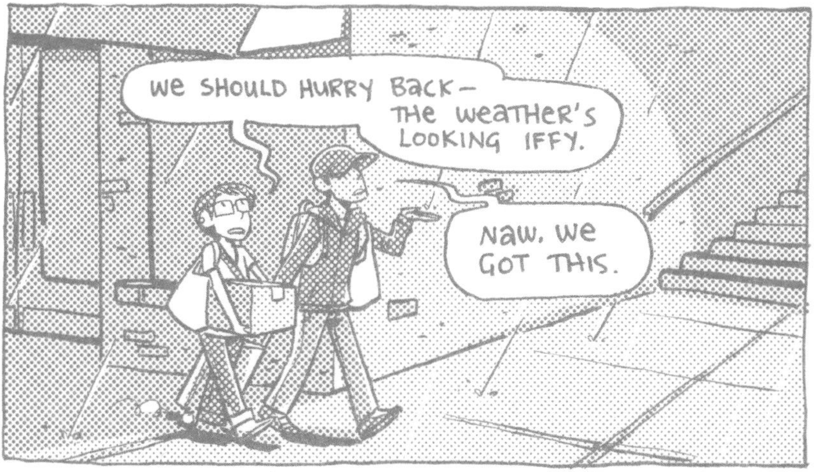
WE SHOULD HURRY BACK—
THE WEATHER'S LOOKING IFFY.
NAW. WE GOT THIS.

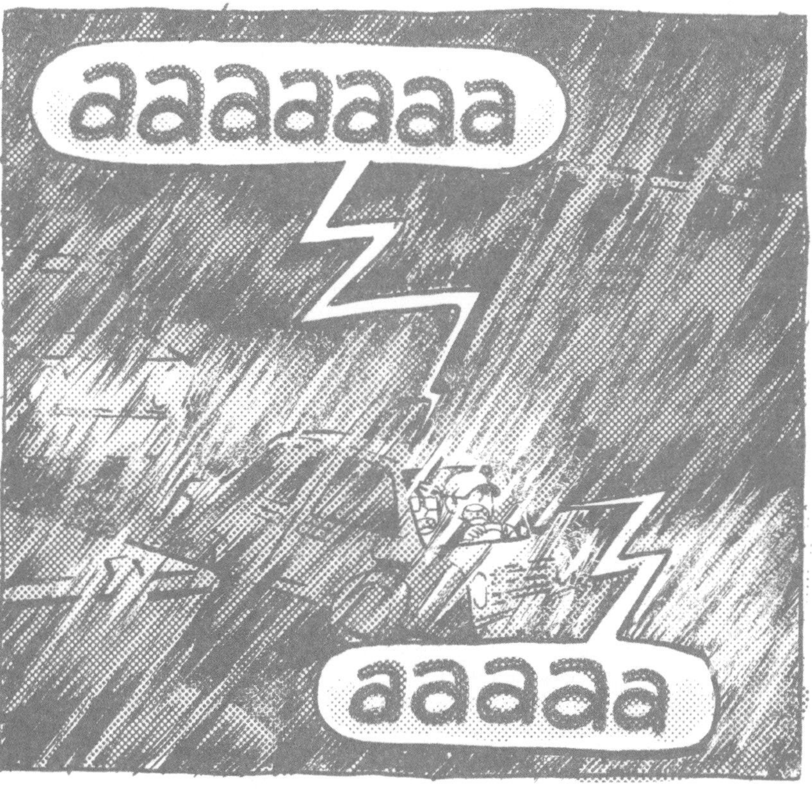
aaaaaaaa
aaaaaa

birthday cricket

CRICKET: SUMMER 2011
CRICKET: SUMMER 2012
DOES THIS MEAN SHE'LL BE A KITTEN...
FOREVER?

kitten coda

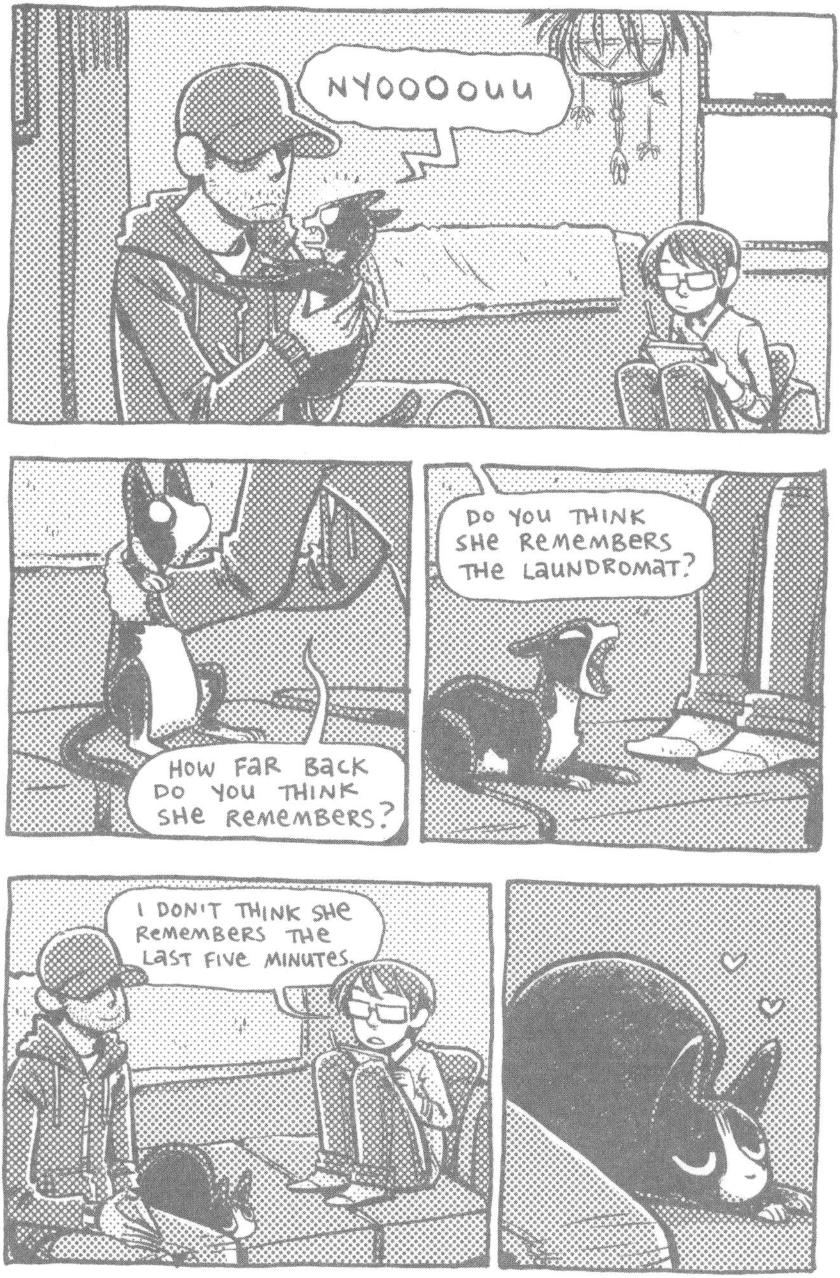
NYOOOouu
HOW FAR BACK DO YOU THINK SHE REMEMBERS?
DO YOU THINK SHE REMEMBERS THE LAUNDROMAT?
I DON'T THINK SHE REMEMBERS THE LAST FIVE MINUTES.

IV.

IN time we'll find a shaded den
All dappled 'cross its dome

Its lady wrapped in splendid black
Upon a splendid throne

And we, away for many miles,
Have not the time to bide a while, so
Lit by her resplendent smile,

Our feet find our course home

everything is fine nothing is broken

carpal tunnel of fun

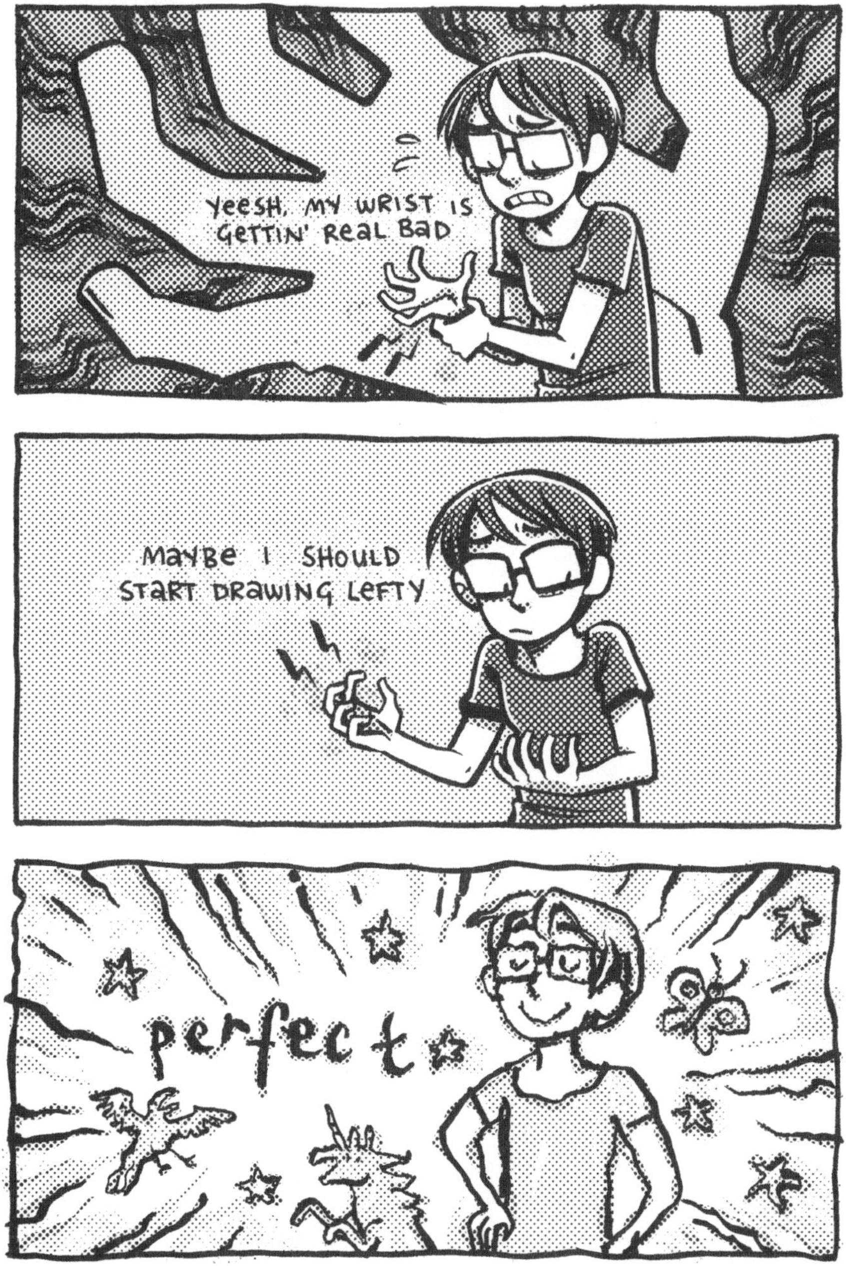
YEESH, MY WRIST IS GETTIN' REAL BAD
MAYBE I SHOULD START DRAWING LEFTY
perfect

non-dominant hand adventures

high five

brush teeth

use chop sticks

text

hwklpo   ohpowe
sarewi   typyt

make sandwich

peel fruit

haunted cat

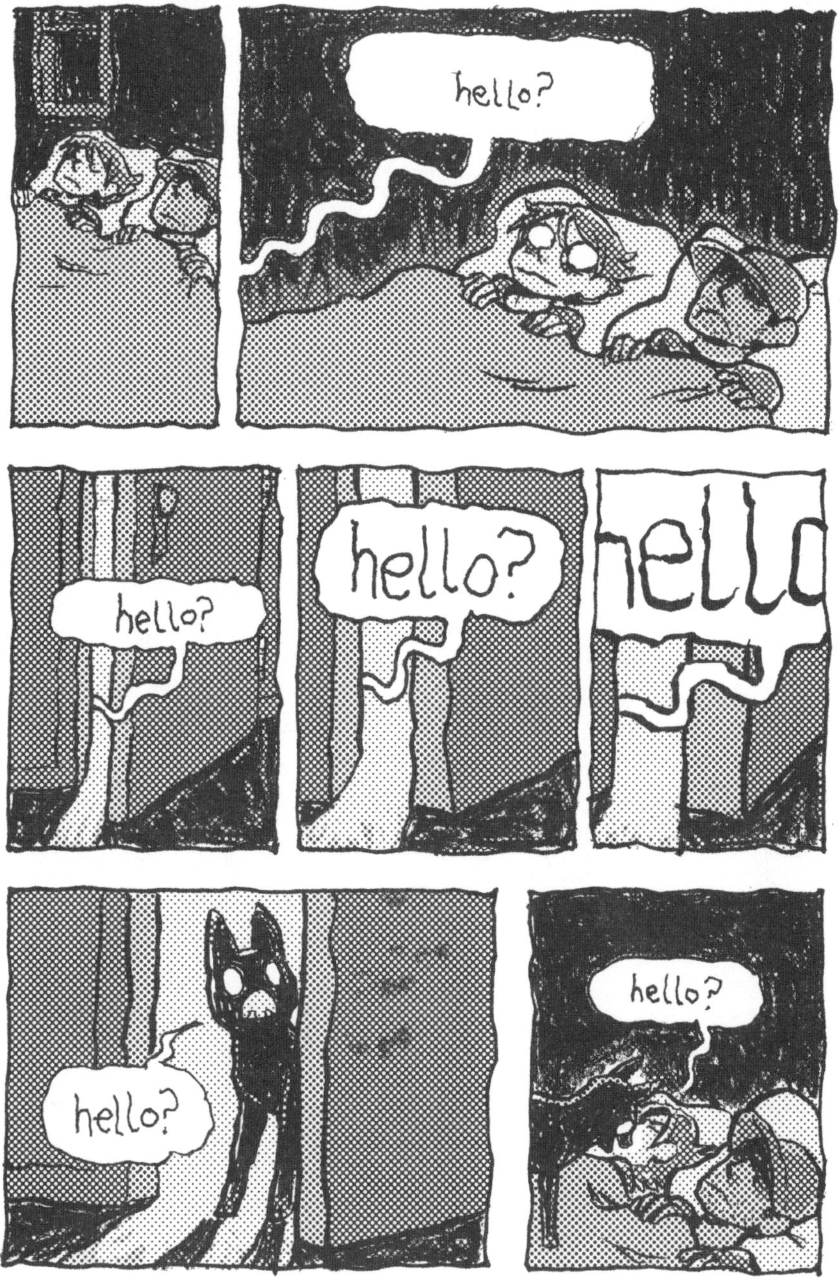

hello?
hello?
hello?
hello
hello?
hello?

spacey cat

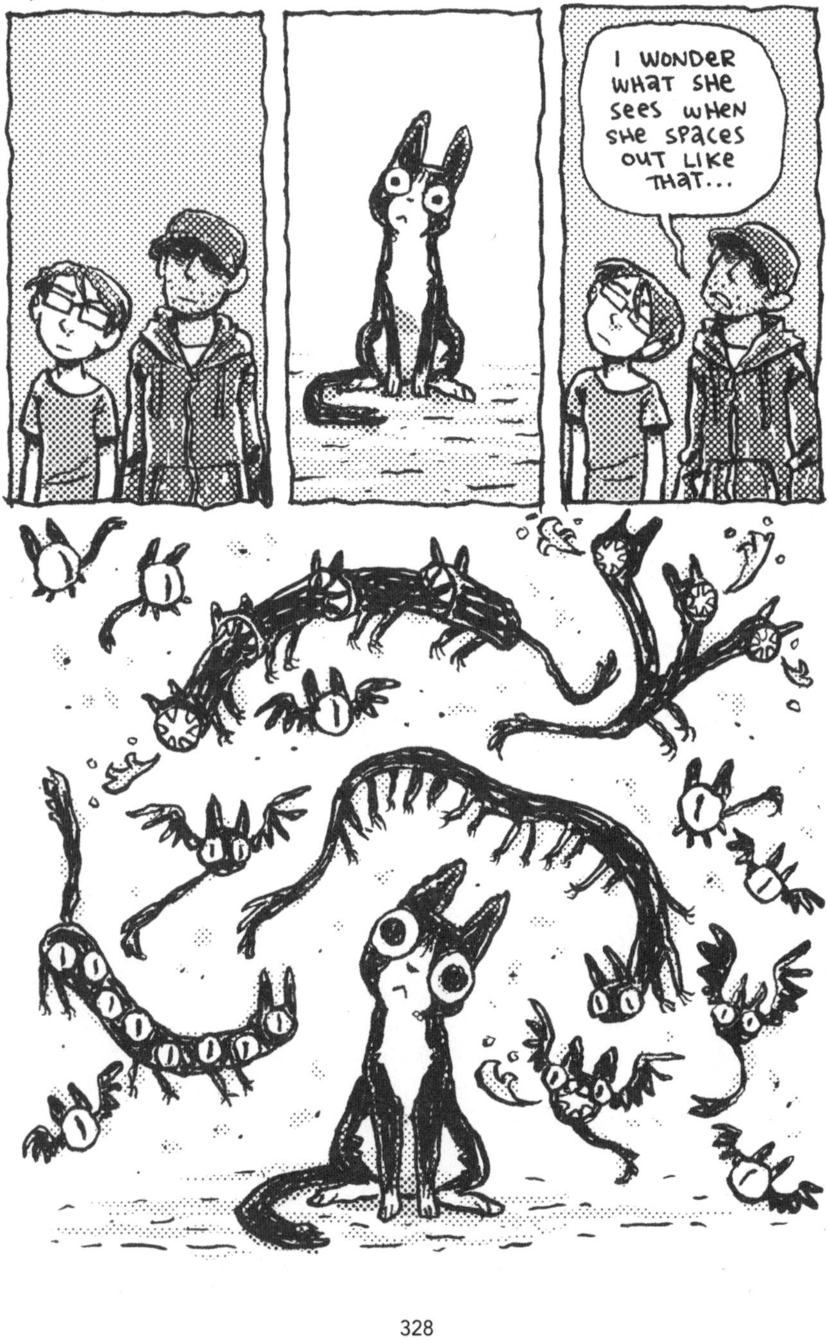
I WONDER WHAT SHE SEES WHEN SHE SPACES OUT LIKE THAT...

burn it down and start over

omnivore cat

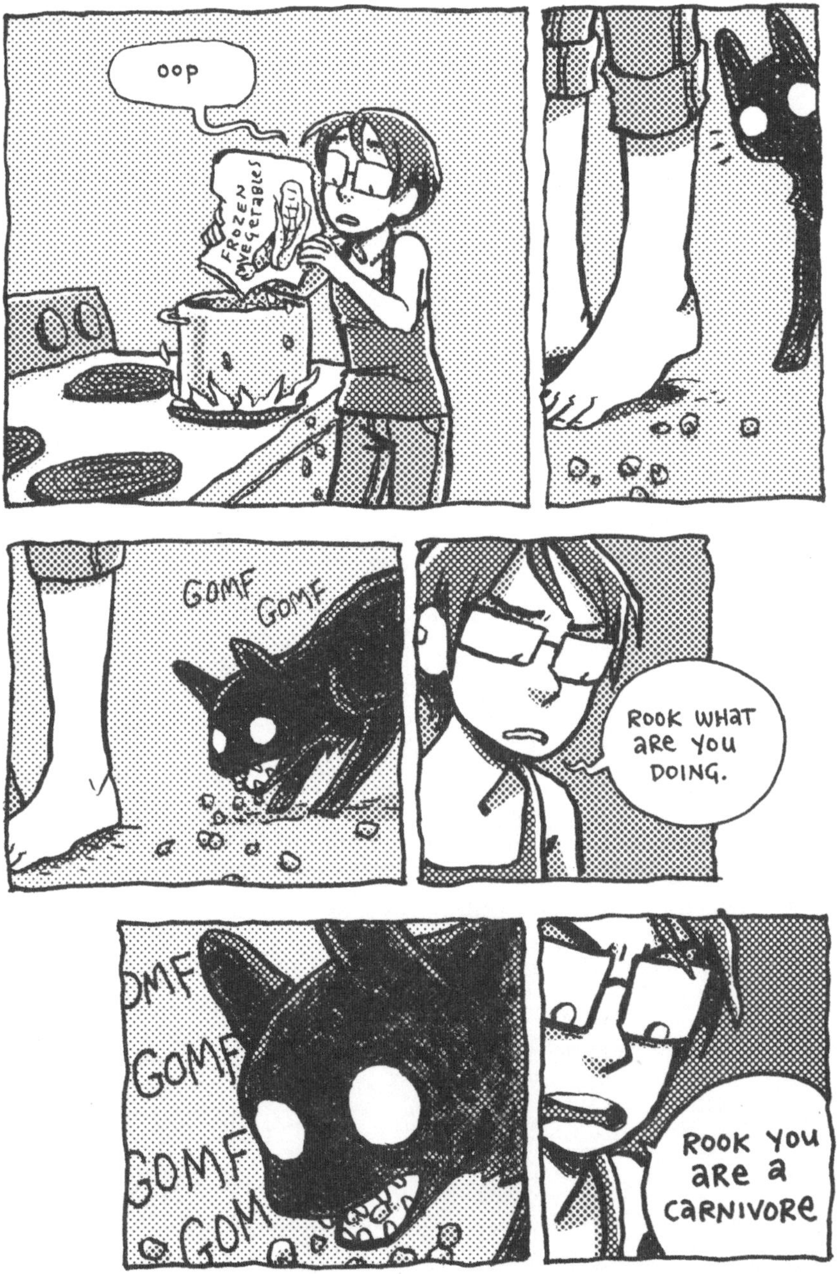
oop
FROZEN VEGETABLES
GOMF GOMF
ROOK WHAT are YOU DOING.
OMF
GOMF
GOMF
GOM
ROOK YOU are a CARNIVORE

hospitality

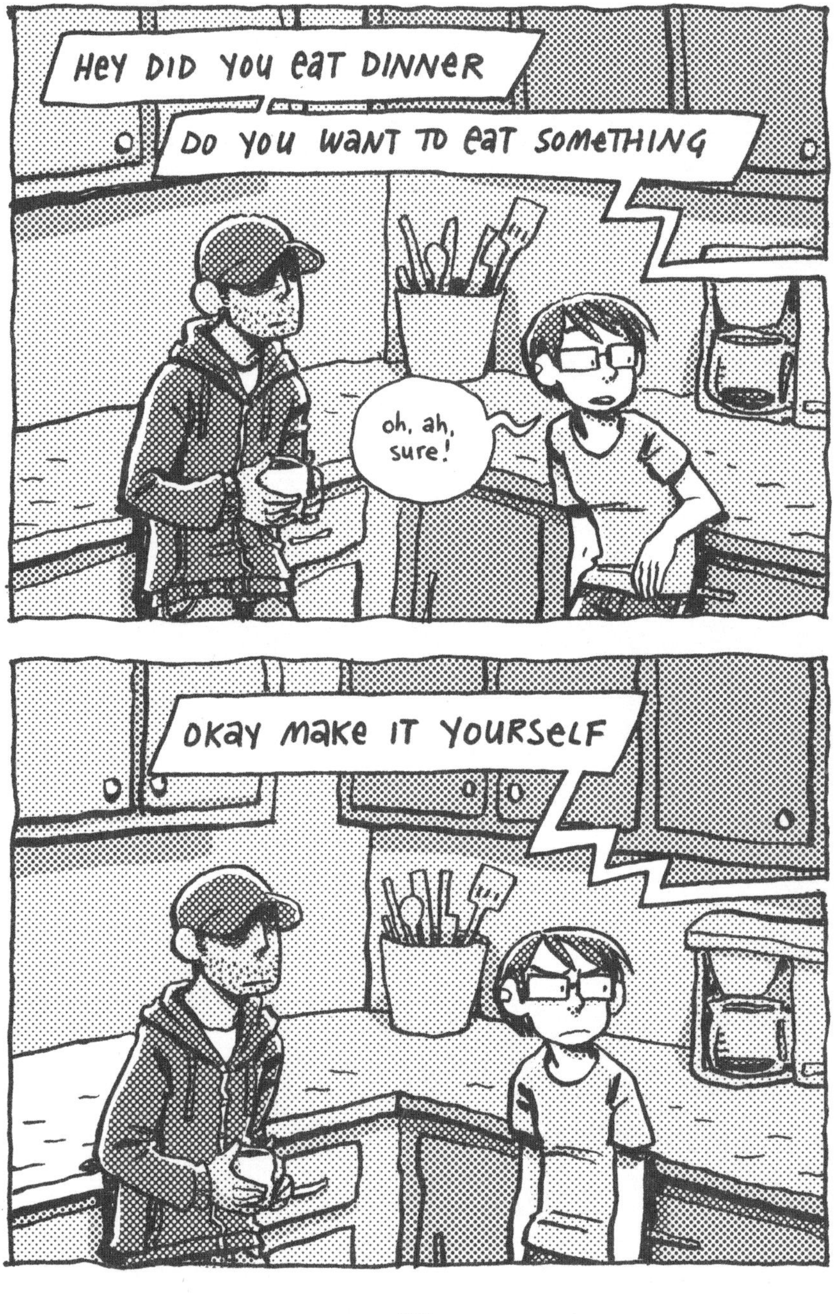
HEY DID YOU EAT DINNER
DO YOU WANT TO EAT SOMETHING
oh, ah, sure!
OKAY MAKE IT YOURSELF

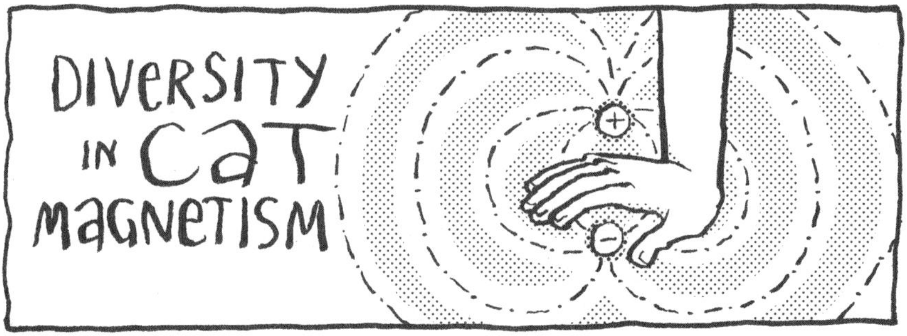
DIVERSITY IN CAT MAGNETISM

FIG 1. ROOK

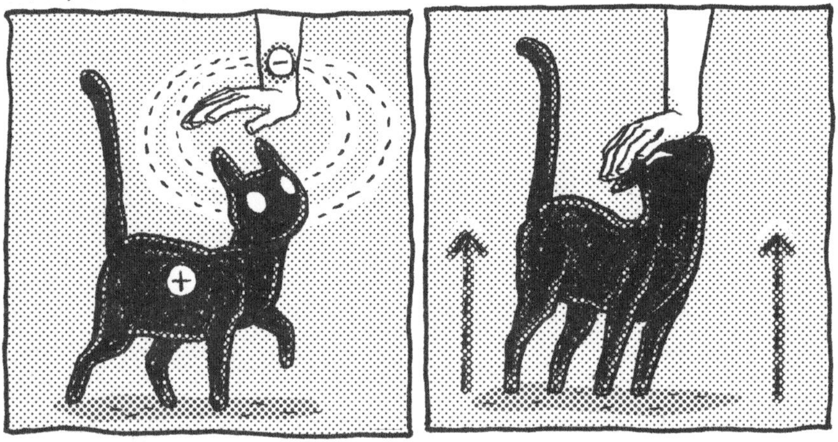

FIG 2. MIKA

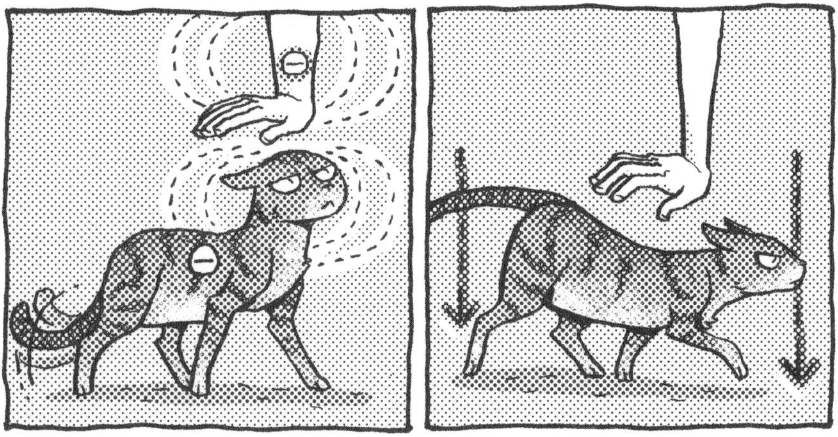

sassycat

meow meo
eow me ow m
meow meo

meow meo
eow me ow m
meow meow
meow meo

I'LL FEED YOU IN A MINUTE, BUDDY.

filing cabinet

HEY, I THINK I NEED A NEW CHAIR.

I NEED TO GO TO IKEA ANYWAY—

WE NEED A—

a, uh...

mmhmm...

most generous baby

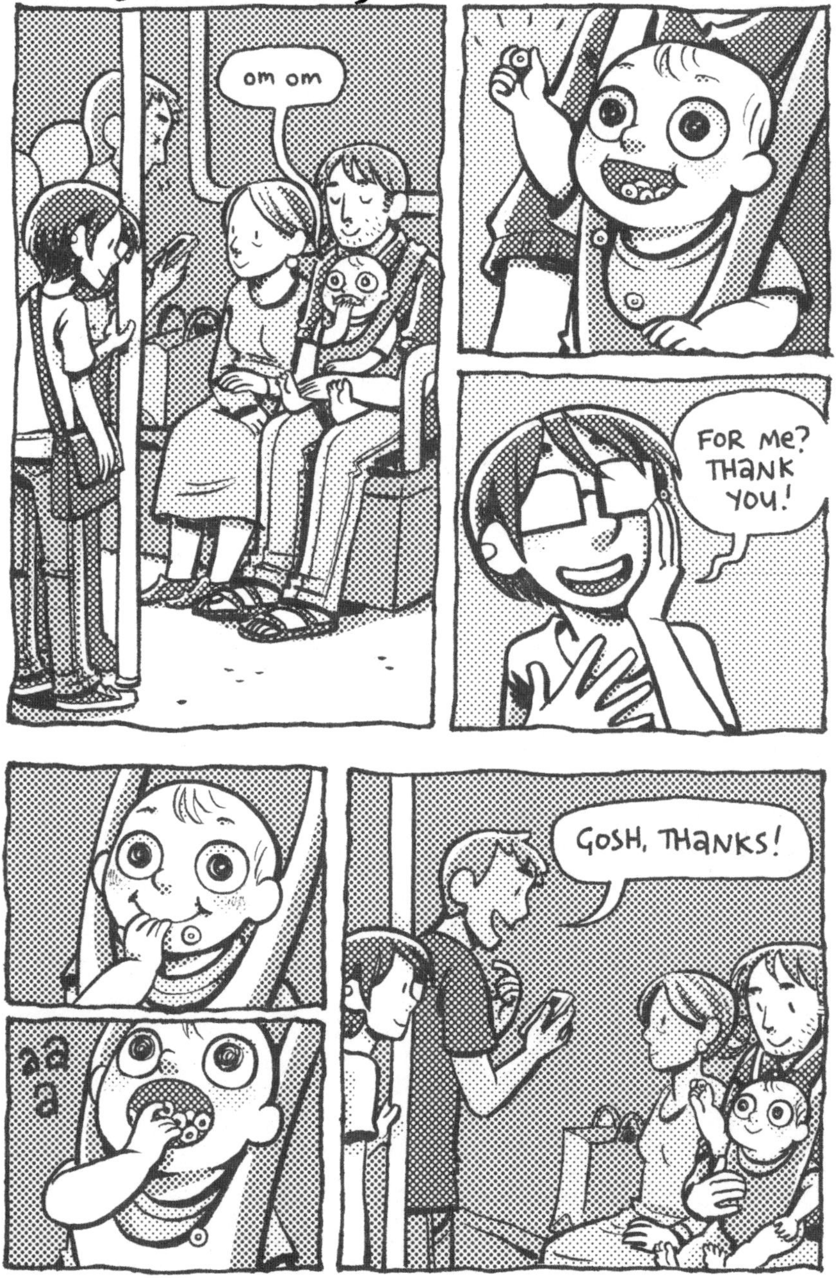
om om
FOR ME? THANK YOU!
aaa
GOSH, THANKS!

a song of ice and aaaablaugh

IT'S PRETTY WARM OUT HERE, HUH?

why-yew-kay-oh

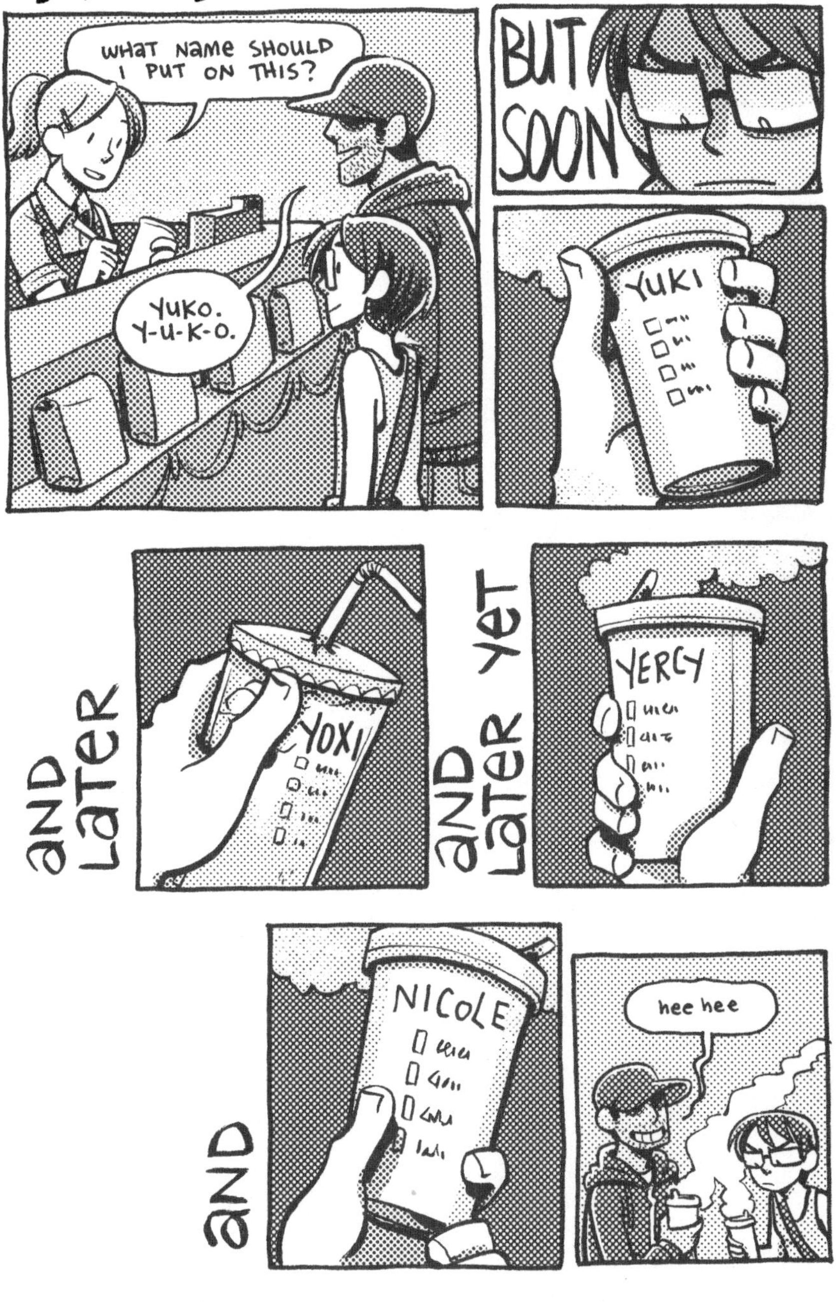
WHAT NAME SHOULD I PUT ON THIS?
YUKO. Y-U-K-O.
BUT SOON
YUKI
AND LATER
YOXI
AND LATER YET
YERCY
AND
NICOLE
hee hee

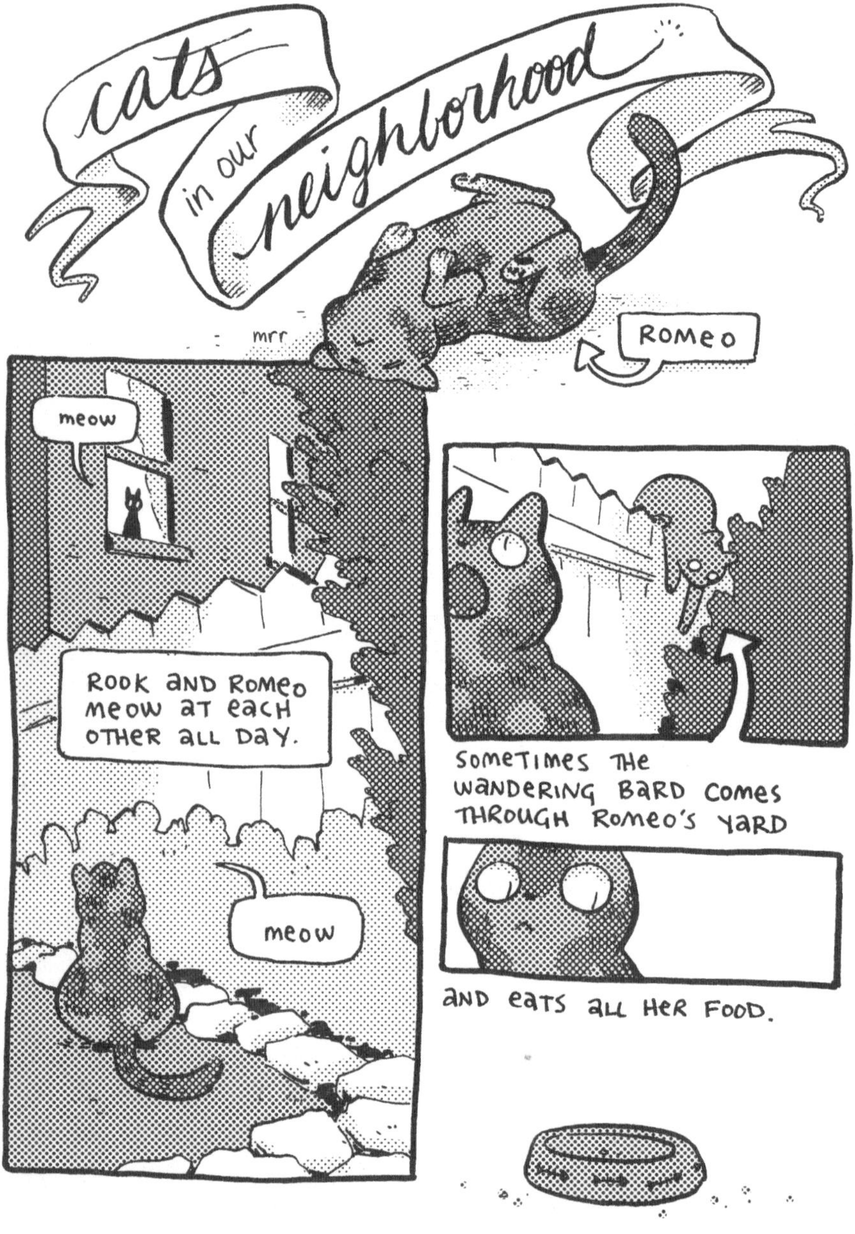
cats in our neighborhood
mrr
ROMEO
meow
ROOK AND ROMEO MEOW AT EACH OTHER ALL DAY.
meow
SOMETIMES THE WANDERING BARD COMES THROUGH ROMEO'S YARD
AND EATS ALL HER FOOD.
IT'S VERY TRAGIC.

there were extras

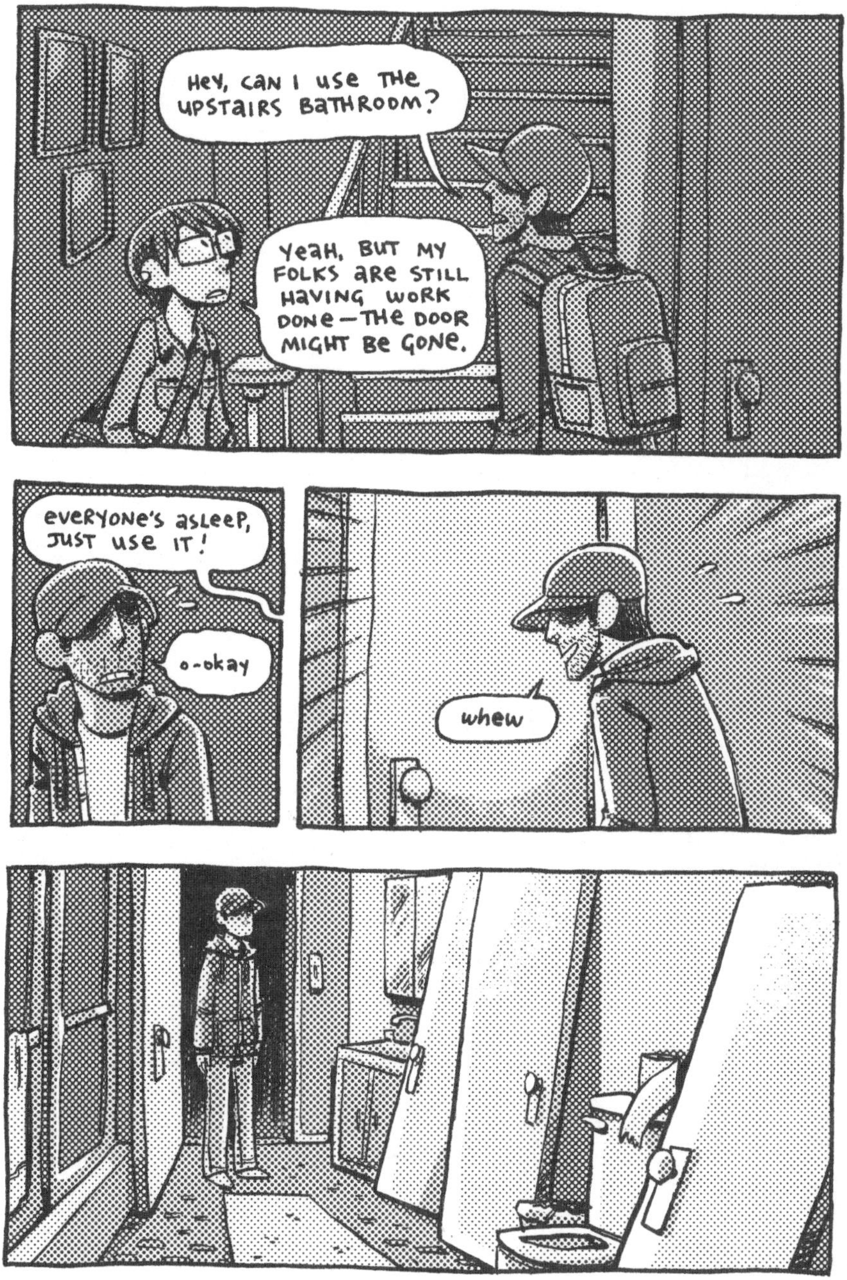
HEY, CAN I USE THE UPSTAIRS BATHROOM?
YEAH, BUT MY FOLKS ARE STILL HAVING WORK DONE—THE DOOR MIGHT BE GONE.
EVERYONE'S ASLEEP, JUST USE IT!
o-okay
whew

katie finds yuko's official classification

YEAAHHH

no belly pets

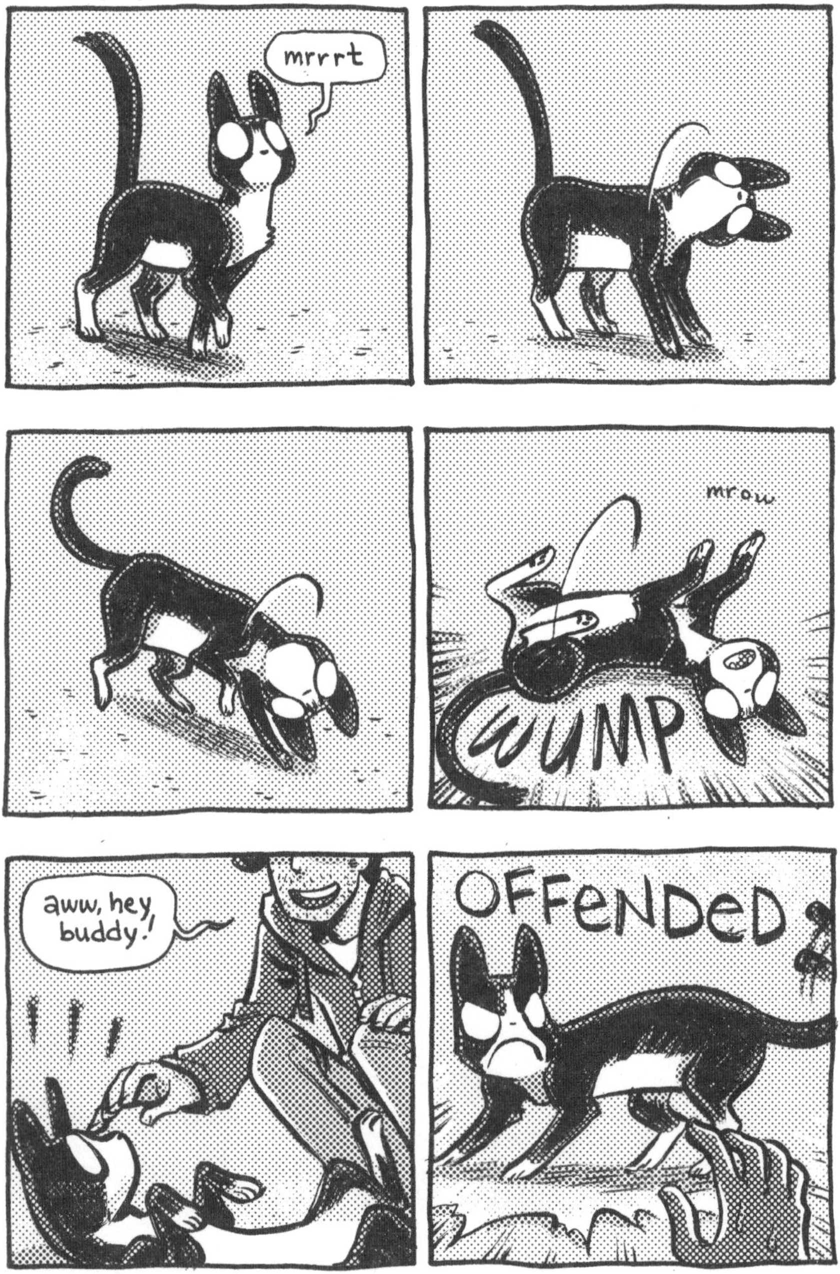
mrrrt
mrow
WUMP
aww, hey buddy!
OFFENDED

depth perception

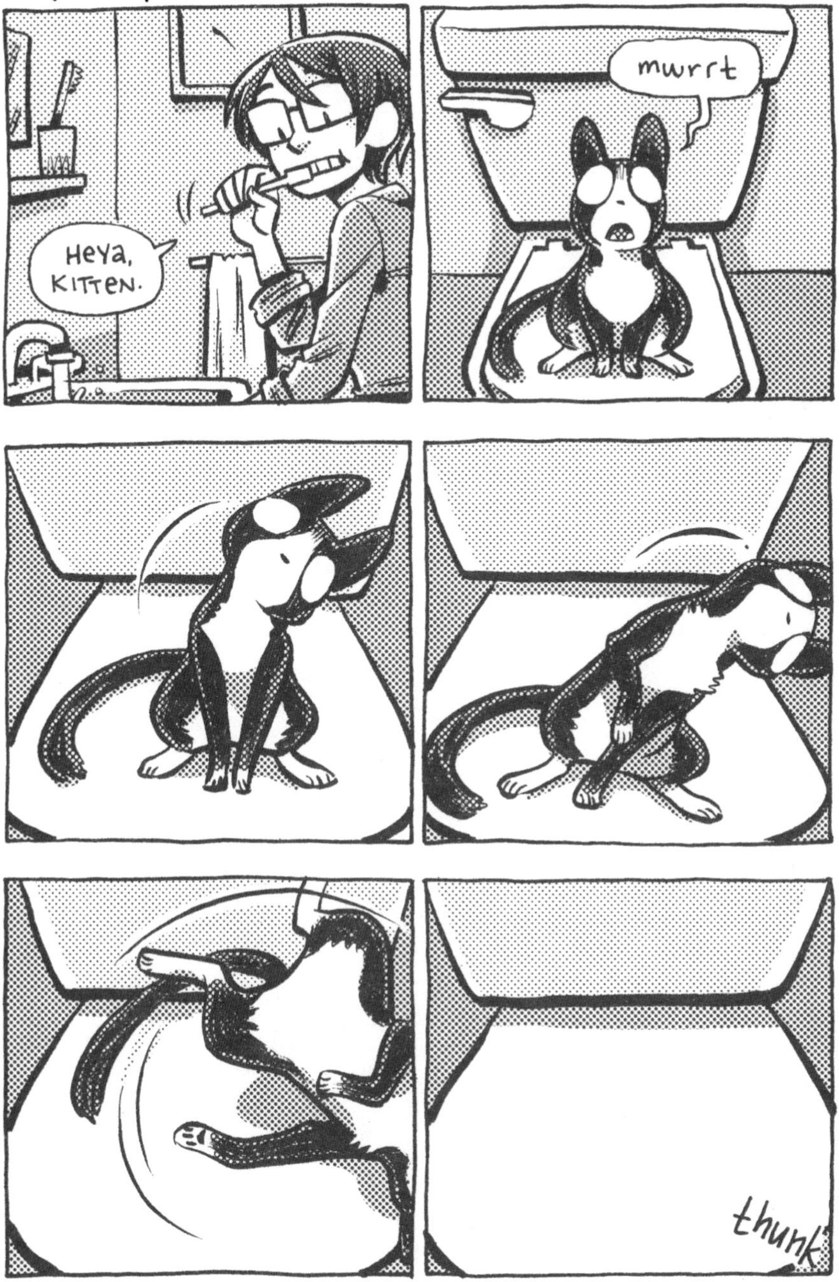
Heya, kitten.
mwrrt
thunk

Classy tea
for lazy people

① loose tea

② put in a cup

③ add hot water

④ whatever

chew chew

Lazy Tea
for lazy people

1. make tea

2. drink tea

3. add new teabag

4. repeat steps 2 & 3 as needed

could you also get some milk and eggs

dream surgeon

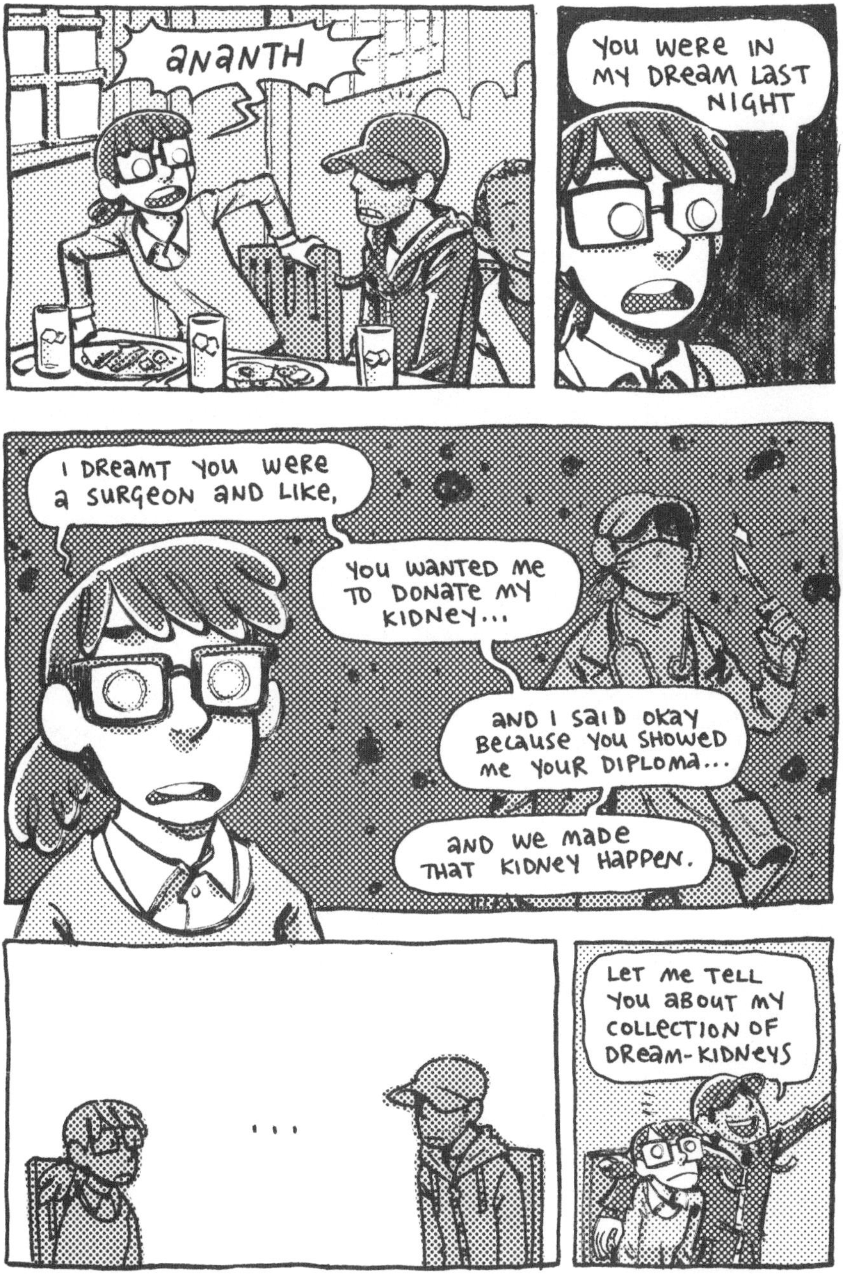
ananth
You were in my dream last night
I dreamt you were a surgeon and like,
You wanted me to donate my kidney...
and I said okay because you showed me your diploma...
and we made that kidney happen.
...
Let me tell you about my collection of dream-kidneys

regret in bulk

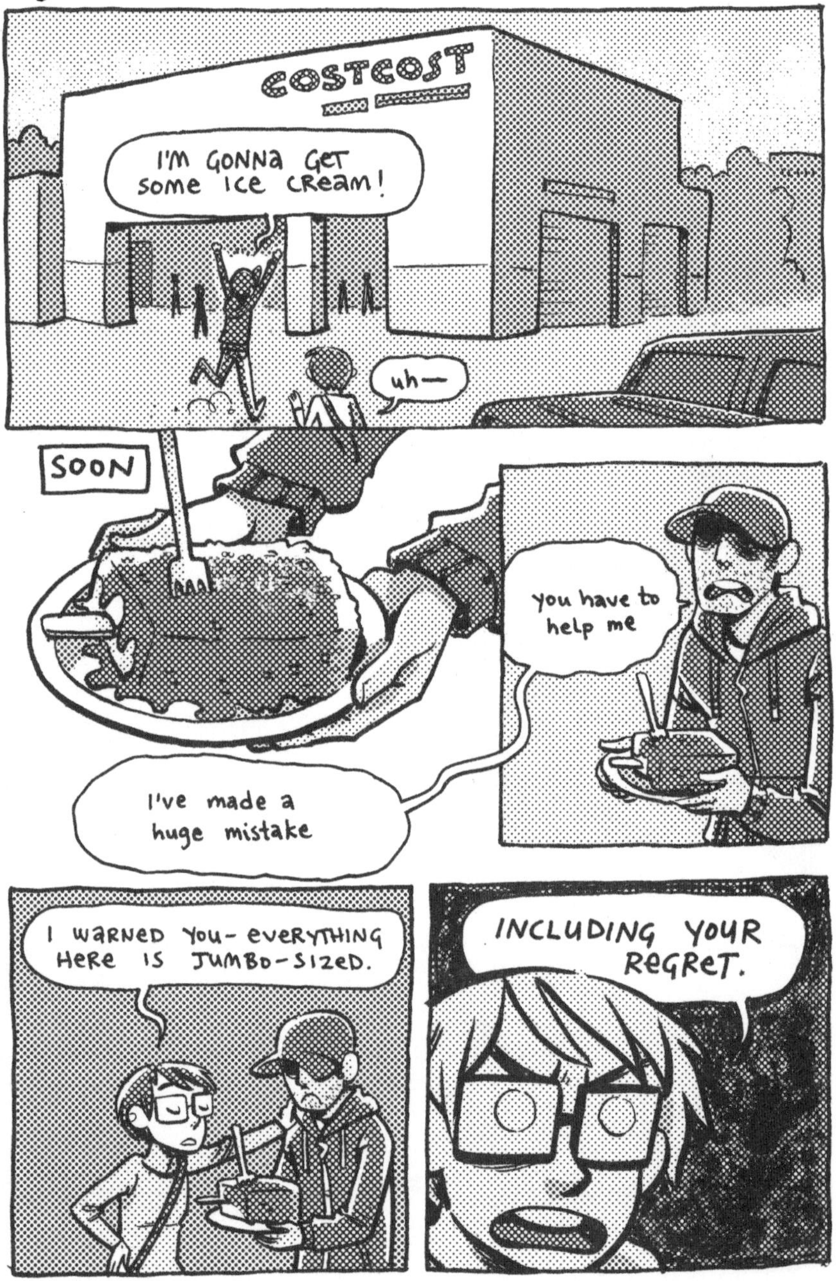
COSTCOST
I'M GONNA GET SOME ICE CREAM!
uh—
SOON
you have to help me
I've made a huge mistake
I WARNED YOU- EVERYTHING HERE IS JUMBO-SIZED.
INCLUDING YOUR REGRET.

shamesgiving

cranberry sauce

ahem.

I saw THAT.

this quickly-turning world

THERE MIGHT BE ONE MORE CHOCOLATE-COVERED STRAWBERRY IF YOU WANT IT.

oooo

NO IT IS GONE

DO YOU THINK THE WORLD MOVES SO SLOWLY

hospitality dad

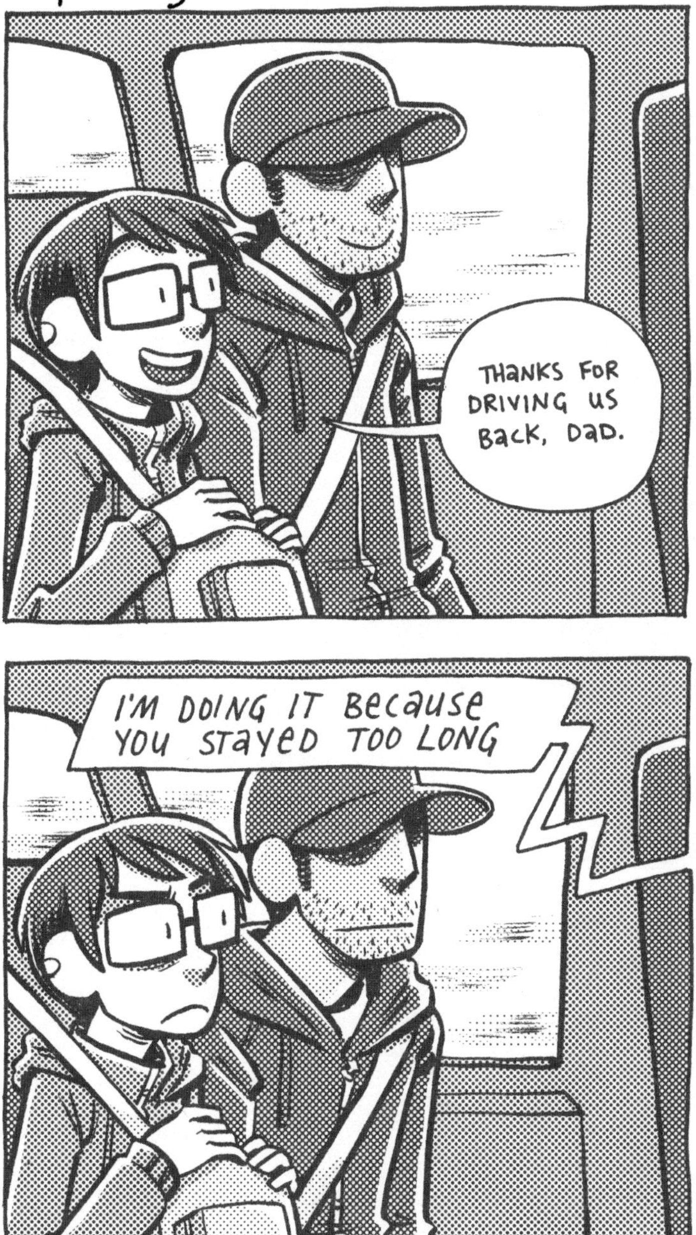
THANKS FOR DRIVING US BACK, DAD.
I'M DOING IT BECAUSE YOU STAYED TOO LONG

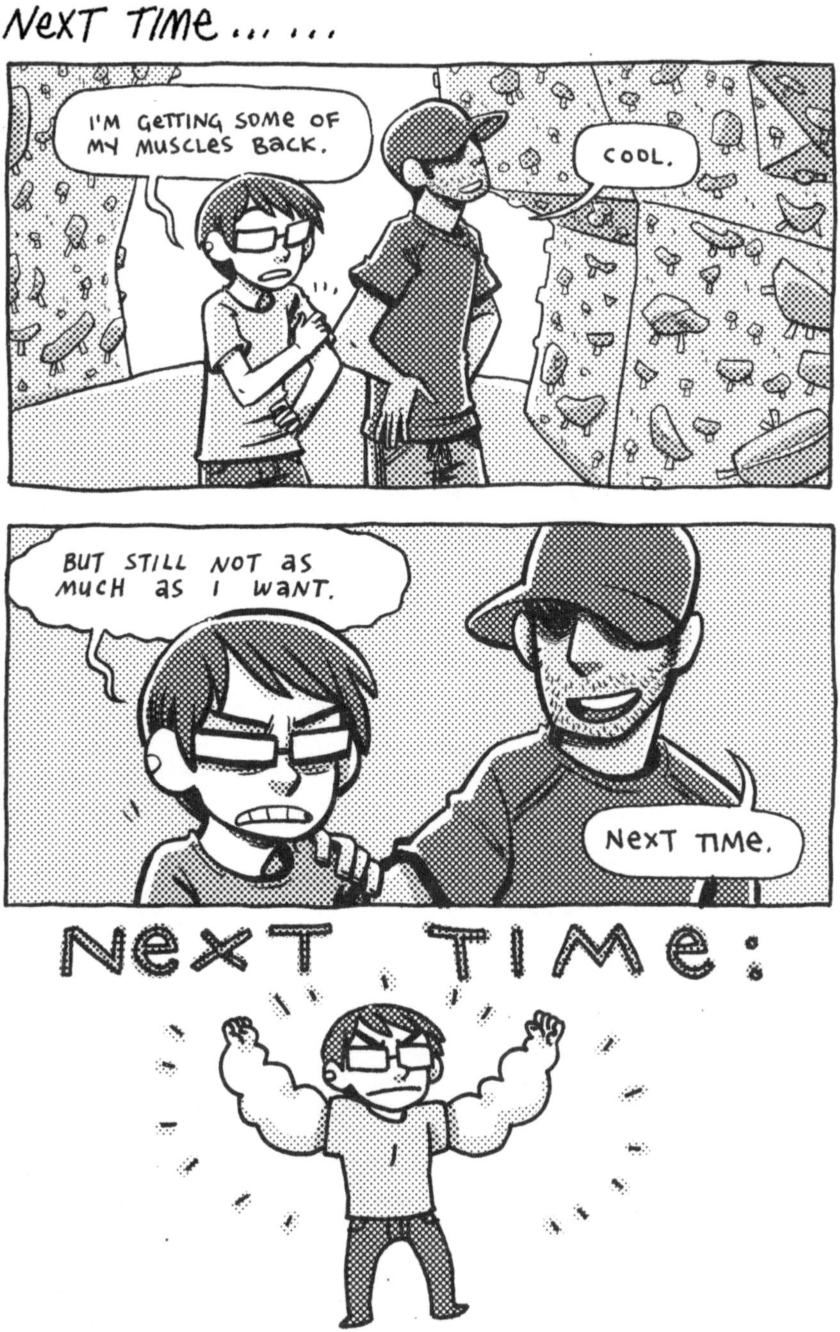
NeXT TIMe......
I'M GeTTING SOMe OF MY MUSCLeS BaCK.
COOL.
BUT STILL NOT aS MUCH aS I WaNT.
NeXT TIMe.
NeXT TIMe:

ananth vs choco croissant

cats in our neighborhood

the viscount

THERE'S THIS CAT AT THE LAW OFFICE.

WE ORIGINALLY CALLED HIM "THE VISCOUNT"

BECAUSE HE'S VERY REGAL

WHEN WE COME HOME LATE WE SEE HIM SLEEPING IN THE WINDOW.

oh, her name is Ivy.

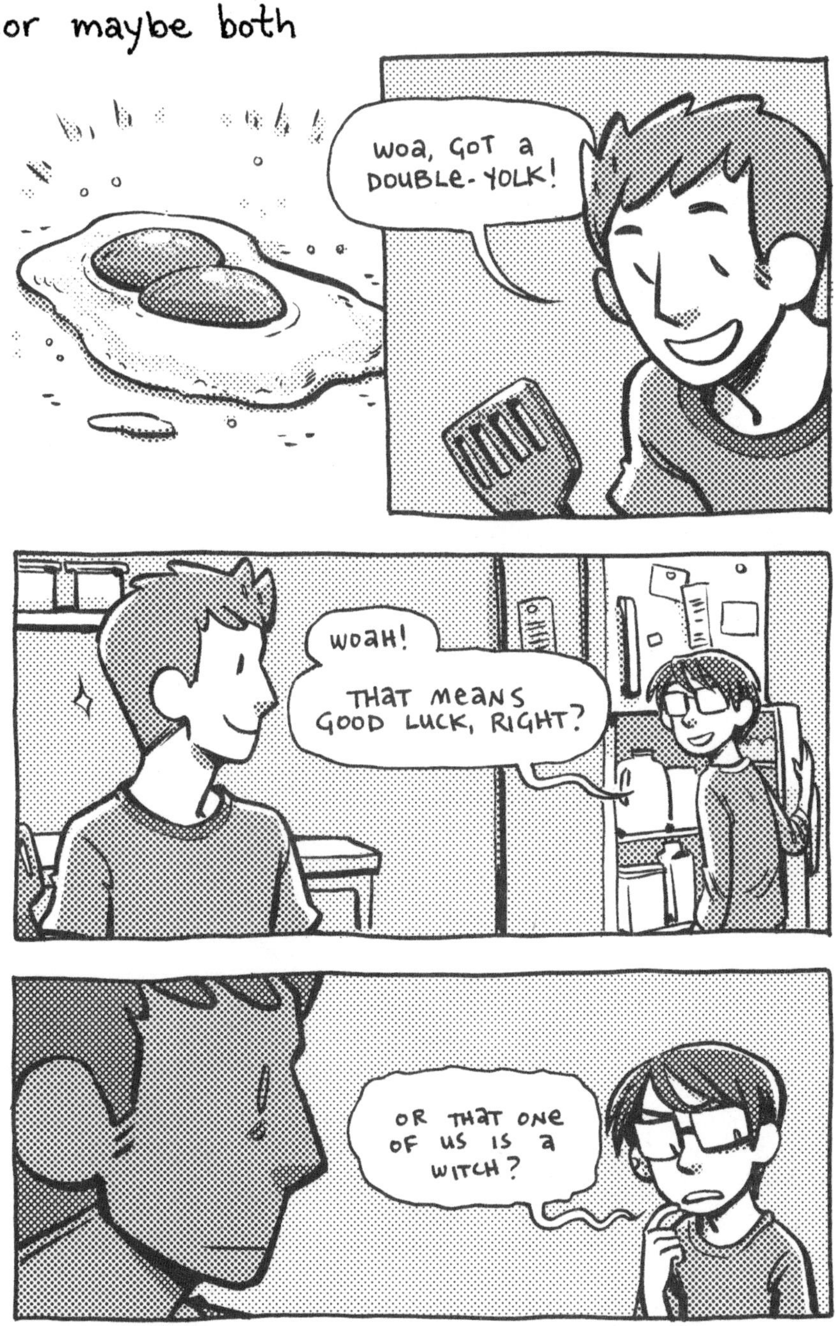
or maybe both
WOA, GOT A DOUBLE-YOLK!
WOAH!
THAT MEANS GOOD LUCK, RIGHT?
OR THAT ONE OF US IS A WITCH?

laydeez cat

PREVIOUSLY:

student drivers

You okay?

WHY IS IT THAT THE ONLY THINGS THAT TRY TO RUN ME OFF THE ROAD ARE SCHOOL BUSES?

HMM...

fig 1.: USAGE OF YUKO'S OFFICE CHAIR: *a pie chart*

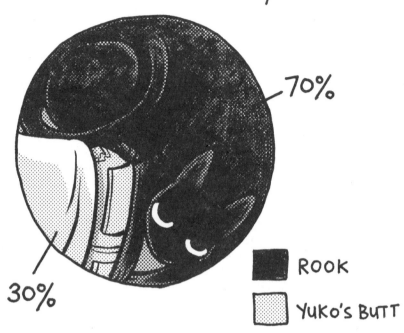

70%

30%

■ ROOK

☐ YUKO'S BUTT

inner ear adventures

whenever I travel out of New York City

I remember how bad my tinnitis is.

small treasures I keep in my pockets

a small red marble

a piece of smooth purple glass

a red & gold D4

a decoder ring

mysterious thrift store undergarments

no not especially

HI, CRICKET!

CRICKEETT

SHE DOESN'T HAVE MUCH GOING ON UPSTAIRS DOES SHE.

ananth only got socks for christmas

fresh homemade dessert

THANKS FOR HAVING ME OVER FOR DINNER.

TO SHOW MY GRATITUDE, I'VE MADE...

HOMEMADE DESSERT

REESE'S PIECES AND...

DID YOU TAKE MY CHOCOLATE CHIPS FROM THE FREEZER?

BON... APPETIT.

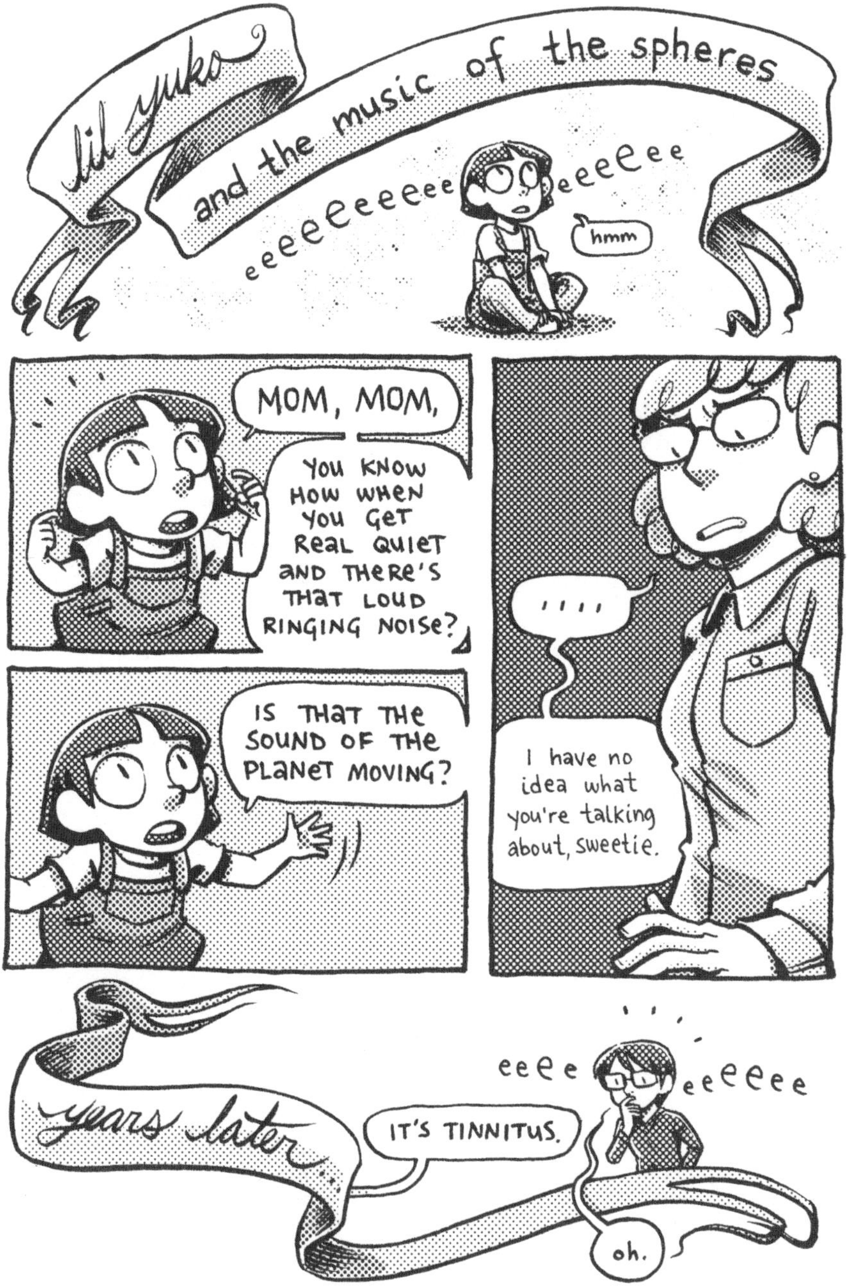
lil yuko and the music of the spheres
eeeeeeeeee eeeeeee
hmm
MOM, MOM,
YOU KNOW HOW WHEN YOU GET REAL QUIET AND THERE'S THAT LOUD RINGING NOISE?
IS THAT THE SOUND OF THE PLANET MOVING?
....
I have no idea what you're talking about, sweetie.
years later...
eeee eeeeee
IT'S TINNITUS.
oh.

an imposter

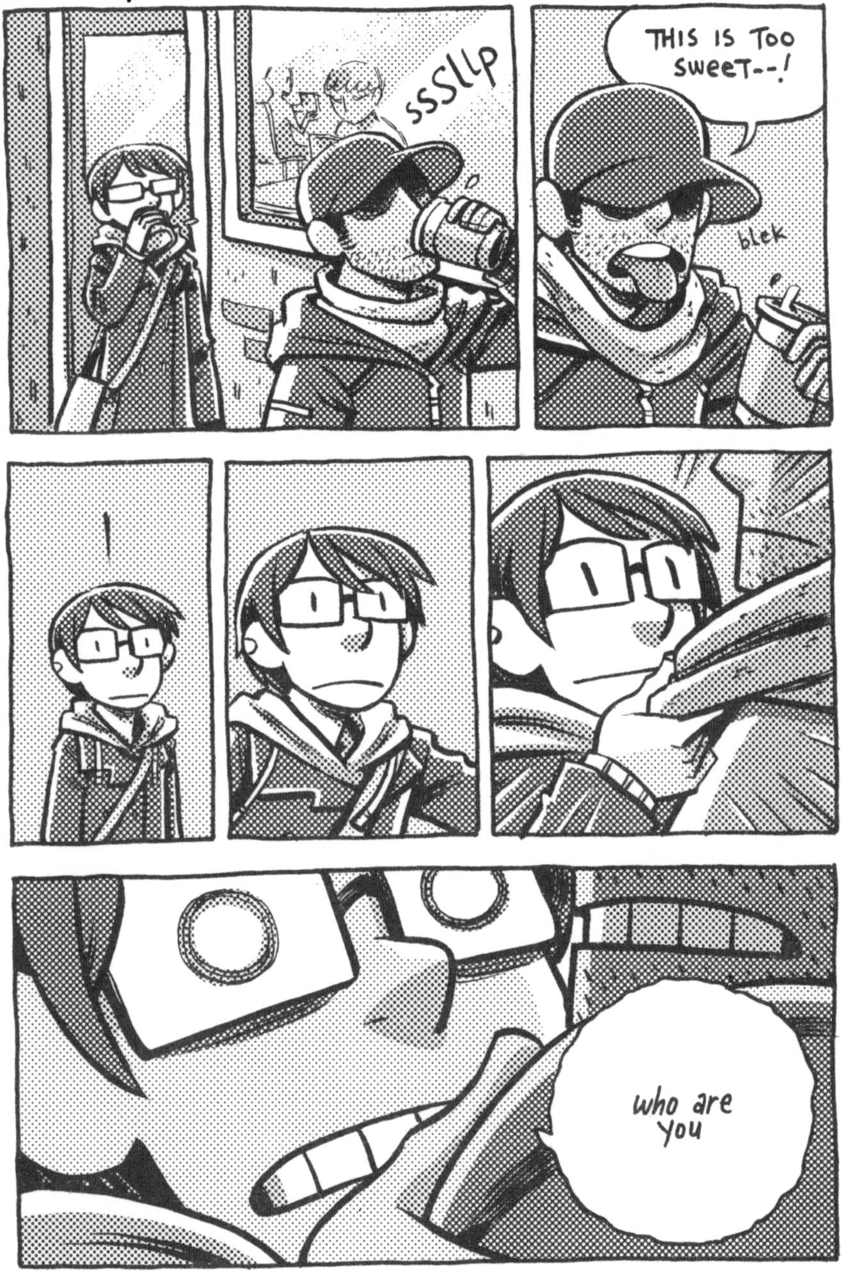
ssSllp
THIS IS TOO SWEET--!
blek
!
who are you

phone master conrad

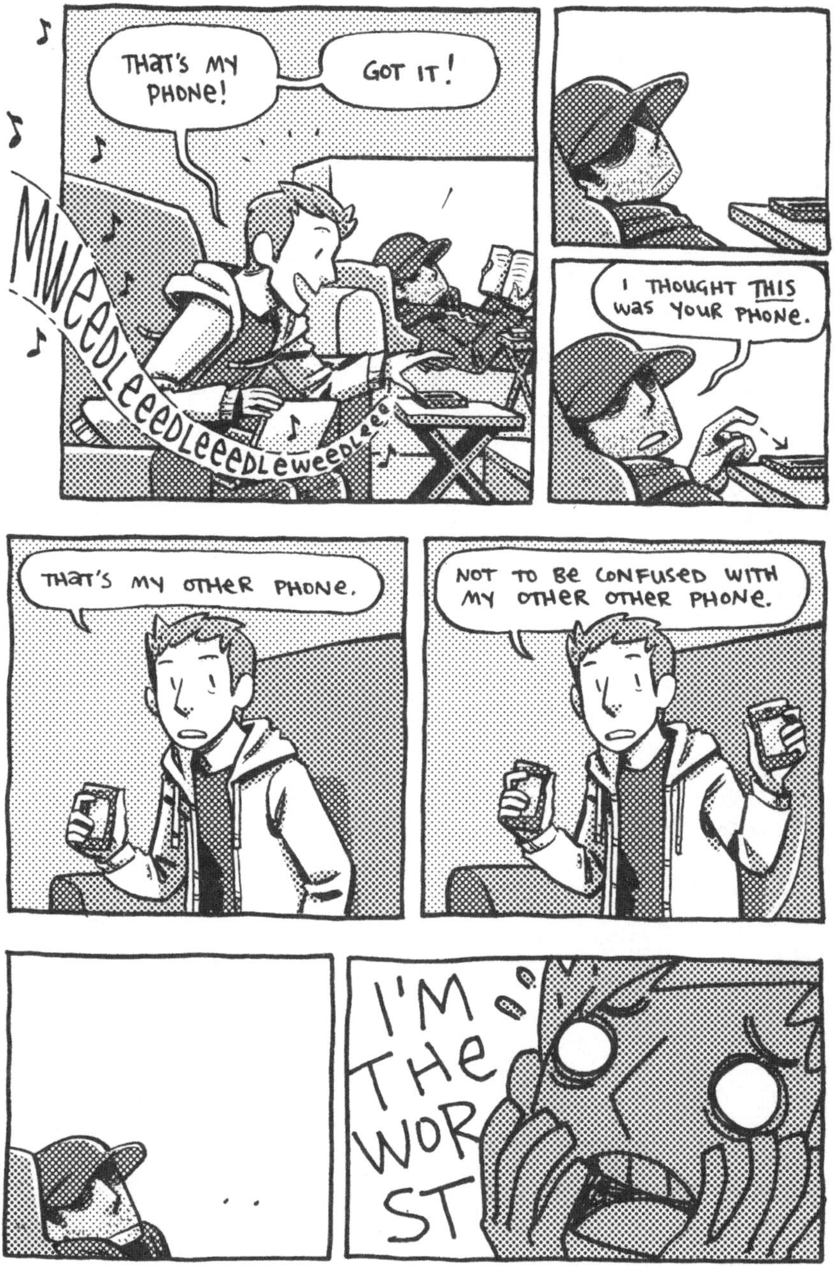
THAT'S MY PHONE!
GOT IT!
MWEEDLEEEDLEEEDLEEEDLEWEEDLEEE
I THOUGHT THIS WAS YOUR PHONE.
THAT'S MY OTHER PHONE.
NOT TO BE CONFUSED WITH MY OTHER OTHER PHONE.
...
I'M THE WORST

no stop

WHERE'S CONRAD, I HAVE TO ASK HIM HIS OPINION ON PHONES.

NO

NO DON'T DO IT

SPOOKY

SPOOKY'S OWNER

THERE'S A CAT AT THE BIKE SHOP NAMED SPOOKY.

ROOK
bigger ears
more shy

HE LOOKS ALMOST IDENTICAL TO ROOK

SPOOKY
yellower eyes
more dander

AND WHEN KIDS STOP BY TO FILL THEIR TIRES

SSSSSS

HE GETS SPOOKED.

guess it's time to use hot chocolate as creamer

the half and half
went bad.

hourly comics
FEBRUARY 1st 2013
9:00 am

THE CATS ARE SLEEPING ON MY LEGS

i'm trapped

10:00 am

MAKIN' MORE COFFEE

this apartment drinks a ludicrous amount of coffee

WWRRMNNNN

SLEEPY AUTOCORRECTED E-MAIL FROM ANANTH

thus nachos som
hugs you've out

11:00 am

RE-ORDERING BUSINESS CARDS

clik clik clik clik

oh my god i am so boring

maybe I should just start over tomorrow

FEBRUARY 2nd 2013
9:00 am

I VOW TO BE MORE INTERESTING TODAY

10:00 am

interneettttt...

11:00 am

it's a baby tapir

oh cool

he's bein' sassy.

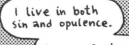

I live in both sin and opulence.

Sin and Opulence are actually my Christian and given names.

I will let you pick which one is which.

12:00 PM

Step 1: look over tax forms

Step 2: freak out

Step 3: post drawings on Tumblr instead

1:00 PM

WORK ON HOURLY COMICS

this is awfully recursive

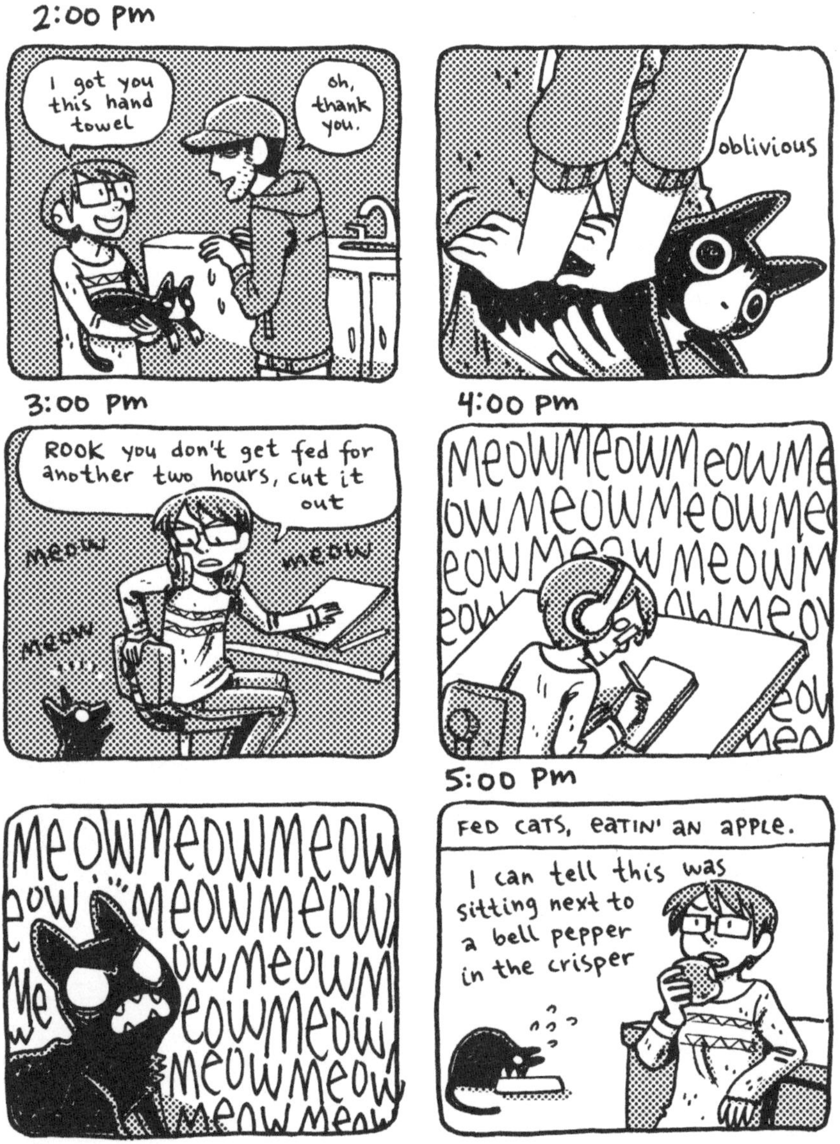
2:00 pm
I got you this hand towel
oh, thank you.
oblivious
3:00 pm
ROOK you don't get fed for another two hours, cut it out
meow
meow
meow
4:00 pm
meowmeowmeowme
owmeowmeowme
eowmeowmeowm
meowmeowmeow
meowmeowmeow
meowmeow
5:00 pm
FED CATS, EATIN' AN APPLE.
I can tell this was sitting next to a bell pepper in the crisper

shower intermission

6:00 pm

lick

lick

lick

everything smells like cat spit.

7:00 pm

OH NO

I FORGOT TO REMIND MY DAD THAT TODAY IS HIS WEDDING ANNIVE RSARY

beep

boop

boop

HE REMEMBERED.

8:00 pm
INSTANT DINNER
9:00 pm
inking
10:00 pm
yeesh
11:00 pm
this audiobook is so trashy

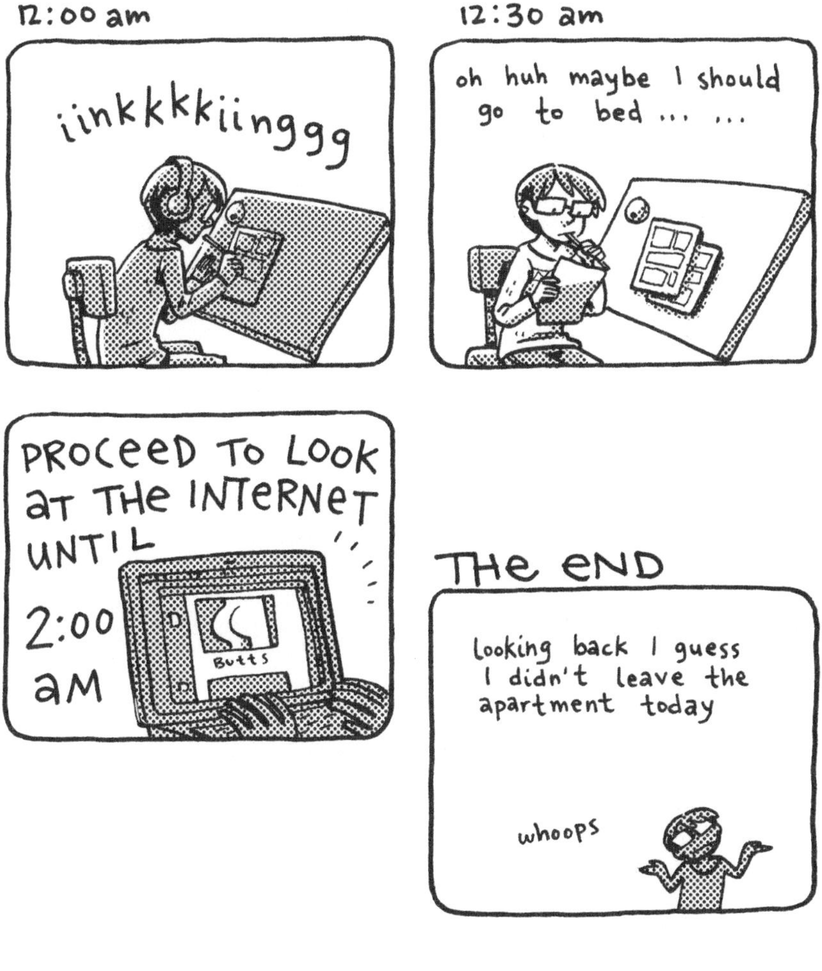
12:00 am
iinkkkkiingggg
12:30 am
oh huh maybe I should go to bed ... ...
PROCEED TO LOOK AT THE INTERNET UNTIL
2:00 AM
Butts
THE END
looking back I guess I didn't leave the apartment today
whoops

tempting fate

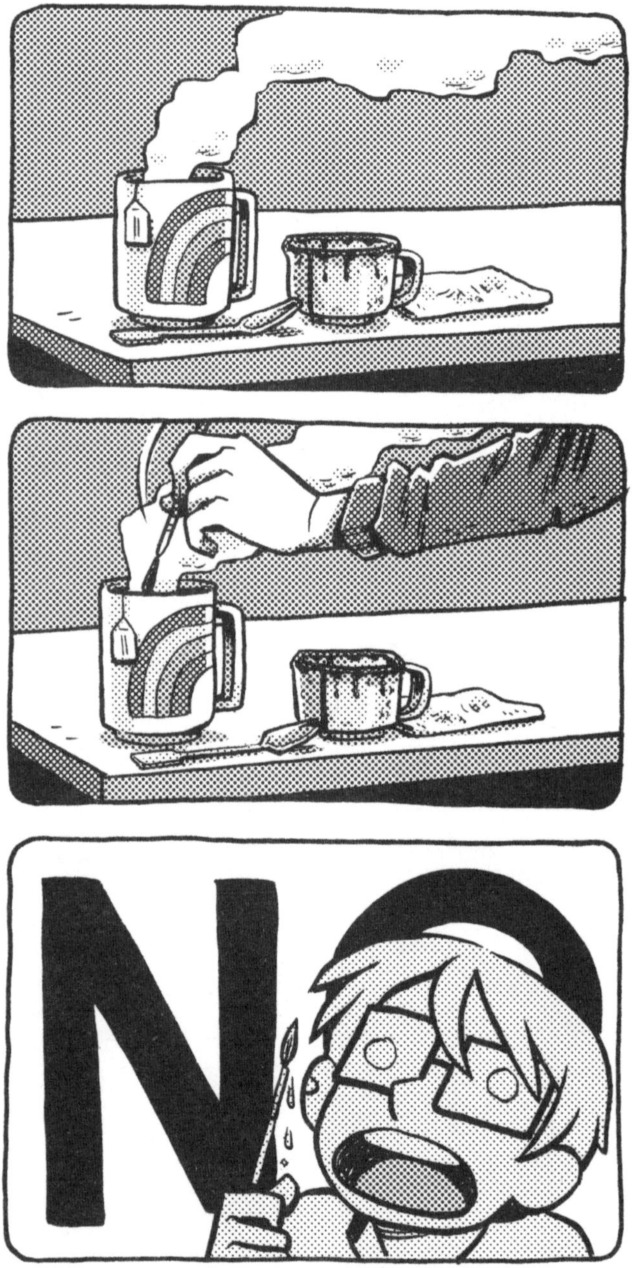
NO

tempting fate once more

an open letter to all registered US voters (2012 ed.)

(it's chard)

IS THIS LIKE... KALE.

NO, SEE THE SHAPE OF THE LEAF?

IS IT ARUGULA.

NOPE.

THIS IS DEFINITELY ESCAROLE.

nuh uh.

FOR A VEGETARIAN YOU'RE REAL BAD AT PLANTS.

watercress.

cats in our neighborhood

BODEGA KITTEN

THERE'S A KITTEN AT THE GROCERY

WHO'S SMALL AND ENERGETIC

SHE GETS INTO EVERYTHING.

EVERYTHING.

many princesses

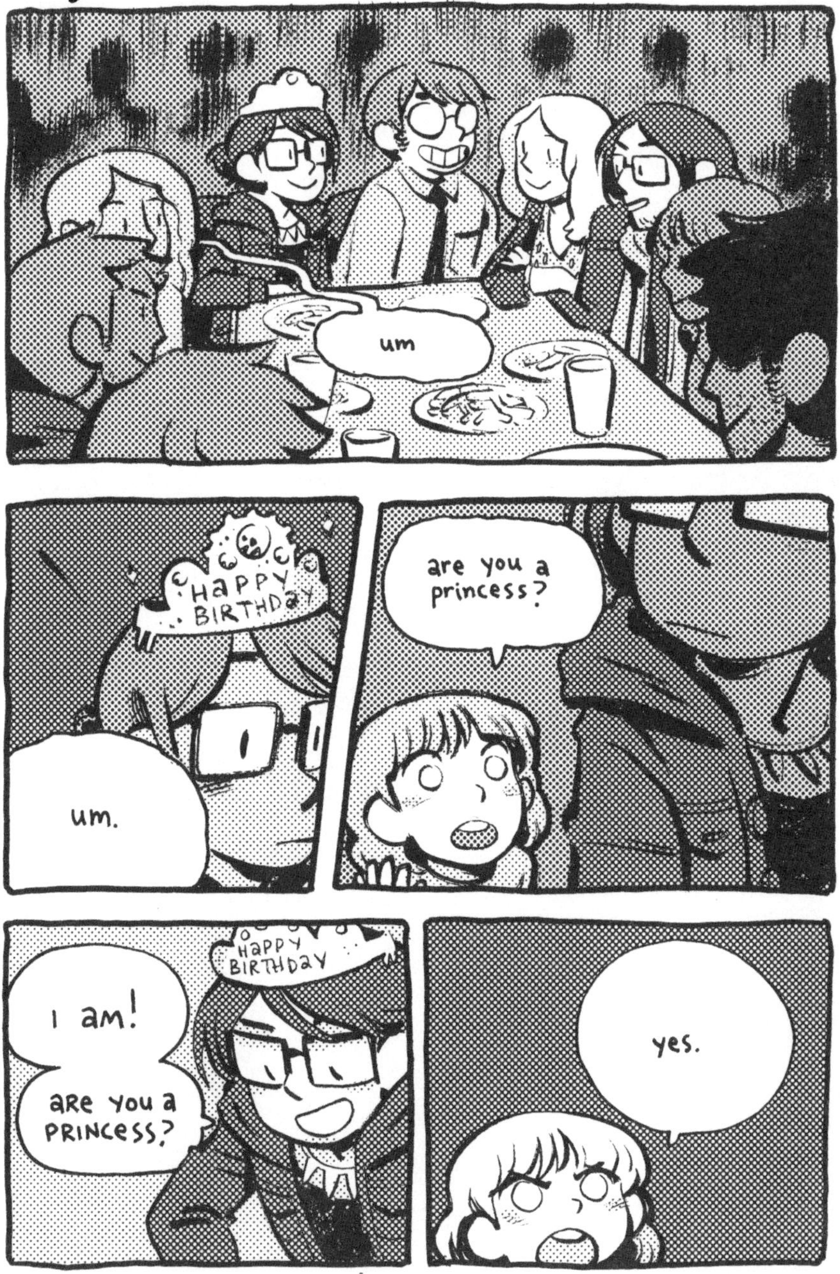
um
HAPPY BIRTHDAY
um.
are you a princess?
HAPPY BIRTHDAY
I am!
are you a PRINCESS?
yes.

freshly brewed

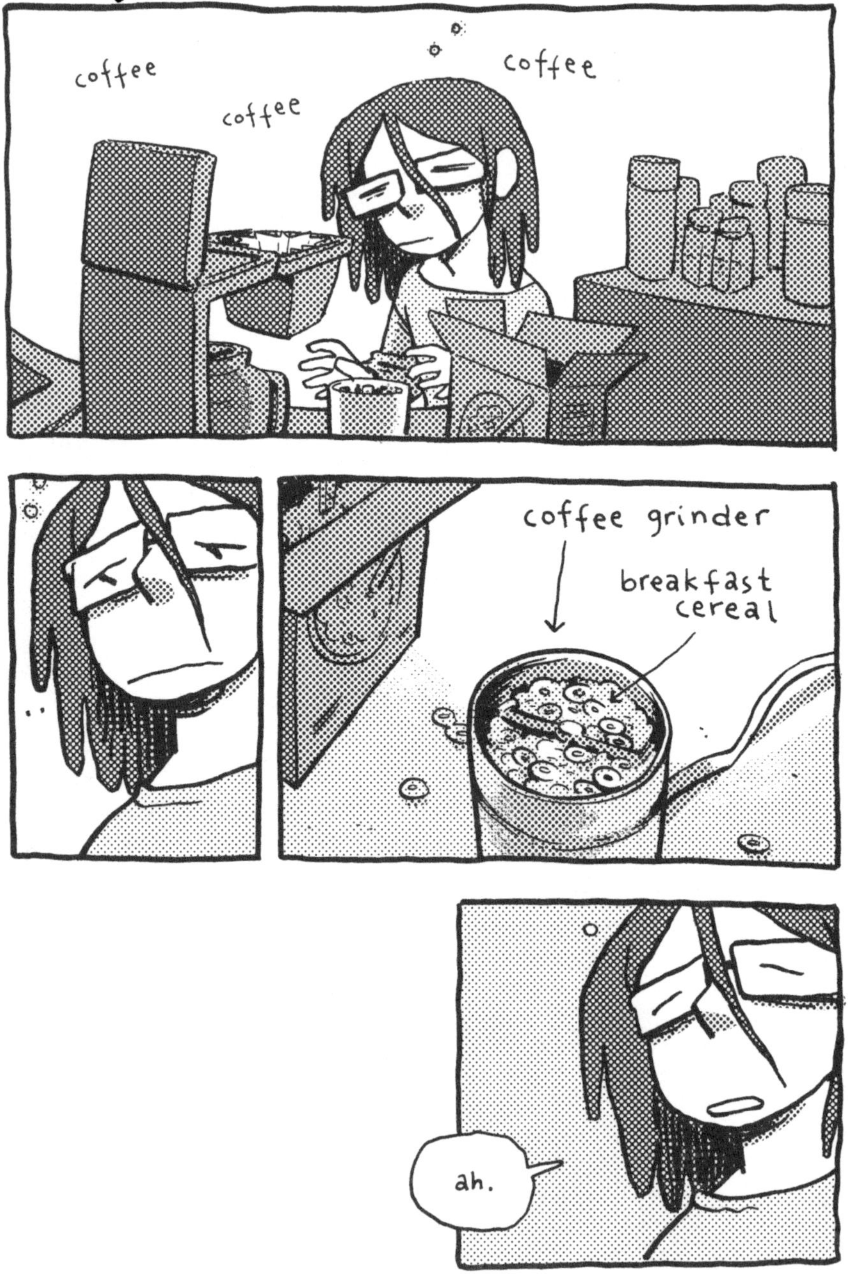

coffee
coffee
coffee
..
coffee grinder
breakfast cereal
ah.

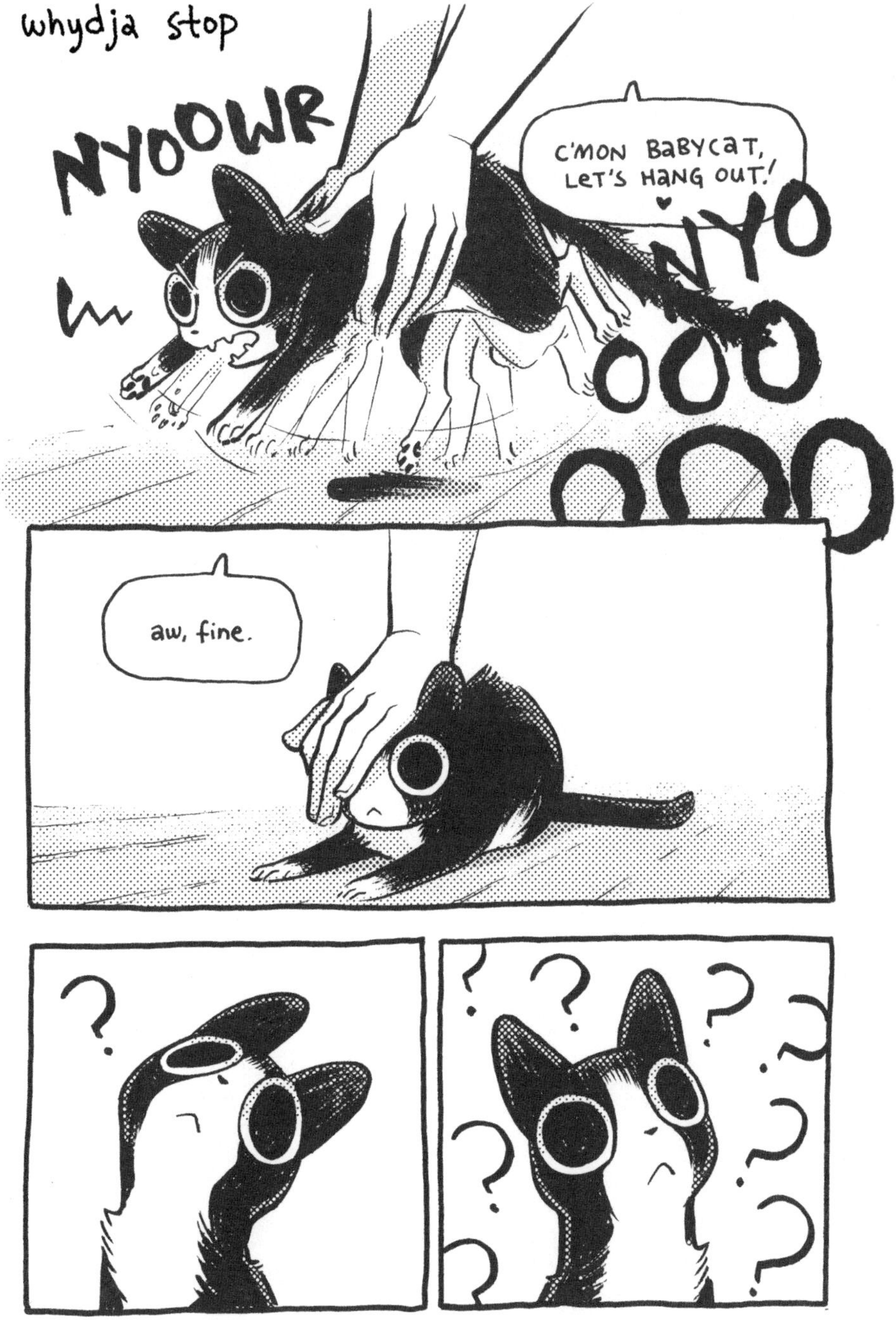

whydja stop
NYOOWR
C'MON BABYCAT, LET'S HANG OUT!
NYOOOOOOO
aw, fine.
?

haunted bhel puri

HEY MOM, I'M AT THE INDIAN GROCERY. DO YOU WANT ANYTHING?

YOUR BROTHER TAUGHT ME HOW TO USE THE CAMERA!

I'LL SEND A PHOTO.

namaste to every grandma

excuse me!

CAN YOU DROP THIS IN THE BOX FOR ME?

OF COURSE!

BLESS YOU!

HAVE A GOOD DAY!

DID YOU NAMASTE AT HER...?

she reminded me of my grandma!

work vacation

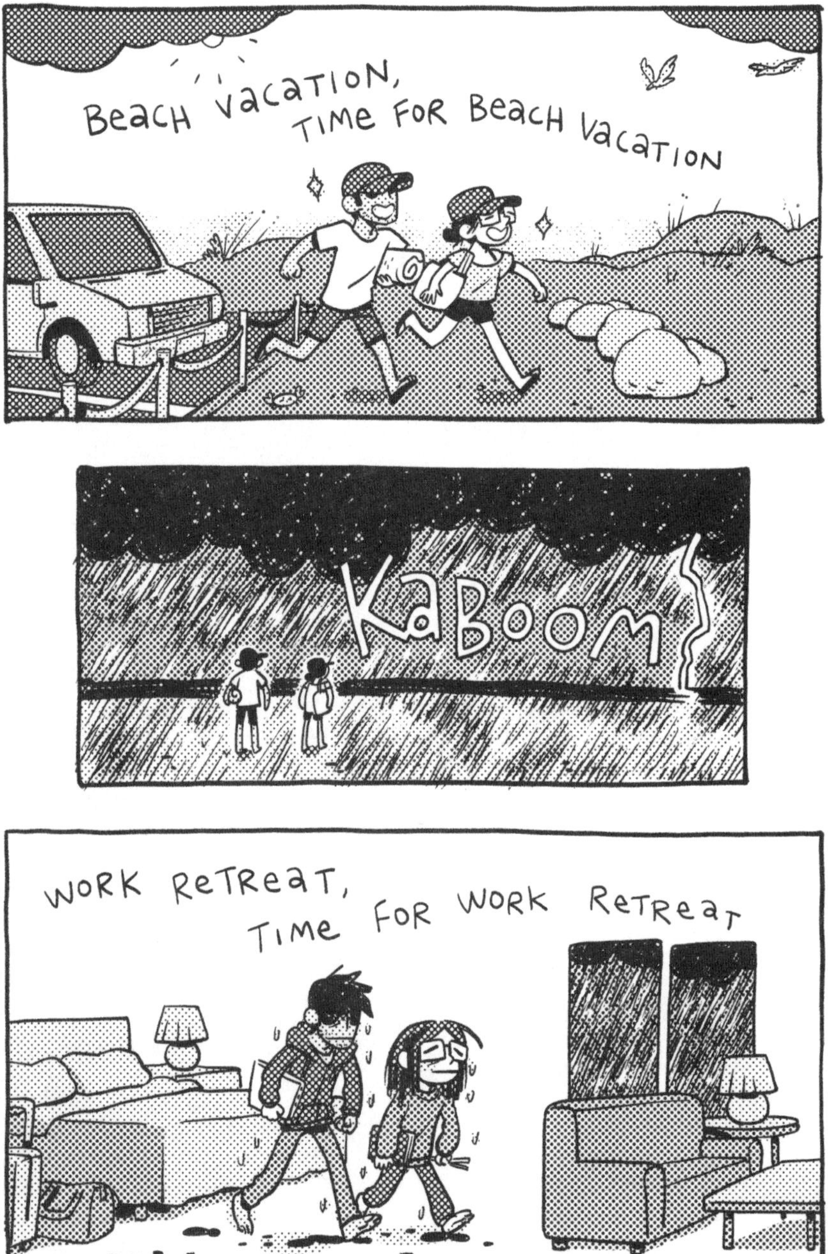
BEACH VACATION, TIME FOR BEACH VACATION
KABOOM
WORK RETREAT, TIME FOR WORK RETREAT

wind storm beach vacation fun times 2K15

HEY IT'S SUMMER, HYDRATE YOURSELF!

let's make some Sun Tea!

YOU NEED:

6-7 cheap tea bags, tags removed

a clear pitcher

OPTIONAL:

sugar

fresh mint

1. water

2. add stuff

3. STEEP IN SUN FOR ~5 HOURS

- take out tea bags afterwards
- keep in refrigerator

WOW THAT WAS easy

cats in our neighborhood
THE BOSS

THE BOSS REIGNS OVER AN INTERSECTION OF OUR NEIGHBORHOOD.

SHE IS A BENEVOLENT AND JUST RULER.

HI, BOSS!

blink

She blinked at me

gasp

a comic about a spider

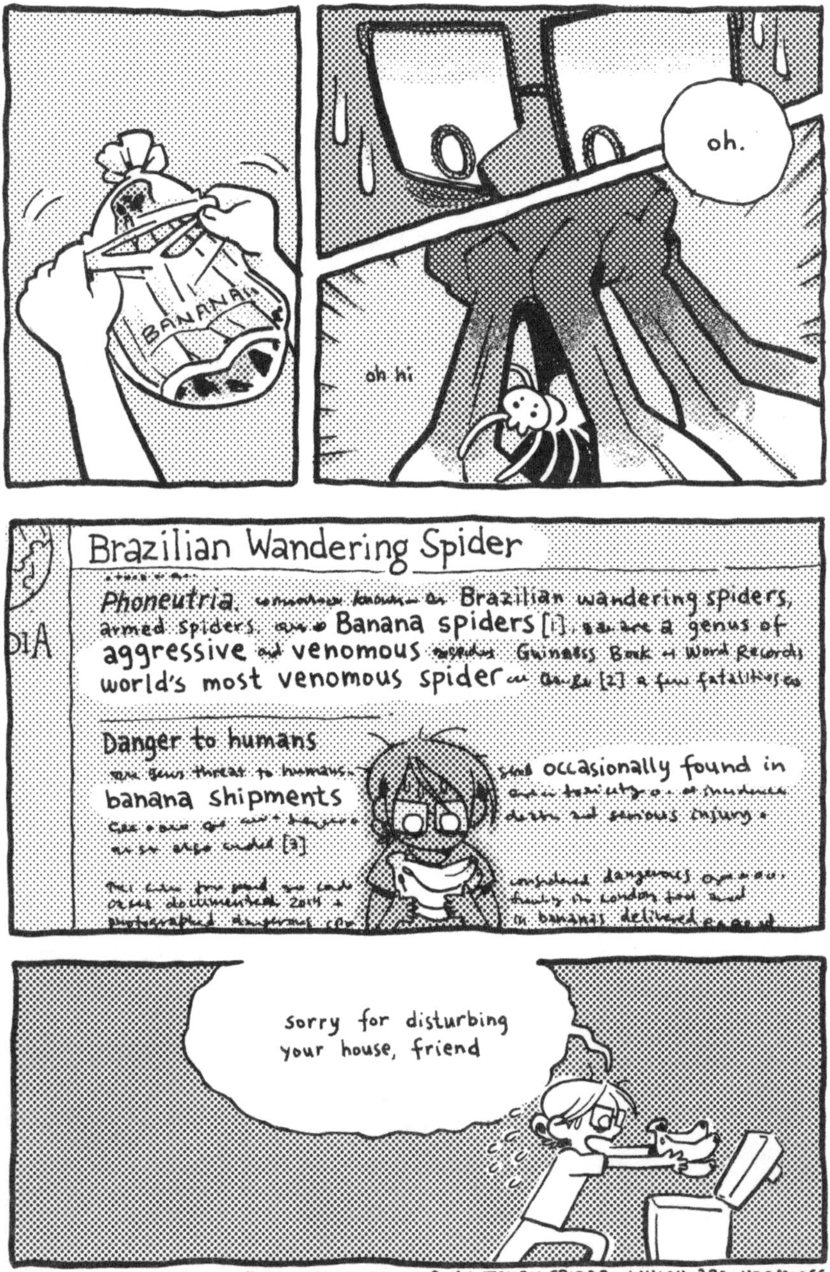
BANANA
oh.
oh hi
Brazilian Wandering Spider
Phoneutria
Brazilian wandering spiders,
armed spiders
Banana spiders [1]
a genus of
aggressive
venomous
world's most venomous spider
[2] a few fatalities
Danger to humans
occasionally found in
banana shipments
death and serious injury
sorry for disturbing
your house, friend

*IT WAS PROBABLY A HUNTSMAN SPIDER, WHICH ARE HARMLESS

sleepy nurse

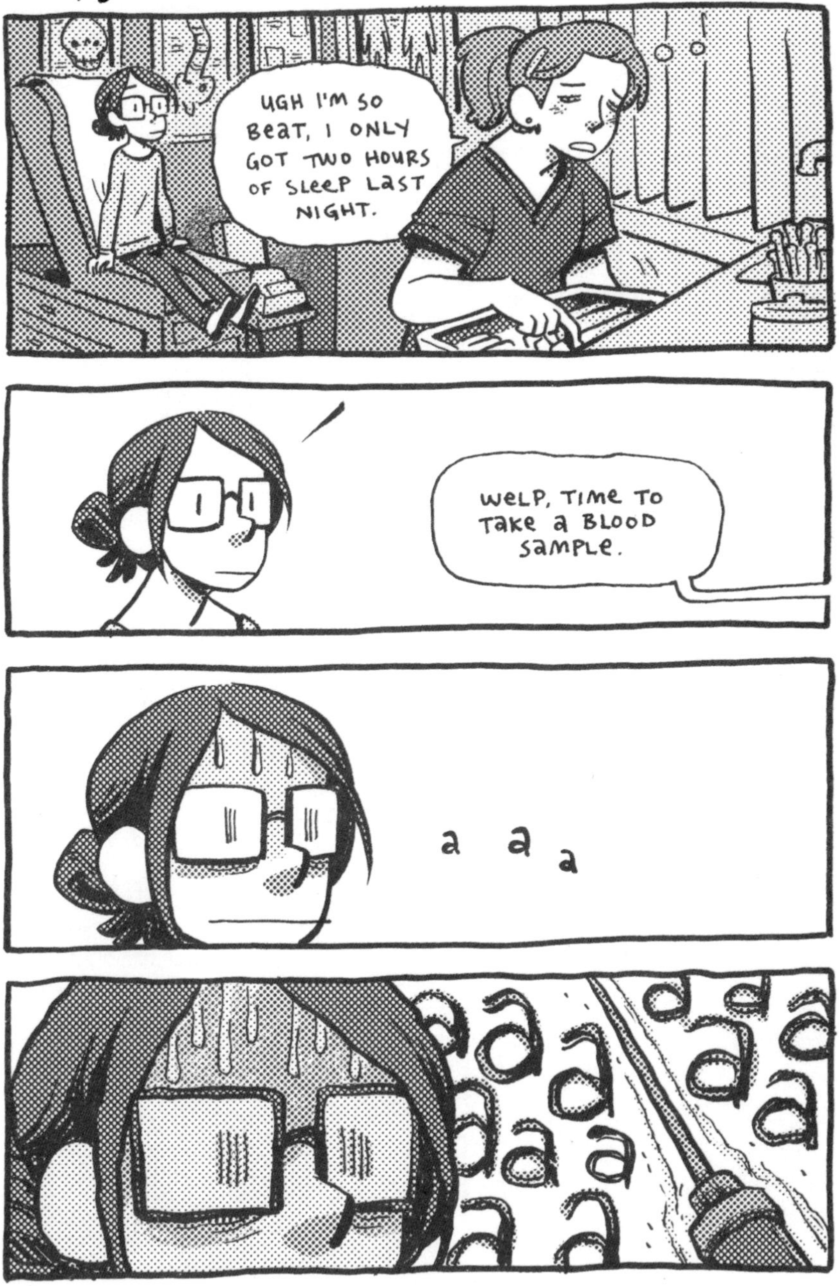
UGH I'M SO BEAT, I ONLY GOT TWO HOURS OF SLEEP LAST NIGHT.
WELP, TIME TO TAKE A BLOOD SAMPLE.
a a a

parallel fashion

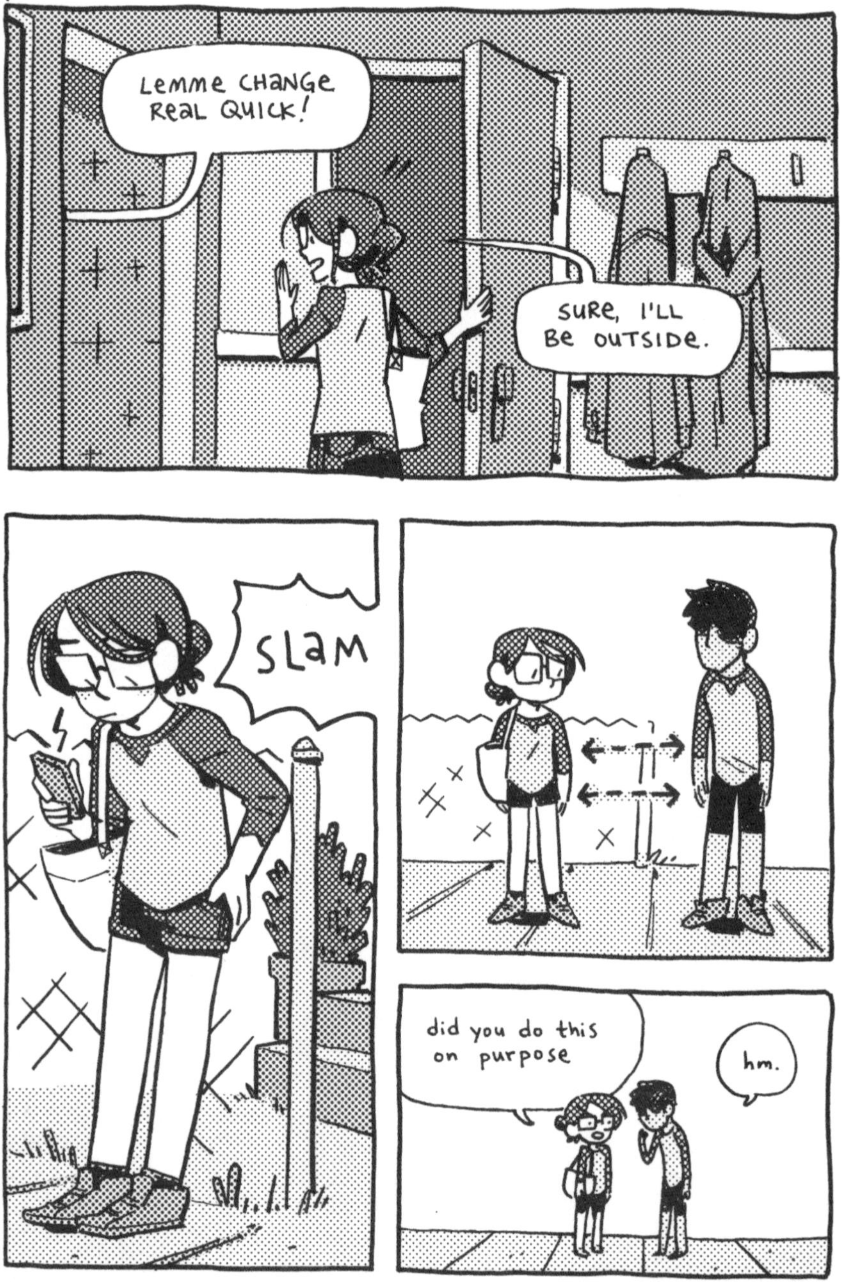
LEMME CHANGE REAL QUICK!
SURE, I'LL BE OUTSIDE.
SLAM
did you do this on purpose
hm.

parallel fashion harder

parallel fashion: with a vengeance

WHY ARE YOU DOING THIS TO ME

hm.

I'M NOT CHANGING

I'M NOT CHANGING.

ARE YOU PLAYING FASHION CHICKEN

AND SOON

WHAT a COUPLE OF NERDS

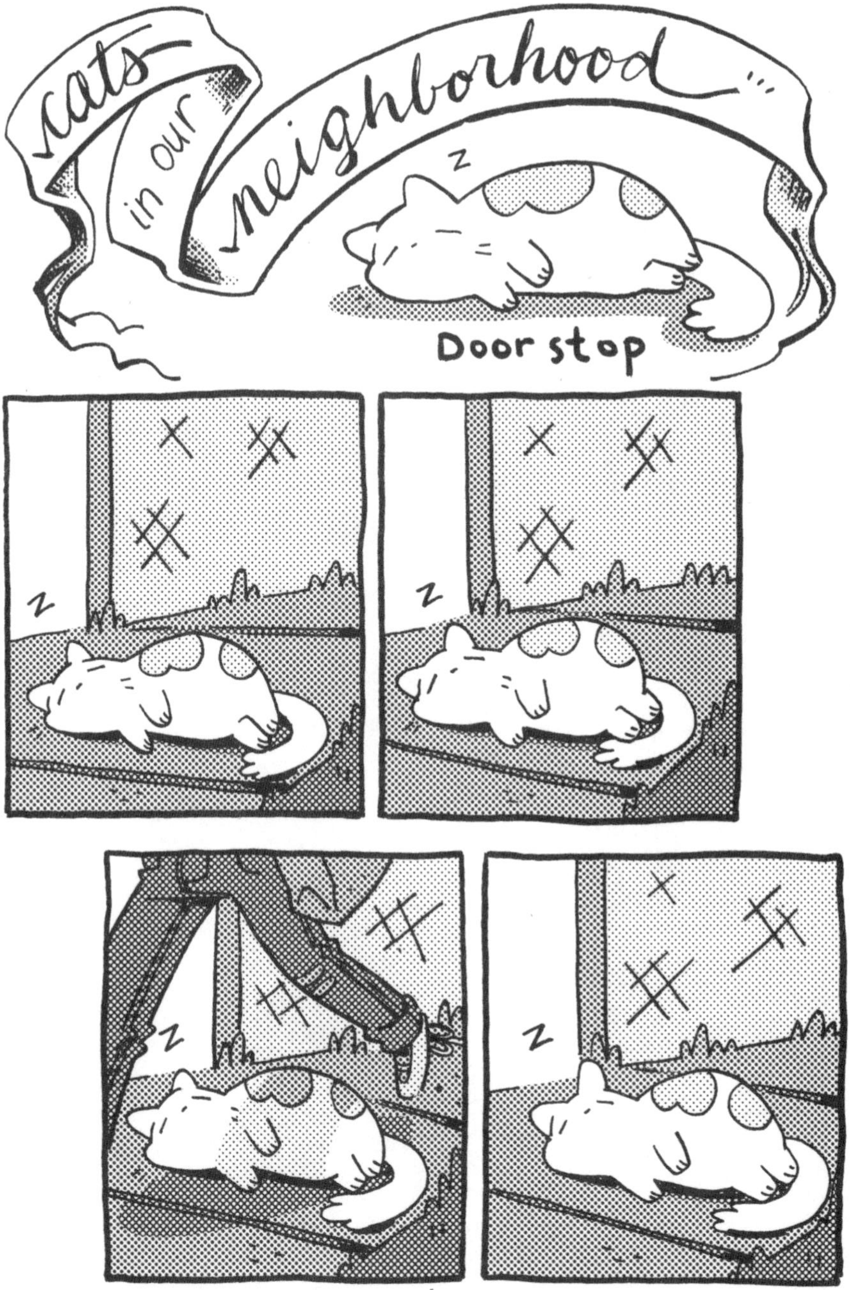
cats in our neighborhood
z
Door stop
z
z
z
z

one time I got a hand-me-down
baby suit from my cousin

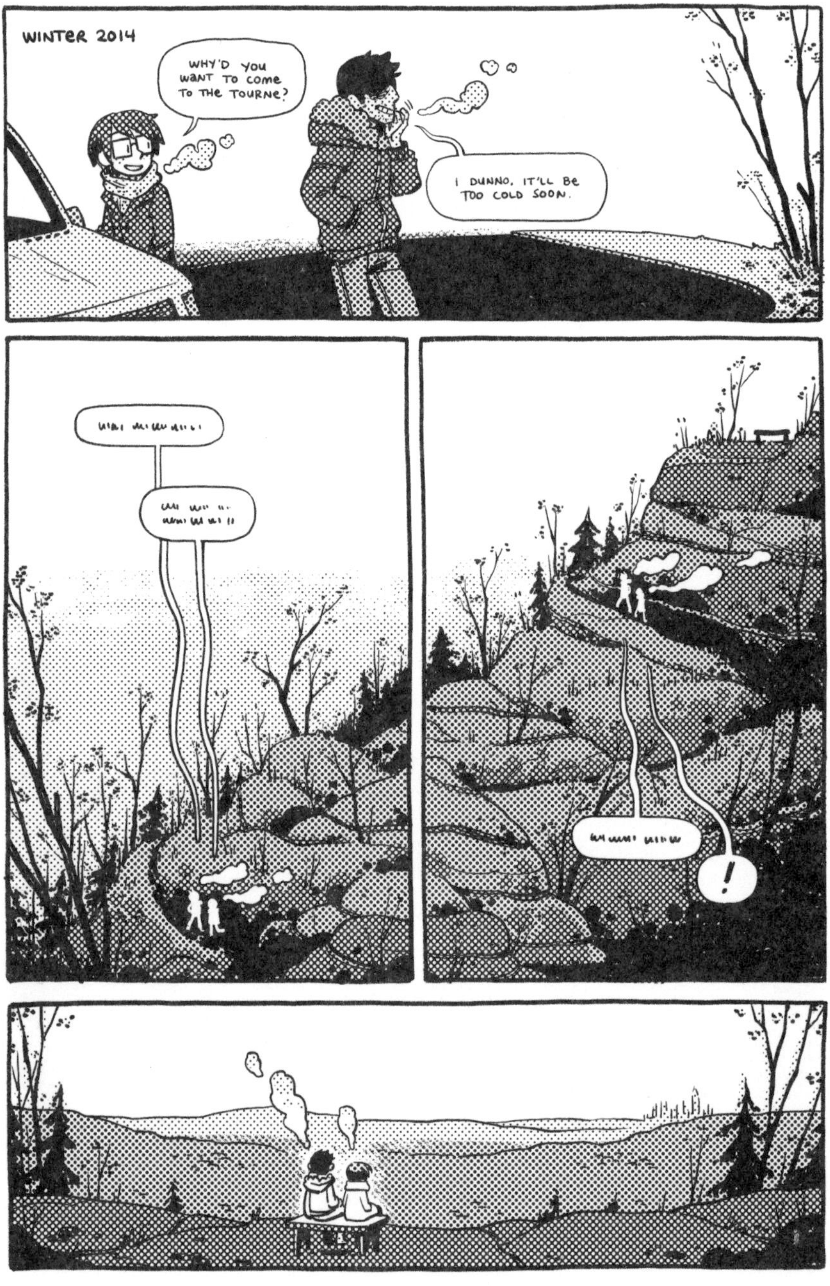
WINTER 2014
WHY'D YOU WANT TO COME TO THE TOURNE?
I DUNNO, IT'LL BE TOO COLD SOON.
!

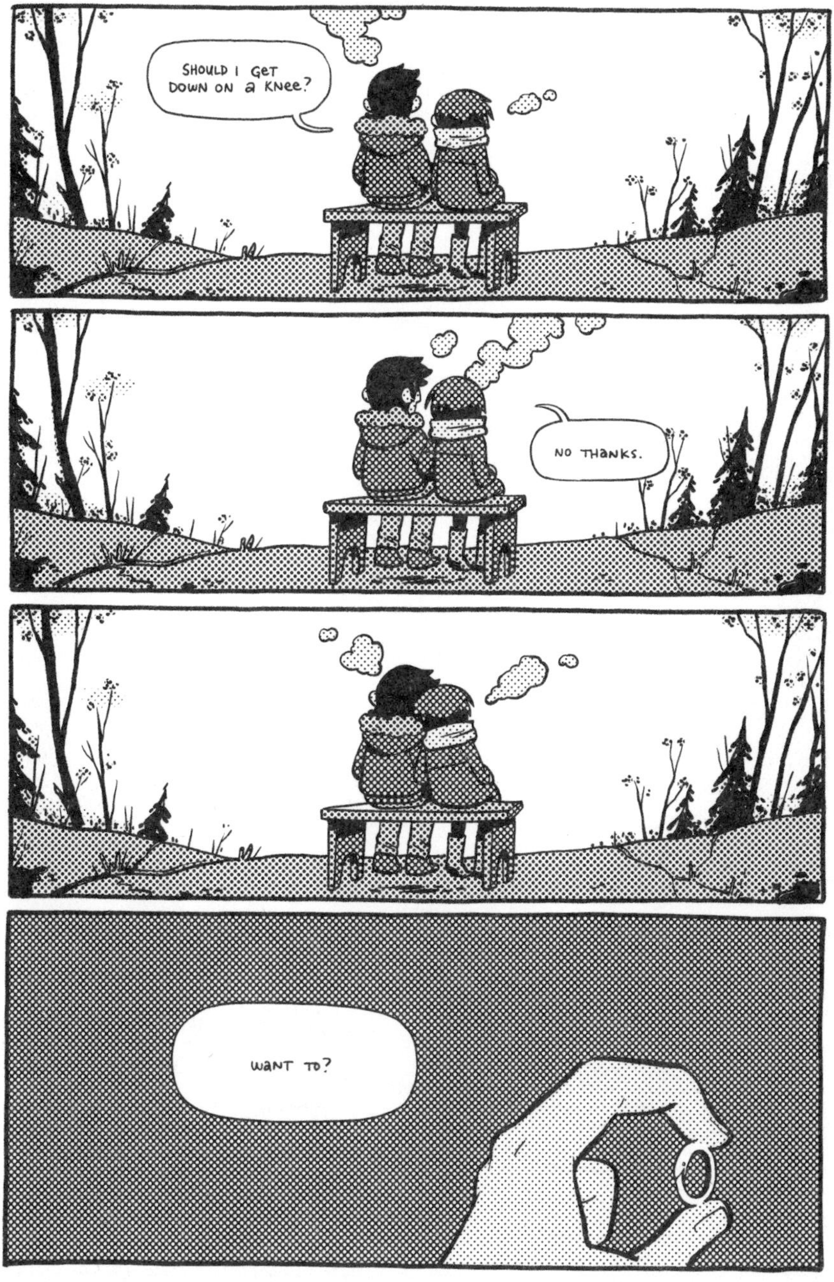
SHOULD I GET DOWN ON a KNEE?
NO THANKS.
WANT TO?

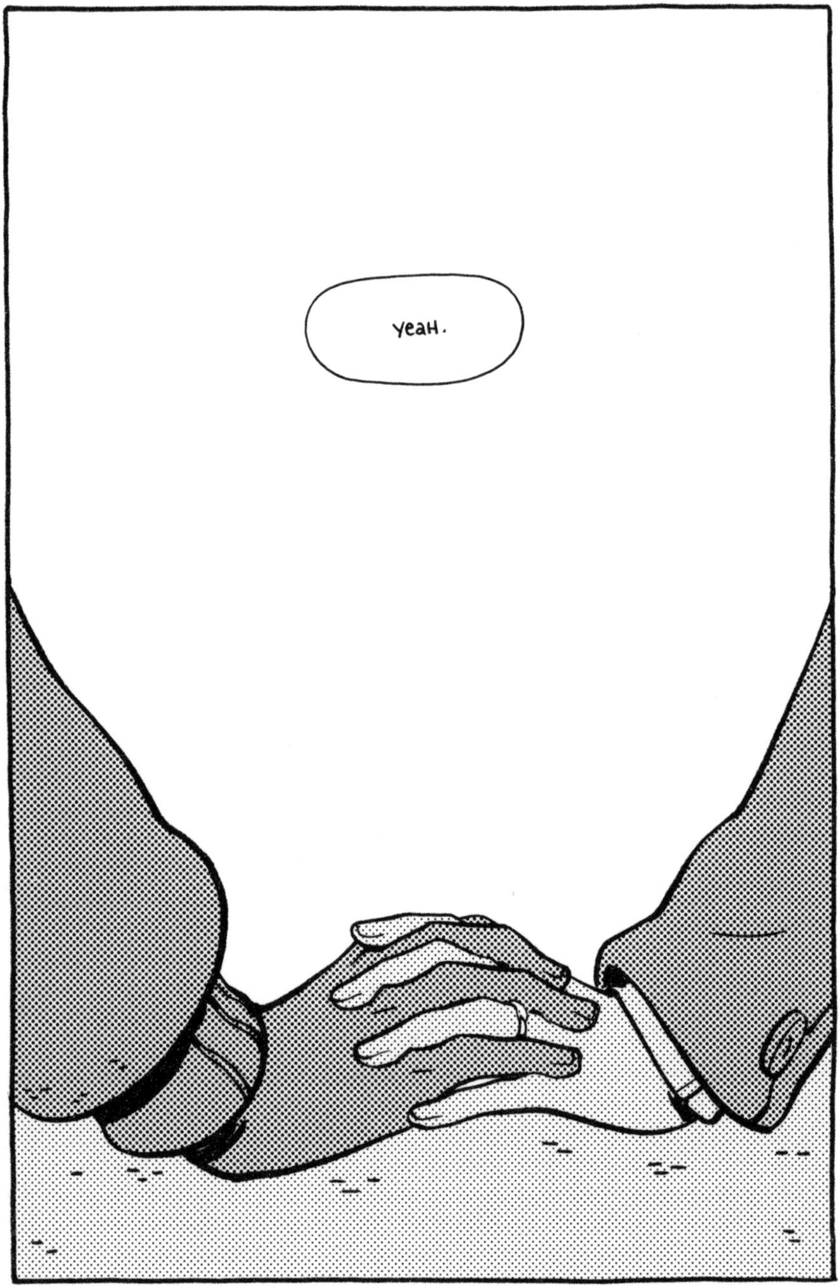
yeaH.

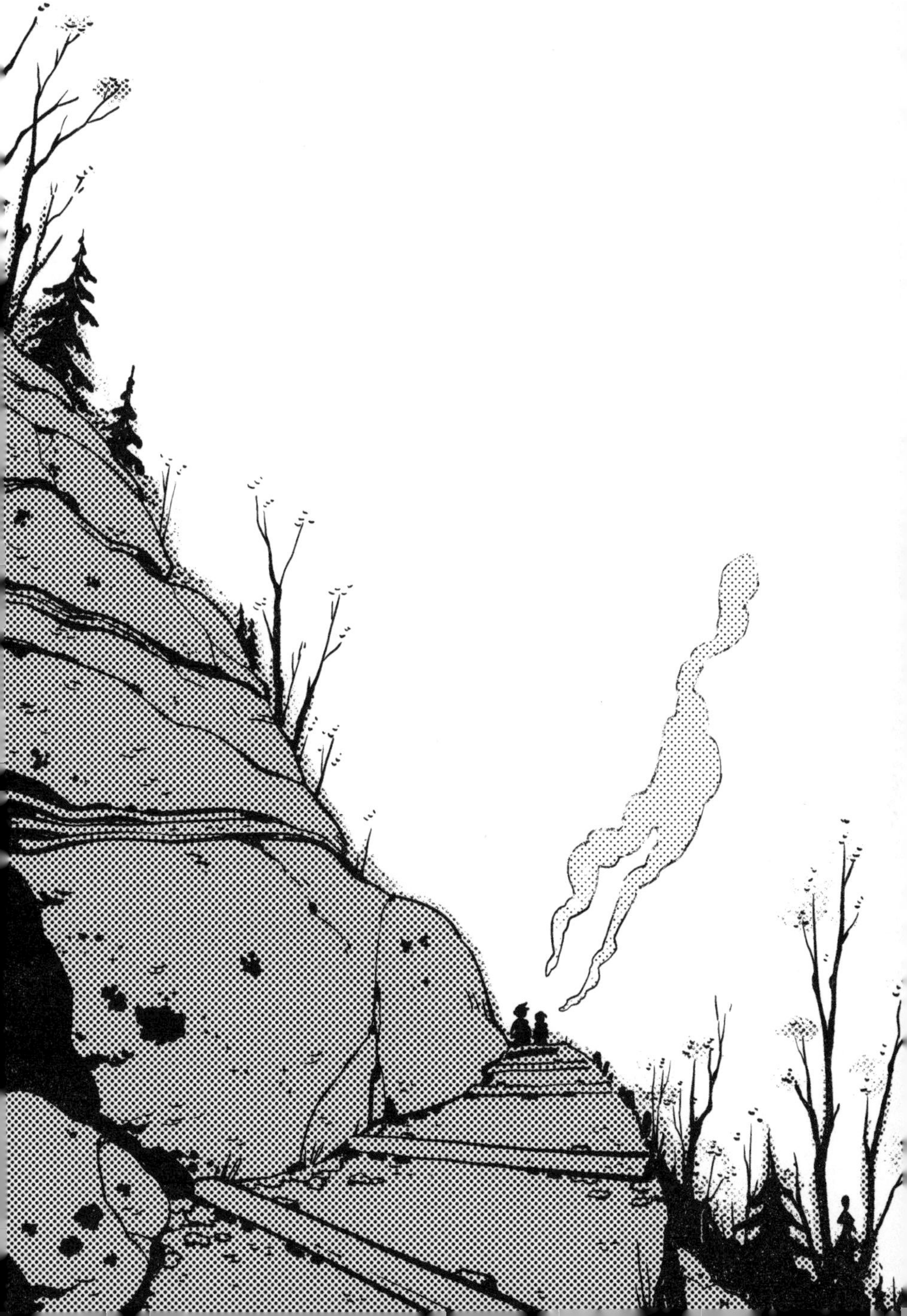

V.

THROUGH the thickest knell of night,
Through milky morning dew,

What wondrous sights I'm set to see
While wanderin' with you

For we could see nigh anything
While wanderin' jus' you an me
For any thing's a won'drous thing

With you, my friend
With you

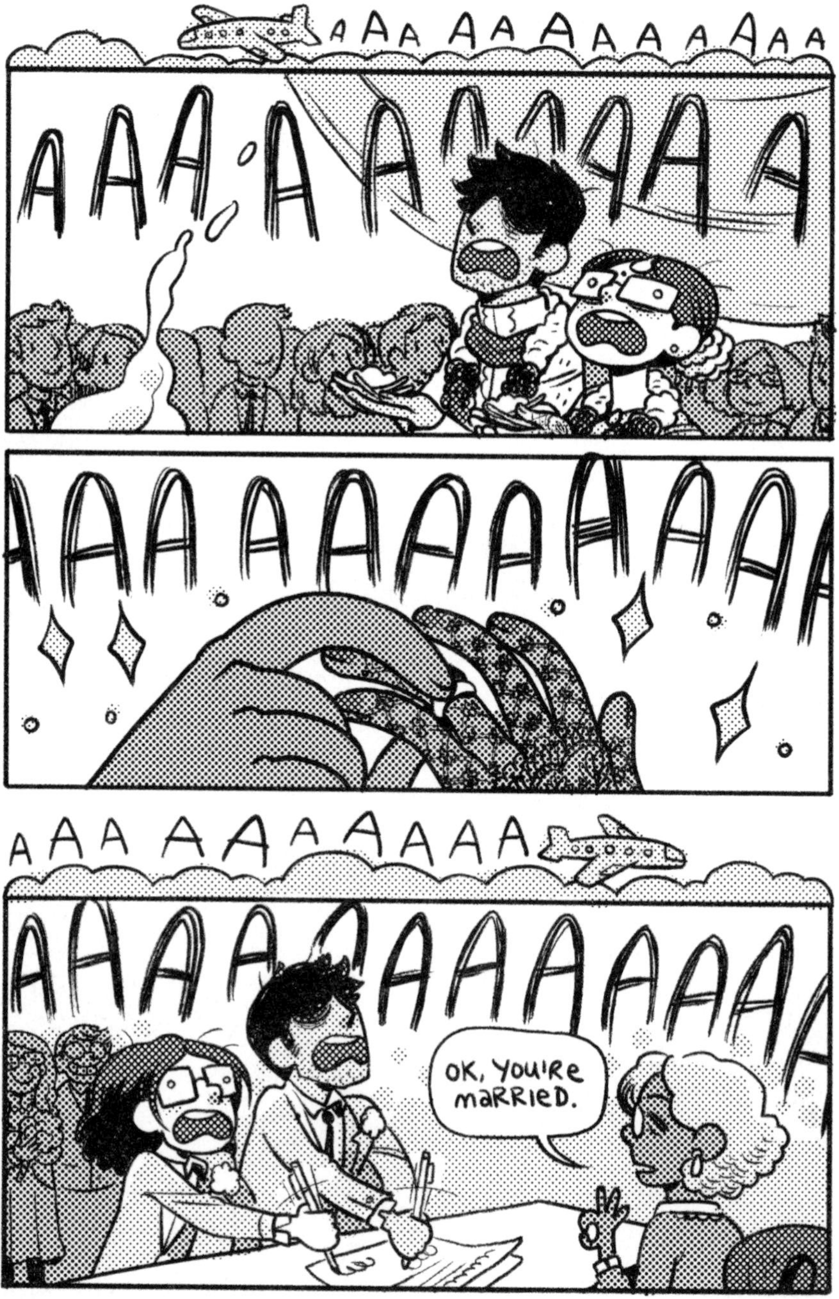
AAAAAAAAAAAAA
AAAAAAAAAA
AAAAAAAAAAAAAA
AAAAAAAAAAA
AAAAAAAAAAAAAAAAAAA
OK, YOU'RE MARRIED.

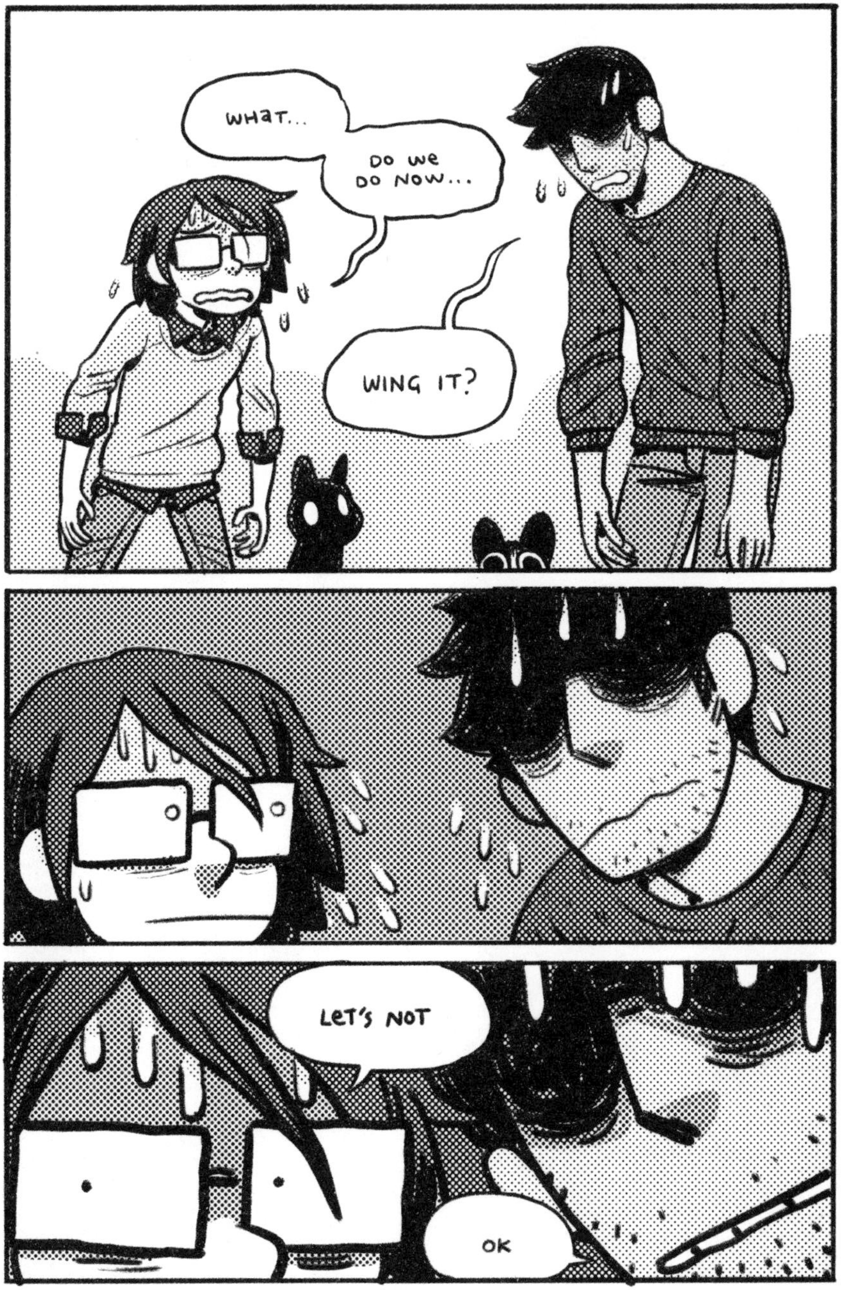
WHAT...
DO WE DO NOW...
WING IT?
LET'S NOT
OK

ACKNOWLEDGMENTS

There are a lot of people who we'd like to acknowledge from over the years. I'm sure some names have slipped my mind– so sorry for that!

Our parents, who can never be thanked enough.

George Rohac, who was there for the whole thing.

Mike Miller, for friendship and artisan marshmallows.

Raina & Dave, for giving us such a warm welcome to New York.

Eugene Ahn, for his enthusiasm and warmth. This dude is magic.

Tucker & Nina Stone, who championed us in a way that means so much.

Bergen Street Comics, for hosting the most killer release parties we ever had.

Magnolia & Jones, two of our favorite people in the universe.

Samm Neiland, for all the cool stuff you sent our way.

L & Xtina, for Math Club.

Lindsay & Alex, for being, like, really funny.

Rachelle, for soju & Boka.

Andrew & Claire, for your kindness and for dessert.

Katie & Jordan, for always meeting us at Target at 1 AM.

Megan & Archer, for decades (and decades) of friendship.

Jamie & Audrey Noguchi, and little Hazel. Can't wait to boulder with all three of you.

Mike Ey. You're the best of us.

Our readers, old and new, for laughing with us.

ABOUT THE AUTHORS

Illustration by
Aatmaja Pandya

Yuko Ota & Ananth Hirsh live in Brooklyn, NY.

Yuko is a cartoonist.

Ananth is a writer.

Their previous book was *LUCKY PENNY*.

They've worked with Oni Press, BOOM!, Dark Horse, Lerner Publishing, Red5, and more.

In addition to their work with publishers, Ananth & Yuko have self-published *CUTTINGS*, a collection of fiction comics and related artwork.

Ananth has a previous book with Oni Press, titled *BUZZ!* You can see more of Ananth Hirsh's work with Tessa Stone on their latest collaboration, *IS THIS WHAT YOU WANTED*.

Yuko and Ananth post comics at johnnywander.com. Their latest project is titled *BARBAROUS*.

thank you to all of our readers!

MANY OF THEM HELPED MAKE THESE COMICS POSSIBLE, AND YOU CAN READ THEIR NAMES BY FOLLOWING THE LINK BELOW. ♥

johnnywander.com/thankyou

ANANTH HIRSH · YUKO OTA
BARBAROUS
BEST GLAMOURS FOR THE SEASON
COLOR MATCH YOUR MAGIC IN 3 EASY STEPS
STOP FEELING LIKE A MONSTER
JOHNNYWANDER.COM

"I LOVE IT! Penny is a human disaster after my own heart!"
- Noelle Stevenson, *Nimona*, *Lumberjanes*

LUCKY PENNY

ANANTH HIRSH   YUKO OTA

A new graphic novel from the creators of *Johnny Wander!*

LUCKY PENNY ™ & © 2016 Ananth Hirsh and Yuko Ota. Oni Press logo and icon ™ & © 2016 Oni Press, Inc. Oni Press logo and icon artwork created by Keith A. Wood.

ONI PRESS
www.onipress.com

IS THIS WHAT YOU WANTED

Ananth Hirsh · Tessa Stone · Sarah Stone

isthiswhatyouwanted.com

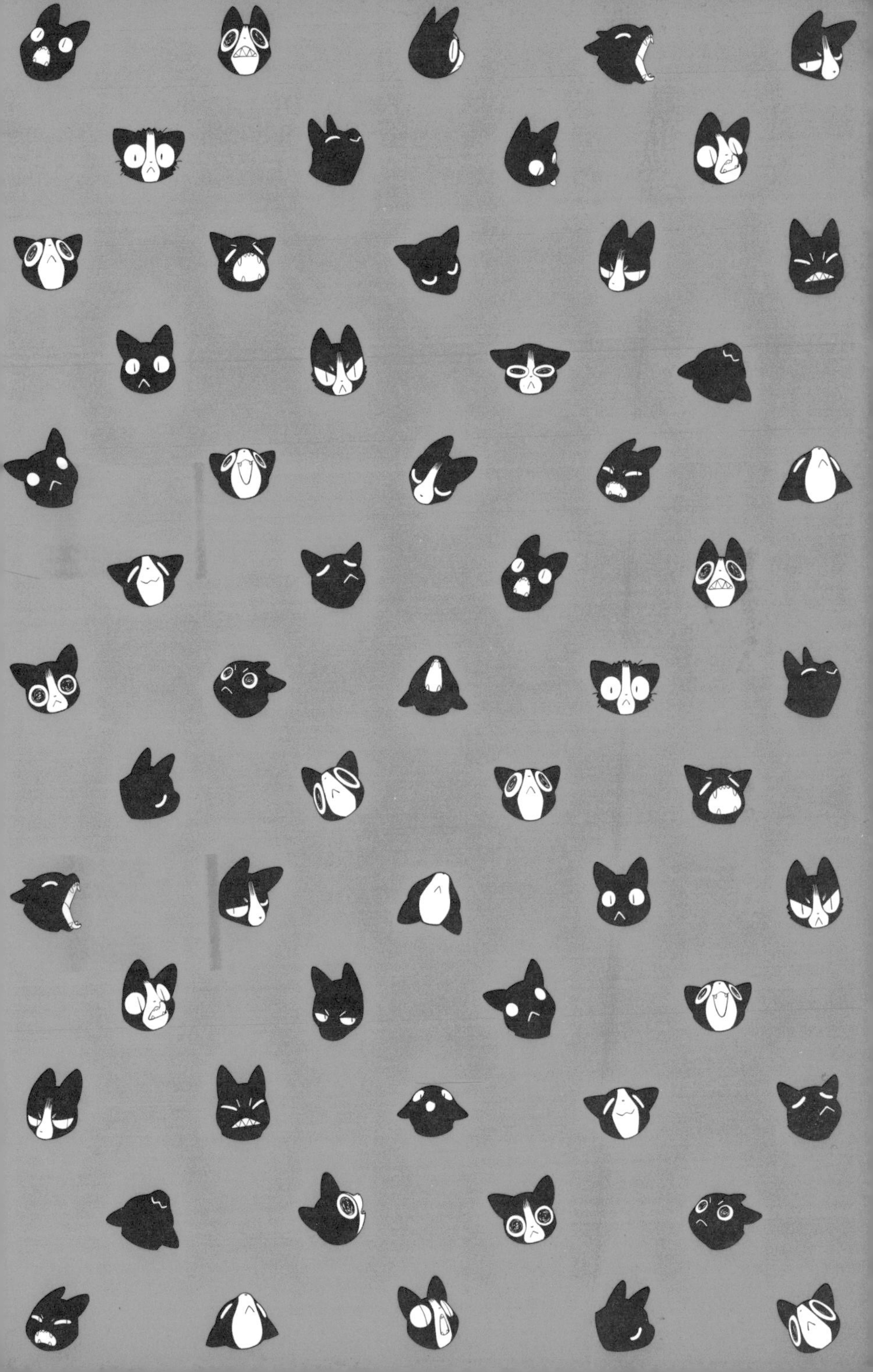

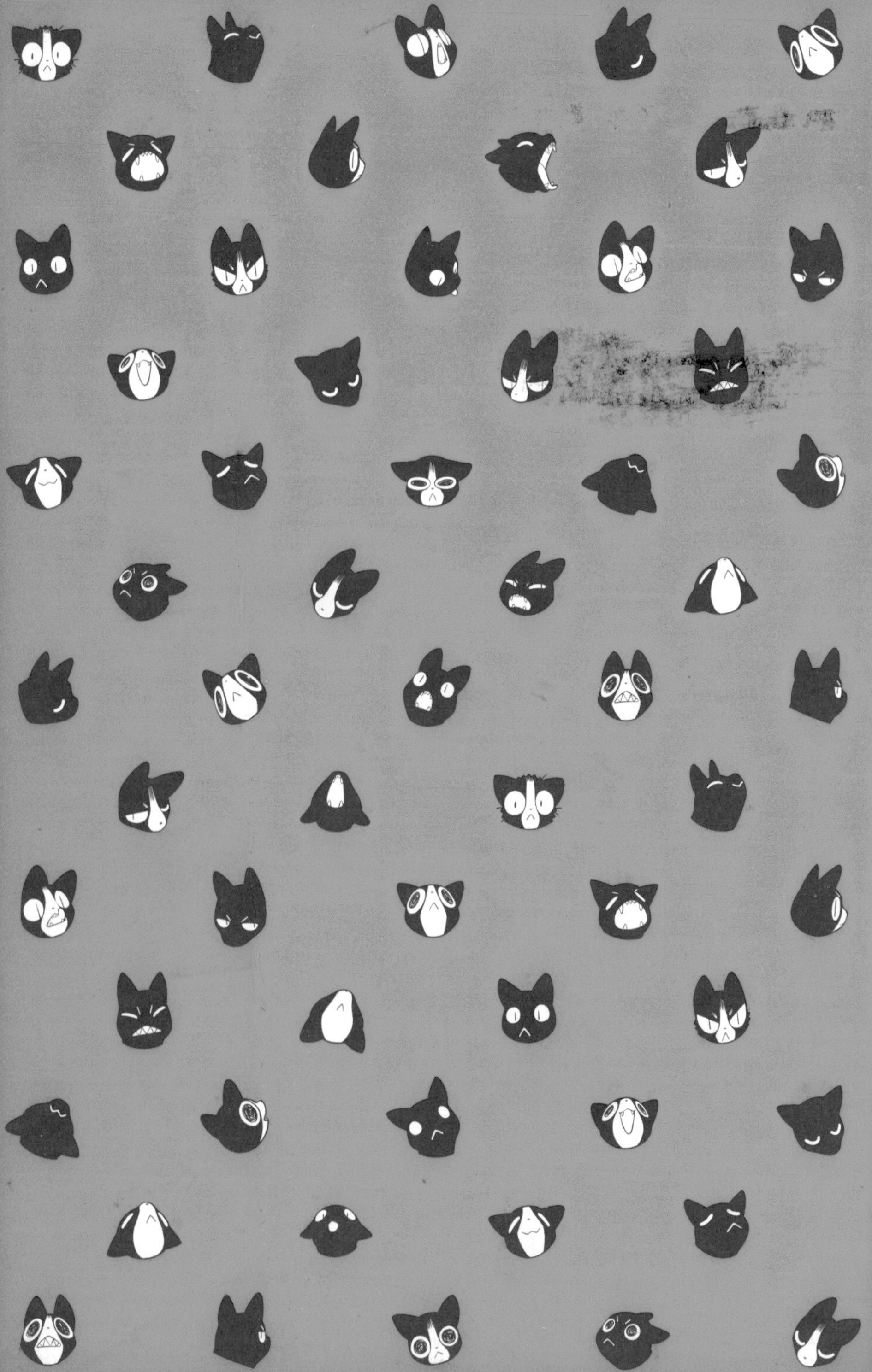